THE ANGUISHED
DAWN

By JAMES P. HOGAN

THE ANGUISHED
DAWN

JAMES P. HOGAN

THE ANGUISHED DAWN

Copyright © 2003 by James P. Hogan

A Baen Books Original

Baen Publishing Enterprises
P.O. Box 1403
Riverdale, NY 10471
www.baen.com

ISBN: 0-7434-3581-8

Cover art by David Mattingly
Maps by Randy Asplund

First printing, June 2003

Library of Congress Cataloging-in-Publication Data

Hogan, James P.
  The anguished dawn / James P. Hogan.
     p. cm.
  ISBN 0-7434-3581-8
  1. Regression (Civilization)—Fiction. 2. Power (Social sciences)—Fiction. 3. Space colonies—Fiction. 4. Disasters—Fiction. I. Title.

  PR6058.O348A85 2003
  823'.914—dc21

                                                           2003006194

Distributed by Simon & Schuster
1230 Avenue of the Americas
New York, NY 10020

Production by Windhaven Press, Auburn, NH
Printed in the United States of America

10 9 8 7 6 5 4 3 2 1

Dedication

To Tim Gleason—in appreciation of
all the help and good advice over the years.

Acknowledgments

The help of the following people is gratefully appreciated:

Dr. Andre Assis, Institute of Physics, Campinas, Brazil, for answering questions on his theoretical work deriving the gravitational force as an electrical effect.

Dr. John Ackerman, for much correspondence concerning his fascinating interpretation of the Indian *Vedas* as a record of Mars encounters.

Larry Kos, of NASA, Marshall Spaceflight Center, Huntsville, AL, for advice on orbits and weird gravitational effects.

Mark Luljak of Fairlight Consulting, Louisville, KY, and Myrranda Hunter of NASA, Ames, CA, for much useful feedback from the first draft.

All those readers who demanded a sequel to *Cradle of Saturn*.

Charles Ginenthal and Lewis Greenberg for their support and encouragement.

Des Butler and Emer Carolan, Des Butler & Co., Sligo, Ireland, for photocopying, scanning, and the like, without which the rest would all be in vain.

(See also the "Further Reading" section at the end of the book.)

PROLOGUE

By the second half of the twenty-first century, Earth had become comfortable and complacent. The military threats that had once spurred technological development were no longer credible, the threat of major war having given way to local counterinsurgency actions and suppression of resistance to what was tending ever more toward the establishment of a global state. With financial institutions finding safe and secure profits close to home and having little incentive to put capital into risky, far-off ventures, the space initiative had not lived up to its earlier vision and promise. Institutionalized science echoed the cultural message of stability and security by reaffirming its doctrine of a universe shaped by gradual, uneventful, evolutionary change under the direction of laws that were immutable and understood.

Not everyone, however, found the notion of material affluence and comfort as the sole aim of life to be a very satisfying philosophy, or accepted the officially promulgated schools of thinking that led to such a conclusion. Landen Keene was one of the restless few who felt that humanity and its civilization were destined for better things. A Texas-based nuclear propulsion engineer who had been battling against complacency and inertia for years to champion meaningful expansion into space, he became a natural ally of the breakaway "Kronian" migrants, who established an advanced technological outpost culture among Saturn's moons to live by their own moneyless value system based on individual merit and cooperative enterprise.

Freed from institutional control and commercial interests, and flourishing at last as the open pursuit of knowledge for its own ends, science under the Kronians opened up new realms of physics and practical application whose pursuit had languished on Earth, and explored academic questions that had been impermissible under the intolerant dogmas that had come to dominate Earth's scientific thinking. What brought about changes in the terrestrial environment that would make the existence of dinosaurs impossible in modern times? Why did conventional Ice-Age chronology have to be wrong? Who were the people who had developed writing and elaborate artifacts long before civilizations were supposed to have existed, and how could they have lived beneath the alien sky that their records depicted?

Finally, the Kronians sent a delegation to Earth with evidence of violent upheavals across the Solar System that had occurred into the times of recorded human history. Keene and others joined the Kronians in warning that such events could happen again, and the human race would be vulnerable for as long as it remained concentrated in one place. But the plea was rejected since it didn't fit with prevailing theory, and dismissed as a political ploy to divert Earth's resources to Kronia. Its proponents were ridiculed, their arguments misrepresented and distorted . . . until, with the ejection of the white-hot protoplanet Athena from Jupiter and the perturbing of its Sun-grazing orbit onto a course sending it toward Earth, a catastrophe that had come close to wiping out the human race once before was about to happen again.

With traditional authority discredited, Keene found himself suddenly elevated to being a principal governmental advisor on the situation. As conditions worsened worldwide with Athena's approach, he was sent to California as part of a team helping to organize the nation's crash program of emergency measures and evacuations. But the planetwide cataclysm of meteorite and climatic storms, flooding and conflagration, gravitational and electrical upheaval, were on a scale that dwarfed anything that had been imagined, overwhelming all attempts to cope. In the final days, with the world as they had known it ending around them, Keene and a small group of companions that fate had thrown together embarked on a desperate cross-continental journey to a site in Mexico, where a shuttle remained that could get them off the surface.

From orbit they watched Earth's final destruction as it gyrated in a final close pass with Athena before Athena detached to career onward toward the outer Solar System. For days they drifted in space, not knowing if anyone else was left alive anywhere, but were finally picked up by the vessel that had brought the Kronian delegation to Earth and which had remained in the vicinity, rescuing survivors who had managed to escape from the surface.

And so they returned with the Kronians to begin new lives in the unique culture that had come to exist among Saturn's moons, now the sole, slender remnant of human civilization—and for all anyone knew, the last refuge of surviving humanity anywhere.

Meanwhile, Athena continued to wreak havoc and disruption among the bodies of the Solar System.

PART ONE

The Kronians

CHAPTER ONE

Delmor Caton, Surface Operations shift supervisor at the industrial constructions in progress or at Omsk, felt an empty feeling taking hold deep in his stomach. His throat tightened in an effort to coax up moisture against the sudden dryness.

It was fear.

He had thought he would grow immune to it after the things he had seen and lived through in the course of the last three years. But it was never long before something else happened to remind all of them that there would probably never be any escape from the danger for the rest of their lifetimes. Earth had been devastated before, and mankind had lived in terror for centuries afterward. . . .

Alarm signals *whoop-whooped* through the domes and tented excavation sites gouged into the ice on Saturn's sixth major moon, Rhea. Simultaneously, alerts were flashed on the emergency bands to mobile units scattered across the surface and to the commander of the military-style training base that the Security Arm operated two hundred miles away. The drills had become second nature. Surface access locks and bulkhead doors throughout the site were closed; all occupants in the first ten levels down from the surface who were not already kitted up began putting on suits;

vehicles caught outside sealed hatches and raced for whatever cover they could get to. Caton glanced at the others in the upper control room overlooking the workings around the main shaft, clearing desks and consoles, shutting down systems, and helping each other secure helmets before evacuating to the communications center below. He snapped a switch to kill the sirens and leaned forward in his seat toward the console microphone.

"Alert is confirmed. Multiple impact hazard zeroed on this area in fifteen minutes, twenty seconds if not neutralized. We're getting everybody underground. Regular drill, Code Orange. Surface operations are closing down. Out."

One of the wall screens showed a view of Athena, currently between the orbits of Jupiter and the Asteroid Belt on the far side of the Solar System—an almost-Earth-size ball of white-hot vapors and magma with plasma tails millions of miles long braided into fantastic forms by electrical forces, giving it the appearance of an animal head glowering between fiery horns. Thousands of years before, when proto-Venus was a similar rogue incarnation recently born of Jupiter, the mythologies of cultures worldwide had depicted it as fiery cow, bull, or wolf deity returning periodically to loom terrifyingly in the skies and wreak destruction across the Earth. Although Athena itself was at present far away, its rampage through the Solar System had effects that could strike anywhere.

Caton rose and turned to find Tanya, one of the operators, stopped halfway to the door, still clutching her helmet and staring back at the image. She was one of the few survivors to have made it to Saturn three years previously, rescued by the Kronians from one of the pilot Terran scientific bases left stranded on Mars. Tears of rage and frustration glistened on her face. Not Kronian-born or raised here from childhood as an immigrant, she was still struggling to adapt to the new ways of living, knowing that everything that had been familiar was gone permanently, and nothing resembling the world she had known as home could exist again until long after her lifetime. "Why? . . . Why won't it leave us alone?" she whispered.

Caton handed her the helmet, ushering her toward the

door. "Because that's the way it is. Come on, we need to go." His tone was gruff but not without sympathy. He hoped that the people up on the LORIN stations were on form today. Everything depended on them now.

A million miles above Saturn, Landen Keene sat tensely in a seat to one side of the Fire Controller's console in the command room of LOng Range INtercept Station 5, between the orbits of the second and third outer moons, Iapetus and Hyperion, and 30 degrees north of the plane of the ring system. A large screen to one side showed a view of Saturn's banded globe seemingly floating in a shining elliptical ocean formed by the rings seen obliquely. In normal circumstances the sight would have been stunning. Right now, however, all attention was focused on the image hanging above the holotable in the center of the floor. It showed a sector of the moon system plane outside the rings on the near side of Saturn. Rhea was close to the center, looking like a mottled gray marble. Titan, farther out and three times its size, sat just inside the image volume as a smoky brown ping-pong ball. And coming in from the side on a slanting trajectory, a pattern of red points, moving perceptibly, denoted the swarm of dark objects that had appeared suddenly from the outer Solar System, hurtling inward into Saturn's gravity well.

The encounter with Athena had deflected Earth into a more eccentric orbit and perturbed the motions of all the inner planets with consequences that were not yet clear. In addition, the attendant debris pulled out of Jupiter at the time of Athena's birth, and the bodies sent off in wild directions by Athena's several interactions with the Asteroid Belt since, had created a multiplicity of rogue objects, some of which traversed paths reaching out almost to the orbit of Uranus. The incandescent ones, such as the several score of new comets torn from Jupiter, and hot material ejected from Athena itself, were fairly easy to track—although prediction of future motions was complicated by electrical disturbances that made the old laws of celestial dynamics unreliable, at least for some time to come. But dark, colder objects could appear unexpectedly anywhere, at any time.

All prospects of support or supply from Earth had gone.

The environment on and around Earth had remained too hostile to contemplate reestablishing a human presence there in the time since the Athena catastrophe occurred. Hence, the survival of the Kronian colony depended crucially on technology in all its forms and the rapid development of more advanced ones. People from Keene's kind of background were invaluable. He was on LORIN 5 to learn more about Kronian operations involving nuclear technology—specifically, in this instance, the system of orbiting defense stations that had been put up around Saturn's moon system for protection in these violent and perilous times.

Jebsen, the Fire Controller, Kronian-born and characteristically tall, with fleshy, swarthy features, moved his head above the neck ring of his pressure suit to scan the updates from the long-baseline search radars and targeting computers. The inside of a LORIN station was cramped and cluttered. The need had been to get them up fast, when the first effects of Athena's raging began manifesting themselves.

An operator called from a position to the right of Keene and above, between a bulkhead support and bank of cable boxes. "Fifty-three objects registering Class C and up. Eleven major Titan hazards, aimed and locked. Eight on miss trajectories. Remainder of scatter pattern implicates Titan immediate sector, nineteen at forty-two percent mean, Rhea fifteen at sixty-eight."

"Pods within range and able to bear total twenty-three rods," another voice reported. Jebsen took in the confirmation from the displays. Not good.

The LORIN stations were adaptations of a space weapons system devised as a precaution years ago, when political tension between Kronia and Earth had raised the possibility of armed conflict—which, as things turned out, hadn't materialized. They carried a complement of ejectable pods that powered themselves to a safe distance of anywhere from fifty to several hundred miles before deploying a cluster of heavy-metal lasing rods that could be independently aimed at multiple targets. The device was pumped by the energy from a fission bomb explosion, focused in the nanoseconds before the rods vaporized into concentrated X-ray laser beams capable of destroying a spacecraft from ten thousand miles.

The problem, however, was that despite the effort that had gone into expanding Kronia's manufacturing capability, supplies hadn't been able to keep up with usage over the past several months. More targets were materializing than there were rods available to shoot them with. Complicating matters further, bodies of solid rock could absorb more energy than hollow structures, which often made it prudent to target two or more rods on something that presented a particularly dangerous threat. In the present situation, the computed probability of impacts on the surface of Rhea was greater, while the consequences of letting anything through to Titan, where more Kronian facilities and settlements were concentrated, would be worse. But Titan had a dense atmosphere, while Rhea was unprotected.

These were the factors that Jebsen had to balance. To risk fewer lives with higher probability, or more lives at a lower probability? Which people were the more expendable? The longer he took, the more the odds would tilt. Keene licked his lips, thankful that it wasn't his responsibility.

Jebsen recited a series of identifications and coordinates in the abbreviated language used for voice input, selecting what he judged to be a compromise of the most menacing situations from both groups. The computers assigned targets and presented a revised fire plan.

"Thirteen minutes to first impact on Rhea," an operator called.

"Go with it," Jebsen instructed.

"Designator acknowledges and confirms."

"Lock-on complete."

Jebsen nodded. "Auto fire."

Twenty-three beams of radiation concentrated a trillion times denser than that from a hydrogen bomb lanced across space, each causing a miniature sun to flare briefly in the remote regions of Saturn's outer moons. Of the incoming objects that remained, two reached Titan to break up in its atmosphere, one of the fragments demolishing a surface dome with twenty-two occupants. On Rhea, the industrial excavation and construction sites suffered relatively minor damage with no casualties this time. However, the military training facility two hundred miles away was devastated under a cluster of impacts. Forty-six individuals were unaccounted for afterward; but the actual death toll probably wouldn't be known for days, if not weeks.

A supply ship delivered more pods to LORIN 5. Jebsen was back on duty eight hours later.

CHAPTER TWO

Flashback. San Antonio, Texas, in flames from end to end, lighting up an orange roof of smoke and cloud that had become the sky. Streets littered with bodies, debris, and abandoned vehicles, figures fleeing aimlessly amid falling buildings and the ceaseless roaring and crashing of incoming bolides. Tank cars exploding in the railroad sidings. A blood-drenched woman wandering demented, calling a man's name . . .

It was in the quiet moments, when there were no external distractions, that Keene's mind would return with a morbid compulsion that he was unable to restrain, to the events of those last weeks on Earth. Just eleven hundred and sixty-two had been brought back to Kronia from shuttles and lifters that had made it up from the surface, or been left stranded in space aboard orbiting structures or vehicles incapable of reaching Saturn. Another sixty-six had been brought from the Mars bases. The number might have been greater if two of the Kronian rescue vessels sent to do what they could hadn't been destroyed in collisions with the debris orbiting Earth, causing the agonizing decision to be made not to send any more missions until conditions eased.

At the time, a mental defense reaction had numbed Keene to the things going on around him and the knowledge that they were happening everywhere. His mind had refused to take in what it meant. Now, as if effecting some kind of catharsis, it seemed to need to purge itself by finally allowing consciousness to experience the burden of horror that it had accumulated and suppressed. It was happening as he lay weightless in his seat restraint aboard the medium-haul transorbital taking him back to Titan two days after the strike hit Rhea, when his scheduled stay on LORIN 5 was over.

He relived again the days of Athena's approach after emerging from its tight turn around the Sun, when its thirty-million-mile-long, outward-directed tail had engulfed Earth, darkening the atmosphere with caustic fumes and incendiary vapors, and bringing worldwide rains of fiery hail. Then had come the meteorite bombardment, pulverizing entire regions, while mounting tides inundated the coasts, and hurricanes stirred stratosphere-high palls of dust and smoke into perpetual night. Had he experienced the rest firsthand, he wouldn't have been here now to reflect on the enormity of it; and whether or not there were any still alive back there who had lived through the final days was unknown. As Athena and Earth, with titanic electrical discharges arcing between them, closed and gyrated about each other inside the Moon's orbit before separating, he had watched the false-color computer reconstructions of the events unfolding beneath the shroud veiling the stricken world.

But the veils that had screened it from his mind were opening. Only now was he beginning, fully, to grasp the meaning of death tolls counted in billions; of entire civilizations, their works, and their cities disappearing beneath walls of water miles high as the Earth's axis shifted and oceans surged across continents; of seas boiling, crustal blocks tilting, rifts opening, lava sheets spreading for hundreds of miles to reenact in hours and days tectonic processes previously thought to require millions of years.

Keene was not the only one to be affected in this way. He could pick out another evacuee, even one that he hadn't met before, maybe sitting on the far side of the cafeteria in an industrial complex on Titan, or passing by in one of the habitats on Dione. They all had the same gaunt look that comes with unsettled digestion and troubled sleep. And they seldom laughed.

It was different for the dozen or so others around him in the transorbital's main cabin, all of them Kronian-born, or at least raised, talking among themselves, reading, following whatever was playing on their vi-spex, or simply immersed in their own contemplations. For Kronians, the impact of what had happened lay more at an intellectual level. Their reality had always been the insides of domes or subterranean galleries, stars seen through armored glass or a helmet visor. Open skies and the rustling of trees, or the rush of surf on beaches was not the stuff of immediate experience. The world that was no more, while perhaps one that they might have briefly sampled, was not a world they had known.

A voice from the chatter around him percolated through his broodings. "Lan's very quiet. Are you okay there, Lan?" It was Bryd, a trainee life-support tech, who was going down to Titan for a few days' break.

The line of Keene's mouth softened slightly. "Just tired, Bryd," he grunted.

Myel, the Kronian girl next to Bryd, had been cook and dietician up in LORIN 5, as well as pharmacist and medical assistant. She was also learning three languages. Preserving as much as possible of Earth's cultures was something that everyone took a part in. "Will you be going straight back to the program you're with at Essen?" she asked Keene. Essen was a fusion-driven materials extraction and processing complex located on Titan. Keene was involved in the development of advanced energy technologies at an electrical research facility called the Tesla Center, that was attached to it. Given his background, that was the most valuable contribution he could make toward the colony's ongoing viability. Contributing mattered a lot in Kronia.

"For now, anyway," Keene answered. "There's no end of things that need to be done."

"You have a family on Dione, though, don't you?" Myel said.

"Not exactly family. A friend who was my business partner back on Earth. Her name's Vicki. She has a son—he's eighteen now. Her husband was in the Navy back on Earth. He died in an accident. That was a long time before Athena . . . happened."

The third member of the group sitting with Keene was called Esh. Like the other two, he was young with an intense intelligence, and imbued with the personal dedication to Kronia and its values that the society that had taken root here instilled. They were similarly clad in plain workaday tunics, Bryd and Myel's olive green; Esh's, navy. Personal adornment was a rare luxury these days.

"I have a son back on Dione too," Myel said.

"What's his name?" Keene asked her.

"Carlen. He's three. Blond hair and brown eyes like Obert—that's his father. And all mischief. He's going to be an engineer too. I can tell. He takes things apart already—but he's still such a long way from being able to put them back together." Keene smiled faintly. By now, he was used to encountering what he would once have considered unusually young parenthood. Myel went on, "He's been in a preschool dorm in between staying with his grandmother. But now Obert's getting some leave too. I can't wait to see them again."

"So is Obert away a lot too?" Keene asked.

"He's with the Swiss Cheese Project—one of the people who make sure the lighting spectra are right." Mimas, the second inner major moon after Janus, was being hollowed into internally heated and illuminated crop-growing spaces that it was said would eventually measure a mile across. Nobody quite knew how far the project would be taken, but if just a hundredth of the 300-mile-diameter volume were to be excavated, the total surface area of the resulting spaces would be over twenty percent that of the former U.S.A.

"Kronia needs him too," Keene answered. "Nuclear engineers are no use without food."

"How could we grow food without energy?" Myel said.

Good manners had been observed without conceding false modesty, which would be considered foolish on Kronia—like throwing away money. It had also been proper for Keene to ask Carlen's name. Establishing names was important. Having an identity meant that a person mattered. Being dismissed as of no consequence was the ultimate Kronian snub.

A thruster fired briefly somewhere, and Keene felt the mild nudge of the transorbital correcting course.

"Weren't you a propulsion specialist back on Earth?" Esh asked Keene after a short lull.

"Yes. But there were always obstacles. The technology and knowledge for advanced systems had been available for a long time. But everything had gotten to be a political battle there."

Esh nodded—although no one who was Kronian-born, particularly of his age, could have understood the historical antagonisms that came with Terran politics and economics. "How does propulsion engineering fit in with power generation?" he asked curiously. "I'd have thought it was more the opposite—using it, not making it."

Keene hesitated, but the other two seemed interested as well. With its anticipated growth and the necessity now for total self-sufficiency, larger and more efficient power sources were one of Kronia's most important needs. Keene's experience with controlling hot propulsion plasmas qualified him for developing better ways of turning raw, violent heat into usable electricity.

"Are you familiar with MHD?" he asked them.

Bryd frowned. "Mag— magneto-something, isn't it . . . ?" He looked at Myel. She shrugged and passed.

"Hydro . . ." Esh supplied.

Keene grinned and rescued them. "Magnetohydrodynamics. It's a way of converting heat to power—well-suited to nuclear. What you do is blast the plasma from a fusion reactor—which consists of hot, fast-moving, electrically charged ions—through a system of conductors to induce a current directly. It does away with the train of machinery that early generating plants had: some kind of furnace, heating a boiler that sent steam to a turbine—all just to turn the generator at the end. A lot simpler; very efficient."

"So didn't they use it on Earth?" Myel said, sounding surprised.

"Oh, it was kicked around for decades," Keene replied. "But the trick is in getting hot enough plasmas, and there were endless political problems with anything nuclear." He made a throwing-away gesture. "But the spacecraft nucleonics that I was working on adapts perfectly for the job. You propel the ship and generate all your power with the same system. It's neat. And you can turn the idea around the other way too. That's what we're working on at Tesla." He nodded at Esh, finally answering his question.

"How do you mean, the other way around?" Esh asked.

"A space vessel capable of functioning as a self-contained generating station when on the ground," Keene said. "Ideal for setting up new exploration bases around the Solar System. No need to transport separate, bulky equipment. And it would be able to deliver immediately."

"Vital work, indeed," Esh observed after thinking it through. "Kronia needs people like you, Dr. Keene. We're glad you made it here."

"The privilege is mine," Keene told them.

There had been more to Esh's remark than simple politeness. Kronia had been founded by gifted but disaffected individuals in search of meaning and purpose. They rejected the doctrine that human existence was no more than a pointless accident as had come to be generally believed on Earth, and sought something better than the abandonment to materialism and personal alienation that they saw as having been largely the result of it. As the colony grew and assumed its own ways and form, notions based on Earth's traditional monetary concepts proved not especially suitable as an indicator of the values of things and a measure of personal worth in the unique circumstances that prevailed there.

In a hostile environment far removed from any naturally renewing source of the necessities of life, the knowledge, skills, and dedication that an individual contributed to ensuring the viability of the colony as a whole meant more than acquiring such tokens as money and possessions, which in themselves were useless to anyone else. Hence, a system established itself in which self-esteem stemmed from the acceptance of duty and obligation and the proficiency shown in discharging them, instead of demands for "rights"—or the laying of obligations on others.

Personal reward came from what amounted to the recognition of one's value in those terms.

The principle had even acquired a name: *appretiare*, from the Latin "to price"—the root of "appreciation." Respecting the real contributions of others—which eventually extended itself to things like motives, and hence judging integrity—became the Kronian "currency" for paying dues. And in its own strange way, which even the psychologists were unable to explain precisely, it worked. In traditional human societies, whether status was won by amassing luxuries, collecting the skulls of vanquished opponents, or having killed the biggest lion, what gave satisfaction at the end of it all was to rank highly on whatever form of totem pole earned the esteem of others. What the Kronians appeared to have done was dispense with intermediates and deal directly in the values that ultimately mattered. In addition, as it transpired, their system eliminated the opportunities for all kinds of misrepresentation and fakery in the process.

Hence, Esh was not just paying a simple compliment but, in acknowledging Keene's status as indispensable, paying the highest tribute that could be given. Like the intricate social etiquette of ancient Japan, the conventions of *appretiare* discerned subtleties of shade and meaning that Keene was still working to master. Kronians raised in the system from birth understood the rules intuitively.

Myel seemed about to say something further, when the call beep sounded from Keene's compad. He took it from his jacket and answered. "Landen Keene here."

"Ludwig Grasse. Am I calling at a convenient time?"

"Yes, it's fine."

Grasse was a former Austrian government official connected with banking, one of an influential group who had gotten off Earth in the final days aboard a European Consortium shuttle commandeered at a launch site in Algeria. They had made it to an orbiting transfer platform for lunar shipments and survived there for almost two months before being picked up by one of the rescue vessels sent from Kronia. Grasse and Keene had met intermittently at reunions of Terran survivors and at several social gatherings. Several days previously he had contacted Keene aboard LORIN 5 to arrange a meeting when Keene returned to Titan. All he had said about the subject was that it involved certain matters that Grasse and others had concerns about, which he would like to hear Keene's opinions on.

Grasse went on, "Is it possible we could bring the time forward a little? I will be leaving later this evening, and there's someone else I need to see also departing. Could we make it for before six o'clock?" Since no common system of timing and dating could fit all the cycles experienced by the various habitats and installations scattered across Kronia, a 24-hour Terran model had long ago been adopted as a universal standard, which the local domains endeavored to adapt to as painlessly as possible.

"We're on distant approach now, due in at Styx in about an hour," Keene replied. "I'm due to meet somebody who might be joining our project, so I have to go straight to the Tesla Center first. Suppose we said about five? How would that suit?"

"That would be satisfactory," Grasse replied.

A little over an hour later, the transorbital detached from holding orbit and sank into the upper-atmosphere clouds of nitrogenous compounds that gave Titan its reddish brown color. It emerged at twenty thousand feet, above a desolate surface of ice, rock, and swamps of liquid methane cloaked in permanent night.

CHAPTER THREE

Although much of Kronia's industry and related research was located on Titan because of its diversity of minerals, the forbidding gloom had traditionally induced most Kronians to prefer habitats elsewhere. Since Athena's occurrence, however, more people were forsaking the human liking for being able to see stars, and moving beneath the protective cover of Titan's atmosphere.

The pioneer group who founded Kronia had established their first base on Dione, naming it "Kropotkin," after the Russian social ideologist who had spent most of his life trying to impress upon people the revolutionary notion that they needed each other, and whose ideas had partly inspired the colony's guiding philosophy. The first exploratory expedition to Titan had been mounted later, after the foothold on Dione was secured, penetrating beneath Titan's cloud canopy to set up a pilot base beside a methane stream flowing from an upland waste of ice and broken crater rims, which for understandable reasons they called "Styx," after the river enclosing the mythical Greek Underworld. Styx was still the name of the spaceport at the site where the original base had stood, now serving the processing complex of Essen, which handled ores and other materials both mined locally on Titan and brought from elsewhere. The Tesla nuclear and electrical research center formed a part of Essen.

The transorbital lander Keene was on descended nose-up, pancake-braking against the atmosphere, and then came around to full-vertical for the final phase of its descent to slide tailfirst toward the opened docking silo. The metal constructions below rose up to take on shape and form with lines of windows and reflected highlights, and then were lost as the ship entered a different world of service gantries and tiers of brightly lit access levels. The half-shells of the covering lid rolled shut overhead, and while the bay was cycling to fill with heated, breathable air, the passengers exited through an access tube at the transorbital's forward door, moving with the peculiar loping gait that quickly became second nature as the most efficient way of moving in reduced gravity. Keene's single carryall was tagged for forwarding to his accommodation address, and he was carrying just a light overjacket slung over his arm, and a portasec briefcase. As he had half expected, Shayle was among the people waiting to meet the arrivals. Small, personal things like that were important among Kronians—even when his destination was only a ten-minute tube ride away. Keene acknowledged her with a grin, exchanged farewells with his traveling companions, and made his way over.

Shayle was characteristically tall but sturdily built for a Kronian, with the buxom fullness and pink-hued, freckly complexion that Keene was accustomed to associating with farmhouse diets and lots of fresh air. Her red hair was loosely braided to below her shoulders, and she was wearing a skirt with a green, hip-length jacket adorned by a tree pattern in brown and tan—reminiscences of an Earth she had never known.

"Hi," Keene greeted. He showed his hands. "The VIP treatment? Or has everyone missed me that much?"

"We just like a friendly face to be the first thing you come back to."

"So how have things been?"

"We've been managing. Pang's waiting for you." Shayle turned, and they began walking in the direction of the elevators that would take them down to the transit-tubes.

"How about Jan— What's his name again? Jan . . ."

"Jansinick."

"Right. Was he there yet, when you left?"

"No, but I called Pang a few minutes before you came off the ship, and he'd just arrived. I don't think Pang wants to go into things too much until you get there. He said he'd just told Jan that he was sure he'd find our work attractive."

"Attractive," Keened repeated, and groaned.

Shayle's tone became more serious. "How was it up there?" she asked.

"More of an education than I expected. It makes traffic control look like a rest home. The Security Arm's training base got hit pretty badly a couple of days ago. They lost a lot of people there."

"Yes, I know. They're talking about abandoning Rhea and setting up a new base here on Titan instead."

"There's no point in rebuilding it out there," Keene agreed.

The boarding area was awash with color from flowering plants in tubs and hanging planters—again, all part of the Kronian dedication to preserving everything they could of Earth. Keene had never learned much about plants and their names. Sometimes, talking with Kronians, he felt as if he should have known more. "It feels like walking out into a palace after a week of being cooped up in a LORIN station," he commented to lighten the mood. "Did you ever see pictures of the insides of old submarines?"

"I'd have thought all this would be almost as bad for someone who lived their whole life on Earth."

"I guess we're just an adaptive animal."

They joined a knot of people waiting at the elevator doors. "Oceans and mountains," Shayle went on. "Open sky from horizon to horizon. I can't imagine such things. You must miss it a lot."

Keene shrugged in a way he had learned to make nonchalant. "Life here is so busy that I don't get much time to think about it. When I do, I'm usually too tired to think." A downgoing car arrived. Keene and Shayle got in with the others.

"How's everything otherwise?" Keene asked as the doors closed.

"Pretty smooth. Nyica has upgraded the V-mode simulation. Gordon's installing the bleed diverters on the rig."

"The swivel bearings arrived, then?"

"Finally—yesterday morning."

"What about the rewiring job that Quane was doing?"

"He moved on. I think somebody in Hybrid is after him."

"Hm . . . We need to find a replacement, then," Keene said.

"Mariel's working on it," Shayle told him.

As with any society that had progressed beyond primitive, Kronia needed ways of coordinating effort and unifying its policies in order to function. Its complex technologies and public services could no more have been sustained by unorganized individuals following their own inclinations than an army could hope to succeed as an unled mass with no plan or strategy. But how could such organization come about without the monetary incentives that had built Earth's corporate hierarchies, or authority structures of the kind that had shaped its military commands and academic tradition? As with so much else of Kronian social dynamics, the solution hadn't been designed or imposed, but had emerged as a consequence of the unique value system.

Keene had begun his professional life in Kronia by heading a small research team working to combine spacecraft drive nucleonics with MHD power generation. He headed it because others had decided they had something worthwhile to learn from him and followed. Shayle was a fusion specialist who had become his second. But the main challenge for him had been not so much in the work itself, but in understanding how a functioning research environment could come together for such work to take place in to begin with.

Pang-Yarbat ran the larger project that Keene had later joined, bringing his group of people with him. But neither Pang-Yarbat nor Keene received monetary funding to hire the people and pay for the services they needed to get the work done. How any kind of cohesion or loyalty could be sustained in such a situation had been one of the first mysteries Keene had faced on joining the Kronian workplace.

The way to be valued in such a system was by doing

work that was worthwhile and demanding. But that worked two ways. What mattered was not so much what *you* might imagine your own level of excellence to be, as the standing and reputation of the people who accepted you as a colleague to work with. Thus, a hierarchy of recognition took shape, reflecting the quality accorded to one's work. The most prestigious teams set the toughest standards, and in the self-reinforcing system that resulted, they attracted the most capable contenders. Making top grade was like being awarded a Fortune 500 directorship or entry to one of the old Ivy League universities—except that it couldn't be bought with money or connections. There was only one way to get accepted: by being damn good.

It had taken Keene awhile to realize fully what a tribute it had been when Pang-Yarbat invited him and his team to join the larger project. It meant that he and those who had attached themselves to him became a section within Pang-Yarbat's group, with a corresponding elevation of status that attracted more talent. The section now consisted of eight regulars in addition to Keene himself. Of these, five were committed to working there exclusively—on the equivalent of a contract. The remaining three worked for Keene part of the time but were also associated with other projects, sometimes competing ones, and not yet decided as to which way they wanted to go. Finally, there were recently qualified students or technicians who moved around until they found a niche that stimulated them sufficiently to want to attach to.

Secrecy was impossible in such circumstances, and clashes of interest inevitable, which would have made such a system unthinkable on Earth. But Kronians valued the flow of information more highly than ownership, on the grounds that it would be more likely to find its way to whoever would make the best use of it. As with material things, proprietary information counted for little on Kronia. Nobody cared about, or was too impressed by, how much a person had; what mattered was what they could *do*.

The tube access point that Keene and Shayle alighted at was in the subsurface part of Essen's central area. They emerged on one side of a concourse where a traffic gallery carrying open-seat electric cars, and pedestrian terraces at various levels came together in a complex geometry that confused newcomers. A children's group wearing an assortment of traditional costumes from Earth was putting on some kind of performance in front of a grotto of shrubs and ferns, where water cascaded down too slowly over rocky ledges to a pond. Around and above were offices and other workplaces, eateries and stores—or at least, the places that came closest to serving the same purpose. For with no money system, people just took what they needed. Terrans had known about Kronian "commerce," of course, but even after seeing it for himself, Keene had remained baffled for a long time as to how it could work. It went against everything he had grown up understanding as making sense. If there was no restriction on what somebody could take, what was to prevent everyone from wanting everything? And given that, how could any system of production keep up?—never mind one as limited in kind and capacity as Kronia's.

But on Kronia it worked. Since possessions in themselves didn't signify anything that was especially valued, acquisitiveness taken too far was not only pointless but the equivalent of passing counterfeit bills. For by the principles of *appretiare*, the act of choosing a particular offering in preference to available alternatives was to acknowledge the value of the provider, thereby constituting payment. People produced—or served, or taught, or advised, or entertained— for the satisfaction of doing worthwhile work. Few greater ignominies were feared than putting one's best into an effort and having no takers—equivalent to bankruptcy, and a sign that one's calling lay somewhere else. But taking what wasn't needed or valued for itself was to tender appreciation that was not sincere and, hence, tantamount to paying in worthless currency.

A short walk along one of the galleries brought them to the front entrance of the Tesla Center. After crossing a reception foyer, they followed a corridor past some offices and then passed through a double-door fire dam and bulkhead lock to emerge on a walkway overlooking a different world of power engineering. The air smelt of hot oil and ozone, and thrummed to the vibration of heavy machinery. Two rotary housings twenty feet or more high stood on concrete plinths in the space below, surrounded by pumps, switch banks, and transformers wreathed in color-coded pipework and cabling. High-voltage insulator stacks stood beyond the supporting columns at the rear, with bus bars ascending to unseen regions above. They followed the walkway for a short distance and then descended a railed stairway to the floor below, crossing beneath a bridge of ducting and lagged steam pipes topped by a catwalk to a passage leading to doors through another double-wall bulkhead.

The surroundings on the far side were different again: more like a lobby, with some concession to color and pattern in the decor, elevator doors to one side, and glass-walled stairs going up to corridors leading away left and right on two levels. Ahead, a concertina drop-screen shut off a work zone where construction was in progress. This was a new extension of the Center, eventually to have its own tube terminal and access shaft to the surface. Pang-Yarbat and his group were just some of many relatively recent arrivals. The administrators took pride in finding room for everyone as their way of contributing to the Center's work, and ultimately, of keeping alive the population that would exist in years to come. Even a laborer with a shovel could watch the spectacle of a fusion-driven interplanetary lifting out of orbit and say, "I helped build the place where the engines for that ship were designed." *Appretiare.*

Pang-Yarbat's office with its lab space behind was roughly halfway along one of the upper corridors. They found him draped in the chair pushed back from his L-shaped desk with its usual litter of hand-scrawled calculations and papers, facing a screen showing some of the group's earlier work. The man seated in a chair drawn up behind him had to be Jansinick Wernstecki. The shelves around them were cluttered with tools, workshop materials, and pieces of equipment in various stages of disassembly. In the area to the rear, Reyd Orne and Merlin Friet were working amid a tangle of instrumentation wiring sprouting from where the outer metal cladding had been removed from the original

Valkyrie array—about the size of a regular door but thicker, mounted horizontally in a steel frame wreathed in tubes and power cabling.

"Ah, Lan!" Pang beamed, getting up. "So welcome back from your shot-in-the-arm vacation. We were starting to wonder if you were transferring up there permanently." It was one of Pang's puns. The Security "Arm," who among other things operated the LORIN stations, was the nearest Kronia had to a military force, while "shot" had doubtless been an allusion to X-ray laser bombs.

Pang was from somewhere in eastern Asia, brought to Kronia at an early age. He was short and chubby, with rich hair cropped short, and deep, alive eyes made more intense by ancient silver-framed spectacles which he refused to change for surgical correction. He had a broad, flat nose, fleshy chin to match, and a rubbery face that could take on an infinite variety of expressions and spoke its own language. His joviality and penchant for puns and expressing himself in riddles masked one of the most agile scientific minds that Keene had ever encountered—or maybe they were an irrepressible byproduct of it. Pang's father and an uncle had played key roles in the Kronian development of fusion energy after hostile politics quashed the chances of any concerted program on Earth, and Pang had followed in the same general field. In earlier years he had directed the design of the drives for the *Osiris* spacecraft that had brought Keene and others from Earth, so Keene's grasp of nuclear-propulsion physics had not been lost on him when it came to his attention. Inviting Keene into his group had been the result—not a bad salary offer at all for somebody relatively new in from Earth at the time.

Wernstecki, who had also stood at Keene and Shayle's arrival, was physically Pang's opposite in just about every respect. A tall, gaunt Caucasian, he had a halo of fair, frizzy hair, thin, pointy nose and chin, and thick lips that looked as if they belonged to another face. His eyes were pale, almost colorless, and took in Keene with a steady gaze, unlike Pang's, which shifted restlessly as if constantly reading in updates from the surroundings. His head was perched atop a long neck protruding from a shirt collar riding atop a sweater, with a light jacket hanging loosely over a gangly frame. Keene judged him to be in his mid thirties.

"Lan, meet Jansinick Wernstecki," Pang said, making an ushering motion. "Jan, this is Doctor Landen Keene, one of the survivors that Gallian's mission brought back, who looks after the power-engineering side of the project. . . . And this is Lan's colleague, Shayle Hartz. Fission and fusion. They make a good combination—or should I say hybrid? I hear Jan is one of the top theoreticians in celestial electrodynamics, Lan. A real live-wire in the field." The corners of the rubber mouth twitched upward. Keene refused to encourage him.

The three shook hands. Wernstecki's fingers were like turkey talons, but the grip was surprisingly firm. On meeting the unwavering eyes, Keene got the feeling of everything readable about himself being absorbed and logged, and immediately sensed an odd but strangely powerful personality. He knew that Wernstecki had been born on Enceladus and had studied under Pang's father for a while. He had gone on to specialize in celestial electrical phenomena, and in recent years had been involved in the frantic work of trying to quantify and recompute the changed dynamics of the Solar System following Athena's disruptive electrical effects. Pang, recognizing the potential value of this kind of experience in electro-gravitic interactions to his own project, had invited Wernstecki to visit Tesla and learn more of what they were doing there. He hadn't said anything specifically about recruiting him . . . but Wernstecki would know how things worked.

Pang went on, "I've told Jan that our work began as a generalization of Weber's force law. . . . But why don't I let Lan come into the act more and take it from here?"

Keene understood that the invitation was as much for Keene to establish his own credentials in Wernstecki's eyes as to help Pang assess Wernstecki's. "You're familiar with that, Jan?" he inquired.

Wernstecki nodded. "Yes, of course. Weber's original work was to derive the Ampère current law by generalizing Coulomb's force law to include second order reciprocal terms in c." He paused, as if for a response. For some reason Keene had expected a reedy voice, but it was deep and firm, like the handshake.

"Unifying electrostatics with electrodynamics," Keene said. "It gave a correct expression for wave propagation before Maxwell."

"Jointly with Neumann," Wernstecki supplied. "They also succeeded in deriving Faraday's induction law from the force law, and formulated the first example in physics of a potential energy that depended on the velocity of the interacting particles."

It sounded like a perfect background for the Tesla project. No wonder Pang's eyes were twinkling. Pang seemed to decide suddenly to put Wernstecki out of the strain of suppressed curiosity that was written all over his face. "We extended the force law further to include still higher terms," he said, turning to face Wernstecki fully. "Then we used it to calculate the average force between groups of neutral dipoles consisting of paired oscillating charges. The results were interesting. It indicated a residual force as a fourth-order effect. Inverse-square. Attractive."

Wernstecki didn't need time to think. Keene saw that what it meant was clear to him immediately.

The velocity of light, conventionally denoted as c, is a very large number. The reciprocal, 1 divided by c, is therefore a very small number. The fourth-order term meant the term in Pang's extended force-law polynomial that contained the reciprocal multiplied by itself four times, which would give an inconceivably small number. That was how small the force that Pang was talking about—an attractive force between the dipoles—would be compared to the electrical force between the charges forming them.

"Forty orders of magnitude smaller," Wernstecki pronounced, after calculating a quick mental approximation.

An electrical dipole is an object carrying positive and negative charges concentrated in two distinct regions, such as at opposite ends. An "oscillating" dipole meant a system of two or more charges bound together in constrained motion. An atom would be an example. Although neutral as a whole, an atom's internal stresses cause the charge of its constituent protons and electrons to be distributed unevenly, making it a dipole. Pang was saying that a tiny attractive force, diminishing as the square of the separating distance, was produced as a statistical residue of the electrical forces between oscillating groups of net-neutral charges.

Such a group would be formed by an assemblage of atoms—in other words, mass. And gravity, the weakest force known to physics, was forty orders of magnitude less than the electrical force. Hence, Pang was saying that gravity appeared as a byproduct of the internal electrical nature of matter. And that much was interesting and exciting in itself, to be sure. But it wasn't exactly new. Speculations and theoretical studies of such a possibility went back a long way. Evidently there was more to it.

Wernstecki looked at the images on the screens again—metal frameworks filled with arrays of unusual electrical devices, typical thrown-together lab efforts. One showed a technician in clean-room garb floating in midair while making some adjustment—clearly a freefall setting. Then he turned to gaze back at the woman and the youth working on the construction in the area at the rear. The exposed section revealed banks of chip-like devices packed in a system of mounting frames strung with bundles of conductors. But the conductors were too heavy for them to be circuit chips; and woven among them was a forced-flow cooling matrix of capacity no electronic system would have needed. A light of understanding came over Wernstecki's face, and the pale eyes shone with genuine astonishment. "Artificial gravity? You've done it? Experimentally? You have verification?"

Pang waved the last of Wernstecki's suspense away with a toss of his hand. "That unit behind us at the back there was actually the first prototype that we built on Valkyrie, before we moved down here and Lan's team joined us. The view on the screen was the final phase of the dipole array wiring."

Valkyrie was an orbiting platform above Titan that housed an odd mixture of scientific and other facilities, including a spherical swimming pool, a 3-D sports arena, an arboretum featuring some strangely shaped plants, and a school of weightless architecture. However, many of the former

occupants had evacuated to the surface since the bombard-
ments caused by Athena began. During his spell on LORIN
5, Keene had learned that the rest of the space was to be
vacated too, and the platform converted into a close-range
defense station for Titan.

"You're talking about huge currents," Wernstecki commented
distantly. He was visibly excited, his mind racing over the
implications.

"One of the problems with the early experiments was to
deliver enough without getting friction or reaction effects that
would have swamped the measurements," Pang agreed. "Solid
conductors were unworkable. In the end we resorted to pinch-
stabilized mercury bridges. Doing it in zero-g eliminated a
lot of spurious background, and the electromagnetic shielding had to be a hundred percent. That was why we stayed
so long up in Valkyrie. But in the end, the effect we achieved
exceeded the attraction of normal matter by a factor of over
fifty. We were measuring tens of nanograms, but it was there.
It was real. We could switch it on and off." He inclined his
head to indicate the direction behind. "With power flowing,
we can make that array act like a twelve-ton mass. And even
with that array, we could improve the figure by a factor of
a million . . . if the structure could stand it."

As Wernstecki leaned back in the chair, thinking, his eyes
came unconsciously back to Keene. Keene could almost read
him fitting the pieces together. Artificial gravity had been
talked about for much longer than Kronia had existed. The
immediate applications would be in spacecraft and satellites,
eliminating the need for ungainly simulations by rotating
structures or whirling modules at the ends of booms and
tethers. Later, larger-scale booster systems could perhaps be
implanted in low-gravity bodies like asteroids or the gas-
giant moons to create Earth-normal conditions at the surface.
And after that . . . who knew? Whole new technologies of
matter manipulation, weight neutralization, freight handling,
earthmoving . . .

But taking it beyond the research stage that Pang had
described would require lots of electrical power. Hence, the
Tesla Center was the obvious place to continue the work.
That was why the project had relocated here and why Pang

had brought Keene's group into it. He had needed power engineers, and nuclear-proficient ones at that—the watts to induce normal bodyweights on spacecraft flight decks or increase Titan's effective mass thirtyfold weren't going to come from any other source. The source would need to be efficient and compact, suitable for being built onto space vehicles. Keene's spaceborne MHD concept had fitted the need perfectly.

"So how far are you now toward a more advanced stage than that prototype?" Wernstecki asked finally. Pang let Keene answer.

"We have a one hundredfold scaled-up engineering proving model almost built here," Keene said. "Down in one of the heavy equipment bays." He looked inquiringly at Pang. "I assume we'll be taking Jan to see it?"

"Naturally, naturally." Pang kept his gaze directed at Wernstecki. "This will open up a totally new realm of physics. New industries will follow one day, revolutionizing engineering, leading to full colonization of the Solar System." In Kronian terms, he was saying that the payoff for being part of such an undertaking, if it succeeded, would be fabulous.

Watching Wernstecki's face, Keene had the feeling it would be only a matter of time before the project acquired a new talent. Wernstecki himself addressed the issue directly, avoiding any pretenses. "When would you want some kind of decision?" he asked Pang-Yarbat.

Pang waved a hand carelessly. "Take your time. I know that the work you're doing at present is important too. Be sure in your own mind what you want." He paused for a moment, tried but was unable to resist it, and grinned an insincere apology at Keene and Shayle. "It's a weighty matter, after all."

CHAPTER FOUR

Keene had arranged to meet Grasse in the bar attached to an eating place called the Rhinehaus, located in Essen's subsurface central area not far from the Tesla Center. A ramp down from one of the pedestrian ways brought him to an open lobby in front of the dining area. The bar seating was off to one side, down a few more stairs. . . .

He remembered an evening when he'd met Cavan in a hotel restaurant in Washington. One wall had been of windows looking out over lawns sloping down to a water's edge shaded by trees. He had nursed a drink and watched ducks swimming close by the shore as he waited for Cavan to arrive. . . .

"Can I help you, sir?"

Keene returned abruptly to the present of false-window walls with fake scenery, to find a girl in a pastel blue workcoat looking at him. He realized that he had come to a halt and was standing, lost in his revery.

"Oh . . . It's all right. I'm meeting someone there." He indicated with a nod.

"Would you like to take a menu through with you?"

"Maybe later. Thanks."

The bar decor was more subdued, with dark carpeting and upholstery and lots of imitation wood—an attempt at injecting a Terran touch. The walls carried framed prints of

35

ships and harbor scenes along with plastic replicas of portholes, ships' bells and lights, rope fittings, and other items of maritime equipage. Grasse was sitting in an alcove booth in a far corner, partly screened by a pillar and plant trellis. He hadn't said anything about bringing company, but there was another man with him whom Keene would have known instinctively to be Terran also, even if the face had not been familiar. Keene carried on over and joined them. The bartender glided across as Keene sat down.

Grasse was a small man with a snub nose, prominent ears, and features that seemed somehow compacted into pink folds and horizontal lines that put Keene in mind of an overripe fruit slightly squashed. The other was long of build and face, with droopy, spaniel-like eyes, and sallow skin stretched into hollows between bony cheeks and a protruding, blue-shadowed chin. Grasse waited while Keene ordered a Celtic Dark—one of the Rhinehaus's preferred beers, brewed in the agroplex on Mimas. The bartender departed. Keene looked across the booth expectantly.

"Dr. Keene, I'd like you to meet General Claud Valcroix," Grasse said. "One of the survivors like ourselves, before with the French defense ministry. We have worked together on and off over many years. We were with the same group that escaped together." He meant in the Eurospace orbital lifter from Algeria.

Although Keene had little inclination to get involved in such matters, he knew Valcroix's face from news screens and a few social functions that he had attended. Valcrois was emerging as spokesman for the Terran evacuees and representative of their interests in the Kronian political scene. The European clique had risen to prominence in this respect, a disproportionate number of their American political and military counterparts having been lost in incidents following the general escape from Earth.

Valcroix and Keene shook hands across the table. "I have heard your story," the Frenchman said. "Amazing."

"Amazing stories were happening everywhere in those times," Keene answered. "I didn't know mine was so famous."

"Your friend, Leo Cavan, told me about it."

Keene's eyebrows rose. "Are you and Leo old friends from the past too?"

"We've had certain dealings since coming to Kronia," Valcroix said.

That fitted. After younger years spent in the Air Force, Cavan had led a shady life as a denizen of the Washington political underworld, but as far as Keene knew his haunts hadn't extended to the European scene.

"Your visit to LORIN 5 was useful?" Grasse inquired.

Keene nodded. "It answered a lot of questions that I'd been wondering about. More to do with the organizational aspects than anything technical." He meant about operation of the Security Arm, which ran the LORIN stations and came closest to fitting a military role. It also functioned as something of a safety valve to disperse the excess energies of Kronians stifling from their life of containment and routine. Many of the younger Terran evacuees had volunteered for the Security Arm. Keene went on, "Did you know that their officers are appointed by consensus from below, not imposed from above?" General Valcroix nodded that he was aware of that, then shook his head in a way that said it made no sense.

The Austrian glanced at his watch. "Anyway, Dr. Keene, the reason I asked to talk to you has to do with matters that some of us feel concerns about. So I decided to invite the opinions of others as well." Keene waited. Grasse cast an eye around as if making sure they were not being overheard. His voice dropped. "Our concerns are with the way of organization here in Kronia. You take my point? Not so much the day-to-day routines of things, but the idealizations that make the foundation underneath it all."

He paused for a reaction.

"I'm listening," Keene said.

Grasse waved a hand. "Their priorities here are in the reverse order of what they need to be if the right things are to get done. And the way of going about achieving them is impractical. I give you as examples—Urzin is again talking about bringing forward the time to send missions back to Earth. He wants a permanent base there. And then it will be bases." Xen Urzin was President of the Triad that headed

Kronia's governing body, formally known as the Congress of Leaders. Grasse continued, "But why do they want to send these missions? As the first step to return and begin rebuilding Earth's civilization? To survey for important resources?" Grasse shook his head. "No. It is for scientists to explore the changed surface and rewrite their geology textbooks. And the best scientists here on Kronia spend their time debating these things of how Venus was ejected from Jupiter and when the Earth was lost from Saturn, instead of how to support the population we will have fifty years from now. . . . I ask you, Doctor, is this a rational way that a tiny colony, isolated out here like this, should be thinking? The first need is to expand and consolidate our industries and their materials base. It is survival we are talking. That is what I mean by priorities."

Keene's drink arrived. Valcroix took up when the bartender had departed again. "The Kronians are making science a religion. Back on Earth, science served practical ends— because it was controlled by people who understood policy-making. But here there is no effective control. Instead, we have this insanity of multiple competing operations all duplicating each others' efforts. We can't afford that—certainly not at the present time. This colony is strung out to its limits. It doesn't have the resources."

Keene looked from one to the other as he took a draft of his beer. It didn't take a lot of imagination to guess who they—and the others that they had alluded to—considered more qualified to exercise that control.

But Keene had seen enough on Earth to know what happened when science sold out and allowed itself to be conscripted to serve politics. The question of resources might be a valid one, but it didn't follow that the solution had to be some centrally directed policy. It was more likely, in fact, to impede finding the right solution. Bureaucratic control virtually guaranteed that the unorthodox and unpredictable— less amenable to forecasts and planning, but at the same time more likely to yield truly novel approaches—would never be attempted.

Now Keene thought he was beginning to see what this was about. Grasse and Valcroix hadn't come here so much to invite his opinion as to sound him out as a prospective recruit to something that they weren't prepared to disclose for the present. Or to be marked as a potential enemy. He would need to play this carefully. He sought for a reply that would avoid commitment, while keeping open his options. Sometimes the Kronian way of going about things seemed so much cleaner and simpler.

"Are you saying they shouldn't be planning on resuming missions back to Earth?" he replied. "For all we know, a general return there might eventually be forced. Or we could find we can't manage without its resources. Either way, it makes sense to have pilot bases there as soon as it's safe, if just for insurance. And then there's the simple humanitarian reason of doing what can be done for any survivors there might still be."

"No, no . . . It's the *kind* of mission," Valcroix said. "They need properly formulated goals, relevant to the immediate interests of this colony. We can't allow such efforts to be misdirected into providing elaborate playgrounds for academics."

Keene nodded in a neutral way. He could see no point in taking issue at the moment. "The Kronians seem to have done a pretty good job of surviving so far," he pointed out instead, taking up Grasse's other point.

Grasse nodded his gnomish head and sighed. "Yes, yes . . . I agree. They are to be commended on a remarkable achievement. But let us remember, Dr. Keene, that it was done by a small population of self-selected idealists. The lack of an economic imperative might seem to work for a while among highly motivated people, all dedicated to their cause. But that will change now. As Kronia grows, all the different views and arguments that we know from Earth will reappear. There will have to be adopted a practical way for quantifying priorities and allocating resources. This we know from our own history of experiences. But the Kronians, they do not have the experience."

"You mean by means of a monetary system," Keene said.

"Yes, of course. Financial controls." Grasse indicated the glass that Keene was holding. "There is an example in your hand. You walk in; they give you the drink; you pay nothing.

It is an absurdity. How can an economy of any sense grow from this basis?" Keene didn't know either. But looking around, he didn't see any drunks. He decided to let the point go. Grasse went on, "However, now it so happens that some of us with skills in just these areas have arrived here from Earth. It could mean the difference between life and death to this colony. So perhaps, when one thinks this through logically, it is not just that we can help the Kronians meet what will become a vital need by introducing our methods. Some would say we have a moral obligation to do so. Wouldn't you agree, Dr. Keene?"

CHAPTER FIVE

Rakki climbed through steep, slippery rain gullies gouged between walls of broken rock, picking his way through tangles of gray, leathery growth, moist from vapors carried by the wind from the swamps below. He moved surely but cautiously, avoiding the thorn thickets and turning aside the limbs of coarse leaves that tried to tear at his arms and legs. His feet were bare. On his body he wore just a loin covering of skin and a vest of some thick, stiff, Oldworld material, open at the chest and with holes for the arms, that he had taken from the body of an enemy dispatched long ago. There was still a blood-blackened patch on one side. Shifting veils of gray formed a permanent canopy overhead, thickening into a black murk above the fire mountains to the east that glowed red at night, where lightning flickered intermittently and nothing lived. Yesterday had seen snowflakes and squalls of wind-driven ice. Yet the rivulets of muddy water running down from the heights above were warm around his feet.

He came up out of the ravine onto a more open slope of scrub and tilted boulders leaning in piles where they had tumbled down. Above him, the slope leveled out into a terrace of broken ground and rock falls along the base of a line of cliffs where the Cavers lived. In front of the openings, connecting surrounding mounds of high ground, they had built a rampart of earth and rocks that closed back to the cliffs on either side to form a walled-in area. The Swamp People had spent many hours watching the Cavers and their movements. The rampart was always guarded. Rakki sniffed the air but could read little from it up here, with the wind. The sound of barking erupted suddenly from above. The dogs had detected him. A barrier blocking a gap between two of the high points of the rampart, fashioned from limbs of dead trees and thorn bush, was raised. Rakki saw the dogs rush out, following them with his eyes in and out among the rocks as they ran down toward him. Human figures followed. He waited.

The dogs emerged from cover—four of them, spreading out to close from all sides. Rakki backed against a boulder and tightened his grip on the edged club that he was carrying—another battle trophy, a length of Oldworld metal topped at one end by a crosspiece sharpened on stone, a grip woven from vine strands at the other. The dogs inched closer, keeping low near the ground, paws stretched ahead, fangs bared, growling and snarling. Five Cavers appeared, following them. Two looked to be no older than Rakki and were carrying spears. *Neffers,* like him—their minds formed by the things that were, knowing nothing of the world that had existed before the fire and the Long Night came, and the earth was torn asunder. The third was older, scrawny, with wild eyes and tufts of face hair, waving a club cut from root wood. But it was the last two that Rakki found himself staring at, for a moment dulling his normally ceaseless alertness to everything around him. They were larger, with thick hair and deep lines covering faces that had seen many years. *Oldworlders!*

Rakki had only seen dead Oldworlders before—who had lived as part of the world that had once been. Although his own earliest years must have gone back to those times, he had no real recollections of them, or of parents or anyone else he had been with then. At times there would come odd fragments of things, like a fading dream that no longer meant anything. Neffers did best in the world that now was. Shaped by it and attuned to it, they accepted its uncompromising reality and lived by its harsh rules instinctively. It was those who seemed to live with part of their mind in one world and part in another who tended to be ineffective and erratic, either withdrawing into long silences that could last for days, or sliding the other way toward craziness like the wild-eyed one pointing the spear. And then, Rakki had heard, there were some left from the Old World, usually older still, with a different kind of strength that had enabled them to pull through and carry on functioning.

The two before him now wore coverings of material that was crinkly like his vest, but not as thick, torn and patched, extending over their upper arms and down their legs, with strange sheaths like animal paws around their feet. One of them was peculiarly pink, the color of hand palms. Rakki had heard of light-skinned humans but never seen one. While the others carried spears, the two Oldworlders were holding implements of intricately shaped Oldworld metal—something like Rakki's club, but without any weighted head or edge. Rakki took them to be the weapons that Jemmo had talked about. But on looking them over now, up close, he was puzzled. There was no way he could see that they could make an effective weapon. Yet Jemmo had said they possessed fearsome power.

The two with spears leveled them to keep Rakki against the rock while the light-skin looked him over. His face behind the hair was twisted and sour, the eyes cold and hard. "Watchoo want comin' aroun' heyah, mud rat?" he demanded.

Rakki forced his expression to remain firm, fighting back his fear reflex. He raised an arm in the direction of the caves above. One of the dogs growled a warning at the movement. "Come in. Weary of killing land. Live with Cave People. Work hard. Fight for," Rakki said. The crazy-eyed one emitted a screeching laugh and spat at the ground.

The darker Oldworlder leered, showing spaces among yellow teeth. One of his arms was heavily scarred and hung in an odd, stiff kind of way. "Jus' a kid, Bo. What kind o' work him good for? Mo' food o' ours he eat. Da's all."

"Bettah use for us if make him dawg food instead, maybe," Lightskin said.

"*Dog meat! Dog meat!*" the crazy-eye screeched, obviously finding it hilarious.

"Juswait! Jusyouwait!" Rakki's chest was pounding. What if he'd misjudged? He felt for the pouch inside his vest. Scar-arm pointed his Oldworld club at him. It made a clicking noise. "Easy now, jus' easy, okay." Rakki's fingers found the four metal fingers that he had brought—yellow-brown at the flat ends, changing to gray where they rounded into points. He brought them out and showed them. "Look, more use than jus' work. Know things and places. Make Cave People strong."

Scar-arm took one of the fingers and examined it, then handed it to Lightskin. "Look like good bullet there, Bo," he said. If that's what it was called, Rakki didn't know what it meant. But he'd been told that Oldworlders valued them highly.

"Wheah you get these heah, mud rat?" Lightskin demanded.

"There's mo' bullet like that, lots mo'."

"Roun' these part? You tell straight, now."

Rakki pointed north and east, where dry heights of unclimbable walls and deep canyons gave way eventually to watery lowlands that connected via a roundabout route to the swamp lands south from the caves, where Rakki was from. "Three days, that way. You see, I know things. Know places. Rakki come live with Cave People. Can tell. Good for Cave People too."

The two Oldworlders looked at each other. "Watch' think, Bo?" Scar-arm asked, eyeing Rakki again dubiously.

Lightskin seemed to turn the proposition over before coming to a decision. "Maybe is so, could be," he said finally. "Take him back up, talk to Mistameg. He know. He say what we do."

The screecher took Rakki's weapon and waved him on as the two Oldworlders turned to lead the way back up to the caves. The two Neffers fell in behind, keeping their spears still leveled, while the dogs stayed close by. The screecher seemed disappointed by the outcome.

CHAPTER SIX

Vicki Delucey had been enthralled by Kronian science long before Athena erupted out of Jupiter. Originally a radiation physicist at Harvard, she had met Keene when he was engaged in plasma dynamics research there. When he gave up trying to fight the politics that had come to dominate academic science, she had followed him south to Texas and partnered with him in founding a nuclear-space-propulsion engineering consultancy catering to the private sector. Keene's dealings with the space business and his conclusion that Terran Establishment Science had taken on a role comparable to that of the medieval European Church brought him into early contact with Kronian scientists and their nondogmatic approach of following what appeared to be the facts wherever they led, regardless of preconceptions and hoped-for answers.

Kronian interest in science was general, pervading the culture as a deeply ingrained desire to know about their origins and understand better the nature of the universe they found themselves in. With the old, comforting picture of the heavens as eternally safe and stable now dead, one of their major endeavors was to reconstruct the history of catastrophic changes that had shaped the Solar System within the last ten or so thousand years. Their approach admitted a broader base of knowledge than had been recognized as "science" on Earth, in that it combined the findings of modern-day physics and astronomy with certain interpretations of the mythologies of ancient cultures that the Kronians accepted as attempts by nontechnical peoples to record cosmic events that they had actually witnessed. Along with this, the Kronians also sought new accounts of planetary origins and evolution, for in the chaos brought by Athena, the old notions of slow, gradual change as the guiding paradigm of geology had similarly died. These questions assumed the role of mysteries in what had become, in effect, the Kronian cultural religion. The need to answer them formed a drive of virtually spiritual dimensions, inculcated in the schools and echoed in every reach of working and domestic life.

Two major upheavals, the Kronians were by now fairly sure, had affected the Solar System in comparatively recent times. The earlier, and perhaps more astounding, of these had been inferred from a discovery that occurred only shortly before Earth's devastation by Athena. For several decades, archeologists had been uncovering evidence of a vanished city-building culture in the region of southwest Arabia and the African Horn. Called the "Joktanian," it had apparently existed long before what were supposed to have been the earliest civilizations. Then, artifacts of indisputably intelligent origin were found by the Kronians in the ice fields of Rhea. The only way they could have gotten there—short of being carried by an advanced technological culture that there was no reason to believe had existed—was through ejection following an impact or some other comparably violent event that had occurred nearby. But when the artifacts were identified beyond doubt as Joktanian, it seemed to follow that the nearby source from which they had come must have been Earth. The implication was so fantastic that Kronian scientists had been scouring the evidence ever since for another interpretation, but the answer always came out the same: At some distant time, but still within the timescale of human experience, the whole system of Sun and planets had been different. Earth was once a satellite of Saturn.

Theories as to the configuration that had existed at that time differed. Since little remained of any physical signature, the only real guide lay in observations recorded in ancient myths and symbolic accounts, which inevitably drew many alternative interpretations. The proposals being argued ranged from various redistributions of the bodies of the known Solar System—minus Venus—to a capture model in which Earth had formed part of a mini-family accompanying a proto-sun Saturn that encountered and combined with the Sun-Jupiter system. In the latter case, the ensuing turmoil could account for just about any arrangement of orbits found subsequently. But in the less radical models, where Earth and Saturn both formed part of a stable Solar System to begin with, the question then arose of what had caused them to separate. The only plausible mechanism seemed to be either a close encounter with, or impact by, another body—either already-existing, or ejected from one of the gas giants in a process of the kind generally accepted as having originated all the minor planets and other lesser bodies.

These fissions had at first been attributed to the buildup of instabilities in a rapidly rotating gas-giant core sufficient to shed excess mass, which was theoretically possible and thought to have happened with Athena. However, a rival theory now held them to be rebound ejecta from massive impacts—in which case Athena and Jupiter's "Huge White Blotch," which now surpassed the Great Red Spot, were results of a freak approach that had occurred on the blind side from Earth. But whatever the detailed cause, the time of Earth's detachment to become a solar planet was generally put at around 10,000 years Before the Present, with the consequences for Earth that had included climatic and geological upheaval, biological mass-extinctions, and collapse of the earliest human civilization.

Regardless of what the final verdict concerning this earlier period turned out to be, nobody any longer disputed that Venus was not something that had orbited the Sun for over four billion years as once taught, but a young, recently incandescent object ejected from Jupiter some time after the Saturn breakup. The reigning Kronian model of what had taken place traced back to heretical challenges to orthodox astronomy that had first been proposed in the mid-twentieth century and held that after its violent birth, Venus had careened about the Solar System as a loose cannon, disturbing the orbits of both Earth and Mars and eventually circularizing its own orbit to become the planetary body familiar in modern times. Stories handed down since antiquity from the Middle East, India, and China, from Siberia through Europe to the Americas, described it as appearing in the sky as what could be recognized as a giant comet, seen universally as a wrathful goddess approaching at intervals to bring times of chaos and destruction. Newly-born Venus was believed to have been responsible for the calamities recorded at the time of the Hebrew Exodus, roughly 3500 B.P., also described recognizably by other peoples the world over. Initial reactions from Earth's scientific institutions had been all but universal ridicule at first, then grudging concessions to catastrophic events shaping at least some features of Earth and other bodies—so long as they were confined to happening in the distant past—and eventually full-blooded confrontation with the Kronians. Then Athena repeated the process and settled further dispute.

After an initial period of adjustment and reorientation on Titan with other Terran survivors, Vicki and her son, Robin, fifteen at the time they came to Kronia, had settled at Kropotkin "city" on Dione, the original base site of the first settlers. Although somewhat glorified in name by the standards that would have designated a city back on Earth, Kropotkin did have the largest residential population in Kronia. After at first feeling as if she were regressing into some kind of human mole in its artificial, machine-supported environment, she had come to accept now that this would probably be home for the rest of her life. Not the home she had planned or imagined she would raise her son in after his father died in the Navy—but at least it was one where Robin would go on, as securely as could be asked for, to lead a full life. The visions of Earth with their midnight sweats and palpitations were fading now, although as with all who had come through it, the nightmare would never entirely be erased. To a large degree, her immersion in Kronian science was also a means of psychological escape.

She sat with Emil Farzhin and their two visitors in a subsurface room of the Planetary Sciences section of

Kropotkin's Polysophic Academy. Vicki had a petite, wiry body that had preserved its leanness despite not working off energy constantly against Terran gravity, a freckled, angular face accentuated by a pointy nose and sharp chin, and light brown, almost orange hair that contracted into curls no matter how she tried to comb or wave it. She was never quite sure how to describe the Academy. It was a mixture of multidiscipline research institute and high school. The classes that Robin had attended for the past three years were held in various parts of it.

As had been the case with Earth's Moon—now broken up and carried away by Athena—Dione orbited with the same side always facing its primary, and major impacts had so far been confined to the "prow" face. All the same, the surface portion of Kropotkin had suffered considerable damage from secondary ejecta, and the population had moved belowground as far as possible. The lines of the walls and ceiling were visibly off square from distortion of the general structure by shock waves, and sounds of riveting and the intermittent shriek of a metal cutter came from beyond, where a work crew were restoring the corridor outside. Pressure-suit-and-helmet packs hung in a rack by the door, ready for immediate use; but everyone knew that a major strike even in the general vicinity would mean total obliteration.

Farzhin was a rotund, balding, one-time Iranian who headed a group that Vicki's interests had brought her into contact with at the Academy and eventually joined. His function embraced the roles that she thought of as private researcher and teacher. As Keene had found too, there was less formal structuring here than at the institutions she had been used to in her previous life. She hadn't applied or had to negotiate an obstacle course of bureaucracy, but just attached herself in a helping-out capacity to begin with, been judged acceptable, and ended up part of the team. The main work of Farzhin's group was reinvestigating the theory of Venus's early history based on new interpretations of the Indian Vedas, which constituted some of Earth's most ancient writings.

"We're not questioning that the Venus encounter happened,"

Vicki said. "But . . . I'm not sure how to put it. Whatever way we look at it, we can't avoid the conclusion that the timing in the standard account is wrong. We think there were two close passes with Earth, not one, and that they happened somewhere around two thousand years earlier than is generally believed."

Farzhin explained, "I'm sure that the hymn describing the birth of the mother goddess Aditi from Dyauspitar, which was Jupiter, refers to the ejection of Venus. This clearly parallels the Greek account of Pallas Athene springing from the brow of Zeus. But dating the event that the Greek version talks about has always involved a lot of guesswork. The Vedic records are more precise. The *Rig Veda* describes two devastating visits by the raging fire deity, Agni, in the years following. Although It doesn't specifically identify Agni as Aditi but calls him Aditya, which means son of Aditi, there are enough clues to link them as the same object. It has to be Venus in its white-hot, protoplanet phase. But the time of menace from Agni ended around 5100 years Before the Present."

The room had a scattering of chairs around a central table, a worktop along one side equipped with screens and a holo-viewer, and closets and drawers beneath. It was used for meetings and mini-conferences. Sariena sat across the table, still striking with her shoulder-length dark hair, dusky brown skin, and sultry, light gray eyes with their curious hint of opalescence, but looking tired. She was one of the Kronian planetary scientists that Vicki had gotten to know from a distance through working with Keene back on Earth, and then had come to Earth as part of the Kronian delegation sent to plead its case for a more vigorous and wider-ranging space effort.

Visiting along with Sariena was a former project manager from JPL in California called Charlie Hu. Of Asian origins, in his fifties, with streaky graying hair and trimmed beard, he had come from Earth with the same group that had included Vicki and Keene. These days he was working with Sariena in one of the orbiting observatories on recomputing the changed Solar System dynamics—a risky undertaking in view of the exposure, but there was no other way for the work to get done. Charlie often said that he'd heard all there could be to make him revise beliefs that he had accepted as uncontroversial when he graduated in planetary astronomy long ago. Now, the look on his face was saying that the Kronians had sent his thinking into a whirl once again.

Sariena and Charlie had come to Kropotkin at Vicki's suggestion to hear more about Farzhin's work. She hoped it would excite their interest sufficiently to bring it to the attention of the people they worked with, who represented the more mainstream view. Although the distances within the Saturnian moon system seemed vast compared to what Terrans had been accustomed to, the small gravity wells and high speeds of Kronian transorbital vessels put journey times about on par with jetting around Earth in former days.

Sariena regarded Farzhin at some length. Vicki could almost sense her checking over what he had said point by point. Finally, she said, "If Venus goes back that far . . . then it couldn't have been a newly created comet at the time of the Exodus."

Farzhin nodded. "I agree. But then I don't think that the Exodus event involved a newly created, planet-size comet. For one thing, it wasn't violent enough. Oh, the calamities that the accounts talk about were bad enough, yes—and the others things recorded around the world at that time. But they weren't on the kind of scale you'd expect with an object that hot, almost as big as Earth itself. Agni, on the other hand, was truly terrifying, searing the Earth, destroying whole regions totally. Humanity came close to being wiped out. In fact, I think that could have been what created the great desert belts—they still hadn't recovered, even after all that time. It's more what you'd expect."

Charlie Hu looked questioningly at Sariena. "You know, after seeing how violent the effects of Athena were compared to Exodus, I've wondered the same thing. This does sound more like proto-Venus." Sariena nodded but was still far away in thought. Charlie looked back at Farzhin. "So are we talking about later encounters with Venus in a cooled-down phase?" He frowned. "But no—you said there were only two."

"I tried fitting Venus with various later events that the Vedas describe, but it just didn't work," Farzhin said. "We chewed it over this way and that, trying to make sense of all the different things the ancient Sanskrit records talk about. And the upshot is, we think that the Exodus encounter was one of a different series that happened later."

"Different?" Charlie repeated. "You mean with something else? Not Venus at all?"

"Exactly," Farzhin said.

"What, then?"

"We think it was Mars."

Sariena's eyes interrogated him silently. Finally, she said, "That would change a lot of things that we thought we were sure about."

The current Kronian model had Venus approaching Earth periodically after the Exodus encounter to bring times of turmoil and unrest—but of reducing severity—until around the Roman era, when an interaction with Mars caused it to recede finally to the orbit found in modern times. However, Farzhin was saying that the interaction between Venus and Mars happened much earlier, and it was *Mars*, not Venus, that had continued to visit the Earth on a repeating basis thereafter. Vicki was impressed that Sariena was able so matter-of-factly to consider a proposition which, if true, would bring tumbling down a whole area of Kronian planetary science that she herself had spent years helping to put together. A comparable reaction from the halls of Terran academia would have been all but unthinkable.

"What led you to think of Mars?" Charlie Hu asked curiously.

"Various lines in the Sanskrit texts that fit too neatly to be a coincidence," Farzhin replied. He smiled faintly. "But one of the things that first pointed us in that direction was Robin."

Sariena looked puzzled. "You mean Vicki's son?"

"Robin?" Charlie repeated.

"He was in one of my classes," Farzhin said. "Some time after he and Vicki arrived in Kropotkin, he came to me with ancient depictions of the deity Shiva that we had been discussing, and pointed out how they could describe features on the surface of Mars. And he was right. The similarities were uncanny."

"It's the kind of thing he comes up with." Vicki sighed resignedly, at the same time shrugging in a way that was almost apologetic.

"We'll show you some examples later of what I mean," Farzhin said. "They fit with things in the Egyptian, Sumerian, and Greek accounts too."

"But this is where we need your input," Vicki told Sariena and Charlie. "Why I wanted you to come here and talk about this. You're the orbital mechanics specialists. We've just been looking at ancient mythologies—and maybe reading too much into them. Tell us if something along the lines of what we think happened is possible."

Sariena and Charlie glanced at each other. Clearly, they were interested. "Try us," Sariena invited.

Vicki looked at Farzhin, but he nodded for her to carry on. She began, "Venus came out of Jupiter on a highly eccentric orbit—possibly sun-grazing, like Athena. After the two close flybys that scorched Earth, it commenced a series of interactions with Mars, which originally occupied an orbit inside Earth's."

"*Inside* Earth's orbit?" Charlie repeated, raising his eyebrows. Farzhin and Vicki nodded. Sariena stared intently but didn't interrupt. Vicki continued, "This is what we want your opinion on. Could the two bodies have exchanged angular momentum in such a way as to progressively lift Mars to more distant orbits, at the same time reducing and circularizing Venus's to an inferior one?"

She watched Charlie in particular as she said this. One of the reasons why Terran astronomers had opposed the young-Venus theory so strongly was the problem of how it could have circularized its orbit in a mere few thousand years. The Kronians had proposed two mechanisms for accomplishing this: the effect of electrical forces in the modified space environment induced by Venus's electrically active plasma tail; and the gravitational pumping of a hot, plastically deformable body to reduce tidal stresses. Charlie had never been convinced that these on their own would be sufficient, maintaining that something else was needed in addition. Well, Vicki was saying in effect, maybe here it is.

Charlie was staring back at her with the incredulous half-smile of somebody who wasn't quite sure whether or not he wanted to believe it. He looked sideways at Sariena in an unspoken question. "It's an intriguing thought," she said. Evidently, she had no such problem.

Farzhin came back in at this point. "From what we can make of the Vedic records, it seems that some kind of recurring pattern established itself, in which the three bodies kept coming back into mutual proximity." He made an appealing gesture at the two planetary scientists. "Could something like that happen?"

Sariena pursed her lips. "A three-way resonance? Yes, it's possible in principle. But whether or not this particular configuration meets the necessary conditions would depend on the numbers. We'd need to set up a simulation with a credible range of limits and run the calculations."

"Would you do that for us?" Farzhin asked.

"Of course . . . How long do you think this pattern lasted? Have you any idea?"

"Almost two thousand years . . . until the beginnings of the Roman Period, about 2700 B.P. So the visitation that brought the Exodus plagues and afflictions wasn't by Venus but by Mars, which if we're right, had by that time already been interacting with Earth for around sixteen hundred years. Although these approaches heralded times of trouble and destruction that the priests and prophets of many religions learned to read, they didn't cause anything like the global devastation that Venus had earlier—"

"And Athena," Vicki put in.

"Yes, of course."

A few seconds of silence fell. Then Charlie waved vaguely with a hand. "It's fantastic . . . but we're all getting used to that by now. I'd like to see how it fits with the circularization criterion." He thought more and shook his head. "Fantastic," he said again.

"You haven't heard the rest yet, Charlie," Vicki said dryly.

"I must admit I have trouble accepting this part myself," Farzhin confessed. "But it fits so many facts. If the ancient narratives are telling us what I think they are, we're faced by a story so bizarre that nobody back on Earth ever managed to understand it, even after centuries of scholarly translations and debate." He paused. Sariena and Charlie just looked at him expectantly. Farzhin got up, moved over to the worktop running along the side of the room, and activated the holo-unit.

The image that appeared in the tank-like viewing zone was of two planetary bodies locked in mutual gyration like a close-coupled binary star system. One was recognizable as pre-Athena Earth, though visibly deformed by a bulge in the region immediately opposite the companion body. The bulge was located in the region of what would normally have been northern India and Tibet—except that it consisted not of mountainous plateau, but ocean. The other body was smaller and more deformed, almost assuming the proportions of a pear. Again, it possessed an aqueous bulge on the facing side. A tenuous bridge of white mist connected the two bodies. Farzhin gazed at it for a few seconds and then turned toward Sariena and Charlie. "The earlier close passes by Venus had raised tidal bulges in the crusts of both Earth and Mars. The massive Tibetan uplift was a remnant of it in modern times. But back in the period we're talking about, starting at about fifty-three hundred years ago . . ."

"Is that when you're saying the Venus encounters occurred?" Charlie queried.

"Yes . . . It was much larger. Likewise on Mars. The Tharsis Bulge still exists as virtually a circular continent uplifted above the median terrain today. But back then, it was a huge deformation of the planet's shape—the smaller body would be far more affected by tidal forces than the larger."

"Wait a minute, Emil," Sariena checked him. Farzhin raised an eyebrow. "Are you saying the other object there is Mars?"

"Yes," Farzhin said. The problem Sariena had with it was plain enough: It bore no resemblance to the Mars of modern times. "That's what we think it was like."

"That recently?"

Farzhin nodded. "When the repeating cycle brought Mars and Earth together, the two gravitational anomalies locked them into synchronism. I'm not sure what broke them up again. Maybe Venus returning periodically disrupted the configuration and started the process again. That's another thing you might be able to help us with."

"How long did each of these periods of mutual capture last?" Charlie asked.

"I estimate around twelve years," Farzhin replied.

"And this went on for almost two thousand years?"

"Yes."

"You're saying they were synchronous. Mars just hung there for twelve years at a time, stationary in the sky?"

"Above northern India," Farzhin confirmed.

"At what kind of distance?"

"About forty thousand kilometers between centers."

Charlie caught Sariena's eye. Vicki noted the strained looks being exchanged between them—but with an unspoken agreement to see it through. Farzhin saw it too. He had been prepared for it. Charlie looked back at Farzhin. "Inside the orbit of the Moon," he commented.

"Well inside. Mars appeared ten times the Moon's size in the sky. The surface details were clearly visible. Faces and figures described in the Vedic hymns correlate with features identifiable on Mars today. Robin was the first to spot Shiva, as I mentioned earlier. That boy is amazing. . . . The Arsia and Ascraeus volcanoes, Valles Marineris, and the contours of the Tharsis bulge form the face. The myth tells of a third eye opening in Shiva's forehead, belching flames." Farzhin gestured at the holo image. "The position of the huge Olympus Mons volcano matches it perfectly."

Sariena sat back, smoothing her hair over the nape of her neck with a hand. Her attitude seemed receptive, weighing things up. "Incredible," she murmured distantly, though Vicki could see in her eyes that her mind was racing.

"The big problem with trying to make sense of the Sanskrit texts as records of celestial happenings was the number of deities named in them," Vicki said. "There seemed to be too many for them to have any connection with planetary objects. But what happened was that people at different times over thousands of years gave different names to the same object as its appearance changed. When you realize that, it all starts coming together. Aditi, Agni, and Varuna, for instance, were all Venus, but respectively as a flare of light ejected from Jupiter, the fire that seared Earth during the early encounters, and the less threatening object that it became later. Mars had other names too, depending on its appearance at varying distances from Earth. Indra was the new, growing Mars when it was being carried outward by its first encounters with Venus. Brahma was the god that dominated Mars transformed by Earth's gravitational influence during the captures. Shiva, the destroyer, brought the collapse of Brahma's rule when the captures ended."

Farzhin affirmed with rapid nods of his head. "And Vishnu, the sustainer, was the name of the permanent Mars deity that returned periodically in the various forms described by the *Avataras*," he completed.

Finally, Sariena came back to the point she had balked at earlier. "And you're telling us that Mars had oceans that recently?" she said, indicating the display. The aqueous bulge was clearly a buildup of the planet's hydrosphere drawn toward the Earth-facing side in an enormous tide. That Mars had once possessed large bodies of water—evidenced by clearly defined flood plains and flow channels—had been known a long time before Athena, but orthodox Terran science had put their existence at billions of years in the past. Charlie was looking very interested. Vicki knew that he had been skeptical of the official view, mainly because the rates of creep for rock under its own weight and of material infall from space meant that such features should have been obliterated long before. This had been pointed out repeatedly, but the Establishment had never budged.

"It fits with the picture of planetary geology happening much faster than used to be believed," he said, looking at Sariena.

Sariena nodded, still keeping her eyes on the image. "So it must still have had an atmosphere then too." The presence of liquid water would have required it.

"If our interpretation is correct, it had a surface pretty much like Earth's," Farzhin confirmed. "The earlier translators could never identify the seas and continents that the Vedas talked about, and so wrote them off as fairy tales. But they were looking for them on the wrong world."

"They seem to describe a living world too," Vicki said. By now, Sariena and Charlie were beyond looking incredulous.

Farzhin elaborated, "The color bands and changes that the texts describe could only be vegetation. The only way to be sure will be to send expeditions to search for the traces. Not by scratching around on the surface the way they did from the couple of bases that Earth set up there. We'll need to go deeper. What's left of Mars today is the remains of a battlefield. First it was torn apart and devastated by Venus, then mangled repeatedly by every tussle with Earth. The entire surface we see today is a blanket of planetwide flood deposits, lava extrusions, and debris from colossal volcanic events. Whatever's left of the original surface is buried way down."

Sariena studied the image for a while in silence, and then got up and came around the table to peer closely at the vaporous bridge connecting Mars with Earth. She looked at Farzhin, still standing by the unit, with a sudden light of understanding in her eyes. "A condition of micro-gravity in the space between them. Low vapor pressure combined with tidal heating of the crust . . ."

Farzhin nodded vigorously. "Yes, exactly what we think. Evaporated and drawn off. Scientists back on Earth kept asking for years where Mars's atmosphere and oceans went. But they were bogged down in their insistence that whatever happened had to have been billions of years ago. And all the time, the answer was all around them. Most of it was transferred to Earth!"

At that, Charlie got up too and came around to join them. Here was another point that wouldn't be lost on him. Evidence had long been known that sea levels on Earth had risen massively in recent millennia from the edges of what in modern times were submerged continental shelves. But there had never been any reason to connect the increase in Earth's inventory of water with the loss from Mars. That was where the influx that had overfilled the oceans came from.

"So you're claiming that this whole area around northern

India was subject to immense flooding," Charlie said. "And it happened periodically, every time Mars returned. Is this what the Tethys really was?" That was the name given to the primordial ocean believed, according to the old plate tectonics, to have existed between India and Eurasia millions of years previously. Farzhin said nothing, letting him fill the details in for himself. "You'd have huge inflows and outflows across the surrounding areas every time the bulge built up and dissipated," Charlie went on. "That could account for the immense sediment deposits all over that region, couldn't it? And what cut the huge gorges of the Himalayan rivers."

"Yes. And now think about the geology and archeology of the Middle East and China," Vicki said. "So much of the architecture in those areas just doesn't fit with the idea of the military constructions that the traditional view always made it out to be. But when you think of them as flood defenses, maybe, or sanctuaries for the population to retreat to when the next approach happened, it all makes sense."

Sariena was stooping to examine the far side of Earth's globe, the face away from Mars. "Antipodal tides in the opposite hemisphere," she murmured. "Maybe a lesser crustal uplift from the Venus encounters, too . . . The Bolivian plateau. Those massive constructions in the Andes. Remnants of sea ports and cultivation up near what was the snow line when you knew it, Charlie."

Farzhin waited, watching the two visitors curiously—and just a shade anxiously. Enough had been said. Charlie and Sariena looked at each other. It was already clear that Farzhin needn't have worried. "I'd like to get those simulations set up as soon as possible," Charlie said, looking back at him. "Would it be possible to go through the data you have sometime while we're here?"

"We can do it right now in my office," Farzhin said, moving to shut down the viewer. "The door up there won't close because of the structural warping, but I'm told it isn't about to fall down anytime soon."

"Can we let you get started without us and catch you later?" Sariena said. "There's somebody else in Kropotkin that I need to see, and Vicki said she'd show me the way.

It's all changed since I was last here. If I let myself get involved in this now, I've a feeling I might not get away."

"Go ahead. We'll see you when you get back," Charlie told her.

"Maybe we could all make dinner somewhere afterward," Farzhin suggested. Everyone agreed that sounded good. Sariena and Vicki retrieved their suit packs from the rack by the door and slung them across their backs as they left. The packs were bulky but of inconsequential weight. In fact, they helped balance. Some people carried lead bricks in backpacks as an aid to walking. Weighted boots were normal.

They came out into a broad corridor where the maintenance crew were working, with screw jacks emplaced at intervals to shore up the roof. "Well, this is a whole new angle you're showing us," Sariena said. "It could change everything."

"And I've got a feeling we're just scratching the surface," Vicki replied. "There are all kinds of references that take on some new kind of significance in Emil's interpretation, but we don't know yet what they mean."

"Such as?"

"Oh . . . for example, not only the Indian texts, but others from Egypt, China, the Middle East, all talk about some kind of celestial staircase, a column or pillar in the sky. . . ."

"You mean like Jacob's Ladder?"

"That's one of them. We're sure they refer to something those people saw, but we don't know what. Then again, you find various symbols and pieces of imagery that turn up again and again. It's fascinating work."

"You seem to have found something that you fit right in with—Emil and his group," Sariena commented.

"It's the kind of work I wanted to do ever since I got involved with you and the others here, working with Lan, back on Earth," Vicki replied. After a pause, she added, "It's what Kronia makes possible—to work at being what you *really* are."

"It sounds as if Robin's doing well too."

Vicki sighed. "He's still not back to his old self. Maybe he never will be. He still has nightmares . . . and long, withdrawn moods. The troglodyte existence here doesn't help. And this stress all the time . . . Maybe none of us will ever truly be our old selves again. Those selves were part of a world that's gone."

They emerged into the labyrinth of interconnecting spaces, shafts, and galleries beneath Kropotkin center. Vicki indicated the way down a terraced stairwell to one of the walkways.

"How about Lan?" Sariena asked. "Have you seen much of him lately?"

"He's been busy on Titan. The artificial gravity project that they're working on at the Tesla Center. Have you heard about it?"

"Oh yes. Jan Wernstecki has been working with us on recomputing orbital changes. The last I heard he was moving to join Lan's group. Are they really onto something?"

"Oh, sure. They've got it working. It's just a case of scaling things up now."

"I hadn't realized they were that far along."

"He'll be back here visiting next week. Leo and Alicia will be here too. It's a pity you and Charlie couldn't have made it for then. It would have been a great reunion." Vicki meant Leo Cavan, Keene's close friend and former political insider. Alicia was the Polish girlfriend that Cavan had brought with him from Washington when he joined Keene in California, as Athena was closing with Earth.

They touch-glided down the steps and carried on across one of the concourses. "How are . . . things?" Sariena asked after a long pause.

There was more in the question than mere curiosity. After the way Keene had risked impossible odds to find her and Robin in the final days on Earth and get them out, most people who knew them had expected him and Vicki to lead a closer life together afterward than had been the case. True, the present conditions on Kronia made demands on everyone, but even so, Keene lived something of a distant life, visiting when circumstances permitted, but spending most of the time immersed in his work on Titan. In a way, it was a reversion to the role he had adopted on Earth, filling a need in Vicki's and Robin's lives that went beyond being just guardian and benefactor, but stopping short of any binding emotional commitment. She still wasn't sure if he was simply one of the kind whose personal feelings didn't extend to such depths, or if other complexities of his personality acted to protect him from such involvements. But it was thanks to Keene that she and Robin were alive and as safe as it was possible to be anywhere. That was enough.

"Lan is one of those complicated people, Sariena," she answered. "If he thinks something needs changing in the world—and something always does—he gets restless if he doesn't feel he's putting his share into doing something about it. You know yourself how many enemies he made among Earth's scientific élite when he didn't agree with them."

"But look at the friends he made here," Sariena answered.

"Yes, he came out ahead in the end. But then he always does. . . . Yet some of the things I hear from him worry me."

"What kind of things?"

"Things that he says are happening among the Terrans. Not all of them are happy with the way things run here. . . . Ask yourself: What kinds of people would be the most likely to get themselves places on the last ships out when the old world was ending?"

Sariena nodded that there was no need to spell it out. "The kind who created the world that Lan ended up spending most of his time back there fighting."

"Exactly. And now he finds them organizing again on Kronia, recruiting a following."

"Have they approached Lan?"

"Not with anything direct—yet. But he thinks they're sounding him out."

"What are they saying to him?"

"That the way Kronia is run will have to change. This way of doing things might have worked when the colony was small and consisted of true believers. But as it grows, conflicts are going to emerge that will call for different methods."

Sariena smiled faintly. "And of course, the methods they have in mind are the ones they just happen to be experienced in. I wonder who they would like to see taking charge of things, if the truth were known."

Vicki glanced sideways as they walked. "Somehow I don't really think this is news to you," she said.

"I hear this and that," Sariena replied vaguely. Then she shook her head in a suddenly decisive way. "But no. There will be no changes. Such people have nothing to offer that we want." Which was about as scathing a remark as was likely to be heard, even in private conversation. *What use are you to anyone?* was the ultimate Kronian insult.

Vicki bit her lip, hesitating for a moment. Then she said, "But sometimes I can't help wondering if they might have a point. Maybe Kronia's priorities *are* guided too much by ideals instead of practicalities. *Can* this system continue to work as the colony continues to get bigger? Or must some quantitative way of allocating resources become necessary eventually?"

"You mean a monetary system?"

"Something like one, anyway."

Sariena touched Vicki's shoulder briefly. "Look, I know you're only saying what seems to make sense. But try to bear in mind that you weren't raised a Kronian. Terrans have only known that way of seeing things, and the mindset that it produces." Sariena's voice had taken on an uncharacteristically hard note. Vicki had evidently touched on something that ran deep.

"Kronia's only experience has been as a small colony of devotees," she pointed out.

"And you think our principles aren't strong enough to survive against harsh reality?" Sariena shook her head. "Don't underestimate us, Vicki. Those who only understand the kind of power that ruled Earth will never prevail here. Nobody is conditioned to hear their message. The kind of wealth that can be hoarded and controlled to buy services and servitude doesn't exist on Kronia. And without wealth that they can control, where is their power?"

Vicki hoped so. She had heard Sariena's arguments before. But she also knew what the people they were talking about were capable of, and that they didn't give up easily. Kronian science might have liberated itself from the ties that had made Earth's a servant of militarism and money, but Vicki had seen for herself how deplorably the Kronian delegation had fared at trying to match Terran political infighting. She just hoped that the Kronians were not miscalculating again, and that here at least, in a system of values that was of their own making, they were judging their opposition accurately.

CHAPTER SEVEN

On Earth, Kurt Zeigler had been a military liaison official with Eurospace and an inside contact there of General Valcroix, for whom he had supplied much valuable information—an impressive position for his relative youth of thirty-four years. He had been one of the few close associates who had escaped from Algeria with Valcroix while the general's own aide remained behind, valiantly leading a force to hold off troops who were trying to prevent the seized orbital lifter from leaving the pad. Zeigler had always been ambitious for power, which, simply put, meant being in a position where others did what you wanted. If it didn't come naturally with birth or wealth, the road to acquiring, he had found, was to become a trusted tool of those who possessed it, camouflaging one's own needs behind an appearance of serving theirs. And as his career up to its untimely termination had shown, he had proved remarkably adept at following this principle. That was why he was here, still enjoying the confidence of those who had arranged his ticket out, while the general's aide, if alive at all—a high statistical improbability—staggered and groped to exist from one lightless day to the next beneath the cloud and smoke canopy covering the cauldron that Earth had become.

He crossed the underground pedestrian precinct in the

center of Foundation, Titan's first settlement after the establishment of Kropotkin on Dione, situated a quarter of the way around the moon from Essen. As Titan consolidated to become the center of the Kronian culture, Foundation had been made the seat of the governing congress. Before Athena, the intention had been to move the administration to Mondel-Waltz City on the far side of Titan, named after two of the principal founders, which had been designed and built to accommodate it. But the new capital—fortunately housing no more than an initial skeleton population at the time— had been wiped out by a major impact, and the Kronian Congress would be occupying its old quarters now for as far ahead in time as it was possible to see.

Zeigler arrived at the steps leading up to the Terrarama, a museum and exhibition dedicated to preserving scenes and relics of Earth, and went inside. The entry hall was darkened and contained rows of rectangular holo-tanks showing images of New York City, San Francisco, London, Paris, Tokyo, Moscow, and other metropolises that were no more. Their glows highlighted the faces of school groups, parents standing with their awed children, and individuals silently immersed in thoughts of their own. The next hall contained scenes of landscapes and life, from cabins in the Canadian Rockies and a desert oasis, to crowded Australian beaches and a waterfall panorama in the upper reaches of the Amazon. Again, everything was in the form of electronic imagery; the pitifully few samples of physical remains actually salvaged from Earth were carefully preserved elsewhere. A major objective of the return missions that had been planned and then postponed had been a Noah's Ark program to bring a variety of Terran animal and plant life back to Kronia.

Zeigler entered a side gallery devoted to selections of local life-styles, costume, and color, and spotted Kelm's tall, blond-haired figure at the far end, contemplating one of the displays. As he drew nearer, he saw that it was a scene of the Miami ocean-front hotel strip and highway—a visitor could call from a practically limitless library of stored images. There was no one else around. Zeigler approached behind Kelm's shoulder and shared the view of glass-paneled buildings and streaming automobiles in silence for a while.

"Everywhere, it was the same," he commented finally. "If you lived south, something needed doing north. If you lived north, you had to be south. Everyone always in a rush to be somewhere else."

The young Kronian turned his head. He looked officer material even out of uniform: trim and athletically muscular, shaped by Security Arm training, features handsome but with a haughty set, artificially tanned. He didn't smile. "The same, everywhere? So many cars?"

"Every city in the world. Millions every day."

"Where did they find enough pilots?"

"Pilots?"

"Whatever the word should be: professionals with the skills to execute such maneuvers. Earth didn't have processors that advanced. . . . I'm not sure that we have anything in Kronia today that could do it. Where did they get all the pilots to take people where they wanted to go?"

It took Zeigler a moment to realize what Kelm meant. "It wasn't a specialized profession," he said. "Everyone drove their own."

Kelm's brow creased. "You mean ordinary people? Even students? The elderly?"

"Everyone."

"I'm amazed. It doesn't seem possible that it could work."

Zeigler shrugged. "Humans are amazing creatures. I guess you've never known big open spaces. Did you ever visit Earth?"

"Never. I was born out here—on Dione."

Zeigler nodded and looked at the image for a few seconds longer. Somehow a part of him still didn't want to accept that it could all be gone, never to be returned to. Then he shook the thought away. There was nothing to be gained from such feelings. They had no bearing on the future that faced him now. "The reason I contacted you is that I think we might be able to help you," he said.

"We?" Kelm repeated guardedly.

"The group that I represent."

"Terrans?"

"They're going to be a powerful force here one day, Kelm. Make no mistake about that. Kronia will need what we know, to become what it must."

"What makes you think I need help with anything?" Kelm asked.

Zeigler moved a pace closer to stand alongside him, facing the display. Having eyes and ears out and about, keeping in touch with rumor and who was saying what, were part of the things he made it his business to cultivate. "Why the Security Arm?" he asked, answering obliquely.

"Everyone contributes something. It's where my skills are." Kelm's tone was that of someone stating the obvious.

"And are you satisfied with your lot there, Kelm? The future it holds? The rewards it will bring?"

Kelm shrugged. "It's what I do. One can't always choose."

Zeigler glanced around. His voice fell to a more confidential note. "Perhaps you have more choices than you think. Your natural skills are military. But Kronia has little use for them and doesn't acknowledge your true worth. We would value them highly. Eventually, the controlling power here will be decided by strength. It has always been that way. Your talents make you a natural ally of the strong. Use them where they will be most appreciated and rewarded the most."

"You really believe you can change things? You who are so few?"

"It isn't how many we are that matters. It is what we know and can do." Zeigler made an open-handed gesture. "Why should your aptitudes be valued any less than those of people who, at the bottom of it all, are just technicians? Nobody has to accept second-class existence as some kind of obligation, Kelm—just because some idealists in the early days stacked the deck in a way that suited them. Eventually things have to change." He nodded to indicate the traffic on the Miami boulevard. "You said it yourself. Without order and discipline, that would be chaos. Unmanageable. But it worked because people imposed rules. The greater human society is no different in the long run. You could be way ahead of the game, Kelm. The ones who help us now will be the ones who will command later. Why be a ranker in a police force whose days are numbered, when you could be a general in the army that will one day rule?"

As he spoke, Zeigler watched Kelm more closely than he let show. While maintaining an outwardly dubious expression—a plus-point testifying to good judgment and control—Kelm's eyes had been flickering over Zeigler searchingly, as if probing for validity indicators. His shoulders had been turned toward Zeigler, as if unconsciously screening off the outside world. He was interested. That was as much as could reasonably be wished for the present. Kelm's mouth turned downward briefly at the corners—but that was controlled consciously and didn't mean anything.

"I don't know. It's something I'd need to think about," Kelm said. "If I decide I want to know more, should I contact you the same way?"

Zeigler had hoped to finish on a more positive note. After thinking for a moment, he said, "I believe you were stationed at the training base on Rhea, before it was destroyed. Is that correct?"

"Yes. I was there." Kelm nodded.

"Then you are familiar with the layout and the locations of the various facilities," Zeigler said.

"There isn't very much left. From what I hear, anything that can be salvaged is being stripped out and brought to Titan. The only things left will be what's buried under the rubble."

"All the same, that is precisely the kind of information that some people are very interested in," Zeigler said. Kelm looked puzzled but didn't pursue the matter. Zeigler nodded at him meaningfully. "And they could be very generous when it comes to rewarding whoever can bring it to them. Think it over very carefully," he urged.

CHAPTER EIGHT

Rakki had no word for the number of people who lived in the caves. They were more than the fingers on his hands, fewer than the feathers on the caw-birds, which they sometimes caught in nets tied from vines. Their names meant nothing to Rakki; he couldn't remember them, and so gave them his own names. While he sat chipping an edge along a flake of hardstone in the way he had been told, he watched Fire Keeper scraping the last scraps of meat from the bones of a long-haired horn-head, cracking open the ones with marrow, and separating the sinews for bowstrings and thongs. The sight produced an aching to eat deep in Rakki's stomach. He had vague memories of the times of darkness, when food had been the only thought and people fought over a sprig of weed carrying berries, fungus found in a rock crevice, worms dug out of the mud, flesh from corpses—anything that could be eaten. Now there was light, and more things were starting to grow. But still the hunger was always there.

The Cavers had ways of making traps for animals that the Swamp People didn't know. Ones like bush-pigs and horn-heads that they didn't kill immediately, they kept captive inside a walled pen built from rocks at one end of the space behind the rampart enclosing the caves. A female that Rakki called Pig Woman brought grass for them

71

and collected the dung to be dried by the fire for fuel. There was also a cleared area outside the rampart that they had crossed the day before when Rakki was brought in, where there seemed to be some kind of attempt being made to induce food plants to grow. All the food that was prepared or collected went into Fire Keeper's stock, which was kept in a guarded recess behind the cooking area. The law against stealing was strict. The Screecher—thus named permanently by now—had told Rakki gleefully of how the last one to be caught pilfering from the common stock had been impaled on a stake by Mistameg's order, and the body hacked into pieces for the dogs.

Mistameg—the Oldworlders called him Meggs—was the Cavers' chief. He was large, even for an Oldworlder, and immensely strong, with eyes and teeth shining white against his face and a mane of hair hanging to his shoulders, tied in a braided leather band. He was fierce, violent, and allowed no questioning of his decisions. Rakki was impressed. He could learn much about power and controlling others to do one's will from such a man. Three of the few Oldworld women were Mistameg's. One that Rakki had dubbed Yellow Hair was pink of face like the man he had thought of as Lightskin yesterday, but knew now was called Bo and held place as Mistameg's second. Although Bo seemed to have a choice of Neffer females, he didn't like Mistameg owning Yellow Hair. Rakki could see it in his eyes and read it in his body talk. But Bo was not enough of a warrior to challenge Mistameg, and so he took out his anger on others beneath him in the order. Yellow Hair might have had other children also for all Rakki knew, but one was a Neffer girl with the same hair and light skin. Rakki called her Shell Eyes, since they were the color of a reed-nester's eggs, unlike anything he'd seen before. The vision conjured itself up in his mind of him one day killing Mistameg and taking Shell Eyes for his female. Then Bo would hate him too, and he'd kill Bo. Then he would be worthy to become a chief. The thought was sweet and helped him forget his hunger.

"The way to become a great warrior is not to let your thoughts show," a voice said. Rakki turned toward White Head, who had to be the oldest among the Oldworlders. Rakki didn't understand all the words that White Head used, but he spoke in a tongue that was closer to the Swamp People's than the one most of the Cavers used. He was sitting on a mat of reeds among the rocks at the cliff base, trying one of the stone edges on a piece of root wood from a fangleaf bush. There were several larger pieces of a firmer, straighter-grained wood than scrub roots in the cave behind him, but they had come from afar and were kept for cutting shapes needed for special purposes. Before the Long Night, so it was said, bushes with stems as wide as the span of a man's arms and as straight as a taut vine had grown higher than a bow could shoot. Dead pieces of them sometimes turned up buried in mud or washed up among rocks, and were highly valued. Rakki sometimes saw images in his mind of huge green growths and the sky lit by a brilliant light, but he didn't know if they were from things he had seen once or just imagination. Far to the north there was supposed to be a land where such things remained, but he had always doubted the story . . . until White Head showed him the round wooden rocks in the cave where he worked. Rakki's edged club of Oldworld metal had aroused great excitement when Screecher presented it on their arrival, and Rakki hadn't seen it since. After being questioned by Mistameg, he wasn't of a mind to protest.

"What you know about warrior? You don't seem like warrior man," Rakki said.

"I know about life," White Head replied. Rakki had little doubt that he had been assigned to keep an eye on Rakki as much as to keep him busy and useful.

"Oldworld life." Rakki said. "Oldworld had great warriors? Make strong chief?"

White Head paused and thought, his eyes distant. "Not just warriors. Gods walked the earth then. Men were as gods. But they grew lazy."

"What are gods?" Rakki asked.

"Like men, but with unimaginable powers. They built shining towers as high as mountains . . ."

"Towers?"

White Head looked perplexed, then made an expansive gesture with both arms. "Like long rocks that stand on end, but hollow. Caves inside. Thousands of caves, layer over layer, over each other, going up and up."

"Thousand? What does thousand mean, White Head?"

"Many, many. More than leaves on a stick-seed tree. Chambers. Like you see in nests the ants make. They made giant birds and flew in them beyond the sky. Floating cliffs that crossed oceans of water vaster than all the land you have ever seen."

Rakki had heard tell of a greater sky that lay above the sky, but he was unable to conceive what it meant. He was about to reply, when a foot kicked him in the back, sending him sprawling onto his arms, still clutching the stones he had been working. He whirled about to find Screecher leering down at him, standing arrogantly, hands on hips, as if lording over some lower form of life. "Mistameg send me, Dog Meat. You come talk real stuff now. We go three days, get bullet like you say. Leave two day from now. Today, tomorrow, you work." Rakki climbed to his feet, his eyes blazing, forcing down the impulse to drive the sharpened hardstone into the Screecher's face. "Bullet better be there, else Mistameg mad." Screecher cackled inanely. "Then you end up dog shit, you see."

One day, Rakki promised himself as he stumbled ahead under another kick. One day he'd settle the score. When *he* ruled the caves.

CHAPTER NINE

Keene stood in the store in Kropotkin, watching as Imel, the assistant, wrapped the synthetic sausage, a slab of "Mimas cheese"—processed from a coagulation of bean curds—carton of bread wafers, and the packs of reconstituted vegetables that Keene had selected, and added them to the bottle of wine and six of Celtic Dark beer in the plastic bags standing on the counter. On the shelf behind, there were also maybe half a dozen bottles of a distilled liquor called Tennessee Amber—smooth, mellow, reminiscent of a good Irish whiskey, which in his previous life Keene had been partial to. It was rare and highly valued. He stared at the tiny display and wrestled with himself inwardly.

The decision ought to have been simple—the bottles were there for the taking; there would be no call to justify himself or account to anyone. And yet, he hesitated. . . .

A quick calculus replayed itself in his mind. He had been back on Dione for two days, the first of which he had practically spent sleeping after several weeks of unceasing effort on Titan, in which the artificially maintained day-night cycles had ceased to have any meaning. To play their part in something that would one day revolutionize engineering and make the colony viable, Pang had said. Yes, dammit, he'd earned himself a drink, Keene decided. He nodded in the direction of the Ambers. "And one of those too," he told Imel.

Imel took down a bottle, rolled a sheet of coarse paper around it, and added it to the contents of the bags. "Will that be all?"

"That's it."

"Enjoy your stay on Dione, Lan."

"Thanks."

"My pleasure."

Keene picked up the bags, went out to the pedestrian way, and turned in the direction that led back toward Vicki's. He didn't really understand the details of the things happening inside his head, but he was becoming a Kronian—he had learned what "felt right."

On Titan, Wernstecki had joined the Artificial Gravity project, which was moving at a pace that Keene still found astonishing, even after all his time here. Pang had insisted on calling the program to build a scaled-up engineering system "Gravestone"—from GRAVitic-Electromagnetic Synthesis Test ONE. The intention was to endow one of the rooms in the group's lab area in the Tesla Center with earth-normal gravity as a demonstration.

A political movement calling itself "Pragmatist" had emerged, initially among the Terran contingent but finding sympathizers too in certain sectors of the Kronian population. Consolidating behind Valcroix, they were making a case to the Kronian governing administration for a "fairer" Terran voice in the making of policy decisions that would now apply to everybody. Yes, they conceded, it was true that Kronia had been founded specifically for the freedom to pursue its own independent ideals. But circumstances had changed since then, forcing a situation whereby, like it or not, Kronia had become de facto the common heritage of all that was left of human civilization. The Terran-originated portion of that civilization along with its views and its values, they argued, was entitled to representation accordingly. The real issue, of course, was finding an angle that would get a bigger say in the way things were going to be run. In short, as always, where the power would come to lie.

Keene left the pedestrian way via a fire door into a side passage and descended in what had been intended as a freight elevator to emerge at a three-way intersection of corridors with floors of metal mesh and ribbed yellow walls interrupted by doors spaced at intervals. It always put Keene in mind of the lower decks of a cargo ship. With the influx of Terran refugees in addition to the general migration of the population underground, accommodation in Kropotkin was still in short supply. Also, damage repair took precedence over new construction, which didn't help matters. The unit that Vicki occupied was the same one that she and Robin had been assigned when they first arrived, hastily improvised from storage levels in the lower parts of the complex as a temporary measure until something became available in the regular residential sectors. More recently, Robin had moved into dormitory quarters with fellow students from the Academy, and Vicki, finding the extra space useful, had stayed on. Keene came to a cross-passage bearing the unlikely sign MIMOSA. The first door to the right carried the number 2 and a sign reading DELUCEY, VICKI. Keene waved his card at the scanlock and went in.

Vicki and Cavan were sitting at the bench seat in the living area, talking across the remains of the meal they had finished earlier on a foldaway table hinged down from the wall. Alicia was in the kitchen alcove, loading dishes into the washer. Vicki acknowledged Keene with a wave as he came in. "How's the weather out?" Cavan quipped, turning his head.

"Hasn't changed much."

"Vicki's been telling me this stuff about Mars coming by periodically and hanging over India. Absolutely astounding, Landen! And do you go along with it too?"

"I'm just the engineer. But Sariena and Charlie seemed to be impressed by it. They're the experts."

"Astounding!" Cavan said again, shaking his head. He was in his sixties, with wrinkles beginning to collect in pink skin about a frame that had once been fuller, and thinning silver hair combed conventionally to the side. But his eyes betrayed him, alive and alert, harboring the same penchant for intrigue and mischief that made him an invaluable ally

to have on the inside of a political situation for as long
as Keene had known him. These days, Cavan spent most
of his time circulating among the various departments of
the governing administration at Foundation. What he involved
himself in there, Keene still wasn't sure.

Alicia cleared some space on the worktop for Keene to
set the bags down and began helping him unload them.
Blond, curvaceous, still managing to look stunning in Kronian
tunic garb and with her once-long hair cut short, she was
little more than half Cavan's age but everyone thought them
ideally matched. Cavan had joined Keene in California with
a military unit from Washington during Earth's final days,
bringing Alicia with them too when it became plain that
there would probably be no going back. Her background
on Earth had been medical. Since coming to Kronia she had
been working to help rehabilitate Terrans suffering from
traumatic disorders and depression.

"Hello, what's this?" Alicia held up the bottle of Tennessee
Amber. "Claiming the good stuff, I see."

"Splendid!" Cavan pronounced. "Good for you, Landen.
Make it a real party."

"You've earned it, Lan," Vicki said.

"Hell, we all have," Keene muttered. "Who'd like one
now?" Everyone did. Keene opened the closet where the
glasses were kept, while Alicia put the rest of the provisions away. Vicki and Cavan resumed talking about the Vedic
Mars encounters.

"You know, I'm still not sure I understand how this works
here," Alicia said to Keene as she opened the bottle. "You
just walk in the store and you take this. You know no one
is going to say anything or stop you. But still you have a
hard time deciding if you should. It happens to me too. Can
you explain it?"

Keene set down four glasses. "I'm not sure I can. I was
talking to Imel yesterday—he's the guy in the store. He told
me he used to be a skimmer once."

"Oh, really?"

"I never knew that," Vicki threw in from across the room.

"And I'm just arrived here. You should get to know your
neighbors," Keene said. "Skimmer" was the Kronian term

for one who took and gave nothing back. "But he said it doesn't last long. Nobody judges or says anything. But something inside gets to them. They need to find a way to pay. So now he works on one of the city repair crews, does a day a week in a shoemaking shop, and helps mind the store up there."

"Careful, Lan. You might start restoring my faith in human nature," Cavan said.

"Restore? How could I, Leo? You never had any."

"Weren't there supposed to have been societies back on Earth at times, where nobody locked their doors or bothered safeguarding their possessions because stealing was unknown?" Vicki asked distantly. "Do you really think it's possible for something like that to work here—even when Kronia gets bigger? I was talking with Sariena about it."

"I think we might soon be finding out," Cavan answered. "There are people here now who'd be the last to let it work if they get their way."

"Because the only power they understand comes from controlling what others create," Alicia said.

"You mean steal," Vicki corrected.

"Ah, now, you can't say that," Cavan told them. "Of course it would be legalized first."

"The really big criminals never break laws," Alicia agreed. "They make them."

Keene came around the kitchen worktop and handed a glass each to Vicki and Cavan. "But you can't run that as a platform to get elected on," Cavan said. "You have to have a front that sounds reasonable."

They were talking about the motives behind the Pragmatist movement. Its stated position was that at this juncture Kronia couldn't afford to expend resources on nonproductive scientific issues far from home that they dismissed as "quasi-religious." Necessity dictated concentrating on the industrial development and construction, here and now, that would mean long-term security for everyone. It was the line that Keene had heard from Grasse and Valcroix when he met with them. The real issue, of course, was *who* would decide the allocations of those resources, and by what means.

"It's a familiar-enough pattern to any of us," Vicki said. "But how many Kronians will be able to see through it? Look at what happened in Washington." The Pragmatists were striving to recruit numbers beyond the Terran contingent by exploiting discontent and resentments among the Kronians wherever possible—and in some instances, by fomenting it. And there were those among the Kronian population who felt that the limited-resource argument perhaps had some merit.

"Yes, I'll grant you that," Cavan said. "The recognizable face of old-style political unrest so beloved to us all is showing itself again." He shook his head. "But they won't win here. I can't see it. The fertile ground they need to grow in doesn't exist."

"That's pretty much what Sariena says too," Vicki said, nodding.

"Well, she should know." Cavan showed his palms, indicating nothing more to add. Vicki still seemed to need more convincing. Cavan looked up at Keene as he tilted his glass. "But things could still come to a fight before we're through. Would you be up to it, Landen?"

"What? Are you trying to drag me into your sordid underworld schemes again, Leo?" Keene said.

"I am, of course. You set thieves to catch thieves, isn't that right? If we've got the kind of situation that we're all too familiar with rearing its head again, we need old hands at the game on our side too."

Keene saw Vicki's pained look and her shaking her head almost imperceptibly. *No*, he told himself firmly. It was time he lived his own life for once, of his own choosing. Besides, if the Pragmatists were playing a lost game in the way Cavan had said, the Kronians should be able to deal with them here, regardless of how they had fared in Earth's totally different, hostile environment. Keene had better things to do than be used as extra insurance.

He shook his head and smiled tiredly. "I had my fill of all that on Earth, Leo. Did my share, if you want my honest opinion. Do you realize what that means to me back there on Titan—at the Center? Finally, for the first time in my life, I'm involved in truly free, creative science—what science should be—without having to answer to bureaucrats, funding committees, or closed-shop peer review panels. We're talking about *artificial gravity*, Leo!— a whole new landscape of physics and engineering." Cavan's eyes were fixed on Keene penetratingly, as if weighing up whether or not to let it go at that. If there was more to go into, Keene would have preferred it to be between the two of them at another time, rather than imposed on the party. He judged it a good time to withdraw tactfully. "Where's Robin?" he asked, looking around and then at Vicki. Robin had stopped by to pay due respects to the visitors, but had been withdrawn and quiet, finally retiring to what had once been his room.

Vicki inclined her head in the direction of the doorway leading out to the hall. "Still moping, I guess."

"Maybe someone should go and cheer him up," Keene said. "Shall I?"

"You can try."

Keene went out to the hallway and tapped at the door to the space that Vicki had made into a study and workroom. He waited a moment, then entered.

Robin was at the triangular corner shelf that served as a desk, looking at something on the screen standing unrolled from a portable compad. He clicked it off and turned his head enough to see who was there. Now eighteen, yellow haired and athletically built with an innate tan that still endured, he would have been a natural for a high-school quarterback or swimming team, had such things still existed. "Hello, Lan," he greeted.

"Hi, C.R. Just came to see how you were doing in here. Not in a mood for the party?" From long habit, Keene still referred to him as Christopher Robin, after the English children's book character.

"Oh . . . I guess not. I'd rather just be on my own right now."

"Uh-huh." Keene nodded to say that was okay by him and perched himself on the spare chair behind the door. In addition to Vicki's books and papers, the room still had relics from Robin's days, including a fish tank, his collection of rock fragments from meteorites and various Saturnian moons, and an array of potted creeping plants weaving their way among pictures of spacecraft, habitats, and astronomic objects, along with maps of Dione, Titan, Rhea, and Mimas. Robin brought up a screen showing part of the Mandelbrot fractal world and watched it with a detached expression. "Your mom was telling Leo about the Mars encounters and the new theory that they're talking about," Keene said. "I thought you'd be interested."

Robin pushed himself back in the chair, frowning awkwardly. He didn't feel especially sociable, Keene sensed, and was struggling to maintain outward civility. "It's interesting, sure, but . . ." He tossed out a hand and left it unfinished, seemingly not really sure what he meant. It was a ghost of the Robin Keene had known back on Earth, who had devoured theories of things like dinosaur engineering, planetary origins, and early human history, and would have driven Vicki to distraction with speculations on this latest development.

"I heard it was you who put the idea into Emil Farzhin's head that it might have been Mars," Keene said. "He was trying to make Venus fit with the records. What made you think of that?"

"I just got to reading some of the translations that Mom brought home. When I was looking at some pictures of Mars, I noticed that the descriptions seemed to fit. Then, when they talked about oceans and continents . . . it couldn't have been Venus."

"Emil had taken them as some kind of metaphor."

Robin shrugged. "I just think literally, I guess."

The simplicity of youth, Keene thought to himself. Just following the evidence wherever it seemed to point, without trying to fit it to predetermined answers. The Kronians hadn't really invented anything new. Keene had listened more than once to older and what he considered wiser heads saying that the wisdom so often prized in later years was little more than rediscovering things that had been obvious at sixteen.

But he could tell this wasn't a time for such things. "Vicki tells me you might be enlisting with the Security Arm," he said, trying a change of subject.

"I'm thinking about it. Leo suggested it. It has its attractions." Robin kept his eyes on the screen, zooming endlessly down through finer levels of mathematically generated, never-repeating detail. Keene wondered if it signified an unconscious need to find structure in life when everything else had fallen apart.

"Alicia says she heard from Mitch," he said. Harvey Mitchell had commanded the Special Forces unit that came with Cavan to California. He and three of the others had arrived eventually at Kronia as part of the group that had escaped via Mexico. "It seems he's working with them too somewhere. You might bump into him again out there if you decide to go ahead."

"Maybe."

"You could get a chance at space crew, too, later."

Robin started to answer, but then turned his head away quickly and straightened up from the chair in the same reflex movement. "Lan, look, I know you're trying to help, but . . ." His voice caught. "Sorry. . . . I need to get out for some air." He scooped a windcheater jacket from a hook by the door and left hurriedly, keeping his face averted. Moments later Keene heard the outer door close in the hall.

He shook his head and stared down at his arms resting on his knees, hands still cradling his glass. *Well, I guess I get first prize at blowing that,* he told himself. But he wasn't sure what else he might have said. His gaze drifted back to the patterns on the screen, descending through endless scales of whorls, traceries, and sunflower bursts. Curiously, he got up, moved across, and killed the Mandelbrot pattern to redisplay the file that Robin had obscured when Keene came in. It contained a list of graphic images. Keene selected one and opened it. A picture filled the screen of a group of grinning teenagers and staff posing in the sunshine for a class photo in front of their school building. Robin was near the center of the third row, standing. The caption read: *Jefferson Junior High, Corpus Christi, TX.* Keene stared at it for several seconds, then closed the image and reactivated the Mandelbrot display. A lump formed at the back of his throat. He got up and went back through to the living area to rejoin the others.

CHAPTER TEN

The party departed at the first lightening of the murky, ever-turbulent skies that signaled the beginning of another day. Bo was in command, again seconded by Scar-arm, both carrying the mysterious Oldworld weapons that Rakki still couldn't see as being effective in any way. Screecher was with them, assigned to keeping a watch on Rakki, who had not been given a weapon. With them were four other Neffers carrying spears and bows: Manuka and Shingral, and two whose names Rakki hadn't memorized but thought of as Gap Teeth and Fish, the latter for no better reason than that he had been gutting a catch for Fire Keeper the first time Rakki saw him. They took two of the dogs with them, one mottled black and gray, the other a ragged brown, both fearsome, and two hill animals of a kind that Rakki hadn't come across before, with long heads, low, straight backs, and long-haired hides.

Rakki had never seen animals led by halters before. The Cavers used them to carry loads. Mistameg had asked him how many "boxes" of bullets there were. Rakki had never heard the word. Jemmo, who had given him the few bullets that he had carried with him—also taken from him, along with the edged club—hadn't said anything about boxes. Bo had made a shape in the air with his hands that Rakki hadn't understood but nodded to anyway. But when asked how many boxes, he hadn't known how to answer. So they had taken two hairhides—which was what he called the animals. If there were more boxes than two of them could carry back, they would make a return trip.

They followed the line of the cliffs, which took them up toward the higher ground above the swamp regions. Although this was not country that Rakki spent extended time in, he knew it well enough from many exploration and food-seeking expeditions. By the next day they would descend again into a valley that opened to the far side of the ash-mud wastes bordering more familiar territory.

As they receded farther from the lowlands the surroundings became bleaker, the slopes of scattered scrub and thorn bushes giving way to a wilderness of shattered black rock standing in angled pinnacles split by fractures that in places rent the ridge into immense blocks already starting to slide apart. Nothing grew here. The earth and rocks threw off an oppressive heat that Rakki could feel on his face. Vapors rose from the chasms and fissures, searing the throat and stinging the eyes. Even the dogs were affected, ceasing their noisy investigations around and ahead of the group, and instead following reluctantly behind, their ears flat, tails hanging down. Partway through the morning, rain began falling but it didn't wet the ground. Rakki's people told him that these were places where new parts of the world were made, when the earth heaved and roared, and fire fell from the sky.

There could be no stopping until they were past the barren uplands. They had brought some water in sacs made from skin and bladders, but the Neffers began squabbling over shares, and the supply was soon gone. The hairhides plodded ever more slowly, tongues lolling from slack mouths, their eyes bulging and taking on a strange crazed look, and the Neffers had to pull them by the halters and beat them with sticks to keep them moving. Bo and Scar-arm were surly at Rakki for bringing them this way, which somehow seemed to make it his doing that the water had run out. Screecher echoed their mood and subjected him to an assault of ongoing abuse interspersed with blows. Rakki's tongue swelled, and his mouth felt as dry as ashes from a fire. He endured the thirst and the insults without protest. The time for reckoning would come very soon now.

Finally, they dragged themselves over the last crest and could look down over folds of falling ground showing patches of lichen and stubby weed before disappearing into banks of mist, beyond which the dark shadows of mountains loomed indistinctly. The animals smelled water, and their lethargy gave way to a sudden eagerness to get ahead, making the handlers fight to keep them back. Beneath the mist were mud hills and then tar bogs that connected roundabout to the swamplands that Rakki was from. That was the route that Jemmo and the others would have taken. Rakki watched Screecher yelling at Gap Teeth, whose hands were slipping on the halter of the hairhide that he was trying to restrain. *Soon now*, he promised himself.

They descended into a basin of shelving slopes, where water rising from the ooze among the rocks came together to find its way down into the head of a ravine opening below. Already the air was cooler. Breaking free, the hairhides forged ahead to plunge their muzzles into the rivulets, while the dogs ran past them and lapped frenziedly. Rakki found a spot where the water spilled over a lip of rock in a trickle, threw himself down, and scooped it to his mouth in cupped hands. It was warm with an acrid, sulfurous taste, but in his condition he would have drunk the tar waters that lay in oily pools among the reeds lower down. Shingral and Fish started refilling the skins.

Rakki waved a hand at them. "Not this, here. Better farther on."

"This yo' country hereabout?" Scar-arm asked him.

"I been up near this part sometime—" Rakki pointed to the direction ahead, "—from down that way."

Bo was standing, studying the cloud cover above. It was showing the first sign of darkening before night came. "Need find place okay for bed down pretty soon," he said.

Rakki pointed ahead again. "Go more, not far. Down from wind. Is food root and berry. Clean water."

"You don't say what we do, Dog Meat," Screecher snapped, cuffing him. "Bo, he the Man. He say."

Bo waved an arm. "Move on," he told all of them. Jemmo

had said the end of the day would be the time, when the Cavers were tired and their minds distracted.

They clambered down into the ravine and followed it over boulders and falls of loose shale between broken walls growing steeper and higher on either side. Thorn bushes and scrub growths began appearing between the rocks, and coarse grass and moss beds by the sides of the water runnels and pools along the ravine bottom. As these thickened into tangles of gray, curling leaves and creepers pushing over the rocks and choking the gaps between, the caustic dryness of the air above gave way to a humid, stultifying heaviness. Rakki's eyes picked out a broken stem of reed, and below on the ground, two crossed twigs—repeated again ten paces farther on. It was the sign he had been watching for.

As he had expected, the dogs caught the scent first. The larger, black-and-gray one raised its head suddenly and growled, its ears pricked. The brown ran ahead and stopped with its front paws on a rock, barking insistently. The party halted around the two hairhides, exchanging nervous looks. Bo jerked his head from side to side, scanning the surrounding crags. "What happening heah?" he demanded. The arrow hit the brown dog in the side, causing it to yelp and whirl around. Another flew from somewhere ahead and pierced its neck. It fell, howling.

Figures brandishing spears rose among the growths and rocks on both sides, their bodies painted blue, white, and orange. Jemmo was at the center, wearing the red headband that was his war emblem. The large black dog snarled. *"Get um! Kill!"* Bo commanded.

The dog bounded up over the boulders and sprang, bringing one of the ambushers down, screaming. A spear flew down and was caught among leaves; another clattered off rocks. Manuka cried out as the third lodged in his thigh. Ahead, beyond the brown dog writhing on the ground, bowmen were running forward into sight, still out of range but fitting new arrows.

Rakki turned upon Fish and gestured at the club slung from his shoulder—a heavy wooden handle with an edged stone lashed at the head. "Need weapon! I fight too!" Fish hesitated, looking to the Oldworlders.

But they were not heeding him. Scar-arm raised the device he was carrying to his shoulder and pointed it. It made a strange *crack*, and one of the attackers above collapsed back out of sight among the rocks. Scar-arm shifted direction slightly and in moments a second did the same, and then a third clutched his side and reeled backward. At the same time, Bo pointed his weapon at the bowmen preparing to rush forward, and even at that distance, before they had begun to move, dropped two of them in the same baffling way. This was all wrong. Only Rakki could save the situation. "*Give!*" he screamed at Fish. Fish nodded and unslung the club. Rakki took it, weighed it . . . and stove in the side of Fish's skull.

He hacked into Scar-arm's shoulder as Scar-arm was aiming the weapon again, but Screecher shouted a warning before Rakki could get to Bo. Bo turned, saw the blood streaming down Scar-arm's body, but for a vital split-second he failed to register the situation. A rock from a sling whirled by a warrior that Rakki recognized as Uban hit Bo in the side and sent him staggering before he could react. And then, screaming, whooping figures were rushing in from all sides. Spearmen had dispatched the black dog and were coming down. One of them—it was Neotto—took Screecher in the back as he tried to go for Rakki. A clubbed blow to the back of the knees toppled Bo, after which he was finished off by spear thrusts, his arms flailing in a vain effort to protect himself. Shingral was hit in the shoulder by a thrown spear.

And it was over. Manuka had sunk onto a rock, one leg useless from the wound in his thigh. Gap Teeth had prostrated himself on his knees, head and arms on the ground in a gesture of submission. "No kill," he whimpered. "I fight for Great Swamp Warrior now. Do work. Make good slave server. You see."

Jemmo, who had come forward, cast an inquiring eye at Rakki. "He would be useful," Rakki confirmed. "And him." He indicated Shingral. "His hurt will mend." Jemmo nodded at his warriors to spare them.

But they killed Manuka, whose leg would have slowed them down too much; also, one of Jemmo's war party, whose stomach the Oldworld weapon had somehow gouged from a distance as if by a spear thrust, and who wouldn't have lasted more than a day or two. Only Screecher was left, glowering fearfully from where he lay propped on an arm, blood running down onto the ground and spreading from the wound in his back. Jemmo stood over him contemptuously and raised his battle mace.

"No!" Rakki said, moving to intervene. "That one is mine."

Jemmo shrugged and turned to supervise the stripping of the other bodies, keeping the Oldworld weapons for himself to be investigated later.

Rakki pulped Screecher's body slowly, breaking many bones. But he stopped short of killing him. "So who stinking dog meat now?" Rakki spat as he stepped back. His pride and his rage were satisfied. They left Screecher there in the ravine, for the flies and the snakes and the vermin that the corpses would attract.

There never had been any cache of bullets. Jemmo had come across a few somehow, and all he knew was that Oldworlders would go to practically any lengths to acquire them. Wiping out the expedition had reduced the caves' defenders by that many. And Rakki had collected much useful information during his two days there.

The Swamp People attacked the caves at daybreak, two days after the ambush—when Jemmo had worked out a plan but before the Cavers would be alerted by the failure of Bo's expedition to return. They divided into two war parties. The main force, led by Jemmo, assaulted the rampart enclosing the area in front of the caves, while Rakki took a secondary group up via a roundabout route to harass the defenders with rocks and missiles hurled from the heights above, which nobody had thought to keep guarded—one of the vital pieces of information that Rakki had supplied. The Cavers fought desperately, but surprised and with their fighting force depleted, they were overwhelmed. The day was not yet halfway through when the last survivors were driven out into the open, and Jemmo in his red headband, his gory mace slung across a shoulder, swaggered along the line to pronounce his judgments.

Mistameg and his immediate lieutenants were killed, of course, both to eliminate the threat that they would always have represented, and to establish Jemmo's authority. So were most of the remaining Oldworlders, since Jemmo didn't understand or trust them. That was why there had been none in the swamplands. He spared a few, including White Head, when Rakki reminded him that some would be needed to show the secret of the weapons that killed from afar. Also the females who were not too old for childbearing.

The Neffer males of fighting age were either clubbed to death or kept to be worked according to Jemmo's whim, depending on how dangerous he thought they looked. The females were taken as mates and slaves for the victors.

It was the way.

CHAPTER ELEVEN

The Kronian Congress of Leaders was headed by a triad consisting of the President, Xen Urzin, and two Deputies. Ranking equally below them were a Legislative Branch, a body of elected representatives called the Assembly of Delegates, and a system of "Directorates" overseeing such primary undertakings vital to the colony's viability and survival as Energy, Food Production, Life and Environment Support, Construction, and Supply of Materials.

The Artificial Gravity project would have an enormous effect on the future Kronian space effort, and its progress was followed closely by those responsible for general planning and equipment specification in the organizational branch designated Space Operations Executive. Although not termed as such for historical reasons, SOE constituted a Directorate in its own right, reflecting the importance of space developments in the overall scheme of things and its relevance to Kronia's longer-term aims. As befitted the AG project's instigator and leader, Pang-Yarbat was the prime contact for the designers and technical specialists at SOE Headquarters, located along with the administrative Offices of Congress at Foundation. Hence, Keene was somewhat surprised when, shortly after returning from Dione to Titan and the Tesla Center at Essen four days later, he received a call from a high-ranking SOE figure by the name of Jon Foy, inviting him to Foundation to discuss aspects of Kronia's space policy that he felt could benefit from Keene's input. Also, he had heard the story of Keene's part in getting his group to Mexico and off the surface, and he wanted to hear Keene's account firsthand and meet him personally. Keene was happy to accept. It was flattering to think that his name had been earning something of a reputation.

His surprise took on an added element of perplexity when further inquiring revealed Foy to be SOE's representative on the Kronian "Consolidation Council," which concerned itself with mapping the longer-term future toward which Kronia was heading. In other words, this was not just an official from one of the Directorates, but a member of the topmost level of the administration, charged with setting the aims that lay beyond merely existing from one generation to the next—the end purpose that the Kronians saw their existence as serving. He didn't seem the kind of person to be interested in details of propulsion system engineering. Keene got the feeling that more was going on than was obvious on the surface. He sensed Cavan's hand at work somehow, but what the motive might be, he was unable to fathom.

Keene arranged to arrive in time to join Foy and some unnamed others for lunch. He made the two-thousand-mile hop to Foundation in a surface transporter skimming at 10,000 feet through the twilight beneath Titan's cloud canopy above a wilderness of ice and rock, broken at intervals by scatterings of lights from a habitat or some kind of construction in progress. Eventually, the capital materialized from the gloom, growing and taking shape as the vessel descended, into another sprawl of domes and arc-lit metallic geometry huddled in the frozen night. Keene wondered how long it would be before humanity could once again flourish across sunny landscapes with coastlines and forests. No wonder so many of the younger Terrans like Robin had sunk into melancholy and dejection.

Keene had been to Foundation a number of times before on space-related business and in connection with energy matters, the last occasion being three months or so ago.

The Kronian Offices of Congress had not been given any grand or imposing character to set them apart from the rest of the city complex. They were housed in a squat, hexagonal structure with several adjoining domes, standing west of the general central area and extending many levels below the surface. The transporter landed on a floodlit pad atop the Hexagon, and Keene deplaned along with several other arrivals via a tube connected to the terminal entrance. He was met by a youngish couple who introduced themselves as Dril and Marna from SOE's Engineering and Development Division, and then escorted him down into a labyrinth of the kind that had come to seem normal for the sanitized metal and plastic environment that the surviving sliver of human civilization was creating for itself. They came to an entranceway displaying the SOE emblem of a gold sun-and-planets on a black background and passed through a lobby to a staircase leading down to a side room adjoining the cafeteria, where a table was set for lunch. The first figure Keene recognized, stepping out from the small, chattering group already assembled and evidently awaiting his arrival, was Cavan. He looked breezy and casual, and his expression was not without a hint of amusement at the look on Keene's face.

"Leo, I had a hunch you were behind this. Did you have to work at being subtle or does it just come naturally?"

"Oh, come on, you know my ways."

"So what's it all about?"

"In good time, Landen. All in good time." Cavan turned to present a man who was waiting. He was white haired with a dusky countenance, wearing a silver-gray robe-like garment, standing tall but relaxed and studying Keene attentively. "Jon Foy. Jon, this is Landen Keene, the man you've been hearing about."

"Leo has enthralled us with his account of your escape," Foy said. He was soft spoken, with a hint of what could have been taken for an Asian accent. His eyes were alert and alive—the kind that seemed to take in much from a distance. "A remarkable story of tenacity and endurance. I've been looking forward to meeting you, Dr. Keene."

"I've been looking forward to meeting you, sir," Keene replied.

Another figure, dressed in a light purple jacket embellished with silky trim and braid embroidery over a black polo-neck shirt, had moved up beside Foy and was exchanging words with Dril and Marna. He was fiftyish, stockily built for a Kronian, with wavy, yellow-brown hair, golden skin—UV tanning was widespread among Kronians—and firmly defined features underscored by a heavy-set chin. His name was Mylor Vorse. He ran Engineering and Development, and had presided over some of the meetings there that Keene had attended. On his other side was a woman in a maroon tunic, who from the compad and document holder she was carrying, Keene guessed to be some kind of assistant.

"And you two know each other," Cavan said.

"Good to see you again, Dr. Keene," Vorse greeted.

"The pleasure's always mine."

The Kronian woman, whose name was Adreya Laelye, turned out to be not Vorse's assistant but his deputy.

"And how is Pang-Yarbat these days?" Vorse asked Keene.

"Always irrepressible. How else?"

"He and I have known each other for many years. I'm hardened to the gruesome puns now. But the last time we met him was . . . when?" He looked at Adreya inquiringly.

"At Essen," she supplied. "Suliman Besso's wedding."

"Ah, yes. We talked about gardening. I told Pang I thought that more space in the Swiss Cheese should be reserved for growing flowers. Wouldn't you agree? Coming from Earth, you must miss them."

"I think I do . . . agree that more space should be reserved," Keene said.

"Of course it should. We need them more than ever down in these mole-holes of ours. What would Besso's wedding have been without them?"

The group parted to make room for a last few who had been holding back. The man at the fore was of crusty complexion and sprightly build, with an upturned, puckish nose and a mirthful expression that broadened to a grin as Keene recognized him. It was Gallian, who had headed the Kronian delegation to Earth that had brought Keene and his companions back. Keene swung his head accusingly toward Cavan. "Leo, why didn't you tell me? You knew Gallian would be here!"

"Oh, you know I always like to have a surprise in store," Cavan returned unapologetically. "Especially if it's a pleasant one."

"Of course, you two know each other already," Foy observed.

"If it hadn't been for Gallian we wouldn't be here," Cavan said—although SOE people would be aware of the details. Gallian had insisted that the *Osiris*, the ship in which his delegation had traveled, remain in the vicinity of Earth when all hope for Keene's party seemed lost. "Idorf wanted to pull out." Idorf had been the ship's captain.

"Which was correct in his position. Safety had to be his first consideration." Vorse sighed. "It was a shame about Idorf. He was one of the best. The *Osiris* was a fine ship." Idorf had also commanded a later mission back to Earth to look for survivors, in which he and the *Osiris* were lost.

"So are you with SOE now?" Keene asked Gallian, to lighten the mood.

Gallian nodded. "I'm hoping to go with the return mission when one's finally authorized."

"Didn't you have enough last time?"

"But . . . to see a whole new world beginning. How could I stay out?"

The remaining few were SOE technical people and a couple from elsewhere who were interested in the AG program at Essen. Vorse, who seemed to be in charge, made a short introductory announcement, and the group spread out around the table to seat themselves. For the benefit of those who were new to the subject, Keene gave an overview of the AG work, describing the early experiments on Valkyrie, the formation of the enlarged group at Tesla, and the design aims of the scaled-up system now being built there. The listeners were quick to raise further speculations beyond the obvious applications of creating normal living conditions in space and on the surfaces of minor astronomical bodies. Was there potential for new methods of excavating and earth-moving, or moving heavy loads? One of the SOE scientists asked about shaping and manipulating the fields on a smaller scale, and if it proved feasible, what kinds of devices might such capability permit? None of this was new, since the team at Tesla spent many hours debating such issues. Keene responded, "Back in the nineteenth century, a Victorian engineer would probably have agreed that the electric motor was a great idea and every home should have one—and he'd have mounted it on a pedestal in the basement, with belts and shafts going all over the building to transmit the power. What he'd never have dreamed of is having motors in just about every tool and appliance he owned. Well, we might be talking about the beginnings of something just as revolutionary that'll be taken for granted a hundred years from now."

Vorse raised the question of how an electrical source of gravity could be reconciled with an alternative model that others were proposing, in which the force didn't arise within the gravitating body at all but resulted from collisions of momentum-transfer agents—analogous to photons carrying electromagnetic energy across space, but far smaller and moving much faster. A cosmic background flux of such agents was posited, acting somewhat like a gas, which an isolated object would feel equally from all directions, giving no net force and imparting no motion. But two objects would "shadow" each other to some degree, giving rise to an imbalance in which the excess forces on the outer sides would drive them together. The result would be an apparent attraction, diminishing with distance as the subtended shadow angle grew smaller. This disposed of the need for "missing mass" that had been vainly sought after for over half a century, since the effect ceased to approximate an inverse-square law over large distances. Vorse's point, however, was that the cosmic flux model put the cause outside the gravitating object, whereas Pang-Yarbat's electrical explanation held it to be inside. Both couldn't be true. How could one view be squared with the other?

Keene was familiar with the momentum-transfer theory. He suggested that the AG model's electrical effects could arise from alterations of a particle's effective cross-section to blocking the external flux, thus influencing its "gravitating" capability indirectly. This led to an exchange across the table that brought in things like supra-luminal propagation velocities, the validity of curved-space models of gravitation, and local Lorentzian ether equivalents as the successor to Special Relativity, which the Kronians had discarded.

They never did get around to any of the space program and propulsion issues that Keene had assumed to be Foy's reason for asking him here, but he presumed that would come later. But he felt elated and gratified. Since coming to Kronia, he had seen what had been his small, relatively obscure engineering research group investigating a standard approach to power generation, become part of a major project that could open up a new realm of physics, and which was now being followed attentively by those responsible for the most far-reaching Kronian decision-making.

Under the intricate Kronian system of protocols and implications, it meant that Cavan's motives in bringing this about ran very deep. And Cavan understood the system very well. Whether or not a scientific venture went ahead and was supported, and if so to what degree, was decided not by funding committees or decree, but by the standing and effectiveness of those who believed in it and chose to support it—from leading theoreticians who attracted scientific talent, to managers of the workshops that made essential instruments and parts. Keene's presence and presentation amounted, in effect, to a funding application.

But a funding for what? Not the AG project itself, since Pang-Yarbat already took care of that. As seemed inevitable whenever Cavan was involved, something devious was going on.

CHAPTER TWELVE

Jon Foy hadn't said a lot during lunch. Physics and technical issues were clearly not his line. Afterward, Cavan excused himself, saying he had things to take care of elsewhere. Foy steered Keene aside, presumably getting down finally to the matter that had been the object of bringing Keene to Foundation. Mylor Vorse joined them.

They ascended in an elevator from the underground part of the Congressional complex and walked a short distance to what appeared to be Foy's workplace—a combination of study and office located in one of the pinnacles by the Hexagon, like a turret flanking the keep of an ancient castle. The suggestion of Gothic sombreness outside was enhanced by the fortress-like lines of the structures outlined in the lights beyond the windows, and the dim form of a nearby crater rim, craggy and black like a Transylvanian skyline against the red-streaked clouds.

The inside, by contrast, was bright and colorful, with an L-shaped desk console facing a mini-conference arrangement of chairs set around a low table, a larger worktable to one side, and a mixture of artwork and Earth scenes surrounding several display screens on the walls. A miniature flower and rock garden stood in a planter below, and the wall opposite the window carried an array of bookshelves—now rare on account of the uneconomic use of space and the effect of more convenient technologies. A large, black, long-haired cat opened its eyes to survey the newcomers suspiciously from a chair by the work table. After a few moments it lost interest, yawned, and went back to sleep.

Foy grinned as he followed Keene's gaze from the bleak scene outside, then back to the interior. "I need the window to remind me that there's still a real universe out there that we need to be concerned about," he said. "It's easy to become focused on the immediate and the immaterial if one's attention is always directed inward—down underground."

"What's the farther-away and the material, then?" Keene asked.

"For a start, a whole world to rebuild. The world that you last saw as radar images scanned through a cloud canopy"— Foy gestured at the window—"a bit like that outside. Would you like to see what's been happening back there?" Before Keene could answer, Foy voiced a command to the room's house manager and motioned toward the table set at a T with his desk. Keene took a chair facing the display wall as one of the screens came to life. Vorse sat down across a corner from him. Foy himself remained standing.

"This is the latest from the probes that we've been keeping in high orbit," Vorse commented. It sounded as if this had been intended—not something that had just occurred to Foy in response to Keene's question.

Earth still looked much as it had from the shuttle in orbit after the escape from Mexico—a dark ball of smoke and cloud stirred into whorls and streamers by storms that could still be ferocious in places. But the chasms cutting down into the murk were less pronounced and sharp than they had been, indicating that the winds were dropping. Debris from Athena's tail was coalescing into the beginnings of a visible ring system. The last time Keene had talked to Charlie Hu, estimates were that the rings would take several centuries or more to decay away.

A pattern in pale blue appeared superposed on the globe, outlining the familiar oceans and continents as they had existed through recorded history. Then a new set in red added themselves, showing the reconstructions from radar mapping of the surface as it had become. Keene still found the implications as stupefying as if he were seeing such images for the first time. Foy and Vorse remained silent, giving him a moment to absorb the meaning fully.

He was looking, literally, at the birth of a new world. It was now no longer questioned that the whole theory of planetary geology as it had been accepted on Earth would have to be rewritten from the beginnings. In the course of three years—and mostly in the early part of that!—Earth's surface had undergone changes which according to the previous doctrine should have taken hundreds of thousands of years or even more to unfold. But the doctrine had been wrong. What had been taken as evidence of slow processes operating over immense spans of time had turned out to be results of a period of relative quiescence between cataclysmic upheavals during which mountains rose, continents were split asunder, and oceans raged across the landscapes, renewing the world not once but several times within the span of human experience. The trifling measures of erosion, sedimentation, and plate movements wrongly extrapolated back to yield time scales in the order of millions of years were just the final, dying phases of events that had happened with terrifying speed—like shrinking puddles and trickles in ditches as all that remains to tell of yesterday's storm.

Earth's passage through Athena's magnetosphere had induced enormous electrical currents in the metal-bearing regions of the mantle and crust, producing heat that had opened up rifts and poured lava sheets over huge expanses of the surface, melted much of the polar ices, and in some places caused the seas to boil. But then, sudden cooling under the pall of smoke and dust from widespread surface conflagrations fed by Jovian hydrocarbons had caused massive precipitations of snow and ice from the saturated atmosphere, in some areas hundreds of feet deep within days. With the Earth's axis shifted ten degrees, new polar regions were appearing, centered on northern Alaska and the area south of Africa, and a corresponding shift and tilt was anticipated for the yet-to-emerge climatic bands. Sea level

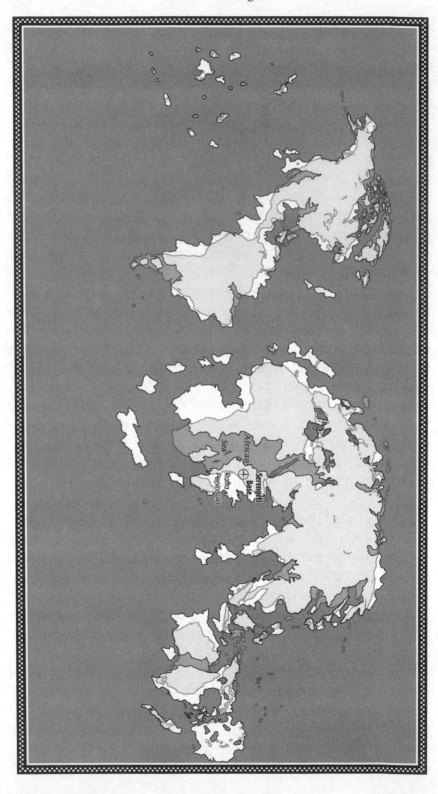

had not altered significantly. The changes that had occurred in coastlines were due mainly to the lateral movements, uplifts and depressions, of land masses.

Athena's main gravitational effect had been a jolting of the Earth's rotation, producing a general pattern of north-south fracturing of the crust. (The similar alignment of major preexisting rifts and mountain chains was likewise attributed to the earlier Venus encounters.) The American continent was generally broader, less pinched in the middle, and shortened. To the north, the still-forming ice cap closed the Pacific, bridging to Siberia apparently on top of a plateau formed by the squeezing out of existence of what had been the Bering Strait. Farther south, the Caribbean was a system of swampy lakes with an arm extending up into the former American Midwest, while the Panama isthmus had broadened toward the Pacific. Land west of the San Andreas fault had not sunk into the Pacific as celebrated in the popular mythology of years, but instead hinged outward to become part of a new land area of uplifted seabed fringed by a chain of mountainous overthrust to the west. On the inland side, the Gulf of California had opened and extended, reaching almost to the wastes of ash and cooling lava fields that covered the sites where Seattle and Vancouver had stood. South America too, had broadened west of the Andes, but to the east large tracts of Argentina were submerged, leaving a truncated mountain spine crumbling into a chain of islands.

The Atlantic had changed beyond recognition. In both the northern and southern basins, large portions of the Mid-Atlantic Ridge had risen to become new, elongated islands of almost subcontinental proportions, with smaller groups forming a chain curving eastward around the tip of Africa to the shifted and reforming South Polar ice sheet. Except that the tip of Africa was no longer where it had been before. Like California's gulf, the Great African Rift had opened into a new arm of ocean cutting north through the Middle East and cleaving Jordan and Syria before curving east to join the Caspian Sea. West of this new arm of ocean, the main body of Africa was pivoting north on huge upswelling lava flows, piling crust and sediment into a coastal mountain chain separated only by narrows from the Mid-Atlantic islands in the south, and in the north forming a mountain barrier below the lakes that were all that was left of the Mediterranean. The eastern side of Africa, meanwhile, had become a jagged peninsula thrusting south from Arabia and bordering an archipelago of new islands extending to a much-elongated India.

Farther east, the western Pacific trench system had propagated southward and cut Australia in two. The western portion, again following the general pattern of north-south shock lines imparted by Athena, was swinging northwest into the Indonesian region to produce an incredible tangle of islands, lakes, land bridges, and channels, while the eastern part seemed to be merging into an area of new southwest Pacific uplift that embraced most of the former island groups and New Zealand.

Although still vastly greater than anything remotely suspected previously, the motions of the new fragmenting and merging tectonic plates were already slowing measurably. It seemed that a new mini-continent was beginning to form in the southwest Pacific, with the west part of Australia destined to become a southern extension of Asia. Elsewhere, the widening of the African rift northward showed signs of meeting another fault opening down from the Siberian coast and dividing the Eurasian land mass to create what might become a new ocean. A number of studies had produced maps of how the face of Earth might evolve over the centuries ahead—all of them highly speculative.

Seeing all this brought back feelings that Keene had experienced in the shuttle above Earth as he watched the false-color radar images change hour by hour, telling their story of cities disappearing beneath mile-high walls of advancing water, nations consumed by infernos of burning air hot enough to melt stone, humans and animals dying in billions. Even now, what else might be happening below the veil of dust and vapor could only be guessed at.

"How low have the probes gone?" he asked finally, forcing his eyes away and looking at the other two. "Are there any signs of survivors?" In his numbness it was the automatic thing to say. He didn't really think so. Any such news would have been known immediately all over Kronia.

Vorse shook his head. "We put landers down at a few places. The views they sent back could have been from Hades." He shrugged as if to say all was still not lost. "But the fraction of the surface that we've sampled has been tiny. There could be other conditions elsewhere."

"Our kind has survived comparable events before," Foy put in. "And they didn't possess the technical resources that the industrialized world had. It's early days yet, Dr. Keene." The cyclic theme of old worlds destroyed and new worlds being born recurred in the myths of ancient cultures as far back as they were recorded. The Biblical Old Testament was not alone in its injunction to go forth and *replenish* the Earth.

"Rebuilding it should go a lot faster this time," Keene said. "Kronia was never here before to direct things. We've got a repository of knowledge that won't have to be discovered all over again."

Foy gave him a long, contemplative look before replying, as if evaluating if this were the moment to broach whatever he'd had in mind in bringing Keene here. Finally, he said, "What we're looking at, Dr. Keene, isn't just the prospect of rebuilding civilization. Because of a quirk in recent times that led to the coming together of some extraordinarily gifted people, the circumstances that we have here at Kronia are unique in the history of human existence. As a consequence, we have the chance to found a civilization unlike anything that has existed before—the kind of civilization that visionaries through the ages have imagined, but which have defied all attempts to turn into reality. Some have concluded that it must always be so: that the harsh rules of reality and human nature make them permanently impossible dreams. But we believe otherwise. We believe that the forced cooperation that has been vital to survival out here at Kronia has produced a workable system of human values that could never have happened in the violent, competitive conditions that governed the development of cultures on Earth. If we can import that system back to Earth, maybe we'll be able to shape a civilization fundamentally different from any that emerged there before, rooted in the same ethic of mutual need and the inherent value of everyone as a unique individual that guides us here." He shrugged. "And if there do turn out to be survivors there, perhaps we can steer their early development in the same direction, before they begin increasing in numbers and organizing themselves into the old, eternal patterns of power rivalries and conflict."

"Who are 'we'?" Keene asked, picking up on Foy's use of the word. "Who decides these things?"

"Those of us who try to consider where our longer-term destiny might lie, beyond just muddling through from one century to the next," Foy replied. "After the present crisis has faded to become just another detail on the cosmic backdrop. When a new race has emerged that isn't divided within itself because of the inherently hostile nature of all its human relationships. Each against all. Take as much as you can in return for as little as you can get away with. That was the underlying rule that drove everything of importance on Earth, was it not? 'Good business.' 'Astute politics.' How could a sentiment like that ever mold and hold together a civilization capable of moving out among the stars?"

Keene took a moment to adjust to the new dimension that the conversation was taking on. What Foy was talking about now went far beyond just an experiment in organizing a complex, technological society on an alternative basis to the monetary incentive that most people on Earth had regarded as self-evidently unavoidable.

Foy completed Keene's thought as if he had been expecting it. "Sometimes our system is described as having invented what amounts to a new form of currency: a trade in the recognition of competence. And in some way it turns out to be a very superior currency. It can't be counterfeited, or stolen, or hoarded—for how can you fake skill or knowledge that you don't possess, take away another person's once they have it, or give it to someone who hasn't earned it? So corruption of the kind that comes with the power to steal legally or to bribe is impossible. And so does enslaving another person to create wealth for your own benefit—for with our kind of wealth the only one who could become rich is the slave."

Keene had heard the analogy before, but he let Foy carry through without interruption. For years, Earth's experts had insisted that Kronia would never last. When it not only lasted but grew and attracted more numbers, they said it was only through dependence on Earth, and they tried cutting the flow of material supplies to prove it. But the restrictions only served to make Kronia more self-reliant sooner.

Foy went on, "But that was said by Terrans who could only think in terms of a model based on economics. Earth was fixated on economics. It had become the global religion, dominating every aspect of life." He waved a hand. "Providing for material needs is important, of course, like eating. But like eating, it merely provides a foundation to support higher things. Look at earlier cultures and their works. Earth had brought everything down to the level of the foundation. It ate compulsively, all the time, with no other purpose."

"An entire Earth culture modeled after Kronia?" Keene said. It was plain enough that this was what Foy meant, but Keene needed a moment to reflect on it. It hadn't been long ago when Grasse and Valcroix were telling him that the Kronian system couldn't survive much more of even the colony's own growth.

"Not just Earth. Beyond it," Foy replied. "I already said, a culture capable for the first time of reaching for the stars." He waited for a few seconds, then grinned at the expression on Keene's face. "The conditioning of a Terran upbringing still shows, Dr. Keene. Forget the dogmas you heard repeated all around you every day of your life back there. This is perhaps the *only* system that *could* hold up on such a scale." Foy made a palm-up gesture with one hand. "How far did Earth's space programs get on its shopkeeper economics after the military incentives went away? Some corporate exploitation of the Moon. A couple of pilot bases on Mars that never amounted to more than glorified field laboratories. No profit. No aims beyond continuing the safe accumulation of capital." He shrugged. "And in any case, profit is a poor substitute for a motivation that will fire the passions of a whole culture. I'm talking about what can only be called spiritual—the kind of drive that inspired Europe of the High Middle Ages to create its soaring cathedrals and spurred the spread of Islam from

India to Spain. The spirit that expresses belief in something beyond individual existence, larger than the individual, that will endure long after the individual has gone and give meaning to the life that was dedicated to it."

"You're making it sound like a new Kronian religion," Keene said.

Foy glanced at Vorse and inclined his head in a way that said he didn't entirely disagree. "Something that plays the role that religion once did, anyway. A universal sense of purpose, a quest that will spur a new Renaissance. Except that this Renaissance will be driven by visions of reality, not myth. All religions founded on myth eventually collapse when the myth is exposed." He paused for a moment. "And what I see playing that role is something that I know is very important to you, Dr. Keene.

"I'm tempted to say 'science,' but I don't mean the dead husk of true inquiry that the word had come to mean in Earth's institutionalized orthodoxies. I mean the free, creative process that functions within and as part of a universe that it recognizes as itself alive—not some soulless observer of a dead machine. What science *should* have been. The driving force that by now would already have carried us across the Solar System, instead of selling out to the power structure as the European Church did before it, and allowing itself to be conscripted to serve politics and commerce. I've talked to Sariena and Gallian. They know you. It was what you stood for through your whole life back there."

Keene nodded distantly. Had the human race been spread out and expanding in the way that Foy described, instead of concentrated in one place, the effects of Athena would have been far less calamitous. As things were, only the lucky fact of Kronia's existence had stood between civilization being obliterated completely, and the future that Foy was painting now. "Is that to be the God of your new religion, then, Jon?" he asked. "Life?"

"Life and love of every creative thing a human being stands for and is capable of achieving," Foy answered. "When Earth replaced the old gods of living nature with its mechanistic science, it reduced nature to inanimate matter running according to mechanical laws, within which life became a pointless accident, thought was no more than a byproduct of life, and morality an invention of wishful thinking. The gods that the new priesthood served were not knowledge or wisdom, but better technologies for accelerating the acquisition of material wealth through legalized theft and violence." Foy looked at Vorse briefly as if for confirmation and tossed out a palm again. "And why not? All other meaning and purpose had been stripped away. The only aspect of individual worth that was recognized and rewarded was efficacy in contributing to profits. No wonder so many knew intuitively that their lives had the potential for better things, and rebelled. That was what drove the migration to Kronia."

"So is that what you see as Kronia's purpose?" Keene asked. "To go out and become part of a living universe?"

"Whatever is in its nature to become," Foy replied. "The High Cultures that have emerged through human history are themselves living organisms that appear, grow, flourish, and eventually die. Each possesses its own unique soul. In the course of its lifetime, everything that a culture produces— its arts; its religion; its mathematics, its sciences; its philosophy and world view, works and constructions—all are an expression of that soul. It can be no other way. Like any organism, it has no choice but to actualize the imperative that's inherent in its nature. Kronia will become what it is destined to become."

"Becoming one with God?"

"I suppose you could look at it that way."

Keene was surprised to hear himself talking in such terms. It wasn't the kind of thing that his work or his inclinations led him into very often. Sariena talked with Vicki about similar things, and how Kronia's scientists saw the universe as an organism designed for a purpose—a view totally at odds with the belief system that Keene had grown up hearing. Now here was Foy, promoting it as the world view of a future star-going civilization. Not that long ago, Keene would have politely respected such sentiments but would have remained unaffected by them. They weren't relevant to what had been his world then—the world of the mathematically and physically accessible, made up of tangible entities. But now, maybe because of the change that had taken place in his vantage point and his situation, as he listened he found himself strangely stirred. Something deep inside was already glimpsing the vision of a race that would one day be, their ships casting off across voids to other worlds and other suns to find their God. Human technology functioning as the essential partner of life, not stifling and replacing life as it had on Earth. It could only have come about in the conditions that reigned on Kronia, where life and technology were mutually interdependent, and neither could exist without the other.

Foy had moved to stand with his back to the window and was watching Keene, letting him form his own conclusions in his own time. Keene stared at the image of Earth again, and then back at the white-haired figure in the silver-gray robe, looking like a prophet of old or the abbot of some remote and fabled Tibetan temple. Vorse didn't contribute but was looking on in silent endorsement.

"That's what you really believe here?" Keene said. "What Kronia believes. There is a meaning to it all, that we— Mankind—can discover." What he was hearing was a repudiation of the whole doctrine of existence responsible for shaping the world he had known—the doctrine that the authorities whom that world had relied on to know had said was irrefutable and unquestionable. The immensity of the implications that it opened up for the future that was portended, and the significance of the roles that he, like everyone, stood to play in it, was dizzying.

"Or maybe rediscover," Foy said. "One of the things that we'd very much like to know more about is the culture that existed out here before, when Earth was a satellite of Saturn."

"You believe that maybe they knew more about things like that?" Keene said.

"We can only speculate. Virtually all of the physical evidence was lost, even before Athena. We only have the scraps of what they recorded, handed down in tradition and legend. But cultures all over the world told of a lost Golden Age, long ago, when Man lived in harmony with nature and the gods, strife was unknown, and the world was plentiful. And in all of those tales, Saturn was the god that ruled the skies."

Keene nodded. Sariena had talked about that too.

Foy went on, "We think Saturn was a benign proto-sun then, pouring out sustenance to give Earth a richness and diversity of life that was never seen or imagined since. But that era was ended by cataclysm in a way we're still not sure of, and Earth was torn away to enter the fiery domain of the Sun. Its forests and gardens were turned into deserts, its animals died in graveyards by the millions. And for the humans who remained, violence and ruthlessness became the code for survival. It became the only way that Man knew, and all the cultures that reemerged subsequently were rooted in it. Eventually they were unable to conceive how things could be otherwise."

Foy paused again, but Keene was still struggling with visions that would probably take him days to come to terms with. Finally, Vorse spoke, turning toward Keene as if he had been waiting for the lead up to this moment. "But, as Jon indicated at the beginning, the difference this time is that Kronia exists. We can prevent the same pattern from repeating again. So I can tell you now, Lan, that it has been decided to go back as soon as possible. The earlier we intervene, the better."

As the meaning of Vorse's words sank in, Keene's gaze shifted to Foy, as if for confirmation. "Back to Earth?" Keene said. Foy nodded.

Vorse resumed, "It will soon be common knowledge. Preparations are being commenced. And this is where you come into it, Lan. One of the first needs will be a building program to replace the ships that were lost in the early rescue attempts. But not just with any ships. It needs the right kind of long-range, extended-mission-support ship. And when we get there, we'll be setting up a full range of seed industries using profab." Vorse was referring to "programmed fabrication," a manufacturing technology based on creating objects by building them up from successive deposition layers, controllable to the molecular scale and capable of producing just about anything, given the right raw materials. "Your combined propulsion and MHD power generation system that would provide full support capability immediately is perfect—just what we want."

Keene made an open-handed gesture. "Well, of course it's yours. And whatever more I can do to help . . ." He checked himself as the broader possibility struck him as to why they might have brought him here. "Are you saying you might want me to leave the AG project, to move into this program?"

"More than that," Vorse told him. "Maintaining bases that can operate viably on Earth will be crucial—both for remote outposts in the kind of venture Jon has described, or as centers to escape to if things go wrong out here. Either way, it's a new design and an untried concept. With what's at stake, it would be too risky to entrust operating them to anyone with secondhand knowledge. We want *you* there, as part of the first mission. We want you to go back to Earth."

Keene slumped back in his chair, too surprised to respond at once.

Foy smiled, as if acknowledging a joke that they had been keeping till the end. "It's ironic, don't you think, Dr. Keene, that because of this calamity that has happened, the new era that might take us back to where the Golden Age was leading will begin once again out here, at Saturn? And, answering your earlier question, that could be the ultimate meaning of everything that Kronia stands for."

CHAPTER THIRTEEN

Eventually, Rakki would challenge Jemmo's leadership of the clan, and one or the other of them would prevail. It was inevitable. Rakki considered himself to be the one who saw more and thought more. It had been his idea to place a second war party above the caves, which had contributed greatly to the speedy success on that day, and he had been the one to say that they should spare some of the Old-worlders to learn the secret of their weapons. And although Jemmo's fighting ability was unquestioned, Rakki had accepted the risk of letting himself be taken by the Cavers, which in his estimation made him an equal in valor. To serve indefinitely as Jemmo's lieutenant and inferior in status would be an insufferable affront to his pride. Jemmo knew it too. Rakki could see it in his eyes as he took in Rakki's measure when they talked, unconsciously weighing him up as an opponent, and he sensed it in the way Jemmo's face would harden, setting a margin of distance between them. And Jemmo, for his part, would never feel safe with the menace of a strong and competent potential rival who might move against him at any time. Rakki knew that too. Each was biding time, waiting for an advantageous circumstance. But the moment would come soon.

He stood near the cave entrance, watching Shell Eyes as

she sat poring over the remnant of the Oldworlder vest that he had once worn, now torn, bloodstained, and almost coming apart into two pieces. She separated some of the strands that it was made from to see if she could devise a way of saving it. Rakki now wore a shoulder-wrap of skin sewn with sinew, which he had wanted ready for the expedition leaving the next day. With Jemmo's approval, he had set her and several other females the task of investigating the scraps of Oldworld materials that were left, such as the pieces of clothing taken from Bo and Scar-arm, and other oddments used as sleeping covers or for cleaning, to see if they could be duplicated. White Head had told them that such things in the Old World were made from the fibers of certain plants and soft down from the hides of animals. The women had collected samples of various plants and attempted to work them, but without success. Everything was too short and stiff, and could never weave together to form the fine, unbroken order that they found in the old fabrics.

"The plants were a special kind," White Head said, squatting nearby in front of the place where he worked, shaping spear tips from hardstone. "Could be they never grew in these parts."

"What they look like?" Rakki asked him. That could be another thing to look out for on the reconnoitering journey starting tomorrow.

White Head made a helpless gesture. "I cannot tell you. It was not what I knew. I was just a herder of cows."

Rakki frowned. "What is cow?"

"Large animal. Bigger than hairhide."

"You own? . . . Like those." Rakki motioned toward the pens holding the animals that had been inherited from the Cavers.

White Head emitted one of his wheezing laughs. "That few! They are nothing. I work for Great Lord who owns them. More cows mean bigger worth. The land his cows needed to hold them was"—White Head waved toward the outside again—"here to the water on far side of swamp lands. More, even. Could be as far as fire mountains."

Rakki couldn't imagine enough animals to fill that amount

of land, and took it as just another of the things White Head said that he would never understand. He turned his head again toward Shell Eyes and lifted his chin in an unspoken question. "This, I cannot remake, my lord," she told him. "I am sorry. I can maybe tie with sinew. It will last a small time longer. I am sorry."

Rakki nodded curtly, suppressing the surge of annoyance that made him want to slap her. It didn't seem worthy of a warrior to beat a female who had committed no fault. He discerned the same disapproval in White Head also when he witnessed it happening with others. It seemed to be part of the Oldworlders' way. Rakki could tell from the way Jemmo looked at her that he resented the way Rakki had claimed her as his female immediately, without deferring to Jemmo's right to choose first. Rakki would be in danger now until the thing between them was settled, one way or another.

Gap Teeth—whose name was Enka, Rakki now knew, but he still stuck to the original that he had coined—and Shingral were nearby as always. Since the day of the ambush, when Rakki had spoken for them to be spared, they had attached themselves to him in the way dogs would to the master who commands them, and appointed themselves the task of watching over his safety. They saw the rising tension between him and Jemmo, and had made it plain by their actions that if things came to a fight between rival factions to resolve matters, he could count on two henchmen who would be loyal. Although Rakki valued the protection, he considered them mildly foolish. Life could not be lived for the benefit of others. The weak tried to harness the strong to save them, instead of learning to be strong themselves. And if the strong let themselves be harnessed, they themselves would become weak—like the hairhides that allowed men to tie lines around their necks and worked for them.

Maybe it had been the Oldworlders' way. But the Old-worlders no longer possessed the caves.

With the Swamp People's domain now extending up to the caves, it had become important to learn more of the territories that lay beyond. The expedition that Rakki would be leading tomorrow was to be a long-range exploration lasting many days to reconnoiter the more distant terrain and search for signs of other habitation and resources that might be of use. Two others would accompany him in addition to Gap Teeth and Shingral. A small, lightly equipped party would move faster and cover more ground than a large group; and in the event of there being any hostile presence out there, they would be less conspicuous and thus not so likely to draw followers back.

Rakki straightened up and reached for the "gun" that he had propped against the rock wall. It was time he went to check on how the other preparations were going. Jemmo carried a gun as a symbol of rank, and he had thought better of trying to oppose the demand when Rakki claimed the right to one too. Even to be confronted by a refusal would have been unacceptably insulting to Rakki's pride and made an immediate resolution unavoidable, which Jemmo evidently didn't want to precipitate yet.

The number of guns they had obtained from the Cavers was five plus another two—White Head had taught Rakki the words for numbers as far as the fingers on one hand. He said there were more that he would tell later. The remaining five guns were kept under guard until it was decided who would have them. But in truth, their value at present went little farther than being just emblems to instill awe. Sims, one of the other Oldworlders who had been spared in addition to White Head and Yellow Hair, had explained the function of bullets, but there were so few of them that Jemmo had been loathe to expend any on learning. But the dilemma then, as Rakki pointed out, had been that the weapons would never be of use if no one could use them. In the end, they had compromised by going out to some open ground beyond the rampart with Sims, taking five and one bullets. Sims had used two of them to demonstrate the technique for directing the bullet to hit a reed basket placed on a rock half a bowshot away. With the remaining four, Rakki and Jemmo tried two each. On Rakki's first attempt the gun kicked unexpectedly causing him to drop it, and he didn't know where the bullet went. He managed to hold onto the gun for the second, but again missed. Jemmo did no better. So the problem remained unsolved of how to learn to use the guns and be left with enough bullets to ever fight with them. One of the hopes for the reconnaissance tour was that it might locate more bullets. Rakki didn't think it very likely, since apart from the things in the caves and a few oddments like his edged metal club—which he had found and reclaimed—he had seen hardly any traces of Oldworld things. But at least, now he had some idea what an ammunition box looked like.

As he lifted the weapon, he couldn't resist running a finger again over its gray metal lines. The precision and form of the pieces and how they fitted together, and the way it opened for the bullets to be inserted, still astounded him. Apart from crude bending or sharpening on a stone, he had never heard of ways of cutting or shaping objects of metal. He remembered White Head's words about gods who once flew above the sky and built shining tower-caves like ant mounds that stood higher than the cliffs. He looked across at where White Head was squatting.

"The birds that the gods flew in. They were made from metal too, like this?"

"Yes. Shells of metal. Like giant eggs with metal wings."

"And all gods carried guns, like this?"

"The god-warriors carried them. Armies bigger in number than the herd of cows that I tended."

Rakki couldn't comprehend how anything could stand before that many guns. He often suspected that White Head exaggerated wildly. He didn't like the thought that White Head might be making a fool of him. "So many not possible." He shook his head pointedly, meaning it as a warning. "You tell me things as they were, Oldworld man. Only truth with Rakki."

White Head cackled and wheezed. "Those, they were nothing!" he said, waving at Rakki's gun. "There were giant-bird weapons that the gods flew in. They sent down giant bullets that burned all the land—like fire mountains. Broke the ground up like the holes that open when the world shakes."

Rakki felt a rush of anger at White Head's ridiculing his newly acquired source of so much pride, but a cautionary instinct made him bite it down. "Attend to your work, old man," he growled. "I have things to do."

He moved to the cave entrance and went out. Rubble and rocks lay strewn over the area inside the rampart. There had been ground tremors in the last few days, and beyond the rampart part of the cliff line had fallen, blocking the trail leading east. Workers were clearing a new path over it. Continual rolls of thunder and deep groaning sounds from the ground were coming from the direction of the fire mountains. With all their powers, the Oldworld gods hadn't been able to prevent the destruction of their world beneath bolts that fell in torrents from the skies and walls of moving water that Rakki had been told devoured mountains. Nobody had been able to tell him what had been the cause of it all. Some said that spirit beings, controlling such things as the earth-fires and the skies, became displeased when men failed to live as the spirits wanted, and so destroyed them. White Head had once talked about "devils," who were enemies of the gods and had similar powers. Rakki wasn't sure if he believed it. To him it sometimes sounded more as if those who talked of spirits invented them as a way of inducing men to live as *they* wanted, which usually meant feeding and protecting them—another way to harness the strong. But in any case, he was usually too preoccupied with surviving from one day to the next to think too much about it.

Jemmo was outside at the far end of the enclosed area, observing the butchering of several animals that had been killed by rocks falling into the pens. Wakabe, another of the Oldworlders, was explaining the procedure. At least Rakki and his companions would eat well before they departed and carry ample provision for the journey. Jemmo had taken to wearing a light Oldworld body garment—originally with sleeves extending down the arms, but Jemmo had found them constricting and had them cut off—with an Oldworld belt above his loin cladding and a cape made from hide, fastened at the neck with a clasped thong. He was also wearing the hide foot-sheaths taken from Bo, but he had removed the thick undersurfaces because they were clumsy and slipped on the rocks. Uncovered soles of feet gave a better grip. *Yes, that's good. Concern yourself with your looks and keep your mind on things inside the caves and the rampart,* Rakki thought to himself. *Worry about being safe and become soft like the Oldworlders. Then, when I return, toughened from travels over great distances, we will face each other.*

IIe was about to move on, when he saw a figure approaching him. It was Zomu, one of the Swamp warriors who had taken part in the ambush in the ravine. He made a sign motioning Rakki back behind a rock flanking the cave opening, at the same time casting a look around them that said he wished to talk privately. Rakki said nothing and waited.

"I say this because I know the day must come when you and Jemmo fight," Zomu began, keeping his voice low, his eyes still roaming. "I believe Rakki will rule the swamp lands and the caves. When your word is the law, I want you to remember who helped you."

"What is it you have to say?" Rakki asked.

"Jemmo is filled with bad blood. A madness burns within him for Shell Eyes. He would see her dead rather than with you. I ask you to be careful. She could be in danger when you leave tomorrow. That is my warning."

"How do you know this?"

"Careless talk by Iyala that I overhear." Iyala was one of Jemmo's henchmen.

Rakki touched Zomu lightly on the shoulder. "It will not be forgotten," he said.

When Rakki emerged back into the open, he stopped and stared toward Jemmo, still talking with Wakabe. Jemmo looked for a moment in his direction, and Rakki knew that he could see him. Then Jemmo turned away.

Rakki thought hard for the rest of the day as to what he should do. Calling off the expedition under some pretext was out of the question—it would seem an admission of weakness. Finally, he took Shingral and Gap Teeth, his two guardians, aside and told them, "The plan for tomorrow is changed. I have information that Shell Eyes may be in danger." He looked at Gap Teeth. "I want you to stay and watch over her. Guard her closely at all times."

"My own life shall be lost first," Gap Teeth confirmed.

"We will make up our number with another who is loyal," he told Shingral. Then, to Gap Teeth again, "If you have doubts or need wise words while we are gone, talk to White Head. White Head, you can trust."

"I will remember," Gap Teeth said.

Later, Rakki spoke again with Zomu. "One of my trusted warriors will watch over Shell Eyes. But we now need another for the journey tomorrow. I pick you as my choice."

"I will come with you," Zomu said.

They left at the first brightening of the next day: Rakki, Shingral, Zomu, and two others whose names were Alin and Dorik. The route took them away from the direction of the swamp lands, skirting the Dry Country of the previous excursion to enter even higher regions where colder winds brought squalls of rain and at times snow that collected as ice in the crevices and gulleys. The party had brought heavier skins, which they put on over their regular garb, and wrappings to protect their feet. Rakki realized the usefulness of the Oldworlders' foot-sheaths now, and wished he had saved some. The surroundings grew harsher and bleaker.

It was late in the afternoon and they were following a trail along the side of a precipice, when Rakki, in the lead, heard a sudden cry behind him. He spun around to find Shingral on his knees, slowly buckling over, with Alin standing behind him, gripping him by a shoulder. Alin drew back his arm to reveal the bloodstained length of sharpened metal as he pulled it from Shingral's back, then released him to let him fall forward. For a moment Rakki could only stare, confused. Then he took in Dorik and Zomu moving around on either side of Alin, leveling their spears toward him as they hemmed him around, his back to the edge of the drop.

Then he understood. Jemmo had never wanted Shell Eyes dead; he wanted her for himself. And he had guessed Rakki's reaction perfectly. Zomu had been serving Jemmo all along. The ruse had been to separate Rakki's two bodyguards. The odds would have been too risky with both of them along. Now it was all obvious. But too late.

Rakki moved to unsling the gun from his shoulder. He

had five of the precious bullets in it—but he would never have time to bring it to bear. Three spears advanced upon him as Alin completed the semicircle.

"What was the price of this teachery?" he hissed at Zumo as they closed, driving him back.

"An Oldworld weapon to carry. And Jemmo would rule anyway."

"You don't get this one!" Rakki threw the gun away behind him, into the chasm, but before he could draw his edged club, they rushed.

He seized Zomu's spear, arching his body to pull it by him, drawing Zomu on. As Zomu pitched forward off-balance, Rakki dropped onto his back, at the same time planting a foot in Zomu's stomach and using his leg as a pivot to carry Zomu onward and over, sending him screaming into the abyss. But the other two were upon him. He twisted away to take the worst out of a thrust from Alin that pierced his side, leaving him lying along the rim of the drop; and then Dorik, declining to present his own spear and risk the same fate as had befallen Zomu, used it instead as a prop to slide his body forward feetfirst, propelling Rakki over the edge.

Rakki remembered nothing of the fall or of landing. The next thing he was conscious of was lying on a rock shelf, his body racked with pain and impossible to move, one leg twisted under him in a way that he knew meant it was broken. Night was falling, and he was already stiff with cold.

PART TWO

The Sky Warriors

CHAPTER FOURTEEN

Vicki had proposed the names in recognition of Emil Farzhin's theories while the ship was still a collection of structural plans and design specifications in the computers of SOE's Engineering and Development Division. The main body of the vessel, which would remain in orbit above Earth, was called *Varuna*, after one of the ancient Sanskrit deities associated with Venus. The inertial-fusion drive section formed a detachable, independently-operable unit capable of descent to the surface, where it could function in low-power mode as an MHD generating plant in the way the Tesla Center team had originally envisaged. This part was named *Agni*, one of the manifestations of proto-Venus that had brought fire down upon the Earth. The entire vessel was a no-frills, utility undertaking put together in minimal time, with space and comfort sacrificed to hold the greatest number of occupants consistent with carrying the essentials of materials and equipment for establishing a bridgehead presence on Earth. Follow-up missions to expand and build upon the pilot program were being fitted out back at Saturn.

A year and a half had gone by since Keene joined SOE at Foundation to head the *Agni* part of the design program, working directly under Mylor Vorse. A year and a half of grueling analysis and drafting sessions often lasting

round-the-clock; of working with the groups involved with
structural configuration, propulsion-power integration, communications and computation systems, instrumentation and
control systems, life support systems; of supervising bench-
marks, test rigs, scaling trials, attending team meetings,
management meetings . . . By the ways he had known back
on Earth, it would never have been possible. Static firings
and full-system testing in orbit around Titan had followed;
then, finally, a shakedown trip out to Phoebe, the outermost sizable moon of Saturn and back. . . .

And now, three months after the shakedown trials to
Phoebe, Keene was once again in orbit above Earth. He
floated weightless in one of the outer-hull observation
bubbles—the *Varuna*'s construction had been too hasty an
affair for elaborations involving gravity simulation—looking
down at what until now he had seen only as images that
robot reconnaissance orbiters had sent back to Saturn: the
graveyard of everything he had once known.

The fires that had raged across huge areas had long ago
been extinguished by massive precipitations from an atmosphere saturated with evaporated ocean water, but the pole-
to-pole murk of cloud and airborne dust still concealed
almost all of the surface detail. Descending air currents over
northern Alaska and below Africa produced clearer patches
that revealed occasional glimpses of the shifted, newly
forming polar regions, but they meant little, even with the
aid of radar-mapped coastal outlines superposed on the
screen image showing on a console to one side. Images had
also come back from probes sent down through the cloud
cover and landed at a number of places. They showed
mountains of storm-driven ocean crashing against the
Appalachian chain, now a peninsula between the shrunken
Atlantic and the new arm of sea inundating the American
Midwest; the new upthrust mountain barrier named the
Barbary range, following roughly the line of what had been
western North Africa and walling in the lakes that remained
of the Mediterranean basins; the confusion of continental
fragments, islands, and waterways, where New Guinea, the
eastern parts of Australia, adjacent former archipelagos, and
uplifted crustal blocks seemed to be compressing together

into a new land mass that had taken over the name Oceania; still smoldering carpets of ash that had been Siberian forests. . . . But contemplating it in solitude through his own eyes directly, without the intermediary of electronic representation, reawakened a sense of communion with the destroyed world that he had not known since the time, almost five years ago, when he looked down from a similar vantage point in orbit while awaiting rescue by the *Osiris*.

Charlie Hu, who had also been present then, had come back with the *Varuna*. As a former Terran planetary scientist, he was impatient to get down to the surface and begin finding out more about the stupendous processes unfolding below. Gallian was back again too, his prior experience in leading the Kronian delegation to Earth having gained him the appointment as overall director of the *Varuna*'s mission. However, because of the difficulties and discomfort that the Kronian-born had experienced even in the comparatively tranquil environments that had existed before Athena, the personnel mix of the mission had been made disproportionately Terran.

Among the Kronians, Shayle, who had gone with Keene from the Tesla Center to SOE, was here as his fusion specialist. Vorse's deputy, Adreya Laelye, represented SOE. And Sariena was back too, with a mixed group of Kronian scientists aboard a relatively small, minimally configured conventional fusion-drive vessel called the *Surya*—a minor deity mentioned along with Varuna in Vedic mythology— that had accompanied the *Varuna*. As well as affording extra carrying capacity, the arrangement provided that in the event of an emergency either ship could act as lifeboat for the other.

They had been in orbit for six days now, along with a gaggle of unmanned freight haulers—little more than containment frames fitted with engines—sent on ahead at intervals before the *Varuna* and the *Surya*'s departure. Teams had gone down to the surface several times to check candidate sites for the first base, but none had been selected so far. When a site was picked and preliminary constructions made ready, the *Agni* section of the ship would detach, leaving the *Varuna* with just an auxiliary power system for orbital corrections and essential services, and Keene would be shuttled down with his crew to integrate it into the base. Expansion of the base proper using materials delivered from orbit would then proceed.

Athena, after making another perihelion turn between the orbits of Mercury and Venus, was currently on the far side of the Sun and climbing outward again toward the Asteroid Belt. Since all of its potential interactions were highly nonlinear, meaning that tiny initial differences could result in hugely varying outcomes, there was no way of being sure of what the future might hold. Hence, reconnoitering and preparing evacuation centers on Earth in case Saturn had to be abandoned had taken on greater importance. Charlie had commented that he understood well now why so many cultures of old had watched Venus and Mars with such terror and built elaborate constructions to track their movements.

From Vicki's most recent messages from Dione, it seemed she would be coming out with the first follow-up mission from Saturn, aboard a new ship being fitted out there, called the *Aztec*. Emil Farzhin was sending a group to begin exploring Athena's biological consequences, and again native-born Terrans were the preferred choice. Keene was looking forward to seeing her again.

In any case, the change would be good for her, now that Robin had gone ahead and joined the Security Arm. He had completed basic training and space engineering school on Titan, and would be leaving shortly on an exploratory mission to survey the primary Jovian moons more thoroughly than had been attempted so far. The intention here was to prepare the ground for an alternative fallback location to be developed—possibly on Ganymede—in the event of Saturn having to be evacuated. The proposal had come from Valcroix's Pragmatist movement, who still argued that putting major investments of resources into the unknowns of Earth was premature, whereas existing Kronian technologies would assure habitable environments at Jupiter. And if the emergency never happened, a foothold would have been made at Jupiter for future expansion.

This concession on the part of the Kronian Congress to consider Jupiter at a time when many priorities were in conflict reflected the progress that the Pragmatists had been making in becoming a recognized political force. Nevertheless, Keene hadn't altered his opinion that in the long run not a lot would come of it, since they had nothing to offer that the majority of Kronians desired, or even comprehended. In any case, he'd seen it all before, wasted enough of his life fighting it, and he was glad to be away. Like Charlie, he was restless to get down to the surface and begin the work they had come here to do.

He was still staring out at the view below, searching for a hint of a coastal outline among the veils blanketing the surface, when a female voice spoke from behind him. "It must be a terrible thing to come home to, Lan." He turned to find Shayle holding on to a handbar in the access hatchway. She was dressed in orange flight coveralls, her red hair cut short now.

Keene grunted. "There isn't much down there that I think I'd call home anymore."

"It must be strange, all the same."

"I've had time enough to get used to it."

"What were you so wrapped up in thought over?" Shayle asked. "I was here, watching you, for a while."

Keene looked down again at the patterns of jet streams and vortexes painted in off-white streaks on the curtain of grays, lusterless yellows, and browns. It brought to mind the storm front that had moved in on the West Coast from the Pacific in the early days of the encounter, when Athena's approach was first being felt. That had been before there was any wide grasp of what would follow, and the world had been hectically mobilizing evacuation plans and emergency services, believing it could pull through.

"I was thinking about a time in the last days before Athena closed in," he answered distantly. "It was in California. We were at one of the airports, trying to get to the Air Force's launch place at Vandenberg. Some people were trying to take it over and grab a shuttle to get out."

"Vandenberg . . . Wasn't that where Gallian and his group shuttled up from to rejoin the *Osiris*?"

"Yes. Most people didn't know how bad it was going to get. They thought that if they got everyone away from the coasts and up to the highlands, the world could make it. . . . Earth was moving into Athena's tail . . . ash and dust falling everywhere. Huge storms were heading in from the west, piling the sea up into black, heaving hills of water. I'd never seen anything like it. Everyone was going frantic, trying to get the last planes out while anything could still fly. I remember the buses and ambulances coming in from the hospitals, and nurses bringing in lines of little kids holding dolls and toys, some of them in wheelchairs. . . . All for what?" He broke off abruptly and turned his head back. "Anyway, you didn't come here to be cheered up like this."

Shayle laid a hand on his shoulder and let it rest for a moment. "I just came to check how you were doing. Anyway, there's eggs and pancakes going with coffee in the crew mess." Pre-made pancakes, heated up. You couldn't make them in zero-g. "I didn't think you'd want to be left out."

Keene managed a grin. "Sure. Okay, come on, then. Let's have at 'em." He set himself gyrating and pushed off with a foot to follow after her.

"Heard anymore about the Colombian station?" Shayle asked over her shoulder as she moved across the compartment opening inboard from the observation bubble. A descent party had gone down to check over a possible base site in South America.

"Not yet. We can stop by Comms for an update on the way to Mess Deck," Keene answered.

They took a shaft that passed by the Communications Room, which formed an extension on the nearside of the ship's Control Center. The Executive Officer was inside when they looked in, conferring with several of the operators. He looked up as Keene and Shayle hovered in the doorway. "We wondered if there's any news from Colombia yet," Keene said. "Maybe some idea of when we might be going down?"

"It doesn't look good. Earthquake activity across the whole region." The EO was a Terran, reporting directly to Gallian. He nodded toward a screen showing figures in heavy-duty surface fatigues and hard helmets, standing amid cases, scientific instruments, and other equipment in front of a couple of inflatable tents. Part of a lander was visible against dark mists behind. "The officer in charge down there doesn't see much point in staying further. So I'm afraid you'll have to remain patient for a while longer."

"Well, we're ready to detach *Agni* any time you say," Keene told him. He turned and resumed following Shayle.

The Executive Officer watched them for a few seconds and then looked back at the screen. Kelm, the officer leading the descent party, was Dione-born, qualified for the *Varuna* mission by previous space and surface engineering experience with the Kronian Security Arm. The two of them worked closely together. The EO himself had had some involvement with Terran space operations too, before the calamity—or at least, with people who ran them. Some of those people were at Saturn now. In fact, they had worked quietly but effectively to bring about his appointment to the *Varuna* mission. But it was considered politic to keep that side of things in low profile—for now.

In the previous world he had come from Europe. His name was Zeigler. Kurt Zeigler.

CHAPTER FIFTEEN

Almost two years had elapsed since the Security Arm's former training base on Rhea was obliterated by impacting bodies that got past the LORIN defenses. The base had provided an environment for weapons familiarization, field engineering instruction, and deployment exercises that typified airless surfaces to be found all over the Solar System; but since the disaster, SA had transferred the facility to the less representative but safer location of Titan. The sites being excavated for new industrial installations at Omsk had taken some damage too, Delmor Caton recalled. It had happened when he was on shift as Surface Operations supervisor.

He stared down over the ruin of the training base from the passenger cabin of the personnel bus making its descent after the two-hundred-mile hop from Omsk. In the seat facing him, Hector Norburn from Operations Management, also suited up for surface EVA, was sitting forward and taking in the view intently. Unlike Caton, he had never had reason to come out in this direction previously and had only seen the pictures.

What had been the area used for firing practice and tactical training, along with the landing pads and vehicle servicing shops, was buried under mounds of secondary debris from a three-mile-long furrow gouged into the surface by a grazing impact. Outlying surface installations such as antenna arrays and ground beacons had disappeared. The transporter used by the Security Arm people who had arrived at Omsk earlier was standing in front of the buckled remains of the main surface buildings protruding from an overburden of rubble and rock. Figures were standing around it, easily discerned in their brightly colored surface suits. Norburn had said the party consisted of a colonel, another officer, and three technical specialists.

Although Omsk was in production now, supplying forgings and pressed parts for the spacecraft construction program, Caton was still there with the Construction Directorate, looking after new excavations for an extension to the ore processing and rolling facility. Tanya, his former Terran assistant rescued from Mars, had completed her certification as a mining and drilling engineer despite her breakdown shortly after the tragedy, and had moved to Titan. She had joined a group at Essen who were developing methods of quarrying rocks and moving them based on the revolutionary artificial gravity technology that had emerged in the past year or so.

Artificial gravity!

Caton shook his head at the thought. Either he was going to have to go back to school, or his professional days might be numbered.

Being closest at hand at the time of the disaster, with vehicles and equipment from Omsk at his disposal, Caton had organized the first rescue teams to arrive on the scene. But after the immediate tasks of dealing with the casualties, searching the remains of what was left both above and belowground for more survivors, and clearing the worst of the wreckage were done, the later work of salvaging what could be used and evacuating the facility had been carried out by the Security Arm's own engineering crews from Titan.

So they had left the remains, deserted and unchanging, apart from the rain of dust and occasional fusillades of larger bodies as Saturn and its moons swept their path through the storm of debris that Athena had stirred up across the Solar System.

And then now, all of a sudden, the Security Arm was

interested in the place again and had requested Omsk to provide local transportation and assistance for a team that would be coming from Titan to conduct some kind of reconnaissance out there. Some hours after the SA team departed from Omsk, administration had contacted Caton to ask if he would fly out to the site with Norburn to look at something the SA group had found there. Caton's name was on record as having been involved in the rescue and cleanup activities following the meteorite impacts, and apparently that was considered significant for some reason.

The bus settled a short distance from the transporter. As its engines died, the flurry of dust around it collapsed in the airless environment like a tenuous balloon deflating. From closer up, the remains of the domes and connecting buildings formed a wall of twisted and splayed metal bordering the rubble-strewn area where the vehicles had landed, sagging out from beneath the debris that had buried it like the spilled content of a gigantic rock sandwich. At one end, part of a flattened dome had been lifted aside—way back, in an operation that Caton himself had supervised—to open the way down to a section of the underground galleries that had escaped being totally pulverized. They'd had to tunnel under a bulkhead wall concertinaed between two levels of flooring that had been crushed together, he recalled. Fortunately, in the gravity of a body the size of Rhea, supporting the load above had not been as difficult as the sight suggested.

"This place certainly took a pasting," Norburn commented, as he sat back from the port and unsnapped his restraining harness.

"You have to see it for yourself to get a real idea of it," Caton agreed.

"Was there much left there below—where the opening goes down?"

"Just parts of a couple of levels. We got a bunch of survivors up from a compartment in the living quarters that had been sealed in. Most of them were just trainee kids. Too dazed to know which moon they were on. Nobody left in that dome up above, though. There was some nasty cleaning up to do in there."

They stood up and took down their helmets from the

rack above. "Well, now maybe we get to learn what this is all about, Del," Norburn said. "Any bets?"

"I couldn't even begin to guess," Caton replied.

The pilot came back from the nose compartment and checked their suit readings before opening the lock. They bounced lightly down the extended steps and joined the group of three figures waiting in front of the tunnel, two wearing suits of Security Arm blue, the other's yellow, all of them carrying hand lamps. The other two making up the party were at the transporter, unloading equipment of some kind. The SA officer in the suit with colonel's insignia had Asian features and the name tag XELU on his chest pack. Caton judged him to be around thirty. He introduced himself, and then the others as Lieutenant Queele, SA, and Bor Ethan, a technical advisor.

"It was you who led the rescue team from Omsk, I understand, Mr. Caton," Xelu said. "The Service will always be in your debt."

"It was my privilege, Colonel," Caton replied. "Just glad that we were here. Only sorry we couldn't do more."

"You did as much as anyone could have," Norburn put in.

Colonel Xelu half turned, at the same time looking back toward the tunnel. "And you directed the digging under the debris there?"

"Right. We could tell from sonar scans that some of the underground levels were still intact farther down."

"Can we go and take a look?"

Caton and Norburn looked at each other. Caton shrugged inside his suit.

"Sure," Norburn said. The question seemed to have been more for form. It was what they had come out here for, after all. They followed Xelu into the opening, Queele and Ethan falling in to bring up the rear.

The beam from Xelu's lamp revealed a path of trodden-down rock fragments and dust descending among fallen floor beams and crumpled wall sections. A cleared shaft going up marked where Caton's team had cut their way through to check the upper parts. It didn't bring back the torrent of memories that he had been half expecting. Too much else had happened in the meantime since the day of those events.

"I suppose we owe it to you to say what brings us here," Xelu's voice said in Caton's helmet as they moved on and down. "The political situation in Kronia is getting complicated these days." It wasn't necessary for him to spell out that he meant on account of the agitation and demands of the Pragmatists. "What's worrisome is that this Terran-instigated movement is being led by individuals who consider coercion and violence to be a legitimate means of achieving social goals—or at least, of imposing the appearance of having done so." No Kronian would have considered results brought about by such means to have "achieved" anything.

The point didn't need elaborating. Even though Caton had been brought from Earth as a child, he was considered a Kronian and he thought like one. It seemed patently obvious to him that if a society appointed leaders from among those who had demonstrated their greatest proficiencies to be in the application of brute force and deception, then that was how their affairs would be run. The nuisance being caused was certainly out of proportion to the numbers and not something that was needed at times like these, and some Kronians were for shutting the movement down forcibly if that was the Terran way. However, President Urzin and most of the Congress were adamant that suppression was not the Kronian way, and relied on the Kronian nature to prevail. If it wasn't robust enough to meet the challenge without turning into that which it sought to supersede, then it probably wasn't worth clinging to, they maintained.

Colonel Xelu went on, "As a precaution in case the need ever arises, the Security Arm is being trained in the capability for taking an expanded role in containing and countering the possible use of violence, sabotage, and suchlike to advance political aims. I trust I don't have to elaborate? I regret the necessity, but it seems that prudence leaves us no choice."

"Everyone regrets it, but it's only common sense," Norburn's voice said on the circuit. "When you think you're threatened, you prepare a defense. Look what happened right here. What kind of state would Kronia have been in by now without the LORIN stations?"

They had reached the bottom of a vertical section of wall. A doorway to one side opened into a large room that the flashlight beams showed to have fallen in at the far end beneath sloping floor sections pressed down from above under a mass of tangled metal. The space was somberly empty, covered everywhere in gray dust. "D-2 Level, Area 3," Xelu commented. "Dormitory and living quarters. This was where you found one of the biggest groups of survivors."

"Over twenty," Caton answered dryly. The memories were starting to come back now. How the place had kept enough air for the time it took to tent the entrance and get down here was something he would never understand. They didn't go through into the room now. Evidently what had brought the SA party here lay elsewhere. Xelu turned from the doorway and indicated a length of corridor leading in the opposite direction, partially blocked by the wall on one side having burst inward, and ending maybe ten yards farther on at a blockage of collapsed partitioning.

"You didn't penetrate through any farther in that direction?" Xelu inquired.

Caton shook his head behind his helmet visor—although in the darkness it would be invisible. "The plan showed there were only sealed storage compartments that way. The access door through to them was closed, and we couldn't pick up any readings of movement or identity transmissions. It seemed better to use the time we had to check other places." He was beginning to wonder uncomfortably if the SA party had uncovered more bodies that they thought he should have found. But in times like that, these decisions had to be made. Xelu would understand that.

But Xelu said, "Let's have a look, then," and picking his way carefully through the wreckage ahead of them, he continued, "One of the things we're doing is increasing our weapons stocks at various strategic locations. But to avoid attracting undue attention with sudden manufacturing requests, we're trying to make as much use as possible of the stocks that were built up during the Emergency period." He meant a time around twelve years prior to

Athena, when there had been fear of the political tension that had existed between Kronia and Earth at that time leading to armed conflict. "Our records showed that there was a considerable inventory here that hadn't been recovered. The reports sent back after the impact wrote them off as inaccessible and probably not worth the effort. But our needs have changed since then, and we were sent out to assess what would be involved in retrieving them. And what we found is this. . . ."

Xelu stepped aside to let the beams of light show a dark opening leading on through what had been an impassible barrier. He ran a finger of his gauntlet over the end of a piece of metal ribbing. The edge was rounded by melting, showing that it had been cut by heat, not broken in the impact. His flashlight beam picked out spatterings of melted metal on the floor below, and beneath more severed members beyond. "It wasn't like this when you last saw it, Mr. Caton?' Xelu asked. "Either at the time of the accident, or in any of your visits subsequently."

"No!" Caton was bemused. "There was no way through there. As I told you, all that we had reason to believe existed there was a closed door leading into a sealed storage area."

"That was where the weapons were," Xelu said. "The door has been cut open."

A gasp sounded from Norburn. "And the weapons?"

"What's left are old or of inferior quality. Whoever took them knew what they were doing. We made a circuit of the area before calling you. The ground in the immediate vicinity was churned up by the activity going on here up to the final evacuation. But there are traces of a ground track leading away toward the east that cuts through the other markings, meaning it was made more recently. It gets lost farther out among the general impact gardening. What it looks like is that whoever pulled this off landed some distance away in the opposite direction from Omsk, below the radar horizon, and came overland."

"How long ago did this happen?" Caton asked. The question was mechanical. He was still grappling with the implications.

"Impossible to say," Xelu answered. "From the degree of

erosion of the tracks, given the current conditions, I'd say six months at least. . . . It could have been anytime in the last year." He paused for a moment, then went on, "It seems there are those among us who would try to impose their wills by methods that are not the Kronian way. We hoped it would never come to this. But if we are left with no choice but to defend against force with force, then that is how it will be."

CHAPTER SIXTEEN

The impression that had registered most forcibly with Keene was the frightening thoroughness with which practically all traces of a civilization that had taken such pride in its global extent and achievements appeared to have been wiped out. Without Kronia, by the time a new order rose again of its own accord, just about all memory of what had gone before would have been lost.

Europe was a wilderness of volcanic desolation and cooling lava sheets, with a two-hundred-mile-long canyon gouged across the center, carved during one of the titanic electrical exchanges that had occurred when Earth's and Athena's magnetospheres intersected. Everything that was once Southeast Asia had disappeared, subducted miles deep beneath crustal plates overthrusting from the south, and from what could be made of the acoustic patterns being sent back from seismic packs scattered about the surface, it was still sinking.

Currently, he was looking down from a height of about three thousand feet over a landscape of marshy valleys and mud flats winding among ridges of sand and gravel below a gray overcast. As far as could be judged, it was where New York City had been. Yet not a brick nor a girder was to be seen, not a sign of turnpike or a piece of dockside wall. Not even the lines of the Hudson or the East rivers,

Long Island Sound, or the New Jersey shore could be found. The entire former seaboard from Maine to the Carolinas lay buried beneath a thousand feet of sediments deposited by immense walls of water surging up the continental slope, leaving the new coastline meandering a hundred to three hundred miles farther east.

Keene banked into a slow turn and began following an expanse of black, oily pools and yellow sulfur sludge extending away into a haze of sullen hydrocarbon vapors. A data set superposed itself on the view, showing the updated bearing, speed, and rate of climb. A zoom-in on one of the pools showed it to be bubbling torpidly. A forlorn tatter of reeds had somehow managed to appear along its edge.

"An anguished dawn," Gallian had called it. The beginning of a new world. New life would be given, and a new story would unfold. Keene thought about the story only now being uncovered of a past far more rich and complex than the simple tale that had once been told of an orderly progression from uncomplicated beginnings leading undeviatingly through the historical ages neatly labeled in generations of textbooks to the civilization that had ended in the twenty-first century. But now a different story was emerging. How many other sagas of human existence had been written and lost in folds of time now vanished between convulsions that had rent and reshaped the Earth—of entire peoples who had lived, loved, died, raised their children and their cities, they and all their works as lost and forgotten as yesterday's footprints on the beach before a storm? How close had even the latest technological-industrial culture, with all its illusions of superlativeness and permanence, come to being just another of them?

"Well, what do you think?" Heeland's voice asked.

"Impressive," Keene replied. "Who ever would have thought that flying could be so easy?" The complete aerodynamic repertoire was controlled by a few set motions of the gloves.

"Some people say they feel the signal delay when they've gotten tuned to it. We're talking about almost ten thousand miles each way just at the moment. Do you notice it?"

"I can't say I do. I guess I'm still too new."

"Do you want to carry on for a while longer?"

"No, that's fine. You can bring me back. I just wanted to get a taste of how it works."

The image in Keene's helmet vanished and was replaced by blackness. Moments later, he felt the helmet being loosened and raised his head to help Heeland lift it clear. He was back in the *Varuna*'s Survey Control section, from where the probes sent down to view and map the surface were controlled, and the landing of instrumentation packages directed. The scene of northeast America that he had been viewing was still showing on a screen above the console, creeping by slowly as the probe continued flying on automatic program.

"Do the probes link directly to the satellites?" Keene asked curiously as he unfastened his seatbelt and nudged with his elbows to drift clear.

"We prefer not to, until we've established full synchsat cover," Heeland answered. "It's too easy to get stuck in a dead spot—especially when you're putting a lander down. We keep a high-altitude airmobile circling as a relay over an area where we're active—as we're doing with the probe you were hooked into just now. The mobile that's relaying from it is up at around sixty thousand feet. They can stay up for months if they have to. We also use them to ferry probes to remote operating areas."

"Months?" Keene repeated.

"Plutonium-fueled, helium-cooled fission pack. Your kind of toy, Lan. Like to see one?"

"Sure."

Heeland pushed off from a structural beam and navigated ahead from the instrumentation room, through a hatch into a side gallery. Keene followed him down to the Fitting Bay below, which was where the probes were equipped and maintained. It was a large space, with technicians working on various satellite packages as well as aerial pods and probes. Heeland indicated a peculiar-looking vehicle at the far end. It consisted of a large disk-shaped body maybe twenty feet in diameter, orange on top and white underneath, with three ducted fans in pivot housings around the periphery, and a pair of black fins above. Three semi-enclosed racks on the underside were obviously for carrying probes, although they were empty at present. They looked as if they hinged open to launch the probes downward, like bomb doors.

Heeland had started to head toward the airmobile, but checked himself and turned when he realized that Keene wasn't following. Keene had stopped beside a sleek metallic gray shape eight feet or so long, secured in one of the berthing cradles. A technician in white coveralls was working on it, using tools arrayed on a magnetic rack at the end of a jointed arm clamped nearby. "Mind if I look? I think I was just flying one of these over New York," Keene said.

"Be my guest," the technician said, gesturing. Keene knew his face from seeing him around during the voyage out, but they had never had cause to talk. He was of heavy-set build, swarthy skinned with a ragged mustache, and had dark wavy hair held down by a cap.

"Is this one of the probes I was in?" Keene called to Heeland.

Heeland moved himself back. "Yes, exactly right. This is Owen Erskine, one of the bay crew here. Owen, Dr. Landen Keene. He's in charge of the power system."

"Yeah, I've heard the name. Homecoming for you too, eh?"

Keene peered more closely but didn't recognize him as being from among the refugees brought back by the *Osiris*. "You weren't one of the refugees, were you, Owen?"

"No. But I'd only just moved to Kronia when it happened. Used to be from Jersey. Did network stuff. How did things look there to you?"

"I don't think you'd want to renew your lease," Keene said.

"But we'll start all over, eh? That's why we're here. That's what it's all about, eh?" Erskine's eyes were bright, hopeful almost.

"Is that why you came back?" Keene asked.

"Maybe . . . Part of it anyhow. Couldn't stand living in those tin cities anymore."

Keene drifted slowly around the probe, touching a part of it here and there, taking in the details. "More elaborate than I realized," he commented to Heeland. Its form reminded him of an old cruise missile, but instead of a warhead it carried a nose unit bristling with lenses and sensors. Panels were opened to give access for whatever work Erskine was doing on it. One of the exposed compartments contained boxes that looked like rations packs. There was also a medical kit, a stack of folded fabric items, and various tools. "What's all this?" Keene asked, gesturing.

Heeland pulled himself closer. "One of those ideas that mission planners come up with," he replied. "In this case, probably not a bad one."

Erskine patted the probe's engine cowling affectionately. "These babies go everywhere, and they can get down just about anywhere," he explained. "There are going to be people all over that vacation heaven of a planet down there, and some of them are going to get hurt, get lost, or otherwise get into some kind of trouble."

"Okay, I get it. Mobile survival units," Keene completed.

"Exactly right," Heeland said.

"A good idea," Keene agreed. "I'm actually with the planners for once. So what have we got?" He leaned over the hatch and began poking around. "Food, medical stuff, uh-huh . . . And these here—a clothing store too?"

"Survival tent. A few keep-you-warm, keep-you-dry kinds of things. Some good stretchy boots," Heeland answered.

"And this looks like a Boy Scout kit."

"Mend it, fix it—everything but the tool that gets stones out of horses' hooves. I guess they didn't reckon on having any horses."

"An automatic and ammo? Who are we starting a war with now?"

Heeland shrugged. "You never know what you might come up against, I guess."

"It's a phone booth too," Erskine said. "That panel at the back—emergency band link via the airmobile, or direct to satellite."

"We like to take care of our customers," Heeland said. Typical Kronian. *Appretiare.*

The compad in Keene's tunic pocket beeped. "Excuse me," he said, drawing it out. The caller was Shayle. She looked excited.

"Lan, we've just heard. The African site has been selected. The descent team is clearing the ground, and the backup crew is preparing to go down now. We'll be following pretty soon!"

"That's great!" Keene said.

The latest candidate site for a base was located in what had been the area east of the Great African Rift, and was now a four-thousand-mile-long peninsula extending south from the crumpled remains of Iran to a splayed tip formed out of Mozambique and Madagascar, between the reduced Indian Ocean and the new ocean forming to the west. The peninsula had been named Raphta, after a large East African trading center described in Roman times but never positively identified. As far as could be ascertained, the area surveyed for the base lay in what had previously been northern Tanzania. Once tropical parkland, it was now a wilderness of crustal upheaval, flood-scoured tablelands, and swamps, its climate cooling under the influence of the new polar region to the south.

"Does it mean the base has a name now?" Keene asked.

Shayle nodded. "Borrowed from the old days. Gallian has decided to call it Serengeti."

CHAPTER SEVENTEEN

The skies had changed in the course of the last year or so—not that Rakki had any clear concept of what a year was or why it was important. It was something that White Head kept track of by marking notches in a piece of bone for every day that passed. There were still storms and lightning, and winds that brought cold, sometimes with snow, if they came from the south; rain if from the west; dry, choking dust from the east. But the sky overhead had lightened and seemed higher, breaking up at times into patches of gray cloud and streamers moving against a ceiling that came close to white. In fact, on one or two occasions, even the ceiling had opened briefly to reveal glimpses of a pale, watery blueness that Rakki had heard was supposed to exist up there but had never known whether to believe. Perhaps the flashes he sometime saw in his mind of a dazzling light in the sky shining down over a world of color and life were real after all. And yet, strangely, he was unable to recall any details of that world—of the trees that White Head said had stood high overhead everywhere, or the places filled with people. Sims said that people's minds protected themselves by shutting out memories that it would be too painful to know could never be experienced again. Generally, the air seemed to be colder, which caused aches in his wounds and in his leg at night.

Even so, the valley was looking greener these days. Slim shoots were appearing in more places, which the Oldworlders said would one day become trees many times the height of a man. When Rakki asked them how long that would take, it turned out—strangely—that none of them really knew.

He took in the view as he and White Head came over the crest of the ridge, riding side by side on what White Head called "mules"; but at the same time he said they weren't like "real" mules, whatever that meant. Being carried on animals had been widespread in the former times, White Head said—but the animals they had then were larger and faster, but apparently were not the cattle that had existed in herds of thousands. Rakki had thought it strange that they would bother riding animals at all if they also possessed metal birds that they could fly in. But he had long given up trying to make sense of the conflicting and often seemingly contradictory things that Oldworlders said.

It had never occurred to Rakki that animals might be made to carry people. With his crooked leg that no longer bent fully, it was his main way of getting around these days, and his only means of traveling long distances. Sims had found the mules petrified in a canyon after an earthquake and suggested using them, initially as a way of moving Rakki more easily. That had been in the times following Rakki's rescue, over a year ago now. All he remembered was returning briefly to consciousness as he lay on the rocky ledge where he had fallen, and then nothing more until a long time after that. He knew the story only from the things the others told him.

It was White Head who had first grown suspicious after Rakki's departure from the caves with Shingral and the others, when he heard Gap Teeth's account of Zomu's warning to Rakki. From his own observations, White Head had seen signs of too close a collusion between Zomu and Jemmo to trust Zomu's story. When he learned of how the result had been to separate Rakki from one of his two staunchest defenders, he became alarmed that this might have been precisely the intention. Convincing Gap Teeth that it was Rakki, not Shell Eyes, who was in danger—and that in any case he, White Head, would watch over her—he had persuaded Gap Teeth to set out after the party in order to aid Rakki and Shingral if they encountered trouble. But before Gap Teeth caught up with them, he had spied Alin and Dorik returning alone and was barely able to conceal himself before they passed. Two miles farther on, as night was falling, he came across Shingral's body lying on a trail above a high precipice, stabbed from behind. On looking over the edge, he spotted Rakki on a ledge some distance below. He could see no sign of Zomu.

With darkness falling, there was not much Gap Teeth could do but find a way to climb down. Rakki had lost consciousness, but there was little doubt that Gap Teeth's attentions in tending and binding his wounds, covering him with skins that he carried, and lending his own body warmth through a long night had saved Rakki's life. Morning found them covered in snow. Rakki was delirious by then, and although he took some sips of water and a few berries, he hadn't known who Gap Teeth was. Trying to maneuver an injured and inert body back up to the trail single-handedly would have been impossible. So, after making Rakki as comfortable as he could and tying a line looped around a flake of rock to his belt to prevent Rakki from rolling off the ledge, Gap Teeth climbed back up on his own and set off back for the caves.

When Gap Teeth returned, Alin and Dorik were spreading the story that Rakki, Shingral, and Zomu had been caught in a rock fall and swept over a precipice. As of then, Jemmo had made no move to claim Shell Eyes—probably to avoid being too obvious and provoking a reaction from Rakki's supporters. But Rakki couldn't be left out there another day. In any case, White Head thought that Jemmo would consolidate his position soon, which meant Gap Teeth would be in danger—and probably White Head too, since Jemmo had never trusted Oldworlders, and White Head's association with Rakki would count against him. They decided it was time for them to leave the caves.

White Head talked to Sims, and afterward told the others that Sims would be joining them. Gap Teeth approached Uban, a former warrior from the swamps, who had always been loyal to Rakki, and told him the story, intimating that

Uban could also be in danger if he stayed. Uban agreed to go with them and in turn recruited another, Neotto, who also felt threatened. Finally, Shell Eyes sensed that something unusual was being planned and accosted White Head, who was frank with her. She had discerned Jemmo's intentions toward her and said she wanted to be taken along also.

To avoid drawing attention, they left individually at different times through the day, taking various loads with them, including several stripped branches and some lengths of vine for lashing together a litter that Rakki could be carried on. They met some distance from the caves and commenced their journey, traveling almost to the end of the day once again before they reached the place where Rakki had fallen. Gap Teeth went down with Uban and Neotto to bring him back up, after which there was little more they could do than find space beneath a boulder to shelter for the night as best they could.

The next morning, White Head, who had some knowledge of treating injuries, was reluctant to let Rakki be moved; but fear of pursuit and Jemmo's vengeance left them no choice but to press onward, taking turns to carry the litter with Rakki lashed to it. They trekked for many days through the Broken Lands, changing direction frequently, erasing their tracks, and living off roots, berries, mosses, and occasional birds or sand rats found among the rocks. Rakki's recollections began again as the party was emerging into a lower region of hills and dunes west of the Broken Lands that none of them had seen before, carved by floods into a maze of canyons and water channels. Scrub and grass began appearing on the landscape, along with the tracks and droppings of larger animals. Soon they began glimpsing ones and twos, sometimes larger groups of them, in the distance. They found scraps of strangely fashioned Oldworld artifacts that not even White Head nor Sims were able to identify, and the bones of huge creatures that the Oldworlders said had lived in areas of water vast enough to submerge all the known land. As Rakki's leg and side healed, he was able to walk for distances that gradually grew larger as the days went by, though always at a pace that forced the others to slow down. It became apparent that the crookedness in his leg was permanent, and he would never run or move with his previous agility again.

According to White Head, they moved from place to place in the region they named Roundhills for almost half a year. During that time Neotto gashed his chest on a poisonous thornbush and died after being consumed by fever, and Shell Eyes began the swelling that meant she would produce a child. Then they encountered a group of people consisting of several couples, most of them crazy-ones, and a number of children, living under makeshift roofs of branches and leaves built over crevices in the rocks. After two of the males were killed in a short but fierce fight, the others submitted to Rakki's leadership. Both the dead Neffers possessed females. Rakki gave one of them to Gap Teeth as a reward for saving his life. She was called Hyokoka and had yellow-hued skin with straight hair and curiously slanted eyes of a kind Rakki had never seen before. Uban challenged Sims over who would take the other, whose name was Engressi, but Sims declined to fight and so she became Uban's. Of the children, two were old enough to fetch, carry, and be given chores. Rakki ordered them to be kept, but not Engressi's boy baby, who was just able to walk. However, Shell Eyes offered to help Engressi with him and suggested he could be raised to be a special attendant for Rakki. "Another leg for you, to replace the one that is crooked," she urged. Rakki had laughed at the joke and relented, and the baby was spared.

But he wouldn't let himself become soft like the Old-worlders, he told himself inwardly. Always, burning at the back of his mind, was the thought of one day exacting revenge on Jemmo. And Alin and Dorik. He sometimes spent long hours visualizing the ways he would watch them die if it ever came within his power to order it.

The location was good, with thick growth around, a creek running down to join a long lake not far below, and although the ground above sloped up to a broken ridge above, it was away from the steep heights that were liable to avalanches of rocks and boulders when the earthquakes came. Rakki decided they would remain there. The people that they had subdued called it Joburg, which they said was the Oldworld name of a place far to the south, now buried under snow according to a lone traveler who had passed through a long time ago. Rakki liked the name and decided they would keep it.

More had joined them in the time since: several couples in a group, again with more children; a number of Neffers traveling in twos and threes, and in one instance, a lone wandering female. All were from the south, where they told of snow and ice covering the land. The clan built more shelters of dried grass thatched onto frames of woven vine, cleared space for growing food plants in the way the Cave People had done, and fenced in an area for keeping the animals they were beginning to acquire. Sims and two of the newcomers made a bowl-shaped frame covered in skins, and floated out on the lake below to find fish.

For the first time that he could remember, Rakki was able to live free from uncertainty and suspicion of everyone around him. Life at Joburg was better than he had known. But still, the thirst for revenge never left him.

He surveyed his domain with pride as he and White Head came down from the ridge side by side astride the mules. Smoke was rising from the hearth outside the open-fronted cooking hut, where a bush-pig was being roasted. The hut for storing a reserve supply of food was nearly complete. A large rock had been levered out of the creek and rolled to one side as part of a plan to clear a portion of it and widen it into a pool for washing and bathing. Rakki felt satisfaction in what they were doing. But he was unsure how long it might last.

"It looks as if they have started working on the creek," White Head observed. "The path down to it is clearer." He turned his head and read Rakki's face. "But you seem troubled."

"How long will we be able to stay in this place?" Rakki replied. "Everyone talks about a world of snow moving closer from the south. Will Roundhills be covered too?"

"That world is far away from us," White Head replied. "I don't think it will reach here."

"But do you *know*?"

"No, I do not know. But a man can only guard himself from what is or what he knows will be. To try to guard against every fear of what might be would make him as the crazy-ones."

"That is good," Rakki pronounced. "We will make Joburg big and find many warriors. Then one day I will lead them back to the caves. We will settle the thing with Jemmo that was never settled, and Shingral will be avenged. Even if I have to walk the whole way there, I will lead them."

"Your fever over Jemmo is more relentless than the one that gripped you after we brought you back up from the chasm," White Head said. "That fever cooled and died with time. This one becomes worse."

"It is our way," Rakki told him. "You understood a different world. This world, *I* understand."

"There comes a time when what's past is better left in the past," White Head said.

Rakki was about to reply, but then directed his attention away when he realized that something unusual was going on around the huts. Gap Teeth and Sims were standing in the clearing in front of the animal pen, both looking up. Hyokoka had come out from the cooking hut, while behind her Engressi was shepherding the children inside. Bakka, one of the newcomers, and his mate, Geel, were in front of the original covered shelter, he looking up, she hanging back under the roof and seeming fearful. More were coming out and calling to others. Rakki frowned and followed their gaze upward. An object unlike anything he'd seen before was hanging in the sky. His jaw tightened as he forced back his fear, at the same time reaching unthinkingly for the edged metal club that he still carried everywhere.

It wasn't a bird, for although it possessed a body and wings, there was no movement of them, and its motion wasn't that of a soaring bird that sailed on currents of wind. It seemed larger than any bird he'd seen, but he couldn't be sure because he had no real way of judging how high up it was. It seemed to be circling slowly around the area where the huts stood, as if studying it. With the wind as he and White Head came over the ridge, Rakki hadn't heard it before, but now he became aware that it was making a steady droning sound. He leveled a hand over his eyes to shield out the background light of the sky.

It was definitely not a bird. There was no head; its lines were too sharp and rigid. It had a dome like the top of a head, but it was in the middle of the body and hung underneath. Its skin was smooth and gray, lighter on the top side, as if it was reflecting the light. . . . Rakki's finger traced unconsciously along the contour of the club he was holding. He looked down at it. Metal. A metal bird? He remembered the strange, distant roaring noises that had been coming intermittently from somewhere to the north for days now; his head jerked around sharply toward White Head as impossible thoughts came into his mind. White Head's mouth was drawn back, showing his teeth. His face and his eyes were shining ecstatically.

"What is this, old man?" Rakki demanded. "What does it mean?"

White Head had to find breath before he could answer. "It means there are some of them left somewhere," he answered.

"The gods?"

White Head turned his face back. Rakki had never seen his eyes watery before. "Yes, Rakki. The gods. They've come back!"

CHAPTER EIGHTEEN

The site that had been chosen for Serengeti base was on a plateau of sediments left by receding floodwaters, close to halfway down the long Raphta peninsula and somewhat west of center, between the shrunken Indian Ocean to the east and the new westward ocean being created by the opening up of the Great Rift, which the Kronians had named the African Sea. North of the plateau, a river flowed westward from a wasteland of shattered rock and dizzying chasms inland, and then turned south to run for some distance through hilly regions to the west and south before turning away again to meander across a marshy coastal plain. The location was judged high enough to be reasonably safe from freak inundations in the still unpredictable conditions, while still offering access for ground exploration over a wide operating range in all directions. Also, it had the potential for expansion to accommodate a sizeable number of evacuees from Kronia, should such a measure ever be decided on.

Keene stood in front of one of the now-assembled prefab laboratories, watching the six-wheeled "Scout" vehicle, just back from a survey excursion. It approached him across the strip of open ground separating the base complex from the landing area, with its gaggle of supply shuttles and personnel ferries down from the orbiting *Varuna* and *Surya*.

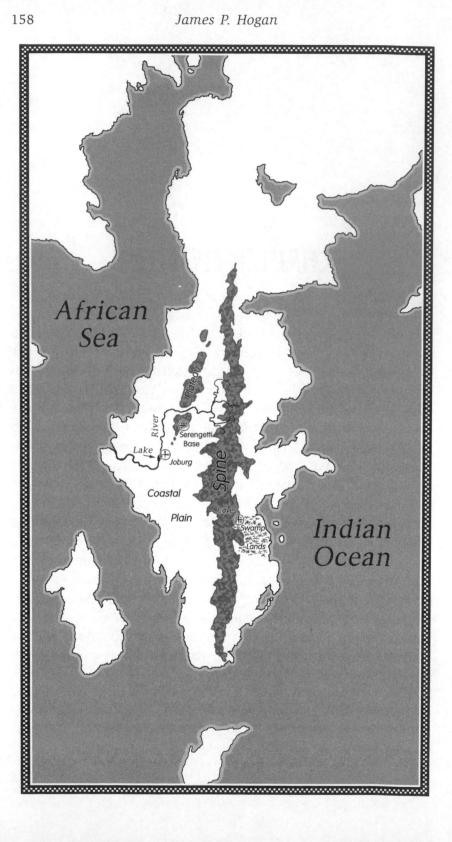

Nearby, outside the storage extension to the lab block, some young members of the mission's Security Arm detachment were unloading a cargo container from one of the shuttles, at the same time getting some acclimatization to handling weights in Earth's gravity. Keene was wearing a surface cover-suit, hood pulled up against the dusty wind blowing down from the mountains to the east. The sky was a patchy gray, like much of the landscape, shifting and swirling and spitting a forewarning of rain. It was not the kind of climate traditionally thought of in connection with what had been the Serengeti Plain. The shifting of Earth's axis to bring the south pole closer had caused a migration of colder regions northward, with the result that the areas that had formerly formed South Africa were now bleak and snowy, with the ice cap extending to the new islands formed from rising ocean ridges south from the Cape. Conversely, Scandinavia and the northwest coasts of Siberia were warming and expected eventually to settle at temperatures comparable to those previously found in California and the American South.

Next to the labs were the Operations Control and Communications Dome and the workshop domes housing fabricating and machining areas. The Kronians built in the manner they were accustomed to. Beyond the domes, a radiation screening wall was being constructed around the open-frame structure of *Agni,* detached from *Varuna* and landed, with power connections coming through to distribution equipment installed in a power control house abutting the workshops. *Agni* could have powered a large town. It was there as a working test of the technology, and to be available to supply the needs of an emergency expansion program should a sudden migration of the Kronian population be forced. So the base was taking shape. Already, the orbiters and probes were surveying for a second site somewhere in the Americas.

Keene's limbs still felt like lead after his time away. He dreaded to think what it was like for native-born Kronians. It was easy to pick them out among the SA recruits, regardless of their height. They were the ones staggering under the weight of cases and boxes that those raised through their formative years on Earth, even after being away for most of their lives in some cases, were able to handle easily. Keene was doubtful as to the usefulness to the mission of an SA complement. There wasn't much in the way of Terran threats to be protected from. But there had been pressure to include them on the grounds that Saturn would be too far away to help deal with whatever unknowns might develop; and in any case, the experience would be invaluable training, and their military-style organization made them an ideal general labor resource in a situation like this. Keene turned his attention back to the Scout as it pulled in and halted in front of the lab block.

A couple of technicians that Keene didn't know well yet since they had traveled with the *Surya* climbed out and went back to the open rear section to begin unloading an assortment of animal cages and containers, trays holding various plants, and boxes of jars filled with rock and soil samples. Keene sauntered over to greet the figure in a padded work vest and Cossack-style hat with the backflap down that had paused at the step below the driver's door to secure a bundle of notebooks and folders that he was carrying against the wind. It was Pieter Naarmegen, also from the *Surya*. Pieter had been a biology teacher in Durban at one time and was with the mission because, in theory anyway, he had some familiarity with the region, and he'd had firsthand professional experience of Terran flora and fauna. He had a pinkish, wrinkly face that gave the impression of being weatherbeaten despite his living the past eleven years in the artificial environments of Kronia, and a short, grizzled beard that he trimmed to a point.

"So, how'd it go, Pieter?" Keene inquired. "You're not wasting much time. Your section of the labs isn't finished yet, and you're starting a menagerie and horticultural collection already."

"Hey, Lan. Pretty good. Well, you know how it is. There's so much going on out there that we'd need a hundred lifetimes anyway. Are we online here with the power yet?"

"The crew are just hooking up to the distribution system now. We'll be ready to go as soon as they've finished the shielding wall." Some of the file folders on top of the wad that Naarmegen was carrying slipped loose. Keene caught them deftly before the wind could carry them away. "It's okay, I'll bring them in," he said.

They walked together to the open double doors leading into the lab block. Inside, the technicians were setting the cages and sample boxes down on benches among others waiting to be cataloged and stored. Naarmegen took the papers into a partitioned area littered with boxes, pieces of furniture, desktop equipment, and miscellaneous paraphernalia that was in the process of becoming an office. Keene looked around while he waited. The boxes contained small animals like mice and shrews, lizards, a brown snake, worms and snails, various insects. He moved closer to contemplate some plant specimens standing in soil-filled plastic pots. They were drab green to dark gray, tough and leathery-looking in texture. One had cactus-like spines along the edges of broad, spade-shaped leaves. Another, purple and gray, growing from a partly-visible tuber, was putting out curly tendrils that were already feeling along the rim of the container.

"Strange-looking things," he commented as Naarmegen rejoined him.

"That's the interesting thing. I'm not enough of an expert to know if those forms are something new or just an unusual variety that happen to be suited to the new conditions. But what intrigues me is the coloring. It's widespread across all kinds of different species. They're getting as much energy as they can by absorbing all across the spectrum. If they did it a hundred percent efficiently, they'd be black."

"Would they have the right chemistry to process it?" Keene asked dubiously. "I thought most plants were specialized to absorb in the red." Which, of course, was why most plants used to look green.

"That's one of the things we hope to find out," Naarmegen said.

Keene stared at the growths reflectively. "Those changes didn't all just happen together by random guesses in the time since Athena."

"Exactly," Naarmegen agreed. "The programs to switch to the new environment were already in there."

It was an allusion to the Kronian version of evolution,

which held that as with their findings in geology and planetary formation, changes didn't happen gradually over immense spans of time as had been previously thought, but in huge leaps, where whole new sets of designs and body plans seemed to appear abruptly to repopulate the Earth after major cataclysms. So maybe "revolution" would have been a better word.

It had long been known that species genera, and whole families appeared suddenly in the fossil record, fully differentiated and specialized, with no traces of the transitional and intermediary forms that gradualist theory said should be present in abundance; but in keeping with what had become so much the practice on Earth, only that which accorded with the theory had been deemed acceptable as fact, and so the difficulty was ignored. Hence, the billions of years required to make the traditional account of things sound plausible were not needed. That fitted well with the general picture the Kronians were putting together of things happening much more quickly and far more recently than had previously been believed. And this was just as well, since according to Vicki, the view among the Kronian scientists whom she worked with was that the traditional account wasn't plausible in any case, even given billions of years. The improbabilities involved were simply so huge as to be indistinguishable from miracles.

"So, do you think we'll be seeing new animals and things coming out of all this?" Keene asked curiously.

Naarmegen screwed up his face and peered into the distance, as if trying to read the answer off the wall at the far end of the room. "It's early days to say yet. But a lot of the niches are vacant now. It will be interesting to see what emerges to fill them. If I had to guess, I'd say we'll probably know within a few generations. Blind trial and error didn't remodel the whole biosphere in a few centuries after the Disruption and the Detachment. But if I had to guess, I'd say that Athena wasn't extreme enough to bring about anything that radical. I think what we'll get will be pretty much variations on what we know"

"Not extreme enough? Hell, it only just about wiped out life as we knew it."

"Not life. Civilization. Look around. I know it might sound crazy just at the moment, but Athena really wasn't the last word."

Despite his sarcasm, Keene knew what Naarmegen meant. The Kronians' current reconstruction put the detachment of Earth from Saturn configuration at around 10,000 years Before the Present, and identified it also as the event that had triggered the replacement of the giant Pleistocene mammals by the more familiar types of modern times. An even greater upheaval at some earlier date was believed to have ended the age of the giant reptiles—involving a large impacting body as known since the twentieth century, but with more yet to the story. Whatever the exact mechanisms responsible, it was fairly generally accepted that on both these occasions Earth's gravity had increased significantly, changing the biological environment sufficiently to induce the appearance of totally new forms of life, not just variations of what had gone before. If such complete adaptations to the new conditions had expressed themselves in the short time scales that the Kronians maintained, then, as with the coloring of the plant specimens that Keene had commented on, the genetic coding must already have been present as components of programs that were immensely more complex than anything that had been suspected before.

Keene asked the obvious question: "So where did the programs come from? How did they get in there?" He had meant it to be flippant, but Naarmegen didn't reply until they had walked back out through the doors and into the open again.

"Answering that is one of the greatest tasks that Kronia has set itself for the generations ahead," he said. "Some say it's the most important single mystery confronting us."

It took Keene back to his meeting with Jon Foy in Foundation. So much to think about. "I often used to wonder why leaves were green and not black," he said, stopping to take in the scene of the hills around the base. "You'd think they'd have optimized by going for all the wavelengths available, wouldn't you?" He gestured. "Like those out there. And then, why settle for the lowest-energy end, the red?" Actually, it had been Robin who'd brought it up, but it made easier telling this way.

"Maybe it was something that hung over from the Saturn era," Naarmegen suggested. "When the Sun was remote. Maybe something near red was all there was." It was a possibility, Keene supposed.

He was about to say something more, when an alert tone sounded from the speakers commanding the area, signaling an announcement. *"Attention. Attention. Descent vehicle due down in the Landing Zone in ten minutes. All personnel are requested to vacate the outside area. Descent due in ten minutes."* It was a nuisance, but something they'd have to live with until sufficient ground transportation was available to service the larger landing area being cleared farther away. Until then, everyone had to be under cover during landings and launches. "I need to park the truck," Naarmegen said. "I'll see you inside."

"Sure. I'll be in Ops."

Keene walked across to the OpCom dome on the edge of the landing area between the ends of the lab block and the workshop buildings, and let himself in via a side door to the lower level. A steel-railed stairway took him up to the operations floor, with its clutter of consoles and equipment, and windows giving an all-round view of the landing area in front and the base complex to the sides and rear. Kurt Zeigler was down from the *Varuna*, supervising, standing behind one of the console operators. As was typical of the Kronian way of doing things, the routine was light on rules and restrictions, and a number of others who didn't strictly belong were also present, either having wandered in to see what was going on while taking a break, or using the operations center as a social gathering point until the general messroom adjoining the two dormitory blocks was completed. The operator in front of Zeigler was talking to a screen showing the head and shoulders of a man in a flight suit, with instrument panels and a figure at another crew station visible behind. Keene took it to be from the incoming shuttle.

"Retros to max. Commencing final. Vector coming around onto . . . ah, three-three-zero."

"You're on the beam, looking good. Wind at the pad is gusting twenty-five to thirty from the east. We're putting you down in slot G-3."

"G-3. Got it. Roger. Any coffee going down there?"

Keene spotted Sariena sitting with Adreya Laelye, the senior SOE representative, on a bench seat by one of the windows on the landing area side and went over. With the work involved in seeing *Agni* landed and brought online, he'd had hardly a moment to talk to Sariena since she came down from the *Surya*. She smiled tiredly at him as he joined them. "Lan, so they've let you have some time off at last. I'd forgotten what it was like on Earth. We're glued to the seat. I don't want to get up."

"Coming up those stairs was enough," Adreya said. "Zeigler took them two at a time. He's kept in good shape while on Kronia. It's obscene."

"You'll be doing it too in a couple of months," Keene told her, although he didn't believe it. He looked at Sariena. "Managed to rest up after the voyage?"

"Yes, finally. It was a very different feeling from last time. But I wanted to come down here, even if we're not in a position to get much work done yet. Damien and the others are staying up in the *Surya* until they've got proper working space set up down here." Sariena had brought a team of planetary scientists from Kronia. Damien was her assistant, left in charge of things up in orbit for the time being, by the sound of things.

"Gallian isn't down yet?" Keene queried.

"Not yet. I think he's still finishing some business with Kronia up in the *Varuna*." Communications delay to Saturn was a little under seventy-five minutes each way.

"We saw you coming out of the labs with Pieter," Adreya said. "Was that another load of specimens that he just brought in? His lab isn't even finished yet."

Keene shrugged. "I know. He can't wait to get started. Can't blame him, I guess." He paused, running an eye around to take in the other things that were going on. "He says he's already seeing signs of what could be catastrophic evolution."

"New genetic programs expressing themselves?" Sariena said.

"Exactly."

"Well, either they wrote themselves or something wrote

them. Which exhausts all of Aristotle's logical possibilities."
Sariena's tone conveyed that she didn't give much credence
to the first.

"Touchdown in thirty-six seconds. She should be just
breaking through," the operator in contact with the shuttle
announced to the room. A screen beside the one still showing
the flight deck brought the view outside the shuttle, of solid
grayness dissolving into wisps and streamers suddenly, and
then the blurred image of an already expanding landscape
with a superposed circular grid centered on the plateau region
where Serengeti base was situated. Several figures got up
and moved to the windows on the front side of the dome.
After several seconds somebody pointed.

"There."

Keene followed the direction and picked out a speck of
bright light against the overcast. As it enlarged and grew
brighter, the sound came of engines braking at full thrust.

The light elongated into the shuttle's exhaust plume with
the ship taking shape and growing above as it slowed in
its descent. It touched down a short distance from the other
craft on the ground, and after a final flare of flame and
smoke the engines cut.

"Switch to local tower frequency five-five-six. Serengeti
control out," the operator said. Outside the window, the
reception vehicles that had been waiting below on the edge
of the landing area began moving out.

Adreya sighed. "You'd think I'd have seen enough of things
like that, wouldn't you. But I never get tired of watching
ships come in. It's so strange to be able to *hear* it! I'm still
getting used to just walking out into air through a door,
without a suit or anything. It doesn't feel natural."

"You might not appreciate it so much if the vaccinations
don't work," Sariena cautioned. In the previous visit by
Gallian's delegation, all of the first-time Kronians had suffered badly from infections and allergic reactions.

"You might not be the only ones this time," Keene told
them. He could feel his own eyes and skin smarting from
something he'd encountered outside. The atmosphere still
carried sulphurous and hydrocarbon contaminants from
Athena's tail.

While they were talking, he noticed that Zeigler, having seen the shuttle safely down and into its berthing slot, had noticed Keene with the two women and was on his way over. For the most part Keene had found Zeigler to be a remote kind of personality, giving a feeling of detachment and never quite mixing in with the confined community aboard the *Varuna*. It could have been that he took his position as Executive Officer a little too conscientiously— although things like that didn't seem to inhibit Gallian from being his old jovial and informal self. Maybe it was just that Keene wasn't used to Europeans. He looked up inquiringly as Zeigler joined them.

"How are we doing with the power?" he asked Keene.

"Connecting to the distribution system now. Shayle's handling that part of it. I talked to her about a half hour ago. We should be running before tonight if they get the shielding finished." Keene made an open-handed gesture. "So, what do you know? I might actually have some spare time on my hands for a change."

"I'm sure we'll find some way to fill it. There's plenty to do. In fact, I was meaning to ask—"

Just then, an operator at one of the other consoles in a different part of the room leaned forward abruptly to follow something on a screen, and then turned her head to call crisply across to Zeigler.

"*Sir!*" The tone was enough to bring immediate silence to the whole room. Zeigler strode across to see what was happening. His body stiffened, and all heard his sharp intake of breath, followed by a slow exhalation of astonishment. Keene was already over there along with several others before he realized he had reacted.

The screen was showing a transmission from one of the probe drones that had been sent out to reconnoiter the surrounding regions. It was looking down over a chaotic area of rocky slopes, piled boulders, and tangles of vegetation with a creek running down the just-visible edge of what looked like a larger body of water below. In several places, crude shelters had been made from roofs of thatch built over crevices among the boulders. And as the probe moved, changing the angle, several simple thatched huts appeared.

Human figures were outside, looking up, including several children. Two more figures were just in sight at one edge of the view, mounted on animals that seemed to be about donkey-size. The probe was being directed from Survey Control up in the *Varuna.* A zoom-in commanded by the operator up there revealed them as both dark-skinned. One appeared to be fairly young, fierce in appearance, wearing a tied headdress, and brandishing some kind of weapon. The one riding next to him was older, white-haired and wrinkled.

"What is it, Lan?" Sariena called from where she was still sitting with Adreya by the window.

"It's coming in from one of the probes," Keene said. He found it was taking him a moment or two to absorb the message. After all the wondering . . . "It's found some, Sariena! It's found people out there! There were survivors!"

CHAPTER NINETEEN

It was a small world—or worlds. Vicki had moved from Dione to Titan for a week of familiarization and briefings at Foundation before going up to join the orbiting *Aztec*, now back from its trials and taking on supplies and equipment in preparation for liftout. With her was a Kronian molecular biologist called Luthis, also from Kropotkin's Polysophic Academy, who would be going as the senior member among the *Aztec*'s scientific complement. *Aztec* would be the first vessel to incorporate decks fitted with experimental Artificial Gravity "Yarbat arrays" on a long-range mission. In the course of their week with SOE's Training Division at Foundation, Vicki and Luthis met a former Terran petrological technician named Tanya, who had worked for a while on excavations at one of the construction sites at Omsk, on Rhea. After the meteorite strike there, Tanya had transferred to Essen on Titan to learn about the new AG-based methods being developed for cutting and shaping rock masses of large dimensions—termed "lithofracture" and "lithoforming"—developed from the technology that Lan had helped pioneer at the Tesla Center.

Aztec would be carrying heavy-duty prototype equipment to Earth to test its efficacy on Terran materials and under Terran conditions, and hopefully to exploit its unique potential as a way of building large-scale structures using the only form of material readily available there. Tanya would be traveling back as part of the engineering-construction team being sent to get the pilot scheme up and running. Two others, going with them as AG consultants, were Jansinick Wernstecki and Merlin Friet—both of them former Tesla Center colleagues of Lan's that Vicki had heard him talk about often in the earlier days, but never met before.

Vicki and Luthis stood watching Tanya in a workroom in a subsurface part of Foundation, where a small-scale demonstration had been installed some time ago for the benefit of government officials and others curious about the new technology. In fact, a couple of news journalists had been recording here that morning for a science-interest piece being made for general circulation.

"What it does is create a high-frequency shearing force across a surface that literally splits the grain structure all the way through," Tanya said, tracking a cursor across the screen to define a wire-frame plane passing through a graphical representation of a piece of Titan rock. The rock itself, about the size of a soccer ball, was clamped in a metal frame on top of the bench beside. Three thick disks maybe a couple of inches across, attached to narrower cylinders, painted red, looking like small top hats, were cemented to the rock at strategic points. Heavy cables from the top hats connected to a rack of equipment by the bench. Tanya continued, "Basically, we use a g-wave to agitate the molecular structure on one side of the plane, and generate an interference pattern to neutralize it on the other." She kept her eyes on the screen, making a few final adjustments as she spoke. "It's like holding one half rigid while you twist the other half off—except that it's not twisted free; it's vibrated free." She was somewhat pasty in complexion and pudgy—not uncommon for Terrans who had moved to Kronia. Tanya had been among those rescued from the Terran scientific bases on Mars, and had suffered some kind of nervous breakdown after the incident on Rhea.

Luthis nodded toward the image that Tanya was manipulating on the screen. "The surface that you're showing there.

Does it have to be a flat plane like that? Or can you make it different shapes?"

"In principle it could be shaped, yes. But that's still in the future."

"Is it good with any material?" Vicki asked.

"As of now, we're limited to brittle things like rock, glasses, ceramics. . . . Metals are too ductile. But we're working on it."

"Okay.

Tanya checked one last time over the readings. "And we should be all set." She brought up a button on the screen, with a query requesting confirmation to proceed. Tanya confirmed the instruction. . . . And nothing happened except that a faint *crack* sounded from somewhere seemingly inside the piece of rock. Vicki stared at it, waited a few seconds, then looked up.

"That's it?"

Tanya smiled, evidently expecting it, as she leaned over to loosen the securing clamps. "What did you expect? A nuclear explosion?" She removed the restraint, and one half of the rock fell away in her hand to reveal a cleaving plane as flat and smooth as cheese cut by a fine wire.

"I'm impressed," Luthis said.

Tanya gestured at a larger mural screen overlooking the bench, which she had been referring to earlier. It showed the proving area about fifty miles from Essen, where the full-scale equipment had been developed and tested. A series of unnatural gouges formed by straight cuts and variously angled surfaces had been cut into the sides of a rock ridge on the surface, with the slabs and forms that had been extracted from them scattered about and in some places piled like gigantic play blocks. "When you get up to that kind of size, the exciters need to be solidly bolted in, not glued. But it works the same way."

"So if we ever have to abandon Saturn and need big shelters back on Earth, is that how we build them?" Luthis asked.

"Yes. And all kinds of other things too," Tanya answered. "It beats having to ship lots of materials all the way from here."

Luthis traced a finger along one of the exciter power cables, then turned to Vicki. "Now I think I'm beginning to see why they were in such a hurry to get that power system there that Landen designed."

"You mean the *Agni*?"

"Yes. The generating plant to power something like this is already there. Did they really anticipate it that far back?"

"But of course," Vicki said loyally. But in fact, she was only just appreciating it herself.

That evening, Vicki sat alone in her room in the quarters the outbound personnel had been assigned while waiting to be taken up to the *Aztec*. It felt depressingly like the unit she had vacated on Dione. Even with Lan and Sariena working most of the time in other parts of Kronia, their visits had meant more than she'd realized. And after the *Varuna* mission departed, the steadily lengthening signal delay eventually made meaningful interaction with them electronically impossible too. Robin had become progressively more withdrawn before finally joining the Security Arm, and now he had been shipped off with the reconnaissance survey sent to Jupiter—which perhaps would be best for him. Leo Cavan still stayed in touch and tried to be reassuring, telling her that it was only to be expected that young people would go through a troubled time when the world they had thought they would grow up to was snatched away from them, and in the long run he was confident that Robin would be fine. Vicki was just a mother, being a mother. . . . But the way she saw it too, he was just Cavan being Cavan.

And so she had immersed herself in her work with Emil Farzhin's group and his account of how Earth and Mars had influenced each other's histories in recent times. In conjunction with other work that had been going on, it was shedding new light on the puzzle of how living forms managed to alter so abruptly in conditions of stress and change. This was the area that Luthis specialized in and what he and Vicki were going back to Earth to investigate further.

The principal mechanism for introducing new genetic information into a species and spreading it rapidly through an initial breeding group, they now suspected, was not the sexual mixing of genes and subsequent agonizingly slow propagation of any benefits through a population. Even before Athena, this had been recognized as a major problem with the orthodox ideas on evolution, but nobody had been able to suggest anything better. Yet a far more effective process had been there all the time, capable of manifesting its effects immediately among adults already at a procreative age, and capable of appearing almost literally overnight: *infection.* But it had been misidentified through being noticed only when the mechanism produced harmful results instead.

The room's wall screen, which had been showing a dance troupe with the sound turned down—low-g choreography could be quite captivating—switched to a head and shoulders view of Claud Valcroix talking. The caption AZTEC MISSION below interrupted Vicki's brooding. "House. Sound up," she instructed in a slightly raised voice.

The Pragmatists were making a bid for greater influence in the Congress by arguing that since the Directorates embodied concentrations of expertise and knowledge in certain vital areas, then by the Kronians' own system of values they represented the interests of entrenched "wealth," thus violating the principles of democracy and fairness. Therefore the Pragmatists, who claimed to speak for typically unrepresented elements of the population, should be involved in their decision-making processes too. It was an obvious attempt to gain greater access to policymaking without having the votes needed for seats in the Assembly, which constituted the democratically elected arm of the Congressional system. Officers of the Directorates were appointed from within, much in the way that senators had been placed by their state legislatures under the original American system. It was an ingenious ploy, Cavan had conceded when he and Vicki spoke a day or two previously. But he couldn't see Congress buying it.

This time, however, Valcroix was criticizing the decision to send the lithoforming technology to Earth. " . . . as we saw in the demonstration given at Foundation this morning. But where are the shelters for the people who are *here,* at Kronia? I ask you all, does it make sense to be sending this capability for cutting and constructing huge works in rock all the way to Earth, where we have just two ships? They tell us, 'Yes, but Kronia may become uninhabitable. We have to be prepared.' I say they have everything backward. Our population, our homes, our industries, and our *future*—for as far as it's possible to see it at the present time—are *here!* Not on the ruins of a distant cosmic battlefield that for all we know contains no other human life and will not be able to for a long time to come . . ."

"House, off," Vicki told the domestic manager wearily. She sat back in her chair and stared up at the cream-painted metal ceiling, the lamp, the extractor-fan grille. Just the thought of getting away from all of it . . .

In her mind, she was soaring out and away, back to a sphere of clouds, earth, and water, close to the warmth and light of the Sun. Even if the clouds were thick and murky, the earth shuddering, and the water thrown into convulsions, it meant being able to breathe without helmets or containment; to see a wind-sculpted sky, and life, however crude, clawing its way up out of the soil. To live from day to day only for her work, leaving politics and jealousies far behind. She thought about Lan, Sariena, Charlie Hu, and Gallian—all of them out there already, and the others who would be going with her on the *Aztec*. . . .

Strange though the word seemed in the circumstances, yes, it would be good to go home.

CHAPTER TWENTY

Midway through the morning two days after the probe's first discovery of the survivors, the Scout lurched its way along the descending line of the ridge, which provided a relatively unobstructed route down from the plateau. With *Agni* online and behaving, Keene had been free of any pressing duty commitment at the time, and Gallian, up in the *Varuna*, had named him as his first choice for inclusion in the party that would make contact when Zeigler reported the situation and requested instructions.

Because of the difficulty Kronians had acclimatizing so early in the mission, the five others in the Scout were also all Terran-born. Ivor, an SA vehicle mechanic and electrical technician was driving. Sitting up front beside him was Jorff, also from the SA, a lieutenant standing in for Kelm. Keene was behind, next to a control panel for various instruments, communications systems, and outside cameras, with Naarmegen sitting opposite, his back to the cabin wall. The two females of the group were in the rear seat: Maria Sanchez, a medic, and Beth, Serengeti base's current nearest thing to a resident psychologist, since she had once majored in psychiatric disorders at the University of California, Irvine. There were no further pictures of the survivors coming in from the probe at the moment to occupy them. Its presence had apparently caused consternation at the settlement, and Gallian had ordered it to be pulled back. Just at the moment, it was hovering a short distance ahead of the Scout, reconnoitering the way. So Naarmegen and Keene were back on the subject of where the genetic codes that directed the formation and function of all living things had come from.

"I talked a lot with Sariena too on the voyage out," Naarmegen said above the growl of the Scout's diesel—it used an independent electric motor on each wheel but was dual-equipped, being able to run them from either a pure electrical storage system or a motor-generator. One of the plans for Serengeti was to set up a fractionation tower to process fuel, oils, and other products from the readily accessible hydrocarbons that Athena had deposited over wide areas. "I was skeptical when I first moved out there. But I think the Kronians have convinced me." It was interesting, Keene noted, that now back on Earth, Naarmegen was already referring to Kronians in the third person.

"That there has to be some kind of intelligence behind it all?" Beth said, leaning forward behind Keene.

Naarmegen glanced back at her. "Right. They've even devised objective ways of recognizing it." He looked at Keene again. "Did Sariena tell you about that?"

"I haven't really talked to her that much," Keene confessed. "Too wrapped up in nuclear plasmas and induction physics for most of the time." But he was interested. "Of recognizing what? Do you mean the results of intelligence at work?"

Naarmegen nodded, hanging onto a handrail. "Exactly."

"Objective ways," Keene repeated.

"Yes."

"Okay, so how would I recognize it?"

Naarmegen made a gesture in the air that could have meant anything. "When you or I see something that's been organized the way it is for a purpose—like the parts of a machine, or the codes in one of those processors behind you—we don't have any difficulty distinguishing it from the results of pure, unguided, physical processes. So how do we do it? There's obviously something we latch onto. Is it possible to identify what it is, even define some rules for measuring it—and then apply them to the natural world and see how it scores?"

Which would certainly be the way to go about it, Keene could see—if it could be made to work. "Is that what the Kronians have done?"

"Yes."

"How?" Maria asked, beside Beth.

"Okay, let's take an example." Naarmegen thought for a moment. "Did you ever play that game they used to have, where you made words out of letter tiles and got double and treble scores on the good places? What was it called . . . ?"

"Scrabble?" Keene said.

"Yes, that was it. So suppose you found a jumble of tiles on the floor that said absolutely nothing at all. You'd have no reason to think they'd been arranged, right? If you had to guess, you'd say they got spilled and just fell that way."

"All right," Maria agreed.

"But now imagine you come across, let's say, a hundred tiles all lined up, and they spell out a sentence from a book that you know. You wouldn't hesitate to say that someone arranged it. It's kind of obvious." Naarmegen waved his free hand in the air. "But why is it obvious? What's different that you've picked out? Can you put your finger on it?"

There was a short pause. "It's too improbable," Beth offered finally. "More complex."

Naarmegen's mouth split into a toothy grin behind his beard, and he nodded as if he had been expecting that answer. "Complex, yes," he agreed. "But more complex? No. Every arrangement of a hundred tiles is as improbable as any other."

"True," Keene agreed.

"The second one—the sentence—contains more information," Beth tried.

"Does it? But you'd need just as much information to construct any of the other sequences too. In fact, if they were random, you'd probably need more. You'd have to specify every letter. There's no way to compress a random string."

Beth shook her head. "No, that wasn't what I meant. I meant it conveys information in a different sense . . . in a language. It carries meaning."

"Meaning to whom?"

"To me—anyone who speaks English."

"What if someone doesn't speak English? It wouldn't mean anything to them."

Beth thought about it. "It doesn't matter. The meaning is still there. It's still encoded in a specific way. Not knowing how to decode it is a separate issue."

Naarmegen nodded slowly, giving all the others time to digest that. "Yes, you've hit it," he said finally. "The key word is *encode*. It encodes—or specifies—meaning according to an independent system of rules whose purpose goes beyond simply specifying a sequence. The Kronians call that property 'specificity.' "

"But you could still get some of that in the first example—the random one," Maria pointed out. "English-language words, I mean. Small ones."

"You mean like 'it,' or 'so,' or 'and'?" Naarmegen said.

"Yes."

"Why did you say they had to be small?"

"Well . . ." Maria shrugged. "They don't have to be, I suppose. But you wouldn't expect long ones."

"Too improbable?"

"Yes, I'd say so. Wouldn't you agree?"

Naarmagen made his gnomish grin again and looked back at her. "But we already said that any other string would be just as improbable anyway."

Maria waved a hand helplessly. "I know what I mean. I'm just not sure how to say it."

"You have to have both," Naarmegen supplied. "The small strings that happen to be English are specific, yes, but not complex enough to rule out chance. When you see a highly complex arrangement that's also highly specific in some form of language, that's when you conclude it was put together that way by an intelligence that understood the language and did it for a reason. So there's your answer."

Keene had been following with interest. It explained a lot of things about the Kronian world view. "And you say they've been able to define these properties rigorously? And quantify them?" he queried. "They've measured them in things like genetic codes and protein sequences?"

"Right," Naarmegen affirmed.

"And what did they find?"

"About as conclusive as you could get. They loaded all the numbers to be biased in the direction of caution—in other words, more likely to miss a signature of intelligence when it was really there and write it off as chance, than to misread a false indication of one where there wasn't any."

"Okay."

"When the complexity becomes too vast and the specificity too tight, you can eliminate chance as the cause. So where's the cutoff? Philosophers typically used to take an improbability of fifty orders of magnitude as a universal bound beyond which chance processes could be eliminated as the explanation. The Kronians applied a boundary—get this, Lan—of a *hundred and fifty* orders of magnitude! And they find organization that exceeds it." Naarmegen smiled expectantly. Keene whistled and looked away for a few seconds to digest the information.

In the front passenger seat, Jorff took an incoming call from Serengeti to check the calibration of the navigation grid laid down by satellites deployed from the *Varuna*. Beside him, Ivor, who had been listening, glanced back over his shoulder as he drove. "You don't need scientific criteria and numbers," he told the others. "It's all there in the Bible, and now it's happened again. The old world became corrupt and abandoned God, and set up its own gods. So God destroyed it, and now He's creating a new world."

Naarmegen glanced at Keene. Keene shrugged and shook his head to say that the ball was Naarmegen's. Naarmegen paused to choose his words before answering. "You could be right, Ivor. For now, we're just concerned with detecting the work of an intelligence. Whether it's the god of any religion or not, or what its reasons are is another matter. Science can't answer that."

"It's all in the Bible," Ivor said again.

Jorff's voice came from up front. "Check three-seven-five and two-oh-nine. We're coming down from the ridge entering a canyon to exit the plateau complex. It's rough going but passable." The Scout had independent swivel-axles for all of its six balloon-tired wheels, and could practically climb a mountain. The Kronians had a lot of experience in designing vehicles for rugged terrains.

"What's your updated ETA?" the operator at Serengeti asked from Jorff's panel.

"Oh . . . maybe a couple of hours, judging by what we're seeing from the probe. There's a scarp of steep, muddy gullies with what look like steam vents that we may decide to go around."

"Is Landen Keene there?" another voice asked. It sounded like Gallian's.

Jorff looked back from his seat. "Gallian is on the circuit, from up in the ship, Dr. Keene. He wants a word with you. You can take it on the panel back there."

Keene turned to activate the panel's screen; Gallian's features appeared on it moments later. They had talked before the Scout departed, when Keene had agreed to be the mission's impromptu diplomat. But with Gallian's ebullient way of going about everything, no plan ever stayed set for too long without addendums and afterthoughts.

"Ah, Lan! How is it to be home?" he inquired.

"I've had smoother rides in my time. This isn't exactly a Texas interstate. What's up?"

"We've been going over the pictures that came up. Those people appear extremely primitive, and they might still be traumatized or otherwise disturbed. Don't take chances. Give all your personnel sidearms. The two SA troopers are authorized to carry rifles. Just as a precaution, eh?"

Only Kronians would have deliberated over the question. It had never crossed Keene's mind not to. "Okay," he replied simply.

"And Charlie's peeved because he can't be in on it too. He says you could have saved some of the interesting stuff." Charlie Hu was still up on the ship, analyzing planet-wide geological data and hadn't managed to make it down to the surface yet.

"Tell him I'm sure there'll be plenty more in store to keep him happy," Keene said.

"Well then . . . good luck. That's really all I wanted to say, I suppose."

"We'll just have to see how it goes. There isn't any set game plan."

"I'm sure you'll improvise appropriately. We'll just watch from the wings and leave you to it unless you call us in. We have every confidence in you and your team."

Typical Gallian. Keene smiled inwardly. "Thanks," he acknowledged.

Gallian cleared down.

"How are the seismic readings?" Jorff inquired in front, to the Serengeti operator. Steady earthquake and volcanic activity had been detected in the regions to the east, beyond the central range of shattered rocky desolation known as the "Spine," ever since the first probes from the *Varuna* landed. Some of the lava lakes there were still molten in the centers.

"Holding steady. No signs of anything unusual building up."

"Uh-huh."

It took the Scout several hours to negotiate a path southward and down through the hilly region, avoiding several difficult patches and following a course roughly parallel to the river. Twice, it was forced to back up and find another route: first, from the top of steep slopes of mud and precarious rock falls that were revealed as more treacherous close up than they had seemed from the probe preview; and again by impassable fissures venting sulfur gases. But finally it emerged onto a boulder-strewn slope above the settlement, with the probe stationed high up and circling at an unobtrusive distance, watching through telescopic lenses. The Scout stopped a few hundred yards above the rude collection of huts and shelters, where smoke was rising from a cooking fire. Figures came out and stared. Some went back inside. After a short delay, a small group came out and approached warily.

CHAPTER TWENTY-ONE

Of course, Rakki went first to meet the apparition. To be seen cowering back, allowing others to take whatever risk was involved would have been unthinkable. He walked slowly up the slope toward where it had stopped, gripping his club resolutely. Gap Teeth and White Head followed him a pace or two behind, and Sims was to one side. Actually, Rakki was more making a show of fortitude to impress his followers watching from among the huts and rocks behind—a wisdom he had learned from Jemmo. White Head's elation on seeing the metal bird, and even a flicker of excitement and maybe hope from Sims, the only other Oldworlder at Joburg, had reassured him that there was probably little to be fearful of. But all the same, Rakki's nature and all of his consciously recollected experiences made him cautious.

There was something about its form and its lines that evoked an echo from the distant past—a fleeting feeling that this was not a totally new experience. He had seen an object vaguely like this before, or maybe an image of one, at some time in that far, forgotten world that now came and went only in odd moments as fragments of faded dreams. The noise it had been making when it appeared at the top of the slope had ceased. It had a heavy, oppressive odor, like the tar marshes, and was colored in red patches separated by white

stripes and lines, like the plumage of some birds that sometimes passed through, usually heading north. But instead
of having legs, it moved on deformable bags that bulged like
skins filled with water, and turned to lay down the same strip
of surface again and again along the ground. The body had
windows like the openings in the walls of the huts Rakki's
people had built, but covered with what looked like sheets
of solid water. He guessed it was like the "glass" that he had
seen small pieces of in some of the Oldworld articles at the
caves. Faces were looking out at them from behind the windows.

"White Head . . . Sims," he said over his shoulder, not
taking his eyes off the intruder. "What kind of thing is
this?"

"There were metal mules, called trucks, as well as metal
birds. That was how they rode," White Head told him.

"Did you ride in them?"

"I never did."

"I rode in trucks sometimes—when we worked making
roads," Sims said. "I never learned to drive one. After the
Long Night and the Terror, I forgot much. Seeing this makes
me remember things."

"Are these your gods or your devils?" Gap Teeth asked,
clutching his spear.

"We have nothing that devils would want," White Head
answered.

Parts of the wall on both sides of the truck swung outward to uncover openings. Two figures emerged, halted
briefly, and then moved forward. A third appeared behind
them but stayed back. Rakki's eyes widened as he looked.
The third was carrying a gun. Then, behind him, two
females appeared from the truck. All except one of the
females were lightskins, like Shell Eyes and Yellow Hair from
the caves, and as Bo had been. The female who was different was not dark but colored a lighter brown. They were
all wearing thick Oldworlder-style garments from their necks
to their feet, and some had headdresses, in one case attached
to the wearer's garment. From somewhere to one side, Rakki
caught a snatch in the wind of the droning sound that told
him the gray metal bird had returned.

Keene came around in front of the Scout, and Naarmegen joined him from the other side, while Jorff climbed out with a rifle cradled non-threateningly at port-arms position and took up a watchful position just ahead of the Scout. Ivor remained in the driver's station with a channel open to Serengeti and a couple of the Scout's external cameras trained on the scene. Beth and Maria got out behind Jorff and stayed by the doors. Keene and Naarmegen went forward slowly, Keene with hands on hips, near his automatic, the holster flap open, Naarmegen showing empty hands. The hope was that Naarmegen's earlier life in South Africa might have left him with the smatterings of some kind of speech that would be understood.

"How are we reading?" Keene checked, speaking to the wrist compad that he was wearing.

"Fine," Ivor's voice replied from the Scout. Then, after a short pause, "Gallian up in the ship says you might be about to make history. He wants to know what it feels like."

"Tell him it's not exactly the uppermost thing on my mind right now," Keene replied.

Four had come up from the huts, all dark-skinned. Curiously, the two who appeared youngest were in the center and seemed to be the dominant ones. They were scantily clad in loin coverings made from skins, and ornamented head coverings, both ferocious in appearance, with wild manes of hair, muscular, sinewy limbs, and hefty shoulders in proportion to their relatively small physical size. Keene was unable to guess at their ages. He'd have said the bodies were in their teens, toughened and scarred, but the faces were those of hardened adults. One, he recognized by his headgear as one of the two riders caught in the first view from the probe. He seemed to be the leader and moved with a dragging limp, which from the shape of his leg was caused by a bad break that hadn't been set properly. He was wearing a tattered cape-like garment and wielded as weapon what appeared to be an old machine part or maybe a structural member, with a wicked-looking cross-piece sharpened to an edge. The other, carrying a small hunting bow with a stone-tipped arrow strung and ready, had something like a vest, with armholes, open at the chest, and was making strange grimacing expressions that revealed discolored teeth, many missing.

Of the two older men, one was shrunken and wrinkled with white hair, probably the other rider from the probe's picture, Keene guessed. The last, carrying a stone-tipped spear, was coffee-colored and looked dirty and somehow unkept, even for a place like this, his body emaciated by sickness or maybe simply the stresses of the past years.

And then the Leader, having evidently selected Keene as the principal, leaped forward with a shriek despite his crooked leg, planting himself solidly, his eyes bulging, brandishing the club in menacing motion. Keene was peripherally aware of Naarmegen a few feet away, open-mouthed, momentarily paralyzed. From behind he registered the *click* of Jorff thumbing a round into the breech of his rifle.

"*No!*" he snapped over his shoulder; at the same time, his mind raced. He knew that the demonstration was to intimidate, a bid to assert rank; but what to do about it? He wasn't about to try and make a point by trading blows with the local head-cracking champion—and quite possibly come the worst out of it.

"*Lan, turn around!*" Beth's voice came through the compad. "*Slowly. Go for the unexpected.*"

Something in Keene's subconscious saw what she was getting at before he did. Overriding the inner pandemonium of rushing adrenaline, he forced his face into an expression of contempt, folded his arms on his chest, and turned his back. Jorff was standing frozen with his rifle at the ready. Beth and Maria were still farther back. For an instant it seemed to Keene that the rest of reality was a movie that had seized up. And then he became aware of a rushing noise and whine, getting louder.

Somebody—either the remote operator back at Serengeti, or it could have been Ivor in the Scout, patching in local control—had kept abreast of the situation and was diving the probe at them. Keene turned his head and saw it swooping in, motor at full power and an audio tone beamed through the on-board speaker for effect. He raised his head commandingly, as if it had been he who summoned it. A cry of fear and scuffling noises came from behind him, and screams from the huts below. The probe *whooshed* overhead, passing low enough for its slipstream to dislodge the hood of Keene's work jacket. Something hit it, disintegrating with a sharp cracking sound; the probe lifted away in a climbing turn, but its engine note had changed and it seemed to be laboring. Still, it cleared the rocks above and disappeared over the line of the ridge at the top of the slope.

Keene turned back in a way that he hoped was majestic enough, to find the mulatto on the ground, gibbering, the old man holding his hands protectively over his head, and the bowman with missing teeth some yards away, seemingly looking sheepish, his bow empty. He looked as if he had started to run away after firing his arrow, and then checked himself.

The Leader, however, still stood where he had been, upright and defiant, his eyes blazing. His expression seemed to be saying, *I did not bend!*

But there was more too. Understanding and respect. Acceptance. He and Keene had passed each other's tests. Now they could treat as equals, each before his own kind. So how would a professional diplomat play it from here? Keene asked himself. He found he had no idea. Then let's just be the engineer, he decided.

Unfolding his arms, he relaxed his features into a hint of a grin and extended an open palm. The Leader looked down at it uncertainly. Keene moved it a few inches closer, nodding in encouragement. The Leader warily released one of his own hands from the handle of the club and raised it until they touched lightly. The tension slackened. Somebody applauded from back near the Scout. Cheering voices at Serengeti base came from the compad on Keene's arm. The others from the Scout started to come forward, but halted when Beth spoke again, cautioning them. "Hold back, people. This is *his* domain. Wait to be invited. His pride and dignity are everything."

Keene withdrew his hand and waited impassively. The Leader remained facing him until his entourage had re formed. Then, seemingly needing to regain some face lost as a result of their poor showing, he pointed first at Keene, then Naarmegen, making his gestures slow and wide to be visible from below, then indicated the settlement, beckoned to them, and turned to begin leading the way.

Beth spoke from Keene's compad. "Don't concede too easily, Lan. He'll take it as weakness. Bargain with him." Keene held up a hand. The Leader stopped and turned awkwardly back on his crooked leg. Keene pointed back at Jorff, still standing halfway between them and the Scout, and then motioned down toward the huts, indicating that Jorff was to go too. The two stood for several seconds, reading each other's faces. Then the Leader nodded curtly and waved for Jorff to follow.

The inhabitants watched in awe, some shrinking back, as the three newcomers were brought down to the cluster of huts and shelters. Keene and the others were shown prized trophies that included some implements carved from wood, a metal jerry can now used to hold water, and a number of garments reworked from recognizable pieces of clothing that had seen better days. They were given morsels of meat and a vegetable preparation to sample—as it turned out, not too bad. Keene caught Naarmegen's eye, conveying that they ought to reciprocate, and inviting suggestions. After a moment of pondering, Naarmegen unclipped the sheath and knife from his belt, and passed it to Keene, who with great ceremony making it plain to all that this was a great honor, presented it to the Leader—whose name they had established by this time, was Rakki. The watchers were suitably impressed. Rakki, whose status had thus been acknowledged before all, beamed his delight, attaching the sheath to his own belt and permitting his clan to come forward and touch the blade wonderingly. To show his magnanimity in return, he made signs that the rest of Keene's party could bring the Scout down to the settlement. *His* settlement. Rakki's.

As soon as Keene got a moment he raised his compad and called Ivor, who was still in the truck. "Was that you who did that?"

"It was. You needed a miracle."

"Oh. Is that how they work?"

"The Lord works in strange ways, Doctor."

"How's the probe?"

"Serengeti says the compressor fan might be a bit chewed. I put it down over the ridge until someone can get out to look at it."

"Okay."

Beth moved over toward Keene as the others arrived. "That was quick thinking, Beth," he complimented. "You read the situation exactly right. I guess we've got Gallian to thank for making sure we had a professional psychologist along on the team."

"Not really," she told him. "I just took a course of psychiatric nursing training when I was a student."

"So which part of it taught you about human nature like that? I'm intrigued."

"None." She hesitated. "It was something I saw a long time ago in a Tarzan movie."

Rakki couldn't understand what kind of gods these were who expended effort on others who could be of no benefit to them. They had total power to command whatever they wanted. If they needed the labor or obedience of him and his clan, they could compel it. And yet they seemed to seek approval and to serve favors. It went against everything that, in his experience of life, was necessary to survive and rule.

He watched with mixed feelings the brown-skinned female inside one of the huts, examining the eyes and mouth and skin of one of the infants, who had been vomiting and emptying body contents continuously and burning up inside with a fever madness. On the one hand, he felt a sense of pride in knowing it was he, Rakki, who had allowed the strangers into the settlement to show their skills. On the other, he was perplexed, for didn't it make more sense to let the inherently weaker die, rather than grow to consume more food than they would ever replace? Outside, the white-faced female was letting others taste foods of kinds that neither he nor his people had ever seen before. Why should these gods care if Engressi's baby lived or died? Why should they give away their food when there was nothing he could see that they stood to gain in return? It made no sense.

Shell Eyes was sitting on skins, tending her own baby—

one who would grow strong and earn its place in the clan. Nearby, White Head was exchanging signs and words with the bearded god. It seemed that the bearded god was an Oldworlder who had once lived somewhere to the south before the Long Night, and they both knew some words of a speech that had been spoken then, although Rakki had never heard of it. The bearded god made gestures upward and looked toward the roof. White Head seemed awed. "What does he say now?" Rakki asked him.

"They went to another world beyond the sky. Now they have come back."

Rakki couldn't imagine anywhere beyond the sky. "What is it they seek from us?" he muttered.

"Why must they be seeking anything?"

"It is the way. They must know this, for they are powerful. The strong only become weak by serving others."

"You lived, Rakki, because Enka came looking for you, and brought us to where you were," Shell Eyes said, referring to Gap Teeth by his name. "You became strong again because of others."

"Others who needed my strength," Rakki said. "You live here now because I lead. You left the caves to escape from Jemmo. Left to him, *you*, White Head, would have died."

"Is that why you think we saved you?" White Head asked.

Rakki scowled and found that he couldn't answer. The question had made him angry. He wasn't sure why. "Everyone must seek for themselves," he said. And turning away to end the conversation, he stalked out of the hut.

The head god, whom the metal bird obeyed, was standing a short distance away, talking with the warrior god who had watched. Rakki studied them and their strange garb again, and his eyes came back to the gun that the warrior was carrying, now slung behind a shoulder like a bow. It looked heavier and larger than the one Rakki had handled briefly at the caves. Sims said it was more powerful, holding more bullets and sending them farther.

Rakki forced himself to control his resentments, remain calm, and think again why he should permit these gods to steal glory before his own people. Because by tolerating their arrogance, he might gain a place as an ally to them in whatever it was they sought. If he and his people became allies, then they would have access to guns too. Then his vengeance upon Jemmo would be total and crushing, and he would rule the Swamplands as well as the caves.

Everyone had to seek for themselves. It was the way.

CHAPTER TWENTY-TWO

The Jupiter survey mission vessel *Trojan* was virtually a sister ship to the ill-fated *Osiris,* which had perished during its return voyage to Earth after bringing Keene's group and other Terran survivors to Kronia. Like the *Osiris*, it had been constructed with armaments during the time of political tension that had existed between Kronia and Earth, and the armaments had been retained as a resource for the Security Arm in case of need. In fact, the Security Arm were crewing and operating the craft jointly with SOE, making the Jupiter mission a combined planetary survey and SA training venture.

Also like the *Osiris*, *Trojan* was built with a unique Kronian variable geometry that combined linear and rotational accelerations to provide a simulation of normal gravity whether the ship was in freefall or under drive. The basic form was that of wheel attached to one end of an axle. The axle was the main body of the vessel and consisted of a relatively thick cylindrical forward end, with a thinner section extending tailward like the handle of an old-fashioned potato masher and containing the fusion reactant tanks and propulsion system. The larger part carried the heavy equipment, cargo bays, and docking port, and also formed the base for six spoke booms (the *Osiris* had been built with four) extending radially to accommodation modules carried at their ends. The modules were interconnected by a circular communications tube to complete the wheel.

The booms pivoted at their bases to be capable of trailing back like the spokes of a partly opened umbrella when the ship was under drive acceleration. The angle they assumed was always such that the forces produced by the vessel's forward thrust and by the rotation of the whole structure formed a resultant perpendicular to the decks in the modules at the ends. Telescopic sections in the connecting ring compensated for changes in the ring's circumference when the trailing angle altered.

Colonel Birt Nyrom, commander of the *Trojan's* SA contingent, stood in the minigravity of the Forward Port Hoist Compartment in the Hub, watching a practice squad completing the drill of bringing long-range attack boosters up from the main armory. The boosters were for attaching to multi-targeting fission-pumped laser warheads, which constituted the vessel's primary long-range armament. The LORIN shield against incoming meteoroids was an adaptation of the same concept. Since the device was triggered— and in the process, vaporized—by a nuclear bomb, it had to be ejected to a safe distance from the ship before firing, typically fifty miles when used as a defense screen. Larger boosters could be attached for carrying out attacks over longer ranges. During the voyage to Jupiter, it was intended to carry out a series of exercises in deploying and recovering unarmed attack-configured warheads over varying distances from the ship. The boosters were being brought up to the ejection stations in preparation.

The rookie lieutenant who was supervising the squad sounded off the final checklist items confirming that the clamp pins were secured, upper feed hoses drained, set to Open, and stowed, and the Feed Hatch Auto Override was returned to Disenabled. "Boosters ready for Condition Yellow deployment and secured," he reported to the chief who was overseeing the operation.

"We're through, Colonel," the chief advised Nyrom.

"Good. Stand down," Nyrom acknowledged.

"Good work, and a pretty fast time," the chief relayed to the lieutenant. "Okay, you can stand the men down."

"Thank you, sir . . . Squad, stand down. Okay, that's it. Good job, guys. Free time until sixteen hundred."

Nyrom watched the lieutenant turn away as two of the others beckoned him over about something. His name was Delucey, one of the intense and dedicated kind who takes everything seriously—good material to have in something like the SA. Terran-born, he had escaped from Earth in the final days as a kid along with his mother and been brought back by the *Osiris* with the group that had shuttled up from Mexico. The intenseness that he brought to the job reflected an escape to the Security Arm from the containment, both physically and psychologically, of regular Kronian life, which he unconsciously blamed for robbing him of a future on Earth. At least, that was what the psychiatric advisers had concluded, who suggested that a long-distance mission to Jupiter might help break down the connections. In fact, quite a high proportion of the SA recruits aboard the *Trojan* were either confused Terrans with repressed hankerings to return to Earth, or young malcontent Kronians who felt the system didn't recognize them adequately. Nyrom had surprised many with his readiness to accept them.

His wrist compad buzzed as he was casting an eye silently over the scene to satisfy himself that all was as Delucey had reported. He raised the unit toward his face to address it. "Nyrom."

"Captain Walsh here." It responded in voice-only. The wording was Walsh's way of indicating "family" business.

"Captain?"

"We have news from home."

"We're just about through here. I'll come on up."

"At your convenience, Colonel." The circuit cleared.

"Carry on, Chief," Nyrom instructed.

"Aye, aye, sir."

Nyrom left the hoist compartment and moved inboard via a transverse gallery, at the same time using the compad to call a capsule to the base of the spoke elevator going "up" to the Command Module. Touch-gliding in a series of slow lopes using feet and handrails, he navigated the labyrinth of passages and shafts to a circum-Hub corridor that brought him to the access point. The door was open and the capsule

waiting. He entered, and less than a minute later the capsule was ascending from the Hub structure. Above his head
through the double-glass wall as he traveled feet-first he had
a view of the intricate spoke pivot mechanism at the Hub,
and beyond the bulk of the ship, a panorama of stars wheeling
slowly. Saturn was still bright in the foreground among them.

The spoke mechanism was ingenious, yes; but as with
just about anything involving large moving parts, high
stresses, and extremes of environment, it could be tempera-
mental. Lubricants leaked and sublimed away into the space
vacuum; pivot arms jammed; the ring when maximally
extended could suddenly begin oscillating with complex
resonances that rippled around the entire structure. He liked
solutions that were solid-state and compact. The Yarbat AG
arrays that they were trying out on the *Aztec* that had just
left Saturn sounded like the right way to go about it. If they
worked out okay, it would make the *Trojan* as obsolete and
cumbersome by comparison as the *Cutty Sark*. Lieutenant
Delucey's profile said that his mother was returning to Earth
with the *Aztec*. That had been considered a factor in his
favor when considering him for selection. His mother had
told the people that she had worked with previously in the
Academy on Dione about her worry over his long, withdrawn moods and detachment from things she had tried to
interest him in. It was amazing how these things got around.

Nyrom could sympathize with the resentments and frus-
trations of the kind of people he had tried to muster. He
himself had felt the gratification of having his profession
and military skills valued back in the days when Earth was
feared as a threat, and Kronia prepared to defend itself. But
then he had found himself relegated to little more than a
trainer of new recruits and administrator in a local police
force when the perceived danger passed. For him, that had
been a personal disappointment as well as a career setback.
In many ways, as a boy growing up on Titan, and for a
while on Iapetus, he had felt deprived in never having known
life on Earth, which he pictured as vibrant and alive, filled
with exciting places and different ways to spend a life. After
his father was killed in a construction accident when Nyrom
was too young to remember him, he had been raised by

an Earth-born uncle, a former military engineer who had migrated to Kronia with his family from somewhere in the Middle East. The uncle had grown to despise war and the suffering it brought to guiltless victims, and come out to Saturn to get away from it and put his skills at the disposal of a better cause. But his nephew had been captivated by his tales of tank duels in the desert, of going out on stealthy infantry patrols at night, of antiaircraft missiles streaking skyward, and he had yearned inwardly for adventure and the exhilaration of competing to exert mastery without pretensions, apology, or disguise. Even with all the space-oriented activity and the exercises on barren moons, the Security Arm had seemed a poor substitute. And then for a while, when the tension with Earth grew, the promise had been flaunted at him . . . only to be snatched away.

Yes, he could sympathize very easily with those who thought they could be worth more in a system that was different from this.

Nyrom felt the pressure under his feet increasing as the capsule neared the ring and his body took on weight. He emerged into the Command Module walking normally and made his way past the Communications Room and Power Direction Center to the Control Deck. Walsh was by the watch console, talking with the First Officer. He saw Nyrom enter, murmured something to excuse himself, and nodded to indicate the door leading aft to the duty officers' day room. It was unoccupied. Nyrom closed the door behind them.

Gray-haired, crusty, square-jawed, and stocky, Walsh was a former brigadier general with the U.S. Army who had also been brought back by the *Osiris*. He had brought a lifetime of military experience that many felt the operations arm of the Space Operations Executive could use more of, and obviously he had not done badly for himself.

There had been some protests back on Titan at the proposal to put a Terran in command of an SOE vessel like the *Trojan*. One of the main objectors had been the other American, Cavan, which had seemed strange to Nyrom then, and he still didn't pretend to understand it. Why wouldn't a Terran, versed in Terran ways, want to see Terran influence expanded in Kronia? But the Triad had ruled against the protests, presumably to placate Valcroix and the Pragmatists in their demands for greater Terran representation in positions of prominence; and then, to appease Cavan and the protesters, they had sent Walsh far from Saturn and out of the way at this politically sensitive time. The more Nyrom saw of political compromise solutions that ended up appeasing nobody and antagonizing everyone, the more he liked the military's simple and straightforward ways of doing things.

Walsh checked the room's monitor panel to make sure that it had not been left with a microphone or recorder on, and then turned to face Nyrom across the table in the room's center, his knuckles resting lightly on the top. "I've received a confidential assessment from Acrobat. His reading of the situation is that it's not going to go through—not by a long way. So we can take it that Blue Moon is a virtual certainty. I'm authorizing you to advance your preparations accordingly."

Nyrom nodded. "Acrobat" was a reference to Ludwig Grasse. Valcroix's bill to amend the procedure for making appointments to the Directorates was about to come before the Congress, and the message meant that the inside word was it had little chance of passing. The news wasn't exactly a surprise. But the record could now be made to show that a constitutional attempt at reform had been rebuffed, and that was the kind of thing that tended to impress Kronians.

The eventuality had been anticipated, and of course there was a fallback plan. The *Trojan*'s part in it depended on being able to persuade a significant number of the SA contingent to come over and throw their lot in with the covert Pragmatist group aboard the ship. That had been Nyrom's reason for seeking out the particular kinds of personnel profile that he had. But that had been about as far as anyone could go toward guaranteeing success, for obviously no actual intimation of intentions could be risked in advance. Hence, Nyrom could use all the time he could get now to begin sounding out the potential support. That was what he understood Walsh was telling him.

Nyrom felt a surge of excitement, the anticipation of action he had always dreamed about. And, if he was honest, relief. Only now did he admit to himself that he had been inwardly worried that the politicians would find some last-minute compromise. New horizons were beckoning, about to open up.

Walsh must have seen it on his face, and smiled thinly with a snort. "Just can't wait, can you, Birt?" he said.

"I envied you, you know, John. I'd always wanted to be a Terran. Suddenly it feels like going home."

"What, even for you?"

"Especially for me."

For, yes, at a time when critical policy decisions were being made that many had strong feelings about, it was understandable why Kronians, thinking the way they did, would send the *Trojan* with its military capability far out of the way to a place like Jupiter when its presence at Saturn could be problematical. And even more so if a goodly portion of those judged to be potentially supportive of the upstart power bid were arranged to be consigned away with it. Of course, Nyrom had seen what was going on when the selection committees pushed all those square pegs and oddballs at him.

But he had been watching and listening and learning to think like a Terran, not a Kronian. True, with the *Trojan* and its complement at Jupiter, life at this politically charged moment would be easier for those involved with calming the waters back at Kronia. But if, on the other hand, the *Trojan* wasn't going to Jupiter at all, then that could make it a very different matter indeed.

CHAPTER TWENTY-THREE

They called the band of survivors simply the "Tribe," for want of anything better. Nobody had lined them up for an exact count, but there seemed to be between forty and fifty souls, including numerous children. From the progress that Naarmegen was making in establishing a kind of pidgin that mixed their speech with parts of a South African dialect that he'd had some familiarity with and a smattering of English as seemed to suit the occasion, they called their settlement Joburg—obviously after the city that had once existed in the now-snowy region to the south.

The leader, Rakki, had led a small band who arrived from elsewhere and asserted their supremacy over an initial group who seemed to have numbered around a dozen. The rest had appeared in ones, twos, and odd groups since. Far from being among the elders of the assortment of still largely dazed and disoriented individuals who made up the Tribe, Rakki maintained his primacy through ruthlessness and sheer battling prowess despite his physical handicap—evidently the ruling currency of the times. Guesses put him in his mid or even lower teens. He himself was unable to give any account of his years, since for a time that the hapless inhabitants wandered among erupting landscapes and falling storms of fire, the notion of "year" had lost all meaning. Most astounding of all was his virtually total loss of all memories prior to the catastrophe, which seemed to be the case with all the younger people. Only a few of the oldest survivors seemed to possess any coherent recollections at all of the world that had once been.

"The best I can make of it is that it's some kind of mental defense mechanism," Beth said to Keene and Sariena as they stood by the landing-area-side windows in the OpComs Dome at Serengeti, watching the shuttle from the *Varuna* that had landed a short time previously being lowered to a horizontal position. The intermittently high winds and persistent ground tremors posed too much of a hazard to leave them standing vertically. The permanent pads to be built on the far side of what was currently the landing area would have silos.

The base was continuing to take shape, and Gallian and Charlie Hu had found time to come down to the surface at last. Keene and Sariena had come over from the now-finished mess facility to greet them. Beth was doing a valiant job as the mission's de facto psychologist and effective psychiatrist. "A collective amnesia is blocking out experiences that were too horrific to be retained consciously. They could have caused mental paralysis to the point of dysfunctionality. Survival needs had to come first."

"There were a lot of theories like that relating to the state of mind of humanity after the Venus catastrophes," Sariena said. "Repressed racial memories that found their expression in myths and religion."

Keene nodded. He'd heard suggestions himself that such buried traumas lay at the root of their reenactment in the senseless aerial bombardment holocausts of modern warfare, and twentieth-century terrors of nuclear annihilation, but had never known how far to believe it. It just seemed to him that the bulk of the human race never passed over any new way of wiping each other out at any opportunity. Or was that in itself another manifestation of what Sariena was talking about? If so, did the Kronians really stand a chance of ultimately producing anything different?

"This looks like them now," he said, staring out. A Scout

carrier was emerging from the huddle of freight movers and forklifts around the shuttle. It turned and headed toward the Operations and Communications Dome.

Surprisingly, in view of the role that physical violence played in determining who would dominate, it was those of smaller stature among the survivors who seemed to have fared better. Presumably their lower minimum nutritional needs had given them the edge through the times when food had been all but nonexistent. From Maria Sanchez's observations, the newborns and infants were small by the standards that had applied previously, too. And similar things seemed to be happening among the strains of animals that were making a reappearance. Naarmegen's surveys had identified pygmy breeds of okapi, hog, eland, hyena, and another doglike species that he hadn't been able to identify, a number of them already showing adaptations to the cooling climate. Again, the animals that Rakki and a few other privileged individuals of the Tribe rode were "mule-like," but with signs of other odd traits being expressed that didn't belong.

In the short time that had gone by, this couldn't have come about through any process of gradual selection from random mutations. Rather, it pointed to the variability already having been there in the genomes, which was the conclusion the Kronians had been coming to for some time. This was what Vicki and Luthis, the biologist also from Dione, and *Aztec*'s senior scientist, were coming out to investigate further. Keene could picture her impatience on reading the latest reports from Earth. The *Aztec* was under way from Titan now but not due to arrive for another sixty days.

"Do you think that everything you ever experience is locked away inside somewhere, the way some people say?" Sariena asked Beth. "Nothing is ever lost?"

"More or less," Beth replied. "But I don't think memory is localized in any place. That's why they were always having trouble finding it."

"So what do you think?" Keene asked.

"The information could be held in interference patterns of some kind of wave process in the brain," Beth said. "Kind of like a hologram."

"Huge capacities," Keene commented. He was intrigued.

"Yes, that's my point." Beth caught the faint smile on Sariena's face that seemed to carry a mixed message of *maybe . . . and then again, maybe not.* "What do you think?" she asked.

"I'm not sure," Sariena answered. "Maybe the information isn't 'in' there in any way at all. What if the brain is just an organ that accesses it from somewhere else?" She gestured at a screen on one of the nearby consoles. It showed a view of Joburg, coming in from a camera mounted on one of the vehicles that was there currently, and had been left transmitting. Kurt Zeigler had gone out with a group to see the place and make himself known. "It would be like looking inside there for a permanent representation of those huts and people. But you won't find any. The information that creates the picture is coming from elsewhere."

"Are we back to where the Kronian designer lives?" Keene asked, smiling. He meant it to be flippant, but Sariena's face remained serious.

"Maybe," she conceded evenly. "You know, Lan, science as the Terrans conceived it ended up really as just bigger telescopes, faster computers . . . better and cheaper extensions of technology. And that's wonderfully effective for understanding and manipulating the material, physical world. But only Terran scientists could have ended up believing that that's all there is to reality. All children know it isn't so."

Keene grinned. "And Kronians?"

"You already know the answer to that. We think things are there for a purpose."

Just then, Gallian, with Charlie Hu and several others just off the shuttle, entered from the level below, bubbling hellos and greeting to all. As was typical of Gallian's style, he was wearing a maroon flight-deck jacket and could have passed for one of the shuttle's crew instead of overall director of the mission. "Landen! Sariena!" he threw across, acknowledging their presence. And then, after an exchange with the Watch Officer and duty staff to check on the situation at Joburg and things in general, he came over to join them.

The puckish face was beaming as usual beneath the mantle of silver, wavy hair, but he was already puffing from the gravity and the stairs. "Well, so here we are back again.

I'm not going to risk any comments, Landen—for fear of being in bad taste. But things have changed somewhat, yes?"

"I don't think there's much you could say that hasn't been eclipsed by the reality, Gallian," Keene said. "But for what it's worth, welcome back to Earth."

"Now you have to grow your Earth legs again," Sariena told Gallian. "Somehow, it doesn't seem so bad the second time."

"Well, that's good to know." Gallian looked at Beth and inquired breezily. "And how are we making out in your new specialty field of shell-shock patients? Any signs of getting through to them yet?"

"It's a slow business," Beth replied. "There's a lot of suspicion and suppressed hostility to deal with. But I think we're learning."

"On-the-job training. It's the best kind. You didn't think we brought you here for a vacation, did you? By the time you get back, you'll be a seasoned psychologist with exclusive experience of dealing with Terran survivors. You'll be known across all of Kronia."

Beth smiled at the thought but sighed in a way that said it would be a long time yet.

"And we have news from Kronia," Gallian announced to all of them. "The latest there is that Urzin and the Congress have finally pulled rank and refused to buy the Pragmatists' stunt to worm their way into the Directorates. I've rarely heard our President speak so forcefully about anything. And both Deputies supported him. They were firm that Kronia has its own procedures that are appropriate to Kronia's ways, and a few malcontents from Earth have no business coming here trying to change them. It's *not* their world too, that owes them any equal voice in its affairs as they claim; it's ours. If they want to come back to Earth and start their own system here again, that's up to them." Gallian peered briefly at the window, grinned, and shrugged. "Well, good luck, I suppose, if that's what they want to do." He cast around at the company again. "But it seems that with luck all this Terran-style political nonsense might be over at last, finally, and now we'll all be able to concentrate on things that are useful." He punched Keene playfully on a shoulder. "No offense, eh, Lan? I wouldn't want to belittle your history or revered institutions or anything."

"Gallian, you *don't* have to worry yourself about that," Keene said. Actually, he was feeling pretty good. It meant that things had gone the way he'd expected. Cavan's attempt to maneuver him into involvement with the politics instead of focusing on the kind of work that he had always felt to be his true calling had been proved overcautious after all, and Keene was vindicated. The old ways of antagonisms and violence, whether physical, political, or economic, were dead. And the new way that Jon Foy had painted so vividly in Keene's imagination long ago had become the new reality after all.

At Joburg, Kurt Zeigler tried to follow while Naarmegen tried with exchanges of words and gestures to piece together from Rakki and the white-headed old man called Yobu, who was miraculously still alive, the story of Rakki and his original group of companions. He had heard the account from Keene and the others of how the Tribe had formed mainly from people drifting in. But he was particularly interested in the group that had come to rule, displacing the original occupants of the place.

They were sitting under a thatched awning by the pool cleared in the creek, since Zeigler didn't like the smells, bugs, and closed-in feeling inside the huts. Some of the women who had been washing skins and recognizable remnants of clothing still watched the strangers with a fear that hadn't gone completely away, some with children clinging to them, equally wide-eyed and awed. Zeigler tried to ignore them. He would have preferred not to have to rely on academics or scientists to translate, because he suspected their ideological tendencies and considered them naive. But he was stuck with Naarmegen for the time being. He wouldn't want him to be involved later, when more serious business might need to be addressed.

"Rakki and Yobu, and it sounds like five others, including Calina"—that was the name of Rakki's fair-skinned woman—"came from another clan, or whatever, who live in some caves to the east," Naarmegen said. "From the sound of it, there were a lot more of them than here."

"So there are other groups too," Zeigler said. That was interesting.

"Seems like it."

"How far to the east?"

"I can't make it out, but it sounds like a long way. They wandered around for a long time before they found this place."

"Not very hospitable," Zeigler remarked. East was the inland direction, where the river that flowed west and then south around the plateau came from—a desolation of earthquake-shattered mountains, volcanos, lava flows, and swamps.

"They're a tough bunch," Naarmegen said.

Zeigler looked Rakki up and down again. His body seemed youthful in some ways, yet it was scarred and muscled like a veteran gladiator's. His face was barely able to support a beard, but at the same time lined and hardened. The eyes were cruel, alert, cunning—but not unintelligent. He looked back at Zeigler with an unbending stare that seemed to say, *So what of your machines and your knowledge of many things? When it comes to the things that make the measure of a man, I, Rakki, can hold my own with the best of you.*

"Why did they leave the caves? Wasn't there more safety and protection with the numbers there?" Zeigler asked.

Naarmegen passed the question on. Anger flashed in Rakki's eyes when he answered. His hand move unconsciously to rub his leg. Zeigler caught the words "one only could rule," "betrayed by lies," "left as dead, for the . . ." something that sounded like some kind of scavenger, or maybe ants or worms, and, "he with holes in teeth," pointing to his mouth.

"There was a rivalry to be chief—one of these to-the-death things," Naarmegen supplied. "He was tricked into going out somewhere with some of the other guy's cronies. On the way they jumped him, skewered the buddy he was with, and tossed Rakki over a cliff. But Yobu sent the one called Enka out looking. He found Rakki just about ready to snuff it, and the others went there and got him. I guess, obviously, they couldn't go back."

"Is that where he messed up his leg?" Zeigler asked.

"Rakki, when you fall from cliff." Naarmegen pointed. "Your leg is broken then?"

Rakki nodded curtly and glowered. "And pierced by spear. Many days, they carry . . ." Zeigler missed the rest. White-haired Yobu added some more.

"The rival's name is Jemmo. He's still there, at the caves. But one day Rakki will rule them. And some swamps—I'm not sure where they fit in. Revenge seems to be an obsession."

Zeigler had noticed how Rakki's eyes would stray toward Kelm when Kelm came close as he ambled about, checking over the surroundings and developing his Earth legs. Rakki watched the other SA troopers who were present too. What seemed to interest him was their guns. He seemed to know what they were. However proud and defiant the eyes that met Zeigler's consciously, the glances when Rakki didn't realize Zeigler was watching betrayed envy of the strangers' power. And that could be the pointer to finding the kind of opening for a mutual advancing of interests that Zeigler was looking for.

A message an hour or so ago from Serengeti had brought the news that the Pragmatists' bid to expand their powers back on Kronia had failed. Before very much longer, therefore, Zeigler expected to receive the code notifying him that Blue Moon was going ahead, which meant he should take any opportunity that presented itself to prepare accordingly. Recruiting the small Tribe here at Joburg would not bring about anything decisive; but they were natural fighters, and it could help. However, if they could lead him to this other group, who by the sound of things numbered considerably more, that could make a significant difference.

And there might well be more still to be found, scattered around in this ruin of a continent, beyond those.

CHAPTER TWENTY-FOUR

Since their emergence as a recognized political force, the Pragmatists had built up their organizational center and focus of support on Iapetus, second outermost to Phoebe among Saturn's principal moons. After their failure to open a back door to power in the Directorate arm of the Kronian Congress, Valcroix and Grasse departed from Titan for Iapetus with a coterie of leading Party names, staff, and sympathizers aboard a local transorbital called the *Eskimo*. Most observers of the scene concluded that the intention was to consolidate after their defeat and consider where they would go from there.

A day out from Titan, *Eskimo* vanished without warning. It was the kind of thing that could happen at any time in a region still subject to hazard from rogue objects of all sizes, and the incident was recorded as "Presumed Impact Destruction. Unconfirmed." Many felt inwardly, though it would have been in poor taste to say so, that perhaps Kronia had been spared much in the way of future complications that it really didn't need right now. Those who believed it was Kronia's destiny to found a civilization intended by Divine Purpose interpreted the event accordingly.

Aboard the *Trojan*, still following the initial part of the course that would take it to Jupiter, Colonel Nyrom met

privately with Lieutenant Robin Delucey in a sparsely furnished staff office in Accommodation Module 3, not currently
being used. Since the ship was carrying a large consignment
of material and industrial equipment for the cache to be
established somewhere in the Jovian system for future use,
occupancy was relatively light for a vessel the size of the
Trojan, comprising the crew and the SA contingent, and scientific groups concerned with the mission's survey work.

Nyrom waited until Delucey sat down opposite him at the
metal-edged table, then took off his hat and leaned back.
"At ease, Lieutenant. What I want to talk to you about is
just between us and the walls."

Delucey made the concession of resting his elbows on the
arms of the chair, but otherwise remained guarded. He said
nothing but regarded Nyrom questioningly.

"We know a lot more about you than you might imagine,
Lieutenant." Nyrom made his voice pointed and confidential,
communicating that this was a time to open up. "You went
through a lot back there, didn't you? Lost everything, lost
practically everybody. And you made a heroic effort to start
out again and make a go of it. I'm full of admiration for the
guts it took. But it didn't work out, did it, son? You're not
happy. Am I right?" He paused, reading the face that without change of expression asked where this was going, then
shook his head. "Kronia isn't for you. Stifling, unexciting . . .
But demanding. And that's how it was going to be for the
rest of your life. That was why you joined the Security Arm.
That was why a lot of young people who are here on this
ship did."

Delucey's eyes retained their detached, mildly cynical look.
"What else is there?" he asked after taking a few seconds to
consider what Nyrom had said.

"There's Earth." Nyrom's voice warmed to the thought
of it. Again the wary look, waiting, conceding nothing. "All
the things you remember are still there: oceans, mountains,
endless landscapes, air you can breathe under open skies.
Except now it's wild again, untamed. There's room for a
thousand lifetimes there, all different."

"They're going back. The *Varuna* . . ."

"And what will they do there? I'll tell you. They'll turn

it into Kronia all over again. Is that what you want to have waiting if you ever go back too one day? Or would you rather have *your* world, that lets you be what you used to be, the way you ought to be?"

"You sound as if you're offering some kind of choice," Delucey said.

Nyrom liked directness, and nodded. "As we all know, the recent Pragmatist proposal to broaden the Kronian political process to a more equitable basis was rejected by those who control the present system. What most people don't know is that it didn't end there. The Congress had the chance to reform within the legitimacy of its own constitution. But since they won't change to something that's fairer for everyone there, we'll take the only alternative . . ."

"We?"

Nyrom nodded. "It's bigger than you probably think. We'll create our own system—the only kind that's workable in the long run—in the only other place available at the present time. We'll build Earth again. And you can be part of it, Lieutenant."

Delucey stared hard at the table. Nyrom could almost feel his mind racing. "But I thought the Pragmatists were against returning to Earth," he said finally.

"Against trying to support a major Earth base from Kronia and sustain Kronia at the same time," Nyrom agreed. "But a self-contained operation on Earth would be something different. And the beginnings of it are right there, waiting for us already."

"You mean the base there? Taking it over?" Delucey's reply followed so easily that Nyrom got the feeling he had been ahead of the conversation all along.

"There's enough aboard this ship to start a pilot industrial operation—and to defend it if need be, while it's becoming self-sufficient. Add that to what's there now, and the things the *Aztec* is carrying, which is bound for Earth already, and we're off to a pretty solid start." Nyrom paused, to let Delucey take it in, watching his eyes flicker unconsciously around the room as if searching for the flaws. "And you wouldn't even be saying goodbye to the family," he went on. "Since your mother is on the *Aztec* too." He noted the surprise that flashed in Delucey's eyes and nodded. "Oh, yes. I told you we know more about you than you probably imagined. And we know how you think too, Lieutenant." Another pause, shorter this time, indicating that he was through. "Whatever your answer, clearly we have to deny you access to communications beyond the ship until our purpose becomes more widely known. But we have to begin detailed arrangements now. When we move to assert control of the *Trojan*, where will you stand, Lieutenant? Will we be able to count on you?"

Delucey answered quicker than most of the others that Nyrom had already talked to, and he had fewer questions. "I'm with you, Colonel," he said simply.

A probe reconnoitering over the southern part of western Asia discovered a band of survivors apparently moving northward out of the devastation that had been the Middle East. Guesses were that they had somehow ridden out the floods in the higher places, and were moving toward the gradually warming, less hostile central area of the continent. Another probe sent back pictures of crude shanty structures built on a high pass in the resculpted North American Rockies, but they appeared to be deserted.

Meanwhile, expansion of Serengeti continued. A transportation depot for surface vehicles was commenced, facing the pad area, which was being extended as planned, and two more storage domes appeared behind the labs and workshops to house the flow of supplies and materials arriving from orbit. Foundations were laid for a General Fabrication Plant to be built around the profab equipment that was on its way aboard the *Aztec*. Capable of producing just about anything commensurate with its size limits and the variety of available materials, this would add enormously to the base's capability and potential for further expansion. Since the profab units could just as easily turn out parts for more profab units, Serengeti would be on its way to becoming literally a self-constructing factory town freed from dependence on supply from Kronia.

Finally, an area outside the base was cleared for experiments in crop cultivation and rearing livestock. Beyond that, possibilities were limited only by what further exploration of Earth might reveal.

These were still surface installations, and therefore vulnerable to strikes by meteorite showers from the debris that Athena had left in the vicinity or strewn liberally in Earth-crossing orbits. However, even at the bottom of its deep gravity well Earth was a large place, and it had been decided that the risk was acceptable until deeper excavations and shelters could be commenced using the lithofracture gear also being sent with the *Aztec*.

The *Agni* system was functioning flawlessly, which meant that until *Aztec* arrived, Keene's commitments would be fairly light. He found his thoughts going beyond the immediate engineering needs of the base and plans for its further expansion, to the longer-term reasons for hastening the return to Earth that Foy had talked about and which Gallian had come here primarily to oversee: the grounding of a new civilization in the ways and values of Kronia. If humanity had been able to accomplish as much as it had by the time of Athena *despite* all the blotches on just about every page of the history of the past five thousand years, then how much more might it stand to achieve without them?

Sariena by her nature was concerned over the same issues too, and they spent a lot of time together and with Gallian debating the philosophy they should adopt toward survivors who were not only uncomprehending of such concepts, but schooled by their experiences in just the opposite direction. The object, after all, was to set the basis for a society that would embrace all its members, not create some master race versus slave situation. No surer way than that could have been devised for insuring that the same troubles, resentments, hatreds, and evils that had shaped the past would one day arise all over again.

Keene and Sariena stood near the workshop domes on the "industrial" side of the base, watching a jib crane swinging a preformed roof truss into position in one of the new buildings, directed by a Kronian using a remote control unit nearby. With the weight under Earth gravity, construction was a trickier and more hazardous business than in freefall or on Saturn's moons, and the Kronians were working to master the requisite skills and judgment. All the same, there had been several accidents already. No amount of briefing and instruction, or attempts at simulation by hologram or in rotating space structures, could substitute for the actuality of being here and doing it, and feeling the real fears of knowing what might happen if something went wrong.

"That guy's getting a hands-on crash course in high-gravity physics," Keene commented. "Everything's dinosaur proportions compared to what he's been used to back home."

He was still finding it exhilarating just to be able to stand outside without a roof between him and the sky, even if the sky was turbulent gray, and the wind cutting and laced with stinging dust. Sariena was acclimatizing, getting outside for gradually longer spells, and spending as much time standing as she could comfortably manage.

"I never thought of it that way," she said. "Remember to tell that to Vicki when she gets here."

One of the subjects that Vicki had been involved in since the days on Earth, which was now just one more puzzle in the story of biological origins and change that the Kronians were trying to piece together, was how not only dinosaurs but the whole world of massive life-forms that they had been part of could have existed, since they simply weren't viable under the conditions of modern Earth. The prevailing theory was that at the time it existed as a satellite of Saturn, Earth's surface gravity had been smaller on the side that was phase-locked toward the primary, and extinction of the largest creatures had been part of the upheaval that had come with its detachment.

"I think I run into my own dinosaur problem when it comes to figuring out the right way to deal with Rakki and his Tribe," Sariena said. "Trying to talk with them can only get you so far. But if nothing they've known or can remember gives them any grounding to relate to what you're talking about, how do you get through?" She sighed. "Sometimes I feel like some kind of moral preacher. There's got to be a better way."

"Definitely not your image," Keene agreed.

"Well, do you have any thoughts, Lan?"

"Did Gallian put you up to this?" Keene asked curiously. It was a subject that Gallian had been lamenting about and asking for suggestions on from all who would listen, both down at the base and up in the two ships.

"Yes, he did. . . . Why, what's wrong with that? It seemed a sensible thing to do."

Keene just smiled and shook his head to himself. Sometimes the Kronians' directness and utter incapacity for guile left him with nothing to be said. Small wonder they had walked into a blender when they tried taking on Earth's political establishment.

He looked back at the riveting crew moving into position to secure the roof member while the crane operator held it steady. The piece had traveled from Saturn on one of the unmanned open-frame freight haulers, after being formed on Titan from ores extracted from Hyperion. All around, work was in progress on the beginnings of bringing a devastated world back to life. He felt again an exultation at the power of creativity of the human species and the knowledge that he was a part of it. . . . And yet it was the same power that could unleash such destructiveness. That was the dilemma that Sariena had meant: How to open people's eyes to the potential within them to reach the stars, when their lives had been lived under a canopy of darkness?

"Show them," Keene said suddenly. "Of course all the talk in the world isn't going to do any good. It never has." He waved an arm to take in the things going on all around them, the constructions taking shape, the shuttles on the far side of the pad area and the excavations in progress behind them. "Bring them here and let them see for themselves what it's all about. . . . Even take some of them up to the *Varuna*." He turned back to Sariena and shrugged. "Why not?"

She stared at him for a moment, then repeated, "Why not? It's too obvious, isn't it?"

But of course, something like that would be a matter of mission policy, not a decision that the two of them could make purely on their own initiative. Keene used his compad right there to raise Gallian, who was bustling about the site somewhere. Keene put the proposition to him.

"A great idea!" Gallian said right away. "Very well. Let's get on with it."

CHAPTER TWENTY-FIVE

The Yarbat AG arrays built into the *Aztec*'s deck structures were working well. They made the whole ship more compact and elegant of line than the ungainly, rotating conglomerations of struts, booms, tethers, and ties that had been gyrating around the Solar System since before Kronia was founded. It was more in keeping with what unaided imagination and intuition thought a spacecraft should look like. Vicki saw it as the beginning of a revolutionary technological era, like those that had brought steamships, trains, automobiles, airliners. And there had been no complaints of the vertigo that affected some people in the older vessels.

She sat in one of the workstation booths provided for personal use, making notes from the latest transmissions from Charlie Hu and Pieter Naarmegen on Earth concerning their biological and geological findings, with comments contributed by Emil Farzhin's group back on Dione. There seemed no escaping the conclusion that the genetic codes that enabled such rapid adaptation to occur had to be present already in the genome. And as already postulated, the most likely mechanism for getting them there, and propagating them quickly through a population, was infection. In itself, however, simply admitting foreign genetic information into cells somewhere in the body wasn't enough. To become a fixed trait in a species, it would have to somehow find its way to the reproductive cells and there be incorporated into the germ DNA to be transmissible to subsequent generations. Farzhin had put forward the suggestion that in fact a mechanism of precisely this nature had been known for a long time, which Terran science had read as reactions to a new class of virus.

It sometimes happened that strong environmental pressures caused cells to begin manufacturing certain proteins on a modest scale, but not a high enough rate to disrupt the cell's normal functioning—unlike "real" pathogenic viruses that caused sickness by killing cells. These packages then budded off through the cell membrane wrapped in a blanket of host protein—the ideal camouflage for navigating the hazards of a hostile immune system—and on arrival at the germ cells were written "backward" into the DNA there by the reverse transcriptase enzyme, tailor-made for the purpose, but whose reason for existence had been baffling researchers since the previous century. In short, Farzhin maintained, the messenger proteins that were the products of some sickness conditions that had been read instead as antibodies to nonexistent viruses. In other words, results were taken to be causes.

The suggestion that alterations to the genome could be triggered by forces in the environment rather than coming about purely through chance flew in the face of what had been unquestionable biological dogma—if not smacking of open Lamarckism, then running perilously close to it. But that was of little consequence to the Kronians, who had seen too many of Earth's once-sacred doctrines come apart in any case.

One of Vicki's favorite examples was the mutations in some strains of bacteria that confer a resistance to mycin antibiotics—at one time widely acclaimed as demonstrating "evolution in action." Of course, the theory had never held that individuals evolve. A cat lives its life and dies with the same genetic endowment that it was born with. What was believed to evolve with the passage of time—either gradually, or in jumps, or however—and get passed down from generation to generation was the accumulating information that makes up the genome. The form exhibited by a species was seen as snapshot of that information expressing itself at the point reached at the time in question. On average, therefore, every meaningful step along the way added some finite amount of information to the growing genome. Or to put it another way, to be considered a meaningful contribution to the evolutionary process, a mutation would have to add genetic information that hadn't been there previously.

But every point mutation that had been studied by generations of researchers turned out to have *reduced* genetic information, not increased it. In the case of antibiotic resistance, the mutations responsible acted in such a way as to lose the specific shape of the docking site on the bacterial ribosome that enabled a molecule of the drug to attach itself there and render the bacterium dysfunctional. The information was lost that was needed to make the fit a precise one. Hence, "evolution in action" turned out to be nothing that could be construed as contributing to the process at all. As in business, where you can't accumulate money by losing it all the time.

Wherever it came from, adaptive genetic information seemed to be already there, in the genome, waiting for cues from the outside to activate it. In another example that Vicki had studied, experimenters had bred a deficient strain of bacteria that normally live on the milk sugar lactose, lacking in the enzymes necessary to metabolize it. But if two particular mutations happened to occur together, they would operate in conjunction to create a path by which an alternative sugar could be metabolized instead. According to calculation, it should have taken about a hundred thousand years for one of the double mutations to occur. In fact, over 40 instances were observed within a few days. But this happened *only* when the alternative sugar was present in the culture. Somehow, the presence of the needed nutrient was triggering the mutations necessary for it to be utilized. This and many other examples like it had been known long before the Athena catastrophe hit Earth, but they had provoked such outrage and controversy among defenders of the faith as to be denied or ignored.

"Luthis tells me it's all coming together," a voice

remarked nearby. Vicki had been too engrossed to notice that Wernstecki had stopped by the booth and was looking in. His gaunt features with their intense eyes and pointy nose beneath his shock of frizzy hair did their best to approximate a smile. "He says Farzhin is firing out one theory after another."

Vicki leaned back in the chair and rubbed her eyes. "And some of the things they're finding on Earth look as if they might be bearing it out already. We're heading for some exciting times, Jan. A complete rewrite of the script. It all happened more recently and faster."

Wernstecki cast an eye quizzically over the screens and notes that Vicki had been working with. Such things were not his specialty, and he didn't pretend to any great knowledge of them. "But doesn't it mean that the whole geological time scale would have to be rewritten too? That's the thing I wonder about when I hear all this."

"Pretty drastically," Vicki agreed.

"I thought it was supposed to have been validated over and over."

"You mean by things like radio-dating?"

"Yes."

Vicki took a moment to save some items on a screen before answering. "That used to bother me once too," she said. "Oh, the theory is solid enough—convert one isotope into another at a known rate, and the ratio will tell you how long it's been going on. But when you get down to the actuality, you run into the problem of contaminants acting to add to or subtract from either or both. That can produce some very different answers. One of the worst can be water, which gets just about everywhere."

"I thought they made corrections for things like that," Wernstecki said.

"But to figure out the corrections, you have to know what the right answer is. And that's where the whole thing got circular. The picture of immense time scales was put together with theories of slow, gradual change already in mind. Radiometric methods came later, and were used to 'confirm' what was already 'known.'"

"The agreements were selected?"

Vicki nodded. "The normal practice was to ask someone submitting a sample the range that was expected. Anything falling too far outside it was rejected as bad data. What was left obviously fitted the theory, and so of course it all held together." Vicki smiled at the expression on Wernstecki's face. "And then you had the assumption that the initial mix of isotopes in the environment hadn't changed. But who knows what changes things like this last incident made in Earth's atmosphere and oceans? That's one of the things the *Varuna* and the *Surya* are measuring." Vicki concluded, "Anyway, Jan, talk to Luthis. He knows more about it than I do."

"I will, when I get a chance." Wernstecki changed the subject by jumping lightly on the floor outside the booth. "Like them?" he asked.

"The AG arrays? I was just thinking before you arrived, it'll change the look of ships forever. No more whirligigs and flying umbrellas. How are they shaping up technically?"

"Not many snags at all so far. We'll see how it goes with the heavy-power, rock-cutting stuff when we get to Earth."

"Lan's department," Vicki said.

"Heard from him lately?"

"Not since they found more survivors." The discovery of migrants in western Asia had been big news aboard the *Aztec*, and presumably back in Kronia. There were unconfirmed claims of other sightings too.

"So it seems that all the people who thought that going back now was premature were wrong," Wernstecki said. "We're just arriving in time to make a real difference."

"Lan thinks so too," Vicki said. She was about to add more, when a message window opened on one of the screens to show the face of Commander Reese, the *Aztec*'s skipper, calling from the Bridge.

"Ms. Delucey."

"Yes?"

"Ahem . . . I wonder if you could come to the Bridge, please."

"Well, yes . . ." Reese's grave expression and tone of voice registered then. "What is it?" Vicki asked.

"There is something I have to tell you. I'd rather it were done face to face, personally."

Vicki swallowed, feeling her mouth go dry. "Very well," she managed. "I'll be there right away." She cut the connection.

"Want me to come along?" Wernstecki asked. "I was heading that way."

"Sure," she said automatically, her mind racing through a score of possibilities.

They arrived less than five minutes later to find Reese waiting outside his working stateroom. "I think this should concern you alone," he told Vicki.

"I'll wait here," Wernstecki told her.

Reese ushered Vicki into the stateroom, which was otherwise unoccupied, closed the door, and indicated for her to sit down. Then he looked at her. "You have a son with the *Trojan* expedition, heading for Jupiter, I understand," he said.

Something tight convulsed in Vicki's stomach. "What's happened?" she whispered.

Reese made an empty-handed gesture, as if to say there was no other way to put this. "We've just received word from Saturn that all contact with the ship has been lost," he said.

A message of sympathy came in from Emil Farzhin and the others in the Academy on Dione not long afterward. Almost two hours later, because of the longer delay times, communications expressing similar sentiments arrived from Keene, Sariena, Charlie Hu, and Gallian on Earth. All of them urged her not to give up hope just yet. But beyond that, there was little anyone could say. It was a time of danger and perils all over the Solar System.

CHAPTER TWENTY-SIX

Rakki and White Head would go; and Gap Teeth would go because he refused to allow Rakki to venture into an unknown and alien domain without his personal protection. It took the Sky People some time to convince him that he wouldn't need his spear.

They summoned one of their winged metal shells that flew like a giant bird—much larger than the one called down by the Sky Being called "Keene," that Rakki had thought of as the head god when they first appeared in the egg with legs that rolled. It descended from the sky a short distance from the huts and opened. Naarmegen, the first of them to use words that were intelligible, came out, along with two others. Rakki and his two companions were taken inside.

Rakki could never have imagined such surroundings. They consisted entirely of strangely shaped creations from metal and other materials that were of the same essence as Old-world objects he had seen . . . but patterned and organized together in a way that formed a totality of purpose that he was unable to comprehend. There were bundles of rods running along the walls and overhead, like vines but straighter and without leaves; patterns of shapes like straight-sided pebbles and slices of berries, some emitting light; constructions that looked the way he had heard ammunition boxes described; flat windows, glowing with designs in colors he had never seen before. Light came from brilliant shapes set into the sides of the interior and above. For the first time since his recollections began of having any coherent impressions at all, it brought home to him the full enormity of what must have been lost. The few relics he had come across of the past that was gone had been just that: oddments and tatters of what had once been a whole world.

They sat Rakki in one of the huge seats that extended past the top of his head, but when they tried to bind him to it with straps, Gap Teeth roared in protest and leaped to intervene. The Sky People seemed amused and were placating, and things quickly calmed down when the three passengers saw that they were securing similar restraints around themselves also. Maybe binding themselves to the Mother Bird was a way of symbolically consigning themselves into her safe keeping, Rakki thought.

One of the Sky People closed the door, sealing them from the outside, and then moved forward to sit at a place near the front, behind the bird's eyes. Sounds like an animal whining and bellowing filled the space around them, and Rakki could feel the bird's life energy pulsing in the floor beneath his feet. Gap Teeth's hands were like claws, gripping the arm supports on the seats. Then he felt the bird move—for a moment his body felt sickened—and he knew they were lifting from the ground. Moments later, through the solid-water windows in the bird's side, he could see the huts of Joburg, the creek that ran beside it, the surrounding rocks and growth, and then the side of the lake where the creek ended, all growing smaller as the bird rose, finally slipping behind and out of view. Soon even the hills were far below, shrunk to the appearance of folds in the mud along the sides of the creek.

Although he had been preparing himself ever since Keene and Sariena, the tall goddess with long hair, offered to bring him to their own settlement, he found himself numbed and awed by the experience. The sense of the power that was carrying them through the skies exhilarated him, as if part of it were flowing from the body of the bird and into his— unimaginable power, like that which could open the ground itself or throw fire into the sky when the mountains thundered; but the Sky People had tamed it to be used, like the beasts that were tamed to carry him. He began to believe that they might really have built another world beyond the sky.

The terrain below lost any similarity to places he could recognize. They seemed to be following the hills northward, beyond the limits that Rakki's people had explored. The hills became more consolidated and grew higher, although not as high as the mountains to the east, which now appeared as black ridges and peaks receding away into the clouds. On the opposite side, to the west, the hills opened out onto jumbled plains of red, brown, and occasional green, again vanishing into haze. There was more water than Rakki had realized existed in the region: rivers hemmed in steep-sided valleys in some parts; chains of connected lakes in others. A wide, flat area that they passed over, where fingers of green and winding channels of water entangled among islands and pools, reminded him of the swamps. In just a few minutes, he had learned more about the lands surrounding his domain than a month of slow, arduous expeditions overland could have revealed.

Gap Teeth seemed just as overwhelmed, and even White Head was unusually silent. At intervals, voices spoke seemingly from the walls and from the flat windows that showed colors. In one of them a female face appeared, as sometimes happened with the things the Sky People carried on their arms. Gusts of wind seized the bird continually, causing it to rise and fall violently. Maybe the straps on the seats were there for more practical and mundane reasons than symbolizing unity with the Mother Bird, Rakki decided. The Sky People left them alone to take in all the strangeness and adjust to it in their own time.

Then Rakki noticed that details of the ground below were becoming larger again and took it to mean that they were going down. A sinking feeling in his stomach confirmed it as the bird's descent steepened. And then he saw what must have been one of the cities that White Head had sometimes tried to describe.

At first it looked something like Joburg, with huts set out in a cluster, rocks and hills all around, and farther off, part of a wide river—running roughly westward, as far as Rakki could judge from the direction of the still-visible mountains. But as the bird came closer, the "huts" gradually revealed themselves as more immense than anything built of thatched boughs and grasses, formed from combinations of sharp lines and curves like the objects inside the bird. And moving around among them were more crawling eggs like the one that had come to Joburg. Rakki made out different kinds of them as the bird came to hover, then resumed sinking slowly. One had a long arm and was lifting something huge, while others nearby were being emptied of things that didn't mean anything. They were for carrying loads, he realized. The Sky People didn't need to tame animals to do their work. They made their own—but with capabilities no animal conceivable in his wildest imaginings could ever hope to match.

The sounds that had been present to a greater or lesser extent all through the journey ceased suddenly. A face was talking from one of the windows to the front again, below the bird's eyes. Naarmegen unfastened his seat straps and stood up, and then did the same for Rakki, White Head, and Gap Teeth, while behind him another of the Sky People opened the bird's side. "This is our base here," Naarmegen said. The word was a new one. So perhaps it wasn't a city, after all. "Name, Serengeti." He then added something that sounded like "Welcome," which Rakki didn't quite get the meaning of either. He stood up, and in response to Naarmegen's waved directions, followed him down the metal steps to the outside.

Out in the open and close-up, the constructions were even vaster than Rakki had guessed when looking down at them. What manner of craft was needed to fashion such things, he had no idea. Farther away in the opposite direction, a number of long columns of white and the silver color showed by freshly scratched metal lay along the ground, and one was standing on end, pointing toward the sky. Something told Rakki intuitively that these were yet larger and more powerful birds that traveled to the domain beyond the clouds. Strange noises came from all directions: droning and snorting like the calls of some animals; banging and clashing; bursts of what sounded like the rapid barking of dogs.

They began walking toward the nearer structures, over ground that was as flat as smoothed sand, yet hard like rock. In one place, a metal animal with an arm bearing a huge bowl, but with flat sides, was digging a trench, scooping as much earth with each bite as a man could move in a day of heavy work. Naarmegen waved a hand and said something that sounded carelessly cheerful. Rakki indicated that he didn't understand. "All a mess. Still lots to do," White Head translated from behind, where he was following with Gap Teeth. Many heads turned to follow them curiously. Some of the figures waved. Rakki was not sure what it meant, and so didn't respond.

They arrived at one of the structures. It was like a cliff or the side of a crag that had been split by a fissure, but made of metal or some other Oldworlder stuff like the made-animals and the birds. Like them, it possessed windows that were solid yet clear. Several steps led up to a pair of doors that opened of their own accord as the arrivals approached.

Rakki's first impression of the inside was that although it was made from Oldworlder materials and lit by their strange light, it felt like being back in one of the caves. More stairs, a greater number this time, took them higher to emerge into a space that was like the inside of the bird, but much larger and with many more people. A group assembled in the center seemed to be waiting for them. Keene was among them, and so was the goddess, Sariena. They greeted Rakki and his two companions, and then introduced another Sky Being called Gallian, whose hair was almost the color of White Head's, but straighter and softer. Everyone was smiling. It seemed strange to Rakki that gods who commanded such ferocious powers should be so apparently anxious not to offend. There was nothing they could possibly fear from these three unarmed visitors who were mustering all of their self-control not to let their confusion and bewilderment show, and yet they were acting as if they conceded superiority of status. It made no sense.

Communicating mainly through Naarmegen, they gave assurances that there was nothing to be feared from the Sky People. They had not come here to make war. Rakki had already arrived at that conclusion. Warrior groups made war because they stood to gain things from those whom they vanquished—food, females, territory, possessions; or simply to eliminate them as potential threats to themselves. His one lingering thought had been that his people might be wanted for slave labor when he learned that the Sky People were building a settlement. But since arriving, he had already laid that fear to rest. They had no need of slaves. They made their own—stronger, uncomplaining, and untiring—slaves who would never drive spears into the masters' backs or slit their throats while they slept.

So what *did* they want?

In the cramped work space that Sariena's planetary scientists had been using aboard the *Surya*, Damien, her assistant, mulled over the results of simulations run from the latest observations of the motions of Athena and the perturbed planetary orbits that Athena's onslaught had induced. The emerging patterns were so intriguing that the group were still up in the ship, even though lab space had been available in Serengeti for almost a week.

There was no doubt now that Athena was circularizing its orbit at a far faster rate than the old Terran theories would have deemed possible. That in itself was no huge revelation. Earlier data had pointed to it; and the old theories hadn't allowed for electrical conditions or the effectiveness of gravitational tidal forces in damping the orbit of a hot plastic body toward lower-energy states. What was unexpected was the way in which the future extrapolations showed sets of resonances in which various Solar System bodies could cooperate in partitioning momentum and energy between themselves in such a way as to minimize further interactions—in other words, establish a new stable configuration—in a surprisingly short time.

"Imagine a bunch of maniac skaters making circuits around an ice rink, all gyrating and flailing their arms," Damien had suggested when trying to explain it to one of the ship's crew. "Every time two of them collide, they send each other off toward other parts of the rink, where there may or may not be someone else to collide with again. If there is, then it repeats until you get to somewhere where there's more room. Eventually everyone ends up with enough space to be left alone, and until something disturbs it all again, you've got a stable system."

Exactly what would happen depended on some very nonlinear equations that made prediction hazardous at best. But the significant thing was that the number of possible solutions being found for them was far greater than anyone had guessed. It meant that the probability of the Solar System rapidly recovering to find a stable configuration was also much higher than had been previously imagined.

What made this even more interesting to Damien was that it added credibility to the suggestion Emil Farzhin on Dione had first proposed, of Venus going into a resonant pattern with Mars and Earth after its expulsion from Jupiter, causing Mars to approach Earth and hang in the sky over northern India for something like twelve years at a time. Damien had found the thought captivating emotionally, but surely too improbable to take seriously without a lot more supporting evidence. Now it appeared the probability of not necessarily *that* particular instance happening, but of at least one from many like it, was not so remote after all.

To add to it, examination of many findings reported on Earth over the years before Athena was turning up more things that were consistent with Farzhin's scenario. No satisfactory explanation had ever been put forward for the sudden rise in sea levels worldwide of around a hundred meters at the time in question, between 3000 and 5000 years previous. Data on ancient lakes and river systems, the depth and distribution of alluvial deposits, and staggering beds of animal and plant remains indicated repeated and massive flooding of the Tibetan-Himalayan region. Yet records from the adjacent areas of China and the eastern Mediterranean told of cyclic patterns in which suddenly receding waters left ships stranded on dry seabeds and ports landlocked far away from relocated coastlines. The number of meteorites found scattered on Earth or in Earth-intersecting near-asteroid orbits with compositions anomalously indicating Martian origins wildly violated all probability statistics based on Mars's always having been where it was at present. And so it went on.

Farzhin's team were continuing their investigations of the Indian *Vedas* and other Terran mythologies. Their latest, even more startling, claim was that under the strange conditions of microgravity that existed between Mars and Earth at the times of their mutual capture, tidal melting of the crustal rocks on Mars had caused immense lava fountains to erupt from the surface, which when cooled on the outside became conduits to convey further flows higher, until enormous, complex, glowing structures were formed, extending as high as a thousand kilometers and clearly visible from Earth. This, they contended, was the awe-inspiring deity that came to be worshiped as Brahma. Shiva, the destroyer, was the power that brought about its eventual collapse when the Earth-Mars bond was broken—in the process producing the layers of peculiarly formed rock shards and fragments covering the Tharsis Bulge region, which had always been something of a mystery. Thus arose accounts of "Jacob's Ladder," "Hamlet's Mill," Atlas supporting the sky, the columns of smoke and fire of Hebrew and Egyptian lore, and various other stairways, pillars, godly phalluses, and the like, that towered above some celestial realm or appeared to offer a bridge for mortals to cross. Damien's first reaction had been to smile and shrug. But slowly, he was being won over.

Now, with evidence mounting to suggest that maybe it wouldn't have needed to be the freak occurrence that had at first been supposed, the question that was coming to be asked was how likely it might be for something similar to happen again. Already, Athena had come close enough to Venus to transfer enough momentum to lift Venus outward several million miles, and future intercepts could creep even closer. One set of possible ways the orbital equations could evolve produced another three-body resonance, this time with Athena in the role previously taken by Venus, and Venus being hurled outward farther to enter into periodic encounters with Earth. Nobody was saying at this stage that it *would* happen; but at least one family of mathematical solutions said that it could. Damien wasn't sure if Earth was ready to undergo another series of Mars-type encounters just yet. Maybe it was just as well, he reflected, that some of the first of the new AG-based technology, capable of cutting and building massive structures out of native rock, was on its way with the *Aztec*. They—or maybe their successors who would one day take over later spells on Earth—might well find they needed it.

A buzz from his wrist compad interrupted. It was Mya Feehn, another of the group, calling from elsewhere in the *Surya*. "What's happening, Damien? Do you know?" she inquired.

"I've been working. What are you talking about?"

The image on the tiny screen looked away, as if wary of being overheard. "Something strange is going on. A pinnace from the *Varuna* docked with us a while ago. And now outgoing communications are blocked—I thought you'd have known."

Damien could only shake his head. "As I said, I was working." But as head of the group in Sariena's absence, it would be up to him to find out—which was what Mya was really saying. "I'll go to the condeck and see what it's all about," he said. "You'll know more as soon as I do."

He cleared the call and got up from the chair, pausing to let the touch of dizziness pass that came from changing attitude too quickly in a small ship. It would mean riding the booms to another module. He set off toward the elevator. But even before he had exited the section that the group's work space was in, a general call over the address system preempted him. "*Attention. This is the Captain. All ship's officers and designated group and project heads, assemble immediately in the Command Module Control Deck. Officers and group heads, come to the condeck immediately. Thank you.*"

There was some congestion at the boom capsule interchange point as persons from different places converged. Nobody knew what this was about. The capsule to the condeck was full, and Damien had to wait through one round-trip before he could board. During transit he saw the pinnace, docked with the *Surya* at a center port. The *Varuna* itself, he was told, was at present out of sight, somewhere on the far side of Earth.

He arrived to find the Command Deck crowded. But strangely, as he looked around for some clue as to what might be going on, he saw that the Captain and ship's officers didn't seem to be in charge of things at all, but were standing in a huddle to one side, looking agitated and subdued. Occupying the center of the floor was a blond, athletically built man in the uniform of an SA major . . . wearing a sidearm!

That was when it hit Damien that other armed figures, brandishing close-quarters automatic infantry weapons openly and ready for use, were positioned around the entire floor. Some were wearing SA uniforms; others, not. Two, standing immediately behind the Captain and officers, were holding unholstered pistols. Damien looked bemusedly at another Kronian next to him. "What's going on?"

"I'm not sure. It looks like they're taking over the ship."

"With *guns*?" Such a thing was unthinkable. Damien shook his head and indicated the SA colonel in the center of the floor. "Who's he?"

"I don't know."

Another man in front of them turned his head. "His name's Kelm. Executive Officer from the *Varuna*."

An amplified voice spoke from a speaker to address the room. "Remain calm. It is not our wish to harm anyone, but if resistance is encountered we will not hesitate to do so. A proclamation will be read on the main screen that should answer most of your questions."

At first, Damien thought it was Kelm who was speaking, but then he saw that the colonel was standing alert but motionless. Before he could ascertain where the announcement had come from, the large view screen facing the commander and chief officers' stations activated. Gasps of amazement punctuated by exclamations of disbelief sounded on all sides. Looking out from the screen was the familiar figure of former General Claud Valcroix, and in the picture a few feet behind, his political partner, Ludwig Grasse. Also in the background were faces that Damien recognized from the political campaigning of recent times as those of prominent former American names from the Pragmatist camp.

"What?"

"But they were all on that transorbital that was lost on the way to Iapetus."

"Where's this coming from?"

"*Wait,*" Kelm called out sharply.

Valcroix began speaking. "I will make this brief, since our position has long been known to everyone. If you are watching this recording, you will already have been made aware of the situation of unilaterally declared sovereignty that it has been our decision to establish over the territory of Earth. The Pragmatist Party of the Kronian world system has endeavored, through the constitutionally approved Kronian political process, to obtain a distribution of representation that would be just and equitable for all its members, regardless of origins, or of beliefs of principle that might differ from those expressed by the present holders of policymaking privileges. We were rebuffed and denied in that endeavor. Therefore, we find ourselves left with no other option but to assert forcibly those rights which we sought to have acknowledged lawfully, but which were refused.

"If the Terran presence in Kronia is to be denied lawful expression, then by the same standard, the Kronians cannot claim to exercise lawful dominion over any territory of Earth. As the representative of, and speaker for, the sole surviving body qualified to exercise authority within those said territories, I hereby do proclaim the existence of the Terran Planetary Government, inaugurated under me as the uncontested President, to take effect as of now. And by that same authority invested in me, I declare all territories, installations, ground works, and other facilities introduced to Earth in the course of the current Kronian invasion of that territory, along with associated spacecraft, air and ground vehicles, and all forms of ancillary equipment and materials, to be rightfully the property of the Terran Planetary Government, seized according to prior international law applicable to those territories in the course of invasion and effective undeclared war. Former Terrans present in those territories are considered subject to such laws that the Terran Planetary Government shall see fit to declare. Kronians not wishing to become Terran citizens or failing to qualify will be regarded as temporary political detainees of status to be determined by negotiation with the Kronian administration.

"My colleagues and I will be arriving shortly to take

direct charge of the recovery operation. In the meantime, I confer upon Kurt Zeigler the title of Acting Governor on behalf of the Terran Planetary Government, and with it delegate full authority to ensure and maintain order across all of the Terran possessions by whatever measures he judges appropriate.

"I ask all of you to help by giving your unqualified support through this difficult period when martial law must take precedence. But until our effective borders are secure, this is forced upon us. The sooner we can consolidate in a socially unified and coherent community, the sooner it will be possible to relax our vigilance and create once again the fabric of more civilized procedures that we all remember." The Pragmatist emblem of a triangular motif pierced by a lightning flash appeared superposed on the picture. Valcroix concluded, "Together, we *will* build Earth again!" The image vanished.

A few seconds of stunned bewilderment passed while the message sank in. Then the protests started.

"They're saying the ships are theirs now? They're *our* ships!"

"How can they get here in that moon-jumper that vanished? It's just the local bus company."

"How can they get anywhere? They're dead."

In the center of the floor, Kelm raised a hand and flipped on the mike attached to a lapel of his tunic. "I think you'll find that rumor was much exaggerated," he said in answer to the last question. He turned his head toward one of the console stations, where a girl with a submachine gun had taken the operator's place. "Transmit the code word down to Zeigler," he instructed.

They had left the cave of metal boxes and talking pictures to move to another of the giant huts. It was less cluttered, with more places to sit, and had great tables, where Rakki and his companions were given food and drink. The food was more varied in composition and tastes than the kinds of things the Sky People had brought with them to Joburg, and consisted of variously colored preparations, some hot, some cold, some wet, some dry, served in dazzling bowls and platters and eaten with metal tools instead of sticks. Rakki still thought of all the beings as Sky People, although Naarmegen had tried to explain that there were two different kinds. Some of them had come back to the world, and others, called Kronian, were from a different world. The only difference Rakki could see was that the Kronians tended to be taller. He had learned other words too, such as "flyer," "ground truck," "building," "screen," "wheel," "compad," and "machine"—although so many things seemed to be described by the last that he still wasn't sure what formed one and what didn't.

It seemed that the intention was for the visitors to be impressed. Sariena, the goddess—a "Kronian" who had come to this world before—and Keene had talked of how all these things were achieved through people working for each other, not through killing and trying to subdue. The message seemed to be that Rakki's people too could learn to command the powers that the gods did and live similarly one day if they changed their thinking and their ways. But if the gods already had the powers they had, and lived in ways that defied comprehension, why would they *care* what Rakki's clan chose to do? They had nothing to gain that he could see; and if over some long span of time they succeeded in turning Rakki's people into another race of gods, then it would only mean risking an eventual clash with them over sharing everything. And yet they seemed to *want* it. There was nothing in his experience that helped him to understand.

The thing that impressed itself on him the most was how utterly unknowing and uncomprehending these gods were, despite all their powers and machines, of even the rudiments of the reality he had lived every day for as long as he could remember. Their smooth hands and soft faces told him that they had never clawed for roots in the mud or under rocks, been swept down a mountainside in a torrent of hot ashes, or fought, crazed by hunger, over a worm-filled bird carcase. He ruled because in *his* world, his way was the only way. The ways of these gods were of no use to his clan. They would quickly be exterminated if they tried to live by them. Was there no other way to command the gods' powers? . . .

Suddenly the gods were no longer paying attention to him and the other two, but talking rapidly among themselves, sounding alarmed. He had never seen that before. Voices were babbling from "compads" and other places on all sides. Keene shouted something at some people across the room. One called back something that sounded like, "Over in OpCom, right now!"

Rakki turned to Naarmegen. "What is this?" But Naarmegen was yelling at someone else and pointing at a screen on the wall.

"*What?*" Rakki demanded again, wheeling upon White Head.

"I'm not sure. . . . Some people have taken over their ship, up beyond the sky."

"What is ship?"

And then a picture appeared on the screen that Naarmegen had been waving at. After a moment, Rakki recognized it as the inside of the building they had been taken to first, the one with many boxes and screens, and windows on all sides. But instead of sitting or standing casually as they had been when he last saw them, the people there were back against the walls, looking tensely at a smaller group occupying the center. One of them was saying something. Rakki couldn't follow the words, but he recognized the figure as the Sky Being Zeigler, who had been at Joburg. Zeigler seemed to be in command, even though the silver-haired one was present who Rakki had been told had the greatest rank. He glanced aside and saw that Keene and Sariena were both staring at the screen in dismay. Something was happening that they hadn't been expecting.

He looked back again. And suddenly a thrill raced through him.

Zeigler and his followers were carrying *guns*! They were asserting dominance and taking command. *This* was a language that Rakki understood. He didn't need to hear the words.

Here, perhaps, was a true warrior that Rakki could follow and learn from.

CHAPTER TWENTY-SEVEN

Armed Zeigler supporters had cordoned off the entrances to the Operations and Communications Dome when Keene approached with Sariena and a string of others from the dorm blocks. They had left Rakki and the other two with Naarmegen and some help to keep an eye on them. The subversives were wearing red armbands emblazoned with the Pragmatist triangle-and-lightning-flash emblem. Most of them, but not all, were SA.

People were converging on OpCom from all parts of the base and being held back, arguing and protesting. Some of them had been inside when Keene was there, and presumably been evicted. As Keene and Sariena pressed forward through the throng, a group of exasperated Kronians surged toward the guards, only to fall back uncertainly when they found themselves facing suddenly leveled weapons. The SA lieutenant commanding the guard detail was Jorff, who had driven out with Keene and the others to make the first contact with the Tribe at Joburg.

"You too?" Keene said grimly as they drew up.

Jorff met his gaze stonily and made the slightest of shrugs. "We're taking our world back. *Our* world."

"And is this how you want to rebuild it?" Sariena challenged. "Starting out the same way, all over again?"

"It's the only way."

A girl in a red armband, standing back nearer the door, had read the name tags on Keene's and Sariena's jackets and was consulting via a compad with someone inside the building. "They can go up," she announced. Jorff stood aside and waved to the others to let them through. Keene was too angry to make any further remark. He shouldered his way past, making sure Sariena was close behind. In the lower level of the dome, a guard watched as a medic attended to a couple of bloodied figures who looked as if they had been clubbed. This wasn't real, Keene told himself.

Pandemonium had taken over the operations floor when they entered from the stairway. Zeigler was still in the center with a number of what Keene presumed were his adjutants. Armed guards were posted around the floor and at places along the walls. A mixed group was confronting Zeigler, in the fore among them, Gallian. The others were mainly Kronian and Kronian-Terran scientific and engineering group leaders, base administrators, and a few Terrans, including Charlie Hu. Keene and those with him in the other building had seen the recording of Valcroix's proclamation, which had been screened there before they left. Everyone seemed to be trying to speak at once. The guards looked on edge and dangerous, no doubt cognizant of the discrepancy in numbers and the magnitude of the risk they were now committed to. Two of the Kronians were waving their arms frenziedly.

"What kind of rule are you talking about?" one of them demanded. "How can there be rule that doesn't emerge from willing support? It makes no sense."

The majority of Kronians wouldn't relate to the concept of subjugation by force. They might be aware of it intellectually from what they knew of Earth's history, but they had no *feel* for what it meant. Overt force was used rarely in Kronia, and then only in *restraint,* to curb behavior beyond what few would question as permissible limits. It wasn't used to impose. A few of a philosophical disposition argued that restraint in itself constituted an imposing of limits; but the rest, for the most part, went about their business happy that the benefits outweighed any cost by a margin huge enough not to be worth quibbling about.

"You can't expect anyone to do anything for you by pointing guns at them," the other fumed. "Why would they? It doesn't make you *worth* anything!"

"After what happened to Limli and Isaan?" someone else was protesting. "You expect us to obey criminals?"

"They were warned," Zeigler replied. "And it should serve as a warning to the rest of you too. Don't underestimate our determination. We shall not hesitate to employ whatever extremes are forced on us."

"Ah, here are Landen and Sariena," Gallian said, spotting them. "Lan, you're a Terran of some practical experience. Tell them this can't possibly succeed."

"Of course it can't!" Keene growled, turning to face Zeigler. He moved a step forward, but two of the guards interposed themselves and Zeigler motioned with his pistol for him to stay back. Keene threw up both his palms. "What's the matter with you people? Can't any of you count? How do you think you're going to keep control of the base and two ships? And even if you could, what good is it going to do you? You have no resources. Developing them is going to need everyone working productively, not split down the middle. This is the fastest guaranteed way to sabotage everything we've worked for. For Christ's sake drop it now, while we can still fix the damage."

"Do you think we thought of this yesterday?" Zeigler retorted. "Just take it from me that such matters are in hand. But to restore some degree of order now, we need to appoint a representative who can speak on behalf of the various interests not yet directly affiliated with us. I was hoping, Dr. Keene, that with your noted organizing and leadership abilities, you might be willing to meet such a need."

"*What*? Cooperate with you? You're out of your mind."

"No. I'm simply asking you to be a spokesman for the various groups that are trying to start a dialog here— Kronians, Terrans. You have experience with both."

"Don't even talk to them," Sariena said.

"You just said we need everyone working productively," Zeigler pointed out. "And I'm agreeing with you. We need your help in organizing just that. Can't you see it's for the good of everyone? Maybe essential to their very survival."

"Then perhaps you should have left things the way they were, running by Kronian methods," Gallian put in. "The Kronians know quite a lot about survival in hostile environments, and about ensuring the resources essential to it." He obviously couldn't resist adding, "Or perhaps you never quite grasped that."

Zeigler looked at him sourly. In his eyes, Keene could see that behind the bold front, the strain was telling. "I suggest that you control your flippancy," he snapped. "Antagonism is not going to help matters."

"*You* accuse *him* of antagonism!" a Kronian woman protested.

Another waved despairingly in the direction of the window facing the pad area and the bleak scene of hilly desolation beyond. "Look outside. You have a world destroyed. The only task is to rebuild."

"Which is exactly what we what to do," another of Zeigler's Terrans chimed in, maybe feeling that Zeigler needed some demonstration of solidarity.

"But you're not. You're starting again the ways that know only how to destroy."

"Look what we built before," the Terran countered.

"And it took, what, five thousand years? More? Look what we built at Kronia in fifty!"

"A few dugout towns and domes scattered across a handful of moons?" Zeigler said dismissively. "We have a whole *world* waiting here. You have no idea what real cities were like, a whole living planet. Just take it from me, your quaint debating-club methods won't do it."

"So you would introduce the methods of what? Of gangsters? Empires? Enslavement all over again? Is that what you want?"

"You don't understand," Zeigler said.

"Damn right! I don't!"

"Will you consider the proposition I put to you?" Zeigler said, ignoring him and looking back at Keene. "As a rational man, you should appreciate that it's in the best interests of everyone. I ask it to make a working compromise possible to best voice the interests of all parties."

"I have considered it, and I already told you: You can

go to hell. If you care about everyone's interests, just climb down and get out of the way."

"I'm disappointed, Dr. Keene. I had hoped for more."

Sariena found her voice at last. "You have to be insane. . . . Do you think you can keep this up indefinitely? A minority like this? Lan already said, can't any of you count?"

"Be quiet, you foolish woman," Zeigler said tiredly. "Do you think there aren't more of us on the way? Of course this was planned to be viable. Not only viable, but eventually impregnable."

"Eventually," Gallian repeated. "Some day in the future? Maybe?" His expression had hardened. He had clearly been angered by the way Zeigler had talked to Sariena. "And what of the reality in the meantime, Mr. Zeigler? Do you imagine that if you insist on bringing your methods back here, Kronians are incapable of adopting them too, if they must. Think about the numbers. Will you ever know who is behind your back? Will you fall asleep easily, knowing you might never awake again?" His voice became quieter, making it somehow more menacing, capturing all the attention in the room. He was advancing slowly, fixing Zeigler with a steady stare. "Will you trust any mouthful of food that you eat? Or where might the bomb be that takes you out, Mr. Zeigler? In your desk? Beneath your bed? Under the path on which you walk?" A guard stepped forward to bar the way, but Gallian pushed his weapon aside contemptuously. The guard looked back at Zeigler for direction. Gallian kept on moving. Zeigler licked his lips. "For that is the world you wish to re-create, isn't it, Mr. Zeigler—your world? And you ask our cooperation? Very well, if you force us, we will cooperate totally in giving you precisely what you ask." Gallian and Zeigler were almost face to face. The rest of the room had become motionless. Gallian continued moving. His hand came up in part of the same unhurried motion, reaching slowly but deliberately toward Zeigler's pistol. "Enough of this, now, I think. Why don't we all just—"

And Zeigler shot him three times, at point-blank range, full in the chest.

✧   ✧   ✧

Far out in space, still beyond the orbit of Jupiter, the *Trojan* had completed a complicated maneuver that involved redirecting its course toward the inner Solar System. But it executed the change in such a way that in an intermediate phase, the vessel's heading was aligned along a precisely calculated minimum-duration trajectory that would intercept the course of the transorbital *Eskimo*, coasting inward from the Saturn system at the best rate its limited design permitted. At this orientation, with the *Trojan*'s forward velocity adding its own maximum component, it launched a freight crate containing six of the boosters that had been brought up from the armory in the course of the SA training drills thoughtfully carried out earlier.

The boosters were intended for carrying fission-pumped laser warheads to a safe detonating distance. But a booster was a booster, and could accelerate any mass that it was properly attached to. Warheads needed to be deployed rapidly, which meant having boosters capable of imparting fearsome acceleration; it also meant that reconfigured for a slower burn, six of them could comfortably gun a moderate-mass vessel up to the kind of velocity usually associated with interplanetary journeys—one the size of the *Eskimo*, for instance.

The crate itself was sped on its way by another two of the same boosters added to its regular propulsion, which still translated into several days before intercept with the *Eskimo*. The *Trojan*'s final course vector set it up to rendezvous with the accelerated *Eskimo* a further week after that.

Walsh was on the Control Deck, rechecking that everything was on schedule and generally keeping an eye on things, when Colonel Nyrom appeared from the Communications Room.

The takeover of the ship had gone more smoothly than they had dared hope, with the number of SA who had agreed to come over exceeding expectations. The dissenters, including a higher proportion of crew, had yielded without too much trouble and were now detained and out of the way for the duration. The scientists didn't much matter, because after their initial show of protest and bluster, they'd prattle for a while, as was already the case, and then get back to the things that concerned them, pretty much regardless of who was in charge. Walsh had never had much time for them when he was an Army man. Lots of smart ideas and blueprints for how the world should be run, and always with themselves in privileged positions of influence. But always from behind the throne. They needed strong men to hide behind and do the dirty work that they didn't have the guts to do themselves. This operation wouldn't be any different.

He turned and raised an eyebrow inquiringly as Nyrom approached. Since there was no doubt who was running the ship now, they could speak openly.

"Regular communications from the *Varuna* and the *Surya* are being blocked," Nyrom informed him. "No confirmation signal yet."

"Already?" Walsh frowned. It could only mean that Zeigler had made his move there. Official notification would come from Party headquarters, currently aboard the *Eskimo*. "It doesn't really affect us yet," he said curtly. "We'll hear in good time."

Nyrom waited to be sure that Walsh had nothing more to add, than said, "And there was another thing, Captain."

"Yes?"

"Delucey did an exemplary job supervising the launch procedure for the booster crate. He's worked conscientiously and efficiently throughout. I'd like to put a request through right away for promotion to lieutenant-commander. We're going to be needing more junior officers soon—and good ones."

"I agree. See to it."

It was clear that Walsh wasn't in a talkative mood. Nyrom took his leave and left the Control Deck.

Walsh moved a few paces to run a cursory eye over the displays at the First Officer's station, then turned to contemplate a screen showing the external view inward toward the ship's hub. He hadn't liked even the delay between takeover of the base on Earth and arrival of the backup force that was in the plan, and had said so when it was formulated. But the political experts behind the throne had theorized that the population there would be easier to handle if there was still essential survival-related work waiting to be done. The feelings of vulnerability would make them more compliant. Walsh hadn't been overly convinced, and behind the glib talk he suspected they knew more about charts and statistics than the nature of real humans. But he was a soldier, and that was the way it had been decided. And now Zeigler had brought the date forward further still. He would be isolated there if anything went wrong. Walsh could only suppose that he had his reasons. They had better be good ones, he told himself.

PART THREE

The Gods

CHAPTER TWENTY-EIGHT

Having taken over the ground installations and the *Surya*, Zeigler was effectively in control of the mission. Thinning down his forces to physically seize the *Varuna* beyond placing guards in the Control Center and Communications Room was not necessary, since with its power module down at Serengeti the ship wasn't about to go anywhere, and without cooperation from the ground it could accomplish little else. Its occupants were not equipped to resist armed boarders, and the ship could be taken over fully when the time was convenient.

The real reason why the SA contingent had been included with the mission and why such a large proportion of them were disgruntled young Terrans who couldn't fit into the Kronian system, was now glaringly clear. They concealed a hard core of Pragmatist sympathizers who, given they were prepared to act ruthlessly enough, might well be sufficient to maintain their position.

Maintain their position until what? For the moment, the majority of the base's inhabitants were at a loss. Even those who might have been capable of acting had been taken by surprise, with no plan or chance to organize. But that would change. The Terrans had a long history of finding ways to resist coercive violence, and Kronians were fast learners. Yes, for now Zeigler and his followers had the guns; but they couldn't imagine it would be possible to dictate to such a numerical majority indefinitely. Hence, they anticipated being reinforced in some way before very much longer, and consolidating their position.

To Keene's mind, it said that taking over the *Aztec* had to be part of their plan too—it was already on its way to Earth with more equipment and materials, accompanied by another flotilla of supply rafts. And who knew how many more Pragmatist supporters might be included among its numbers? But it didn't necessarily follow that they would make their move there at the same time as Zeigler. In fact, it would make more sense for them to bide their time until the events on Earth could be concealed no longer. That meant there was a fair chance that the most effective way of throwing a wrench into the Pragmatists' works might be to contrive some way of getting a warning out to the *Aztec*—thus depriving the Pragmatists of that whole factor in the equation.

But how? Zeigler's people controlled all communications beyond the *Varuna*. Keene still hadn't come up with a means that seemed viable a day after Zeigler's coup. Then Zeigler summoned him to be brought over to the Operations and Communications Dome for a "discussion."

Zeigler summarized from behind the desk in the room he had taken over in the office section on the upper level. Two armed guards stood inside the door, a short distance behind Keene's chair.

"I expect you and your staff to maintain power from the *Agni* module as normal. Failure on that account will merely prevent the continued growth of the base toward full functionality, putting everyone out there that much the more at risk. I trust I make myself clear."

It was blackmail. By "everyone out there" he meant all of Keene's kind—those who were not part of the takeover. Zeigler and his cohort had moved in to take full control of the OpCom dome, installing quarters for themselves on the lower level, surrounding it with a wire fence, and posting guards at the two gates. OpComs had its own standby generator, which meant that if Keene cut off the power from *Agni* it would only be depriving everyone else, and stopping further development of the facilities. In other words, it wouldn't do Keene a lot of good, but it could cause friction between him and some of the others out there. It was Keene's call.

Right now, Keene could see nothing to be gained by creating further disruption. He was up against a classical no-win bind: either cooperate or risk incurring the kind of resentments that those who would divide and conquer just love to precipitate. Zeigler had also intimated without threatening openly that if forced, he would resort to taking hostages. Keene had no doubt that he meant it. Zeigler was past the point of no return and had nothing to lose by going to any extreme now. Maybe that had been his purpose.

"Do you really think you're going to get away with this?" Keene asked. No prizes for originality, but he was fishing. In his answer, Zeigler might give away something useful.

"Why don't you let us worry about that, Dr. Keene?" Zeigler suggested.

"Gallian said it all. Do you think you're ever going to sleep easily at night now?"

"I've tried to address that issue tactfully. We'd prefer not to be driven to taking extreme measures. But if you compel us . . ." So the victims, not the perpetrators, would be responsible. The old terrorists' and kidnapers' ploy. But some of the Kronians had already halfway bought it.

"Time isn't on your side," Keene said.

"Don't you believe it."

"Really? Why not?" What did Zeigler think was going to happen to change things?

But Zeigler showed no inclination to elaborate. "In fact, time could be something you might profitably put to use yourself while you have it," he said. "Eventually, a new state will take root here. A state based on realistic understanding of the forces that must inevitably emerge and then clash in the running of a complex society. We have a world rich with resources. Kronia has a few balls of ice. Don't be caught on the wrong side when the real test comes." Zeigler paused pointedly. "Ours could be very generous in its rewards for those who worked with us from an early stage."

Keene's fists snapped shut, and he almost sprang from the chair, but checked himself as he remembered the guards behind. "I already told you, you're out of your mind," he said tightly.

"I wasn't asking for an answer now, or expecting one," Zeigler said. "But something for you to think over, nevertheless. As I suggested to you before, things would be considerably eased for all if a single spokesman were appointed for the others. Perhaps we can resume this conversation when the time is more opportune." He nodded to the guards. Keene started to say something but Zeigler cut him off. "That will be all for now."

One of the guards came forward. Keene stood. The other opened the door, and they ushered him out.

Shayle was still numbed when Keene joined her in the power distribution house, next to where *Agni* was sited, behind the workshop domes. She and two technicians were running power factor and frequency tests, watched by a couple of Zeigler's guards. Keene told her that it would better serve the interests of everyone if they carried on as normal for the time being. The decision didn't seem to come as any great surprise to her. As a Kronian, she would have been hard put to conceive in any concrete form exactly what else they were supposed to do. Just at the moment, Keene was far from having much of an idea himself. They moved through a switchroom annex behind the control room and went outside via a door at the far end, where they could talk away from unwelcome ears.

"What else did he say?" Shayle asked. She stood in the pose of women gripped by anxiety, pulling her jacket tighter around her as if she were cold. In fact the wind had shifted to the south and did have a chilly nip to it.

"The proposition about being a spokesman and making it easier for everyone, again," Keene answered. "Only this time laced with a dash of promise of being well looked after when they run their Brave New World."

"You didn't agree, did you?"

Keene shook his head. "No . . ." He let it hang for a moment. "But things could reach the point where something like that might be the best course. The strategy of people like that is always to divide the opposition among themselves. That's how tyrants stay in power. Speaking through one person could keep us united and make it more difficult."

"You mean you'd cooperate with them?"

Keene sighed. "See how they get you? They've got you doubting me already."

"I'm sorry, Lan." Shayle put a hand to her brow and shook her head. "I've just got no instinct for dealing with this. . . . None of us have."

"I know."

Shayle stared out past the domes and structures of the base at the hills outlined against a dark, angry sky. "So how bad could it get? How does a minority like this keep control over a whole community?"

"You've already seen how," Keene said grimly.

"But they can't shoot everybody. There's got to be a line. Push people beyond it and they'll simply revolt en masse because they've nothing to lose. I do know something about Earth's history, even if I never lived it."

Keene shrugged. "It's like I said. You divide them against each other. Single out individuals and make examples of them. Take hostages. And if you've got the guns, you can do things like control the food"—he gestured at the wall shielding *Agni*—"or the energy supply. When you have power over people's ability to make a living and survive, they'll do what you want." As an afterthought, he added, "Controlling the distribution of wealth created by others was how the elites who ran Earth operated for centuries. If 'slavery' means being coerced to work for the benefit of others, maybe it never really was abolished. They just replaced the blatant physical kind with things that were more subtle." He looked at Shayle curiously. "I never thought about that before. Maybe there are more reasons for Kronia's determination to stay away from introducing a monetary system than I realized."

"But for how long?" Shayle persisted. "How can something like this it last?"

"Look how long it lasted on Earth," Keene replied. "Even then, it took Athena to end it."

Shayle shook her head. "But surely this is different. That was a whole world of mutually supporting interests. We are just . . . this. They're obviously not so stupid as to believe that they can hold on indefinitely as things are. They must be expecting some kind of reinforcement."

Keene nodded. "Yes, I'd already come to the same conclusion."

"But who?"

"What else can it be but the *Aztec*?"

Shayle stared at him in the kind of disbelieving way that said it was too obvious. "Of course," she said tiredly.

"It's got the AG lithoforming prototypes to make big, secure constructions here. Profab equipment to create a diversified industrial base. That would give them a start to expand from."

"Would it be enough? Obviously there won't be any more follow-up missions from Saturn now."

Keene could only shrug. "Maybe that's a gamble they decided to take. With a whole planet full of resources here for the taking, waiting to be developed . . ."

"By whom?—if they have to spend all their time keeping the rest of us in line."

"By us, working for them. That's what it's all about. And in any case, we don't know how many more of them there might be coming with the *Aztec*. That could change the balance of numbers a lot."

Keene gazed around restlessly. One of the guards had come through into the switchroom to keep an eye on them, but he was staying back at the far end. Keene dropped his voice. "Saturn will figure out that something's wrong here from the communications blackout, but it might take them awhile. So the Pragmatists might not have made their move on the *Aztec* yet. It still might not be too late to get a warning to the ship somehow. We need a way of getting access to the *Varuna*'s or the *Surya*'s communications."

Shayle stared at the bank of cable ducts and piping running from the power building through the shielding wall around the *Agni,* and then looked back into the room full of equipment behind them. Something was taking shape in her mind. Keene watched her face silently and waited. When she spoke, her agitation of a moment ago had given way to a deeper, more distant thoughtfulness.

"Suppose we staged some kind of problem with *Agni*'s power system down here that needed diagnostics and repair directions from the *Varuna* to fix. At least that would put us in touch with the engineers up there."

"But *Agni*'s self-sufficient. It wouldn't need any help from up there," Keene pointed out.

"You and I know that. But Zeigler doesn't."

Keene stared at her. Of course! The shadow of a grin softened his face. "And then we play it by ear from there," he completed.

"Something like that."

Keene checked it through in his mind again. There was no obvious flaw that he could see. And time was crucial. He nodded. "The sooner the better, then. We'll need to cue Gus and Blinda in on what we're doing." They were the two Kronians back inside the power house. He thought for a few seconds longer. "Can you dream up something, Shayle? It would probably look better if I weren't around when it happens. Let Zeigler's people come to me when you discover the 'emergency.' "

"That's fine. Leave it to me," Shayle said.

They made a cursory show of checking displays and equipment in the switchroom, then went back into the main distribution control center. "I'm done here for now," Keene said to the guards. "I need to go back to the dorms." It stuck in his throat to have to ask it, but the formality was already established. One of the guards nodded. Keene left via the door connecting through to the workshop domes.

CHAPTER TWENTY-NINE

Keene found Sariena in one of the partly completed work areas in the Laboratory block, where the planetary scientists had been in the process of moving into from the *Surya*. The next phase of their program involved adding a hangar at the base to accommodate ground-launched probes for detailed mapping of the Raphta peninsula to supplement the longer-range surveys being directed from orbit. They were carrying on according to the original plan but in a mechanical kind of way, with the enthusiasm gone, as if unsure anymore what the point was of any of it.

Adreya Laelye had approached Zeigler, claiming that her capacity as SOE's senior representative gave her the authority to speak on behalf of the rest of the base. Probably she felt an obligation to show some such responsibility, since officially Zeigler himself had been next in the mission's line of command after Gallian. Zeigler, however, had been unimpressed, stating that he would deal with a representative of his own choosing at such time as it suited him to do so. Keene had expected something like that and had confided as much to Sariena. But both of them had agreed that Adreya should be allowed her chance to try. The outcome had left Sariena feeling all the more despondent.

"It isn't just confusion over this setback we have right

now," she told Keene. "But suddenly it seems as if"—she waved an arm, as if searching for words in the air— "everything we've been working for could be in danger. It's going to be the way it always was, all over again, isn't it? Nations and then empires built on crushed human spirit. Tacitus said it over two thousand years ago, didn't he: 'To robbery, slaughter, plunder, they give the lying name of empire; they make a desert and call it peace.' "

Keene looked at her in surprise. "Did he? You know, it never ceases to amaze me how much Kronians know about Earth."

"What makes people that way? Can it be something about the planet, do you think?"

"Oh, I'd say more a question of being conditioned there."

"Not something inherent in human nature—permanent, unchangeable?"

"Then why not the Kronians too? Aren't they human?"

Sariena shook her head, not wanting to pursue it. "Just now, I don't know what to think."

Owen Erskine crouched in the cover of a trench leading into a pit at the rear of the Lab block, where concrete was due to be poured for a foundation. He had come down from the *Varuna* to help set up the ground-based probe mainten- ance hangar intended for the base. But since then a new priority was demanding attention, and nobody else seemed to be doing much about it. Landen Keene, whom Heeland had introduced in the probe bay up in the ship, had struck him as the kind of person who might take the lead in standing up to somebody like Zeigler, but his crew were continuing to provide power for the base as if nothing had happened. There was a rumor going around that Adreya Laelye from SOE had gone in to see Zeigler with some kind of demands that morning and been thrown out. Others had done a lot of talking but not much else. It seemed that everyone was paralyzed after the Gallian shooting. Well, things like that had always happened, always would, and life was the art of working around them. Someone would just have to make the first move in shaking them out of it.

The two guards were posted together as had been the

pattern since yesterday, at the base of the crane behind the stores buildings, from where they could watch the rear area of the base. The location also meant that they were screened from most of the other directions where activity was going on. From time to time, one of them would patrol to the far end of the stores complex, check past the corner toward the workshops and the power installations, and retrace his steps. The moment Erskine had chosen was the next time one of them was halfway along the route, out of sight from the rest of the base.

Dru, a one-time Turkish landscaper, was in position by a stack of pipe sections, hidden from the guards but in view from the trench where Erskine was. Ida, also Terran-Kronian, was up on a work platform in the scaffolding behind the crane, securing lighting cables, again in sight of Erskine and waiting for his signal. The two Kronians who had agreed to join them were concealed among crates stacked behind the storage buildings. Kronians were no different from anyone else in having what it took, Erskine was convinced. All it needed was for someone to show them how. With a couple of weapons in their hands, it would be that much easier to acquire more. Then the rest of the base would get the message and follow suit, and the whole thing would be over by the afternoon. Erskine hadn't come all the way home to be pushed around by a bunch of jerks like this.

The guards exchanged a few words, and then one of them detached to commence another slow amble along the familiar line. Somehow, just from the way he moved, Erskine could tell he was Terran. Erskine touched a button on his compad twice. Three answering flashes on the "channel" light told him the two Kronians waiting in that direction were ready. He signaled to Dru, who raised a hand in response, and Ida, who touched her nose. Erskine watched until the guard was almost at the point he had marked, then made a "go" motion in the air with his hand.

Ida emitted a cry and tumbled from the platform to a plank forming part of a walkway from a ladder a few feet below. The guard by the crane turned toward the sound, and simultaneously Erskine and Dru emerged from cover.

It was only a matter of a few yards; a quick, silent rush was all it needed. . . .

But something—either Ida's fall wasn't convincing enough, or maybe the way her gaze was directed—made the guard look back. It was like one of those moments when a person is about to have a car accident and can see everything happening in slow motion, but finds themselves powerless to intervene; or a dream where running seems to be through jello and doesn't consume any distance. The guard's gun was coming up, and Erskine was still too far away. The plank walkway should have enabled Ida to arrive quickly too, but she had barely picked herself up. Seeing the situation, she hurled a wrench in desperation but it clanged harmlessly off part of the crane base as the guard fired. Erskine found himself reeling, folding out of control like a boxer whose legs have gone, then his head thudded into the ground as he fell heavily and drunkenly. He knew he had been hit in the stomach, but for the moment he felt nothing and was only aware in a detached kind of way of Dru staggering backward as the guard fired again. Another shot sounded in the direction the patrolling guard had gone. Erskine rolled over to look along the rear of the stores building and saw one of the Kronians kneeling, clutching his chest, the other standing a yard or two back with his hands raised, the guard covering him. Running footsteps were already approaching. The voice of the guard who was closer came, directed at Ida. *"Drop everything you are carrying. Now come down from there, very slowly."*

Erskine let his head fall back in the mud. Yes, the whole thing was over. And well before the afternoon.

" . . . as soon as Shayle figures something out," Keene told Sariena. "The idea is to get access to a channel up to the *Varuna.* Then, hopefully, we'll find a way from there."

Sariena went quiet, thinking over what he had said. "Valcroix and those others with him aren't going to get here in the *Eskimo,*" she replied finally. "Which means they'll have to transfer to something faster."

"Another reason for taking over the *Aztec,*" Keene said.

Sariena looked uncertain. "So what does it do? Coast while

the *Eskimo* catches up? Or would it be quicker if they went back to meet it?"

"I'm not sure. You're the orbital specialist."

"And you're the propulsion engineer."

They were both tired. Keene showed his hands. "Either way, the sooner for them, the better. So we need to do something fast. The more I think about it, the more it seems it has to be too late already."

Sariena smiled thinly. "That doesn't sound like you, Lan. But you'll try anyway, right?"

"Damn right."

After another pause, Sariena added, "Although, if it's true, it means that *Aztec* won't be getting here so soon. So Zeigler can't be counting on it for reinforcements anytime soon. Why did he make his move when he did? It means he has to hold out that much longer. Why wouldn't he have waited?" She raised her eyebrows. Keene could only shake his head. "Could he be expecting to strengthen himself in some other way?" Sariena asked.

"What other way is there?"

"Maybe there are more Pragmatists here than have shown themselves yet."

That was a thought. "Maybe . . . which could make loose talk very dangerous," he mused.

"That was my point."

The door from the lab area burst open to admit Charlie Hu with bustle and haste, which was unusual. Voices were babbling somewhere behind him. "There's been some shooting!" he said. "Behind the stores."

"Anybody hurt?" Sariena asked as they followed him back out.

"I don't know yet."

"It was only a matter of time," Keene muttered.

They came out of the building behind a gaggle of figures who had stopped in the face of several guards brandishing guns. "*Back inside,*" one was yelling. "*Everybody back inside.*"

"What's happened?" Charlie Hu asked one of the construction people.

"Some guys got shot trying to rush the guards."

"Oh no. Anyone killed?"

"We're not sure."

"I saw Ida being led away," a Kronian girl said. "She looked as if she was all right, though."

"Not Ida," Sariena groaned. They had been friends on the *Surya*.

Keene was shaking his head. "Never mind how it works in movies. You don't go for guys who have guns and nervous fingers. It's not the way."

One of the guards looked up from talking into a compad. "Is Maria Sanchez, the medic, here? She's needed."

"I think she's back in the dorms somewhere," somebody answered. The guard relayed the information.

"*Everybody, back inside,*" the one who had spoken before ordered again.

Kurt Zeigler returned from the lower level of the OpCom dome to the office on the floor above where he had installed himself. Kelm, who had left an occupying force aboard the *Surya* and come back down to Serengeti during the night, accompanied him. The Kronian woman and one of the two Kronian men were unharmed. The other Kronian was shot in the legs and would recover, as would the former Terran who had been wounded in the stomach. The second ex-Terran, shot twice in the chest, was in serious condition. "I want a portable cabin set up behind OpCom as a secure medical facility and detention building, another for guard quarters, and the perimeter extended around them," Zeigler said. "Also, we need elevated watchtowers. Give me a plan by eighteen hundred tonight for a minimum number and recommended sites. Fast and basic. We can start work on them under arc lamps tonight. Also, put out a general order, effective immediately, that until further notice gatherings of more than five persons are prohibited unless express approval is obtained. And a curfew, effective twenty-two hundred to six hundred."

"I'll see to it," Kelm said.

Zeigler sat down at his desk to scan the low-priority reports listed on his screen. "So it seems that Kronians can have some fighting spirit too," he observed. "Could it mean that some of them might turn around yet, and see things our way, do you think? We could use some volunteers."

"I can't say," Kelm replied, trying to be tactful. "It's all so unprecedented. Anything could happen."

News from the *Trojan* was that the maneuver to boost *Eskimo* onward toward its rendezvous point had been executed successfully, and everything was on schedule. A message from *Eskimo*, however, had strongly questioned Zeigler's decision to act now, far sooner than had been planned. But the plan hadn't taken any account of the opportunity to strengthen Zeigler's force from an unexpected source with natural killers. The recruits might be rough raw material, but they were the kind that, with discipline and training, fanatical followers are shaped from. To do something about it, however, he would first have to be in control. So he had gambled that by risking the short term, during which potential opposition would be confused and in disarray, his grip would be firmer in the long run, when they'd had a chance to organize.

"How are Rakki and the other two doing?" he asked Kelm.

"Just sitting, waiting it out. At least they're smart enough to know when they don't have much choice," Kelm said.

The three natives who had been at the base yesterday when the Gallian incident occurred were still being detained, the main reason being simply that there had been more urgent things to take care of than taking them home. But it also saved Zeigler the trouble of having to go out to Joburg himself to put his deal to them. Keene's timing in bringing them here couldn't have been better.

"Then maybe it's about time we had a talk with them," Zeigler said.

"Shall I have them brought here?" Kelm asked.

Zeigler thought for a second. "No. We'll go over there," he replied. "And use that translator of ours who's been studying the tapes. We need to get her up to speed. Obviously the South African can't be involved in this."

CHAPTER THIRTY

The room that Rakki, White Head, and Gap Teeth were being held in was formed from the same kinds of materials as the crawling shell that had come to Joburg, the bird that had brought them to this "base" they called Serengeti, and the few other parts of it that they had seen since. The structure was not woven from anything, but consisted of unbroken sheets of a size and extent that amazed him. And how it was all fastened together such that the greatest force he could bring to bear failed to produce even the slightest bend or movement was a mystery. Doors opened silently of their own accord; light appeared at the touch of a finger; shining handles gave forth endless streams of water, hot or cold, and clearer than was found in the pools of high-mountain streams. How it was possible to create such things intrigued yet confounded him. He had seen the strange shapes from which the Sky People were constructing the base, and from which, presumably, they had also built their even vaster cities. And then, beyond that, what manner of knowledge of forces and powers enabled other creations to move themselves across the ground and fly in the sky?

Surely, Rakki would have thought, these were the god-beings that White Head had talked of, which people had once believed were to humans as humans were to animals and came from the sky. But no. White Head said they were human, just like himself, Rakki, or any of the others at Joburg or back in the caves. And that in itself was a challenge both to Rakki's hunger to know, and to his pride. For if they were human, it meant that *he* could learn too. And if other humans commanded such powers, a leader of any stature would have to show himself as capable of possessing them too.

"You say they are humans like us." Rakki brought the subject up again. He sat with his legs stretched along one of the fine woven-hair beds, his back propped against the wall, and addressed White Head, sitting in a chair at the table, causing pictures and lines of strange symbols to appear on a screen. White Head seemed to have an idea what some of the symbols meant. Gap Teeth was sitting cross-legged on the floor, silent and unmoving. He said the chairs were the wrong shape and too soft. They made him feel as if his bones were dissolving like salt stones dropped in a cooking pot.

"Just like us," White Head said again.

"But they are *not* just like us. You tell me they make these things from essences that lie hidden in rocks. But I have broken rocks and examined them, and I do not see these things. Why can we not make machines from essences of rocks if it is not because the Sky People are different?"

White Head pushed himself back from the table but kept his eyes on the screen. "They are different only in what they know. In the same way, you know much and Shell Eyes's baby knows nothing. But it is as human as you, and will become like you."

"Are you saying we are nothing but children?" Rakki challenged. He didn't like the comparison and felt anger at the suggestion.

"When it comes to learning the things the Sky People know, yes," White Head answered, refusing to compromise. Rakki knew it was true and let it go. White Head called the achievements of the Sky People "miracles"—things that required knowledge that was beyond normal understanding. It had been discovered little by little and passed down from generation to generation, always growing, for longer spans of time than Rakki was capable of grasping.

He still didn't know what to make of the confused impressions he had been getting ever since these gods who were not gods first appeared at Joburg. Keene, whom had first thought to be the head-god, and the long-haired goddess had told that the knowledge White Head spoke of came from people working with each other; that the ways of war prevented learning and brought only sorrow, pain, and destruction. They had brought him to Serengeti to see, and he had met the greater god Gallian, that even Keene served.

But what Rakki had seen was that the world of the gods did not exist as all working together in the way Keene and the long-haired goddess had said. They fought each other too—as those who burned with the inner flame that compels them to command and to rule were always driven to fight. And Zeigler's gods had proved the more powerful. He ruled, and Gallian was vanquished. Gallian's gods were reduced to servants as the Cave People had been made to serve their conquerors from the Swamps. So what was Rakki to make now of the things that Keene and the goddess had told him? If the gods didn't achieve their miracles by working for each other after all, then why had they tried to convince Rakki otherwise? Perhaps as a way of inducing Rakki, and hence all those he too ruled over, to work unconditionally for *them*. Now *that* would be a ploy that he had no difficulty understanding.

He heard the door opening and looked across. One of Zeigler's warriors came through and stood aside to make way for Zeigler himself, followed by another, muscular of build and fair like Yellow Hair. A female was with them, yellow-skinned and with slanted eyes. She put Rakki in mind of Hyokoka, the woman that Gap Teeth had claimed back at Joburg. Rakki swung his feet down and stood to meet them, and Gap Teeth rose from the floor. White Head turned in his chair.

"The warrior chief comes to us?" Rakki muttered, surprised.

"It is captives that are summoned to their captor," White Head said. "He is telling us we are as guests."

The female came forward. She seemed to know that White Head did most of the speaking and addressed herself to him, though acknowledging Rakki with glances of her eyes. "She is the talk-between for Governor Zeigler," White Head supplied—although Rakki had understood that much himself. "Her name is Leisha. The Governor regrets making us stay here. There are many troubles in Serengeti." Rakki nodded, satisfied. He felt he was being treated like a leader, not a child.

"We are not offended. He rules the mightier tribe," Rakki said. White Head seemed to take a long time passing it on, probably adding some words of his own.

Zeigler pondered while he studied Rakki searchingly, as if for a hint as to how best to broach the matter. Probably head-on and direct, he decided. The undisguised awe that Rakki had shown toward firearms ever since the first contact at Joburg, and the evident impression that yesterday's action had made on him, said they spoke a common language. "Tell him, more of us will arrive soon. Then we will be a truly mighty tribe."

Leisha interpreted with some trial and error. "From the . . . it sounds like 'gods' place,' beyond the clouds?"

"Yes." The image suited Zeigler fine. "But until then our numbers are small. Rakki and his Tribe could help make our position stronger."

An exchange ensued between Rakki and the old man, who was called Yobu. Leisha did her best to follow, at the same time keeping up an intermittent commentary. "Zeigler has the guns. . . . Why doesn't he just kill his enemies? . . . Because then they couldn't work for him. . . . They have the knowledge to . . . the nearest I can come up with is, 'perform miracles.'" Then Leisha concluded, "But Rakki says the Tribe does not have a large number of warriors. . . . He would be honored to help the god-Governor . . ." Zeigler had to bite his lip to prevent a smile from softening his features, " . . . but he wonders how much difference they would be able to make."

"He spoke before of more who live in caves and swamps to the east, beyond the mountains," Zeigler said.

"He does not rule that tribe. His enemy rules there."

That was something Zeigler hadn't known. He glanced automatically at Kelm, but Kelm's expression said he had nothing to offer. Zeigler frowned. And then the obvious angle suggested itself. He looked back at Rakki while continuing to speak through Leisha. "Suppose that in return for helping us, we help him remove his enemy. Then he will rule all the tribes. And we will have more allies." The flash in Rakki's eyes told Zeigler the answer before Leisha had finished translating it.

She went on, "But even with greater numbers, how could his warriors be a worthy addition to yours, who possess wondrous weapons?"

"If they join us as I ask, then they will have such weapons too," Zeigler promised.

Just then, the compad in Kelm's tunic pocket beeped. It was set to accept priority interrupts only. He took it out and raised it to his ear, keeping it on audio only. His eyes flickered unconsciously over Zeigler as he listened. "Yes, he's here with me. I'll put him on." He passed the set to Zeigler. "It's OpCom. The power control room is reporting some kind of problem with the *Agni*. They've put out a call for Dr. Keene."

"I should get over there," Zeigler said. "Stay here and make arrangements to get these people back to Joburg. See who we can spare to make an instruction fire-team. I want a dozen at least of Rakki's fighting men to begin small-arms familiarization right away. Also, find out what you can about these other people over the mountains. They sound like the material we could really use. Maybe that chief of theirs that this guy here is ready to take out is the hook that'll get them for us."

Aboard the *Aztec*, Vicki sat playing a solitaire game, her eyes following the cards as she turned them but not really seeing them. Tanya, who had ended up as Vicki's cabin mate, watched from a folding seat on the far side of the cramped space. She and Vicki's other friends had tried to arrange things such that someone was always with her ever since contact with the *Trojan* was lost. There had been no further news from Saturn.

"His father was killed in a Navy accident when he was just a boy," Vicki said, almost to herself. "So I did the single-parent thing for a lot of years. Then Lan appeared and we started the consultancy in Texas, and he was probably the nearest thing to a father that Robin ever really knew. But he was always more of the loner kind of a kid— forever with his head in a book, or immersed in some project that he'd found on his own. Finally, he did start getting something of a life and friends together . . . and promptly lost all of it. Of course, everyone was affected. But Robin never really got over it. He was bitter and withdrawn the whole time we were on Dione. Nothing seemed to get through to him. Lan tried, so did Leo Cavan—he was a friend we'd known since Earth. Joining the Security Arm seemed almost like an act of defiance sometimes—as if he was trying to get some kind of message across. But then maybe it was just a way of escaping. I remember when he said he was going on the Jupiter mission, Lan and I thought it might have been the best thing that could have happened."

Tanya sat, letting her talk it out. At least she wasn't insulting Vicki's intelligence by reciting inane things like "no news is good news," or any of a dozen other platitudes that the occasion might have prompted.

Vicki contemplated the situation, conceding defeat, and shuffled up the cards to begin dealing out the array again. "Did you ever meet Sariena?"

"The Kronian scientist who was with the delegation that Gallian took to Earth?" Tanya shook her head. "No, but I've heard of her. Why?"

"She used to talk about the Kronians' belief in us and the universe being here for a purpose—the opposite of what they used to teach on Earth. You were on Kronia long enough to know. Is that the way you see things too?"

"You mean about there being some kind of intelligence at work at the back of it all, that it was designed for a reason?"

"That's part of it, yes. But more than just that. The whole experience of existence serves a purpose. Not so much what you become or who you end up being in worldly terms; but the *experience* itself. Period."

"Well, yes, that's how I was raised to think back home,

so it comes pretty naturally to me. So many things make more sense that way. The particular person that you happen to be right now isn't especially significant—like a vehicle that you use for a while, and then you're done with. But there's a more permanent something behind them all."

"You mean a soul?"

"I'm not sure. I don't know if people mean the same thing when they use words like that. But something that creates personalities of the right nature and in the right circumstances to undergo the experiences that it needs to learn and to grow. At least, that's the way the Kronians I've talked to described it. I'm not really sure what I think, though."

"Yes, that's what I was getting at," Vicki said. She wanted especially now to believe that there were good reasons why things happened the way they did; she needed to talk and hear about such things. Before she could put it into words, however, a buzz sounded, signaling that someone was at the door. Tanya touched a button on the remote lying near her.

"Yes, who is it?"

"Jan Wernstecki here. Is that Vicki?"

"Hi, Jan. No, it's Tanya. But Vicki's here too." As she spoke, Tanya touched in the number to open the door.

Wernstecki came inside. "Hello," to both. "How are you feeling, Vicki?"

"I'll get by," Vicki said.

"What is it?" Tanya asked.

Wernstecki looked mildly perplexed, as if at a loss to explain something. "I never believed in jinxes before," he told them. "But you know, I'm beginning to think there's one over this whole thing that we're involved in. I've just heard it from the Bridge. Now there are communications problems with Earth. Electrical disturbances are swamping the whole region and affecting the links to both the *Varuna* and the *Surya*. They're restricting traffic to official use only—and that's very intermittent. The last that came in beamed at us said to hurry up with the lithoforming gear. They think maybe they're going to need it."

Which meant there would be nothing more coming in from Lan either—at least, for a while. Vicki's dismay must have shown on her face. Tanya leaned forward and rested a hand lightly on her arm. "I know. Don't let it get to you, Vicki," she said. "Just try and believe it's all for a reason."

Keene and Shayle did a good job of simulating problems with the *Agni*'s delivery system, which they solemnly diagnosed as being due to instabilities in the plasma focusing fields. Keene concocted a line of mumbo jumbo to the effect that they would need cooperation from the engineers up on the *Varuna* to rectify matters, and Zeigler authorized a communications channel to be opened. But the *Varuna* engineers were unable to make a lot of sense out of what Keene was telling them, not the least reason being that it didn't make any sense, and he was unable to clarify things further because Zeigler's people insisted on monitoring the link closely.

For the same reason, it quickly became clear that he wasn't going to gain access to anyone connected with the ship's communications, let alone initiate any kind of outward-going message for the *Aztec*. So, after playing the charade through for what he judged was long enough to be convincing, he announced the problem to be magically cured and signed an engineering report to that effect, leaving the *Varuna* crew bemused and confused—and Zeigler's observers, he hoped, none the wiser.

He then went out to the edge of the landing area to stand staring at the hills and brood on his own.

CHAPTER THIRTY-ONE

A bulletin put out by Zeigler's office the following day brought the news that Dru had died from chest wounds; Erskine and one of the two Kronians involved were wounded but not critically; Ida and the other Kronian were unhurt. The four survivors of the incident were being held under arrest according to the martial law condition that had been proclaimed. By the same terms, perpetrators of further such attempts would be liable to execution by shooting automatically. Entry to the extended secure zone around the Operations and Communications Dome and its annex was not permitted without authorization; a general curfew would apply to anyone not having business outside after 22:00; and until further notice, outside gatherings of more than five persons other than for recognized work groups was prohibited. The design of a triangle pierced by a lighting flash, along with the words *Together, we* will *build Earth again!* were appended.

Keene and Adreya Laelye drove out with a relief crew in one of the general-purpose site runabouts to view progress with the shuttle silos and launch pads being constructed on the far side of the landing area. The runabout had four wide wheels on independent axles like the larger Scout, an enclosed cab that could hold three with a squeeze, and an open rear section like a pickup, but which could be tipped to function as a dump truck also. The work going on currently involved forming revetments and foundations from a ceramic foam that dried a fraction of the weight of concrete but with strength of the same order. It was intended as an intermediary measure until heavier construction and full industrial startup capability arrived with the *Aztec*. The talk, however, as most of the time, concerned the takeover and its implications. They stood by one of the trenches, watching the skeleton of alloy mesh being emplaced, around which the foam filling would be blown.

"We've all read about it," Adreya said. "But to actually witness it is something completely different. Even the idea of a minority having control without general support of the followers is inconceivable. Never mind imposing it."

"Yes, I know," Keene told her. "Sariena's been saying the same thing."

"The obsession for amassing wealth beyond any conceivable need is something we just can't relate to. To us it's as pointless as compulsive eating." Financial obesity, Keene thought to himself as he stood with his hands thrust into the pockets of his parka. That was an interesting way to put it. Jon Foy had said something similar. Adreya went on, "But now that I've seen it, and what people can be driven to in pursuing it, I think I know what it is that motivates it." Keene cocked an eyebrow at her inquiringly. "It's insecurity. Fear. They have nothing to offer that anyone freely wants, but they depend totally on others for everything they need. So to feel secure, they must have the power to compel."

Keene had listened to similar things from Kronians but never heard it put quite that way before. He remembered being told in earlier times that one of the big fears of the fabulously rich was very often that of finding themselves penniless, even when simple arithmetic showed it to be something they'd have a hard job achieving if they devoted the rest of their lives to trying, but he'd never really understood it. "Well, they can always build bureaucracies," he commented. "That way, you create lots of rules that don't benefit anyone, and then make a comfortable living catching people for breaking them. And you do it at their expense. Pretty neat when you think about it."

"I never understood how someone could possess ownership rights to the wealth created by another." Adreya sighed. "It seems that whenever things reached the point of there being money in something, that always destroyed it."

How true, Keene thought, looking back. Small wonder the Kronian leaders were set on the unique economic system that their experiment had brought into being. He was about to respond, when he saw Pieter Naarmegen approaching beside the low wall forming the top of one of the molds. He was wearing a quilted cap with ear muffs, his face pink in the wind behind his straggly beard. He looked at Adreya uncertainly for a second, seemingly trying to convey that he wanted to talk to Keene privately; but then his expression changed to one that seemed to say, *Heck, if I can't talk in front of the representative of SOE . . .*

"What is it?" Keene prompted.

It was a good place to bring up subjects that weren't for general audiences, since the guards hadn't attempted to secure the far sector of the pad area. For one thing, there weren't enough of them to spare any for such a task; and for another, there was little out here that it was necessary to guard against. None of the ships could move without clearance codes from ground control, and there was nowhere to bring unloaded cargos back to except the base. And the background of construction noise made a good privacy screen against other ears that didn't need to know.

"A group of us have decided to split," Naarmegen said, directing himself at Keene. "Your name is one that was voted to be invited."

"Split? Where to?"

"Anywhere. Just out. We're not prepared to play ball or live like this. There's no way they can seal this part out here. We arrange to leave a Scout here at the pad, stock it with gear and supplies, and then move out to it in small groups early in the evening. Hell, Lan, there isn't anyone out here to stop us. We take off at night, in the opposite direction from the base. By daybreak we'll be miles gone."

"When?"

"We haven't fixed it yet. When we've got the Scout fitted out. Probably tomorrow or the night after."

"How many?"

"A dozen so far."

"Big load for a Scout."

"This is Earth, not some moon without an atmosphere. We can put some on the trailer. Zeigler doesn't have the manpower to come after us."

"He can still send out probes and recce drones. They'll find you in an hour."

"And what would they do? They're not armed. And even if they were, what would be the point?"

"Who knows with someone like Zeigler? Maybe just to demonstrate who's in charge, and that you don't step out of line."

"That's a risk we'll take," Naarmegen said.

Keene eyed him dubiously. The practicalities were a secondary issue, he could see. It was a gesture that Naarmegen needed to make. He wasn't asking for Keene's endorsement— just a simple yes or no as to whether he wanted to be included.

"I wish you luck, Pieter, but I don't think it's the way," he said. "I need to be here."

"To do what?"

"I don't know yet."

"So what is the way, Lan?" Adreya put in.

Keene made a shrug that said there was no glib, ready answer. "You observe, you organize, you prepare . . . and wait for your opportunity."

"And if one doesn't happen?" Naarmegen asked.

"Then you find a way of making one happen."

In the Communications Room of the *Trojan*, Captain Walsh viewed a decoded message from Grasse's assistant on the *Eskimo* that the consignment of boosters had been retrieved successfully, and they were being fitted to the vessel on schedule. There was also news from Zeigler that the situation at Serengeti was stable and under control after some minor reactions. There was still no indication of why Zeigler had moved the date forward from that originally planned.

✧   ✧   ✧

Kurt Zeigler had made a name for himself around Europe in the circles connected with arranging finances for international sales of sophisticated weapons systems. The deals that he specialized in were frequently engineered to bypass the laws and technology-transfer regulations of the governments involved, sometimes making expedient use of third parties; at others, by contriving ingenious shell games involving holding companies and transfer agencies to confound audit trails of exactly who was being paid by whom and for what; and on occasions, resorting to outright falsification of documents describing the equipment involved or its intended purpose.

Larger-scale conflicts deserving of being called "wars" had become a rarity by the time of pre-Athena Earth, not so much as a result of any marked advance in the direction of humanitarian restraint on the part of the world's governing eminences, but more because military solutions to capturing markets essential for continuing capital expansion and denying them to non-approved economic systems were becoming too expensive and unpopular. However, ongoing tensions in various places between ethnic groups that had been inappropriately mixed or forcibly separated, and the reluctance of many local populations to appreciate the benefits of the global financial and economic order that was going to bring the Millennium, had kept business buoyant and profits respectable. Zeigler had graduated to the big league by buying out the interests of a pair of overly-trusting business partners at a discount when a negotiation was cooling, and then making a killing on a fast sale to a second buyer, whose existence he had been less than forthcoming about. That was when he came to the notice of Valcroix and his associates, and his rise to a position of influence in the international political-military scene quickly followed.

The same processes shaped business and politics as produced people who were fit to rule others and build empires. The weak and the inept were consumed to make room for the strong and the skillful. Dominance and survival were the rewards of excellence. The rules might be harsh, but it wasn't he who had made them. They were

the same rules that had directed life's upward struggle from
its emergence out of primeval ooze, and through ruthless
competition and selection eventually produced minds capable
of comprehending them. They were the rules of the real
world. The world of the Kronians was a dreamland based
on a naive ideology that could never survive outside the
artificial protectorate they had created. That was why they
rejected things that science had known for two hundred years
and invented fanciful, supernatural purposes to account for
inconvenient facts and contradictions they were unable
otherwise to explain. Ironically, the "primitives" who had
survived understood reality better than the sophisticates who
would presume to teach them.

But then again, was it so ironic? They were both products
of their respective worlds, after all. The Kronians brought airy
ideals from the starry, uncontaminated halls of Kronia. The
survivors had already qualified by every test Earth had to offer.

Accompanied by Leisha and two guards, Zeigler walked
out with Rakki, Yobu, and Enka, to where the flyer was
waiting inside the OpCom perimeter fence. He had had red
shoulder tabs sewn on his tunic as a mark of his rank. It
was just after dark. Lieutenant Jorff and the two troopers
who would also be going to Joburg to commence the
weapons training were standing outside, silhouetted against
the lights—a small enough number, but as much as could
be spared. Rakki turned as they got to the machine, and
raised a hand toward Zeigler in salutation in the way he
had learned. Zeigler returned it. He had declined to introduce the custom of shaking hands.

"When we meet next, your guards will carry weapons like
these too," Zeigler said.

The reply came back as, "He will make sure they are
worthy. . . . I think he means worthy to be sent here to help
out."

"I'm sure he will perform the task well."

"And then we will make him ruler of the caves?"

"And then he will rule the caves."

Leisha joined the departing party as they climbed aboard.
Zeigler watched with his guards while the flyer taxied
away a short distance before opening to full power and

climbing steeply to clear the fence. Then he turned and led the way back to the OpComs Dome.

These natives were material that definitely had potential, he reflected. And yes, he could use the additional manpower. But beyond that, the existence of such a force, armed, trained, and loyal to him, could prove a factor very much to his advantage when the Party leadership arrived, and the internecine disputes and clashes of interest that reality said were inevitable sooner or later began breaking out. And now there was news from the *Varuna* of more survivors, numbering possibly several hundred, spotted on the eastern coast of the Raphta peninsula, trekking northward toward the warmer zone. He didn't have the time or the resources to create a trained army. But if he moved fast enough to at least get them aligned with him in the way he had done with Rakki, it would go a long way to making him a formidable force to reckon with indeed.

On arriving back in his office, Zeigler was informed by Kelm that Naarmegen and a group of others were planning to desert either tonight or tomorrow. Their plan was to use a Scout vehicle that would be left for the purpose among the constructions in progress on the far side of the pad area. How did Zeigler want to deal with it?

"Do we know who they are?" Zeigler asked.

"A dozen in all. I have six of the names other than Naarmegen so far. All from the scientific and clerical staff."

"Where do they think they're going?"

"There doesn't seem to be any clear idea. It's mainly a demonstration—to get away."

Zeigler turned it over for a while. "And how far are they likely to get?" he said finally. "There was enough trouble getting to Joburg overland." He tilted his jaw. "We do nothing at this stage. Let them proceed. Just follow their progress for the time being. If they get into trouble, it will serve as a warning to the rest."

"We're happy about letting the vehicle go?" Kelm queried.

"It was only used for scientific work. That's low on the list. And it will be a dozen less for us to watch for now.

Let them go." Zeigler thought for a moment longer, then added, "And in any case, why reveal that we have our information sources out there to no useful purpose?"

Keene learned about it from Shayle later that evening, when they were having supper in the dorm blocks cafeteria. "He went out himself to see them off? And Jorff went with them?"

"Plus two troopers and the girl who's been their translator. A couple of welders who were working on the annex roof watched them go. They left in a GP personnel flyer."

Keene chewed on his food and frowned as he tried to divine some meaning from it. Supper was Kronian chicken-flavored soy compound and reconstituted vegetables with a salad from the *Varuna*'s hydroponics unit. Although he should have been used to such fare by now, he hoped it wouldn't be long before Serengeti got some tilling and stock-rearing of its own under way. "What do you make of it?" he asked when he'd swallowed finally.

"It seems like the flattery and camaraderie line. The only thing I can think of is that he has plans on recruiting them."

"For what?"

"Presumably, to add to his troops."

"Rakki's Tribe? But there aren't enough of them to make a difference that would be worthwhile."

"What about the others to the east, where Rakki and his band came from? Weren't there supposed to be a lot more there?" But even as Shayle said it, she was shaking her head. "No, that couldn't work, could it? Rakki and their chief are sworn-to-the-death enemies."

"It seems that way, doesn't—" Keene halted in mid-sentence. "Unless . . ."

"What?"

"The idea is to remove the other guy and put Rakki in charge of the whole roost. That would be an old enough trick. You couldn't get a more devoted follower than that. And that would add significantly to the number of soldiers Zeigler could expect." Keene stared distantly at the wall as further implications opened up. "More soldiers not just for now, but for later too, maybe . . ." His voice trailed away.

Was Zeigler playing a longer and more complex gamble—

to strengthen his hand for when potential rivals arrived, perhaps? But what quality of recruit could he expect to produce in the time he had available? Keene thought back to the first contact with the Tribe at Joburg, their total unfamiliarity with even the rudiments of an advanced technology, the near panic that merely a low pass of the probe over their heads had caused. . . .

And then, suddenly, a completely different light came into Keene's eyes as everything he had been thinking about a moment ago was forgotten. He turned his face back and stared at Shayle with the expression of someone who had just received a beatific vision.

She stopped eating and waited. Finally, she invited, "Lan, what is it?"

"The probe," Keene answered distantly. "That probe that sucked in an arrow and was grounded the first time we went to Joburg. It's still there, somewhere up over that ridge up above the place. Owen Erskine was supposed to be arranging for its retrieval, but he's been having other problems lately. . . . It's still up there, Shayle, up on that ridge. And it has its own independent emergency channel to Survey Mission Control up in the *Varuna!*"

CHAPTER THIRTY-TWO

Sariena found Charlie Hu in one of the cubicles in the Lab block, contemplating a screen showing analyses of atmospheric samples that the probes had collected from various places. He seemed to have detached himself from recent events by turning inward and immersing himself in his work. "This is interesting," he said, inclining his head. "Athena has changed the isotope mixes of carbon, argon, nitrogen . . . all of the elements we've studied. If the same thing happened with the earlier Venus and Mars encounters, it would invalidate the assumptions that most conventional dating was based on. . . ." He turned his head finally and registered the look on Sariena's face, saying that other matters were preoccupying her just at the moment. "What?"

She kept her voice low. "Lan and Shayle came to talk to me. Lan's had one of his ideas again."

Charlie pushed himself back from the worktop where he had been writing. "What about?"

"Did you know that a probe was disabled at Joburg on the day the Scout made the first contact there?" Sariena asked.

"Was it? No, I didn't. I was still up in the ship then."

"It's still there, grounded somewhere up above the Joburg

settlement. With everything that's been going on, nobody has done anything to retrieve it. Apparently, the probes are equipped to function as mobile emergency relief posts. More to the point, they have a communications system that bypasses the regular net and uses a special band to link via the circling airmobiles to the probe control section up in the *Varuna*."

"How do you know all this?" Charlie asked.

"From Lan. Owen and one of the controllers showed him the system when he was up there."

"Owen Erskine? The guy who got shot?"

Sariena nodded. "Yes. But the thing right now is that Lan's talking about using it for another try at getting a warning out to *Aztec*."

Charlie looked perplexed. "But how can he, if it's at Joburg?"

"That's the whole point. He thinks he can get there. But it isn't like getting from California to Texas and Mexico this time. Everything has changed since then. And he had others with him then. He'll get his chance, but he needs better odds than these. Shayle agrees. But we're not Terrans, Charlie. How can we try to tell him what he'd be taking on? It needs someone from Earth, and who was with him then. We want you to try and talk him out of it."

"How do you think you're going to get there?" Charlie demanded. They were standing with Keene on the edge of the pad area, outside the *Agni*'s shielding wall. Farther away, in front of the silo and pad constructions, a shuttle was being elevated in readiness for launch. Keene turned to gesture back toward the excavations on the far side of *Agni*, where various vehicles and machines were working.

"One of the general-purpose runabouts. They've got the right torque and speed for the terrain, wide wheels to get through the sticky patches, and you could turn one on a dime. Given the kind of going I'd estimate from what I saw with the Scout, I'd say a day, maybe a day and a half."

"But they're electric. They don't have the range."

"Rig one up like the Scouts. You put a diesel-generator set in the truckbed and drive the motors off that. I figure that thirty-eight gallons of diesel fuel should do it. A regular drum holds over fifty. I plan on taking two."

"Wouldn't the generator set need to be secured somehow?"

Keene shrugged. "Drive out for an hour on the fuel cells— which will also mean a quiet start. Then drill a few holes and bolt the set on before switching over to the generator. Okay, so add another couple of hours."

"You think you're just going to load up a runabout and drive away? Like no one's going to notice or say anything? And even if you managed to just disappear, they'd have probes out searching within hours."

"There are always some runabouts left out at the pad workings. Naarmegen's group are leaving from there tonight. If I arrange to disappear at the same time, it will seem that I decided to join them at the last minute. Any probes will be looking for the Scout. A runabout's a lot smaller. And visibility from anywhere above a few hundred feet tends to be pretty hazy and patchy in any case." Keene nodded decisively. "I think there's a good enough chance of making it." He waited, watching the contortions following each other across Charlie's face, as if somehow able to read from them the thoughts forming within. Finally he emitted a knowing sigh. "Okay, Charlie, I'll spare you the agony," he said. "Shayle and Sariena think it hasn't got a chance, and they asked you to try and stop me because you're someone that I'll listen to. Is that close enough?"

Charlie nodded. "Yes, that's about it, Lan," he admitted.

"Okay, then, let's hear it. There are just too many hazards and unknowns out there. Zeigler's too far gone now to stop at anything. If the *Aztec* hasn't been taken over already, it will have been by the time I get there." Keene listed the alternatives in a weary voice. "What's the line, Charlie?"

"As a matter of fact, I wasn't thinking anything like that at all," Charlie said. "What I was thinking was that Kronians found this world intimidating even before any of this happened. Four hands are better than two for things like bolting generator sets to trucks. And that anyone getting hurt on their own out there is going to be in real trouble." He tugged at his tuft of a beard and met Keene's eyes squarely. "The only thing I'd try and talk you out of is this crazy idea of doing it alone. I'm coming too."

Keene's position of running the primary power system for the base made him responsible for overseeing backup arrangements too, so there was no difficulty in acquiring a generator set. He had Shayle collect one from the stores in a GP runabout, along with an assortment of tools, and then ferry it out to the construction area, ostensibly for a standby installation to be located there. She then came back with a returning work crew in a site bus. Keene and Charlie took the rest of their gear and supplies out at intervals through the remainder of the day. It really was as straightforward as that.

Shortly before midnight, a transformer located in the rear part of the base experienced a mysterious short circuit to the accompaniment of spectacular arcs, clouds of white smoke, and considerable noise. The diversion had been requested by Naarmegen, but there was no reason for Keene and Charlie not to take advantage of it too. While guards ran around hurrying the on-duty technicians from the power house, and searchlights that normally wove desultory patterns around the pad area were turned rearward to illuminate the scene, the two escapees slipped away from the main complex and followed a roundabout route along the side of the pad area. Keene had arranged for Shayle to leave the runabout at a remote spot on the outskirts of the construction workings, which was also well away from the storage sheds for unloaded shuttle freight, where Naarmegen's Scout was concealed. There was no point in taking a larger than necessary risk of getting involved if the other group encountered trouble. Another reason why Keene had chosen to stay apart and not reveal his own intentions was the possibility that Naarmegen's approaches in recruiting for the larger group, despite his best attempts to exercise discretion, might have been picked up by informers.

They lay low, watching for a while, but the surroundings remained quiet and undisturbed. Keene concluded that his fears had been groundless. By this time, a pump was running over in the base complex to clean up the foam from the transformer fire—and also to cover any sound from across the pad area of the Scout starting up and leaving. It was also as good a time as any for Keene and Charlie to be on their way too, they decided. They emerged from cover to climb into the cab, Keene taking the driver's seat.

He had equipped himself with night-vision goggles to help navigate through the darkness, since they wouldn't be able to use the runabout's headlamps until they were well clear of the base. However, there had been no time to put them to any practical test, and as things turned out their value proved limited. They operated by intensifying the images produced by low-level sources like starlight, but in the near total blackness below the post-Athena clouds there was precious little of anything to intensify.

As soon as they left the cleared area of the base, Keene found himself running into rocks and sliding down slopes of soft-formed sediments. He knew straightaway that this was going to be a very different affair from traveling overland in a Scout, which with its balloon-tire wheels and swiveling axles could traverse just about anything. After a particularly violent lurch off a clump of boulders that felt for a moment as if the runabout was turning over, they resorted to the expedient of Charlie shining a flashlight ahead through the windshield, waved in response to Keene's hasty directions. But at best it could reveal only incoherent glimpses of what lay in a few tens of feet immediately in front, keeping their progress down to a crawl. Already, Keene was finding himself forced to revise his estimates of how they could expect to fare tomorrow.

CHAPTER THIRTY-THREE

As dawn approached, they were still on the ridge leading down from the plateau, following the same route that the Scout had taken on the first contact journey, but having covered less than half the distance that Keene had estimated. With the runabout's fuel cells almost exhausted and its yellow-black marking designed for easy visibility, they couldn't afford to stay up on such exposed ground any longer. It was imperative to find some kind of concealment where the diesel generator could be fitted without inviting detection from search probes.

The ridge ran roughly north-south, and consisted for the most part of heavy flood deposits laid over the scarp of a tilted crustal block falling gradually in the westward direction toward the coastal plains of the newly forming African Sea. Naarmegen's plan had been to head that way, seeking some kind of temporary haven in the valleys lower down. The eastern side, by contrast, formed the edge of the uplift and was steep and rugged, with faces shaped by immense fractures marking the line of the fault, and breaking lower down into a chaos of rock falls, fissures, and volcanic extrusions. But Joburg lay that way, farther south among the hills beyond the end of the ridge.

As the first light began filtering through the overcast,

Keene steered toward the east, looking for a way down. "Why don't we give that a try?" He waved his hand, indicating ahead and to the left. From the shelf that they were following, a ramp of loose rock and shale, with a steep drop on one side, sloped down toward a broad, gravely basin. The far side of the basin was lost in banks of early mist, and whether or not it offered any continuation on down was anyone's guess.

"Looks pretty slippery and flaky," Charlie said.

"It's probably the last chance we're going to get before the power runs out."

"I guess that decides it, then. Go for it."

Charlie's caution about the descent being slippery turned out to be too true. The rocks were covered in an algal slime, which with the morning condensation turned them into skating skids. Before they were a quarter of the way down, the runabout was sliding and swerving on a moving wave of scree, its steering alternating between intermittent and nonexistent. The ramp narrowed alarmingly between the drop to the left and a bulge above, but they were carried on through by the tide of rocks converging into a funnel, while Keene wrestled the wheel without effect. Then the ramp widened but tipped outward, sweeping them toward the edge. Keene had lost all control and could do nothing but hold on and let whatever was going to happen, happen. But at the last moment the wheels grounded on the solid rock forming the rim of the drop, and he was able to crash to a juddering halt, slamming the heavy generator set into the rear of the cab behind them. Charlie let go of the hand grips to wipe his palms on the thighs of his jump suit, emitted a long, shaky breath, and managed, magnificently, to say nothing. Keene licked his lips, reengaged drive, and kicked them off back toward the ramp's inner side.

They reached the basin to find it cut into a maze-like confusion of sandy ridges and fissures, causing frequent changes of direction and doubling back. Some parts of the depression became miniature canyons, with slopes of greasy clay giving treacherous passage past pools of oily sludge, and cracks of unknown depth. By this time Keene was watching the charge indicator anxiously. If they had to, they could have tried rigging the generator here, but the whole area was a trap for sulfurous fumes venting from below-ground, stinging in the nose and eyes, and catching the back of the throat. It wasn't a place to stop, so long as there was any choice.

By now, the ridge they had come down from was no more than a darkening of the mists behind them. The general incline of the basin floor was increasing, but more rapidly in the center which fell toward what turned out to be the head coomb of a valley. The lower reaches narrowed to a chute, while the sides rose to become walls, depositing them finally in a long, sloping amphitheater that ended in a pool fringed by banks of rocks, reeds, and mud. Keene steered gingerly along one side of the pool and halted. Before them, the pool emptied as a waterfall between rock shoulders into a boulder-choked ravine falling away below. There was clearly no way farther down from here. The only course would be back up to the basin, and to try for another route from there.

"We'll probably be better off out on the ridges than try-ing to follow the streams, anyway," Keene said. "Water takes the steepest way down."

"As long as the ridges don't end in cliffs," Charlie agreed.

But for the time being, it was as good a place as any to stop and mount the generator—not that there was much option in any case, since the cells were about done.

In fact, this place was better than many they might have picked. An updraft from below the waterfall played against the vapors drifting down from the basin to create an enhanced haze above, which also helped keep the air around the pool breathable; and in its position between the rock walls, the runabout would only be visible from directly overhead. But before they would be in a condition to do anything, they needed to rest. They snacked from the sup-plies they had brought with them and a flask of coffee, still refreshingly warm, and then settled down to doze in the cramped cab as best they could, improvising padding and pillows from packs and folded parkas.

✧   ✧   ✧

"A fraction more to the right . . . Okay, hold it right there."
Keene tapped the last bolt through the lug in the mounting
frame and the hole he had drilled in the bed of the truck,
while Charlie applied pressure to keep them aligned, and
checked that it was sitting squarely. The generator set looked
okay, although it had dented the rear wall of the cab enough
to tear the metal when it had been flung forward. "That'll
do it."

Charlie relaxed his grip. "You know, Lan, it's as well we
brought that extra drum of fuel. The way we've been zigzag-
ging about and backing up already, I'm beginning to think
we might need it."

"Well, see, that's what you get from being an engineer,
not a scientist, Charlie. Scientists straddle their best guesses
with error bars. Engineers assume worst-case."

"But you were both, right? Didn't you do theoretical work
on plasma physics at Harvard?"

Keene straightened up and heaved a leg over the edge of
the truck, feeling with his foot for a step to climb down. "Can
you pass down the wrench and the nuts for the outside?"

"Here."

"That's right. But science had become an intolerant
religion more concerned with putting down heresies that
challenged its theories than finding out how things really
were."

"I know. I've seen the list. It's been a long road from
JPL to Kronia."

"There—in that box. I'll need the locking washers too. . . .
At one time I used to say that science was the only area
of human activity in which it actually mattered whether or
not what you believed was true. In just about everything
else, what was important was *that* you believed, not
what you believed. Then I decided that scientists were no
different. So I changed it to 'engineering.' You can fool yourself if you want, but you can't fool nature. If you get the
wings wrong, your plane won't fly."

Keene ducked down to locate the first of the bolt ends
protruding through the truck bed. An ugly, lizard-like creature
was staring with huge, unblinking eyes from a muddy niche
between the rocks. Keene didn't like the look of it. He waved

the wrench at it threateningly, and it vanished between some clumps of moss. He threaded on the nut, semi-tightened it, and rose back up to collect the next.

"What's your take on this Kronian belief in a higher power?" Charlie asked.

"The only answer I can see is that you can't rule it out."

Charlie nodded, but, it seemed, reluctantly, as if he didn't want to agree but could find no alternative.

Keene went back down below the truck bed, raising his voice to continue. The air down off the ridge was heavy and muggy, making him perspire. Serengeti was well placed up on the plateau. "It's tough readjusting when the only thing you've been told all your life is that the nuts and bolts are all there is to it, for no reason."

"It doesn't seem to have bothered you too much," Charlie commented.

"Oh, I've always gotten fun out of tilting against the orthodoxy. . . . And anyway, a lot of it rubs off from Vicki. You'll need to talk to her some more after the *Aztec* gets here."

"I already know. She was terrific when Sariena and I visited her on Dione, with Emil Farzhin."

There was a silence until Keene came out from under again. "Do you really think there's still much chance of getting through in time?" Charlie asked.

"Whatever it is, it isn't something I can change," Keene replied.

Charlie eyed him curiously. "Have you ever given up on anything in your life, Lan?" he asked.

Keene paused to think about it. "I don't think so, not really. . . . I guess I've always been too scared to."

"Scared?" Charlie looked surprised. "How come?"

"It seems like one of those things where once you start, it could too easily become a habit," Keene said.

Charlie filled the tank for the diesel, while Keene secured the electrical connections to the runabout's drive system and set the transformer taps and rectifier control. The diesel started after a few seconds of coughing and spluttering. Keene checked the generator output, and after a couple of adjustments the motors were responding with all power indicators reading correctly. The last thing they did was camouflage the vehicle by smearing on a layer of mud, paying special attention to the bright yellow stripes, and adding some leafy sprigs and clods of grass for good measure. Keene was quite pleased with the result. "That's it. We're ready to go," he announced.

But they were far from where they had planned to be by this time of day. And having to detour back up into the basin would set them back more. They agreed they would try to force a way through without going all the way back up the scree ramp to the ridge—which was probably impractical anyway. Instead, they would try to leave the basin over the shallower rise on its south side, beyond which what looked like a descending spur seemed to extend in roughly the direction they needed to take.

Jorff reported to Zeigler from Joburg that the fifteen native males of fighting age that Rakki had supplied were proving to be quick and efficient learners. Leisha was working with Rakki and Yobu to produce a map, based on their recollections of the journey they had made, showing the region where the larger cave and swamp clans lived. When they had made the best job of it they could, Zeigler would order a probe reconnaissance of the area to pinpoint the locations. From Yobu's accounts, and allowing for growth in numbers since the exodus of Rakki and his followers, Zeigler though it might be possible to increase his force by at least a couple of hundred. And then there was the new band of survivors on the far coast to be investigated.

He had just cleared down from Jorff's call, when the message indicator flashed again. This time it was Kelm, from the new hangar that had begun operating ground-launched probes. "We've found them," he informed Zeigler.

"The Scout?"

"Right. It's about sixty-five miles west, following the river, making for the coastal plains."

"That was fast work. Did we get a break in the weather for once?"

"Even easier. Something on board has got a locator

transponder that they didn't turn off. I sent a probe there to confirm visually—from long range."

"Good." There was no point in tipping them off. "Just keep them under observation for now."

"And there's another thing," Kelm said.

"What?"

"Apparently, no one's been able to raise Keene this morning. The people who deal closest with him are vague. I have a hunch that maybe he changed his mind and went too."

"How vulnerable are we if they have any more trouble with the power system?" Zeigler asked after a pause. "Is that second of his still here, Shayle?"

"Yes, she's here. I checked."

Zeigler pondered for a while. Maybe they would have to institute more stringent measures to make sure that key personnel stayed around. That was something he'd hoped to avoid until the new recruits began arriving. He couldn't afford to have his credibility put to the test and found lacking. Hence, at this stage, letting the people in the Scout go had been preferable to trying to stop them. The risk now, on the other hand, was that it would send a message to all the rest.

"We can't be seen not to react," he said finally. "Have all vehicles either locked in the depot overnight, or parked on the near side of the pad area, under lights and guarded." Kelm nodded, but his expression said that he wasn't satisfied with it either. With all the activity going on around the base, it would be impossible to guarantee policing against one slipping away even in daylight. What was needed was an effective deterrent.

"When we decided to let them go, we said that if they got into trouble, it would act as a warning to the rest," Zeigler went on. "It would be very convenient if something like that were to happen."

"An accident? . . . I don't really see a ready way of arranging one," Kelm answered. "And an overt attack on it could hardly be disguised."

Zeigler leaned back, rubbing his chin. "An attack by *us*," he agreed.

"I'm not sure I follow."

"Have you forgotten those natives out there? Violent, savagely disposed. Wouldn't a handful of people camped out in that wilderness with all those pickings be an obvious target? Think of the effect it would have here, when we go out to intervene but are too late, and bring back the bodies. What better way could there be to convince everyone else at Serengeti to stay put? You get my point now, Kelm?"

CHAPTER THIRTY-FOUR

Jorff stood on the edge of the clear area a few hundred yards up from the huts and watched as Lanserm adjusted the grip of the trainee dropped on one knee in a firing position. The Kronian shifted the rifle stock a fraction to fit more snugly against the native's shoulder, and stepped back, at the same time nodding to Enka with the missing teeth.

"Five shots, slow and aimed," Enka ordered. Rakki had appointed Enka to oversee the proceedings, and was standing watching, a few yards back, his arms folded. Jorff's orders were to keep Rakki sweet. Behind Enka, the other recruits in the squad waited for their next turn. Yesterday they had been through a starter on handguns and knew the basics. Today was the single-shot primer on rifles. Automatic fire would come later.

The one who was firing sent off five careful rounds at measured intervals. Two of the five ration tins placed on a flat rock fifty feet away flew back, while one jumped a few inches from a grazing hit. Rakki glanced at Jorff for a verdict. Jorff gave an almost imperceptible nod. "Good," Rakki pronounced.

"Next, Bakka," Enka said. The one who had fired stood

up, set the safety on his weapon as he had been shown, and returned to the line. Custom did not permit a change of expression, but there was pride in his eyes. Enka signaled, and a young girl ran in from the side to reposition the targets.

"Carry on, Lanserm," Jorff directed.

"Sir."

Gralth, the other trooper with the party from Serengeti, who had been standing a short distance back, moved forward to assist. Jorff turned and began walking back down the slope to the settlement. The children and several others who had been watching from behind a line ceremoniously drawn across the ground to mark off the shooting range drew back, giving him plenty of room to pass. A lot of the "god" image was still there. Jorff strode by them commandingly. It felt good to breathe wind-driven air again, and feel his boots crunching into the soil of a living world. They might not rebuild it in his lifetime. But he would see the beginnings.

He was of Swiss and Malay parentage in Java, one of the major Indonesian islands, and had come to Kronia at age eighteen. One of his brothers and a cousin had been chemists, and the family business had revolved around complicated dealings in variously priced substances and preparations, not all of which were approved by the lawmakers of the state. Besides illegal trafficking of the kind that thrives on prohibition universally, there was also a vigorous local trade in cheap and effective but banned medicinal drugs. Having fallen out of favor with both the underworld and the law enforcement agencies, Jorff's father decided that a change of scene would be beneficial for the health and probable longevity of self and immediate family, and organized a hasty move to the Central Americas. However, his work habits and penchant for falling foul of local politics soon got him into trouble again, and a sudden revelation to find new horizons and spiritual rebirth via a shuttle from Guatemala to a Kronia-bound orbiting transporter quickly followed.

But, truth was, young Jorff had missed the excitement, perceived glamor, and the adrenaline kick that came with the riskiness of the life he'd known in those years. Compared to the images that memory furnished him with—and who was he to say what kind of selection and editing might be at work, even if he'd thought about it?—Kronian life seemed dull and stultifying. He saw a lot of hyping of abilities he didn't have, recognition of people he didn't particularly want to be like, and heard endless talk about how all the trouble with Earth had stemmed from the upside-down way of apportioning the rewards among makers, traders, and takers. Somehow the assumption seemed to be that the providers had a moral superiority that entitled them to make the rules for everyone else, and anyone who thought differently just needed some friendly tutoring to see the error of their ways.

The problem was, Jorff had seen the tedium, thankless-ness, and plain hard work that came with the socially responsible life style, and he didn't find anything particu-larly redeeming about it at all. To him, it all came across very much like the sheep solemnly agreeing to observe vegeterianism and deploring the aberrance of any other taste. But in his experience, it had been the takers who drove the big cars, wore the stylish clothes, and pulled the sexiest chicks. It was too bad that the Kronian boss had to go and get himself shot, but as Jorff's uncle Siggi, who ran the "heavy" side of the family business used to say, "You have to let people know who's in charge." There was nothing he could see to find any error in or feel remorse about. He *liked* being a wolf.

The flyer they had arrived in was parked a short dis-tance above the huts, guarded by two natives with spears that Rakki had posted, more to keep inquisitive children away than from any serious risk of interference. Rakki's people took notice of his orders. Between some boulders to one side, Sims was directing a group, mainly women, who were building an armory from rocks and mud for the weapons and ammunition to be stored in. Sims had some firearms background too. Jorff was toying with the idea of training him to be the Tribe's resident instructor and quartermaster, but hadn't decided yet about some of his personal qualities. He reminded Jorff of too many types he'd known in Jakarta who would squeal to either side for another hundred dollars.

He found Leisha with Yobu in the porch extension to Rakki's hut, working to make cleaned-up copies of the maps. Nobody went through to the two inner rooms, which were Rakki's personal space. Rakki's woman, Calina, with the strange, light-colored eyes, was sitting on a rug of skins at the rear, tending to her baby. Jorff cast an approving eye over Leisha as he stepped up under the reed roof. Nicely built, with the kind of cute face and come-on eyes that would have made her a natural as a hostess or dancer in the bars. With all the tension back at Serengeti, it wouldn't have been very smart to try anything that might have provoked Zeigler's displeasure just at the present time. But there could be some good chances out here, away from all that, where he was in charge, he told himself.

The sounds came of another series of shots commencing outside. "Working hard out there," Leisha commented. "You've been at it all morning."

"That's the only way it's going to get done."

"How are they shaping up?"

"They're doing okay. Enka's cutting a good figure as sergeant." Jorff came over to the folding table where they were working, which was from the items brought with the flyer. "You're right. We're working too hard. If we're going to be here for days, there needs to be some relaxation to break it up. You want to schedule some free time later?"

Leisha gave him the kind of look that was calculated to keep men guessing. "Let's see how it goes," she replied.

Jorff looked over the papers strewn on the table. An imaged version of the main map was showing on the extended screen of the compad on one side. "So how *is* it going?" he asked.

She pointed her pen at a contour representation of an area in Raphta's east-central region, reconstructed from orbital radar scans. "It's looking like somewhere around here, three to three-fifty miles southeast, on the other side of the Spine. It's amazing that they were able to make from there on foot. They had to cross a whole new uplift zone."

"Do we have enough information to schedule a recce with probes?" Jorff asked.

"Well . . . this is about as good as it's going to get."

"Then package it up so I can get it off to Zeigler. He's waiting to get started."

Leisha pointed at the compad. "Working on that right now."

Jorff moved closer, making a pretense of looking over her shoulder. "Talking about recce probes, there's that one still out there somewhere that needs to be located for recovery," he murmured, twining a finger in a curl of hair at the back of her neck.

"One still out where?" Leisha kept on working, but she didn't pull away.

"The day that Scout first got here. I was part of the crew. There was an incident that involved a probe coming down low, and Enka put a stone-headed arrow up its intake in a freak shot." Leisha snickered. Jorff went on, "It probably didn't harm anything, but the thing was making unhealthy noises, so we put it down until it can be checked out. It's still up there somewhere, over the ridge."

"Oh. I see." Leisha's tone said that she saw several things.

Jorff toyed lightly with the curl of hair. "So . . . what say you and I take a walk up that way and see if we can find it? Nice and peaceful, away from all these people . . ."

"As I said, we'll just have to wait and see, won't we?"

Behind them, Calina said something to Yobu from where she was sitting by the wall of the inner hut. He spoke, and Leisha turned her head. Jorff looked at her and raised his eyebrows.

"She asks why people from the sky who can do anything need our young men to fight for them," Leisha said.

Jorff wasn't going to get into any of that. He wasn't sure he could have explained it if he'd wanted to. "We'll make Rakki a great chief," he replied, thinking that should suffice.

Leisha conveyed it back. "Rakki brought Jemmo to the caves and made him a great chief too," was the gist of Calina's answer.

"What does that mean?" Jorff asked Leisha.

"I'm not sure."

"No great chief will ever stay second to another," Yobu supplied. "Even the gods fight already in their city to the north. She wants to know, when their chief has made Rakki like themselves, how long will it be before they and he turn on each other? And when the power of the gods turns into anger, what will become of her people then?"

CHAPTER THIRTY-FIVE

"Fridays, when it was clam chowder," Keene said to Charlie. "And a good seafood salad bar. I was never that much into lobster, though. Too much like groceries. You know—one bag of them always made three bags of trash. But maybe some scrod or flounder, or a nice piece of whitefish . . . *What?*—"

For a moment it was like the loss of steering when a car slides on ice. They were crossing above slopes of rock outcrops and mud slides overlooking tracts of reedy marshland, and trading visions of their best-remembered restaurants in Los Angeles and Boston, when Keene felt a lightness in touch on the wheel. And then the whole cab seemed to rise from the ground, and he was seized by a sudden vertigo, as if he had been transported back into space and become weightless. Charlie was clinging to the bar on the door pillar and flailing with his other hand to find purchase, but some relentless force seemed to be lifting him from the seat and sending him sideways against Keene. Keene became conscious of a juddering, roaring noise, seemingly all around, and an octave below it, a groaning from deep in the ground that he *felt* in his stomach more than heard. Then came the punctuation of a series of immense, violent shocks that stung in his ears like the reports of nearby artillery. The runabout

seemed to bounce and leap upward again, the scene outside turning. He registered in a detached kind of way that
the tilt of the piece of ground they were on was changing.
The runabout was thrown up and bounced several times
more, becoming part of a jumble of loose boulders all
tumbling and bounding downward in a melee as if they had
taken on life. The force reversed and carried Charlie away,
pinning him against the far side of the cab, and Keene found
himself in turn hugging the steering column and trying to
brace with his leg to avoid being flung on top of him. And
then the whole section of hillside beneath them detached
and slid away, sweeping them down toward the fringe of
the marshes. The windshield shattered into a shower of
pieces, and Keene found himself first bracing across the gap
to prevent himself from jackknifing out over his seat harness, then slammed back against the rear wall as the runabout rolled and turned over. His head struck something
hard, and his vision kaleidoscoped; but he remained conscious of them thudding to a halt in an upended position,
straps cutting into his body.

Still, the shaking and thundering continued, with more
rocks tumbling and crashing into them from above. The rear
wall of the cab was torn and bulging inward, wedging Keene
awkwardly toward the driver's-side door, with Charlie hanging
above him beneath the slanting seatback. Hot, caustic gases
seared Keene's nostrils and his throat. There was fresh blood
on his sleeve. He felt his arm and shoulder, but apart from
probable bruising they didn't seemed to be injured. It wasn't
from inside his coat. Finally, he traced it to his shoulder
and found wetness down the side of his face and neck. There
could be no thought of getting out until the turmoil outside
eased.

His mind had gone into a state of numbness; he lost track
of how long it lasted. It could have been ten minutes or
an hour. Gradually, the heavier lurches gave way to a slowing
clatter of pebbles striking the runabout or the rocks outside.
Then Keene felt water inside the cab seeping into his boots.
"Charlie, we have to get out." He waited for a second or
two, then jabbed upward around the bulge in the cab's rear
wall at Charlie's shoulder. "Charlie, are you okay?"

A pang of worry hit him, and then Charlie's head turned sluggishly. "I think so. . . . Just a bit shaken up." His voice was wheezy. "Man, look at you!"

"What?"

"One side of your head's got blood all over it. You sure *you're* okay?"

"Just a scalp thing by the feel of it. But we need to move. We've got water coming in. I can feel it."

There was no question of opening the driver's door. It was partly on the underside, its window disintegrated, embedded in mud and by the look of it, buckled firmly in place anyway. Charlie felt for the door latch on his side, released it, and heaved with his arm and shoulder, but the door wouldn't budge. "It's no good," he announced, breathless. Keene released his seat harness and leaned past Charlie to add his strength as well, but it didn't help.

"Then it'll have to be the front," Keene said. He searched around and checked the dash compartment. The only object he could find of any weight was a metal-cased flashlamp. He used it to clear the remaining windshield shards from around the edge of the frame; then, with Charlie assisting, lifted his legs up along the dash panel and hauled himself over the wheel to squirm downward and out through the opening. It would have been easier if the runabout possessed more of a hood, which would have left a bigger space between the windshield and the ground. As it was, Keene had to worm his way feetfirst toward the passenger side, where the gap was higher, before he could turn and straighten up. Charlie followed, managing more easily since his reversed position brought him out the right way around. The squeeze had left both of them smeared with mud and soaked along their bodies.

The runabout had come to the end of its trail. It was nose-down in a mud slide that had surged into the marshes, its back end lifted by a rock lodged firmly underneath, and the rest of it looking as if it had been used as a practice target for field artillery. The generator had torn loose and was partly immersed in ooze maybe thirty feet away. Looking up to take in more of the general surroundings, Keene was dumbstruck.

The slopes that they had been traversing above had been broken and rugged before, but they had been continuous. Now they were split by two enormous, vertical fissures that had opened up all the way to the summit line, from which palls of black smoke or dust were spilling out over the lower slopes. Rivulets of rubble could be seen cascading down into the nearer fissure in places. But even more than that, the whole line of the slopes was tilted drunkenly forward, as if it had been torn from the greater massif behind by the opening up of a fault running lengthwise but invisible from where they were standing. Charlie was standing, staring up as if mesmerized. "Awesome!" was all he could find to murmur.

Moving mechanically for want of any better inspiration just at the moment, Keene clambered up to the truck bed, and leaving Charlie to his rapture, began hauling out what was left of their gear and supplies to take stock. Most of what had been stowed in the open bed of the truck was gone, which had included the drums of diesel oil—now neither here nor there anyway—but more importantly the main fresh water container. However, there were several bottles clipped in a rack. They still had the food, medical kit, spare clothes, and carrying packs, which had been in the closed compartment behind the cab. Then a fit of nausea and dizziness came over him. He stumbled across to some nearby rocks and sat down.

Charlie came over with one of the water bottles, a tin cup, and the medical kit. He gave Keene a drink, and when Keene had recovered somewhat, began cleaning the gash in his head and began closing it with suture clips. At least, Keene had been right in guessing it was mostly a scalp wound. The amount of bleeding had made it look worse than it was. "We should move from here as soon as we can," Charlie said. "Those rocks up there look precarious. There could be more falls at any time."

Joburg lay ahead to the south, where the ridge they had been descending from eventually broke up into a region of rounded hills. Obviously, the information from probe flights and the Scout's journey stored in the runabout's on-board system would no longer be of any use to them. They had compads, but using them to access copies from Serengeti would be an invitation for the transmissions to be traced. "I estimate about thirty miles," Keene said. "The settlement shouldn't be too difficult to find when we get in the general area. There's a conspicuous peak to the east that should give us our bearings. At the rate we're likely to manage in this kind of country, say, three days. Maybe four? . . . *Ouch!*"

"Sorry, Lan. But it looks a lot cleaner now. I'll put some of this on and cover it up."

"So what do you think?"

"You still believe there will be any point in trying to warn the *Aztec*, after all that time?"

Keene realized that it hadn't occurred to him to wonder about it. But there was no way to change any of that. "What else can we do?" he answered simply.

"After all this time away from Earth? Do you really think either of us is up to it?"

"There's only one way we'll ever know, isn't there?"

A few seconds of silence followed. "We do have two choices," Charlie said.

"What's the other one?"

Charlie shrugged as if reluctant to state the obvious. "Accept reality, Lan. Admit that it was a good try, but it's over. Call Serengeti to have them pick us up. . . ." Keene raised his head. Charlie saw the look on his face. "You're right. There's only one."

They laid out what they had and sorted it into piles. The food, fresh water, cooking gear, personal hygiene items, medical kit, foam-quilted bed covers that they'd brought to substitute for sleeping bags, and a minimum of the spare clothing they had brought were obvious selections. Keene added some of the lighter-weight tools and a few oddments like electrical tape, twine, repair aids. Would there be a need for some kind of weapons, just in case? Charlie wondered. Keene didn't know. The best improvisations he could find were a two-foot pry bar and an alloy survey stake used for ground marking. Finally, he ducked down through the passenger-side window of the cab to retrieve whatever he could find that was useful from there. The on-board processor was still working, and twisting uncomfortably, he transferred a copy of the Scout's map from its store into his wrist compad. That should get them to within sight of the landmark peaks, he told himself.

When he straightened back up, he found Charlie staring thoughtfully out at the marshes. He followed Charlie's gaze but could see nothing especially significant. "It isn't duck season, Charlie," he said.

"The Bolivians used to make boats out of reeds like that," Charlie answered distantly. "I got to ride in one once up on Lake Titicaca. So did the Egyptians long ago, too." There were clumps of tall reeds lining the water in places.

Keene's head hurt, he'd ricked something in his back, now it seemed the rest of his body was stiffening up too, and given the choice he would have preferred just to lie down. "You know, Charlie, I was just wondering about that," he said.

"Maybe there is another option."

"What?"

"Going directly south from here, inland of the ridge, we know the going's rough. But if my memory is correct, the upper part of one of the rivers parallels it on the other side before it turns west farther down, toward the sea."

"That's right," Keene agreed. "I just copied the map."

"If we got to the other side, we could make a raft and use the waterway. I'm almost certain it would have to flow into the long lake below Joburg. It would halve the time. And we wouldn't have to go back and over. Not much farther south from here, there are ways through to the west."

"Assuming there are reeds over there," Keene pointed out.

"There's bound to be some kind of suitable material around a river." Charlie turned his gaze back finally and looked at him. "Which would you rather risk, Lan? A thirty-mile trek over this? Or trusting we'll find something, in return for riding the current downstream and taking half the time?"

Put that way, it didn't need a lot of thinking about. "You're right. The river, it is," Keene agreed simply.

They checked over the pile of discarded items for anything vital they might have overlooked. It contained two packs of inflatable plastic air beds that some Kronian back in mission planning had thought to provide for overland expeditions. Keene and Charlie had been about to leave them to save weight, but then Keene realized they would be ideal aids for raftmaking. He retrieved them, passing one to Charlie. "Pontoons," he said.

Charlie took it and added it to his pack. "What have we got to cut reeds with?" he asked. The planners evidently hadn't seen much use in the runabout's tool kit for things like sickles or machetes. After some rummaging, Keene produced a general-purpose handsaw with exchangeable blades, and a pair of hand shears. He put them in his own pack with a shrug that said that was it. Then, wincing from the bruises they had collected, they heaved the packs onto their backs and began picking their way, slipping and sliding, across the foot of the slopes.

The ground became firmer as they moved off the mounds of fresh debris, with pools of intruding water already forming among them, and they were able to increase their pace somewhat. But Keene's legs were soon beginning to feel leaden. Being away from Earth had affected him more than he'd realized. After maybe a mile, they stopped to catch their breath. A low rumbling sound came from behind them. They looked back. One of the towers above where the runabout lay was collapsing, burying the area in an avalanche of dust and rock. They glanced ominously at each other but said nothing. Hitching their packs higher on their shoulders, they turned away and resumed a slow but steady pace toward the south.

To President Xen Urzin of the Kronian Congress, it was so obvious that the universe and everything in it were fashioned by some creative force with a purpose that he was hard put to understand how rational minds could ever have thought otherwise; even more, why they should have been so insistent on contriving ways of clinging to their view after repeated demonstrations that all the numbers and probabilities showed it to be simply untenable. He suspected it was a hangover from the period of Terran development when notions of conquest and exploitation being the right of the strong, and survival the natural reward for excellence, served as a convenient justification for the political and economic ideology of the times.

It seemed as self-evident as anything could be that the cosmos functioned as an immense materials-processing factory for producing planetary systems and the suns to nurture them; planetary systems provided assembly stations for constructing living organisms, the purpose of life was to support consciousness; and consciousness existed in order to undergo experience. Beyond that, things got more conjectural.

Many believed that the entities experiencing consciousness were products of some higher, more spiritually directed form of intelligence pursuing objectives of its own. Urzin liked to think so too, but he admitted that this was largely for reasons of emotional appeal and internal conviction—although why this should be seen as an admission, indicating some kind of weakness, he wasn't quite sure. However, he did believe that the ancestral humans who had inhabited the Earth when it orbited Saturn had been more directly attuned to such realities, and in something comparable to a collective amnesia that had befallen the race as a consequence of the cataclysms that had occurred since, that awareness had been lost. He believed it was part of his role to help the race rediscover whatever future had been destined in those far-off times, and that they would find it out among the stars. Interestingly, it had been the very ordeal brought on by the fall from that earlier idyll that had spurred the technological advancement that now made such a migration possible. Without the hardships and insecurities that it had endured, and the restlessness and ambitions which those things had engendered, humanity might have existed indefinitely in a state of blissful but stagnant ease. Maybe the religious believers from Earth who stated that their Lord, Buddha, Allah, or whatever worked in strange ways had a point.

He stood in his suite in the Hexagon at Foundation on Titan, contemplating a panorama of waterfalls in a rain forest beneath a sunny sky of blue and shining white clouds. Jon Foy, higher up in his tower, liked looking out at a dead surface in the gloom, but Urzin preferred internal graphics creations that he could choose to suit his mood. The latest theory he had been invited to consider was from the school that sought a naturalist explanation for things, and posed the many-universe version of quantum mechanics as being potentially capable of originating the complexity of living systems that confounded conventional attempts at explanation. Essentially, the suggestion was that if in a sufficiently vast totality, everything that could happen would happen somewhere, and if some mechanism existed for communicating information between the all-but-infinite number of universes making up the totality, then life having emerged in one part, however unlikely, could propagate itself to the rest.

In effect, it was an attempt to put traditional evolution on a more solid foundation. Urzin didn't really think it mattered that much. Whether or not living things had arrived at their present form through some process of change from simpler beginnings, or appeared abruptly as expressions of complex genetic programs whose origins could at present hardly even be guessed at, wasn't the issue. The real question was, had the programs written themselves through the accumulating effects of unguided natural processes, or had something that knew what it was doing written them? Urzin liked his own theory better. And he was quite happy to concede that emotional appeal was probably the real reason why most people ended up supporting any theory, whatever other reasons they might profess. He was still cogitating over the issue, when the house manager informed him that Mylor Vorse was at the door. Right on time as always. Urzin acknowledged by voice and had him enter. Vorse appeared from the outer room of the suite moments later. He was carrying two dark bottles with maroon labels embellished in gold lettering.

"Mylor. I haven't seen you for a while. You must be busy. My! What have we here?"

"A dry merlot from Mimas. Superb, Xen! The manager there sent me a crate on behalf of the work force. I thought you'd like a couple of bottles to add to your reserve."

"My thanks, indeed." Urzin raised one of the bottles to inspect it. "And what did you do to earn such esteem from the winemakers on Mimas?"

"Oh . . . I think it was in appreciation of the shipping we've provided for their crop produce generally. Personally, I think we've all got more to be thankful to them for. But it was a nice bonus, anyway."

Urzin took the bottles over to a cabinet by the wall and found a place for them in the mildly chilled section. "But that wasn't what you wanted to see me about," he said, straightening back up and turning.

As was his way, Vorse spent little time on preliminaries. "We're still getting intermittent messages claiming electrical disturbances blanketing communications with Earth. What's come through has been from Zeigler or his staff. Nothing from Gallian for four days now. With the sudden blackouts from *Trojan* and *Eskimo* too, I'm suspicious. It's all too much to be a coincidence."

It wasn't the first time Urzin had heard such thoughts. A number of people in the higher levels of Congress and the Directorates were talking about a Pragmatist coup with a lot of Security Arm involvement. More than one had criticized him for allowing the SA too much power and freedom at a time when their real reason for existing had passed. He had seen it as a needed safety valve for unsettled youth and the more adventurously disposed, but on reflection conceded that he might have been too trusting. The Security Arm had presented an opportunity that Terran political interests couldn't pass by, and Terran politics simply wasn't something that Urzin pretended any instinct for anymore than did most Kronians. Leo Cavan had probably discerned the risk sooner than anyone. But few had listened to him back then.

"Yes, I'm aware of the concerns, Mylor," he said. "In fact, I was intending to call a meeting of the Triad and inner policy heads, including yourself, to go over it. The problem right now, to be quite frank, is knowing where anyone's true sympathies might lie. I have a feeling it's a lot more complicated than we might have thought."

"I appreciate that," Vorse said. "But in the meantime, there's the question of the *Aztec*. If there has been some kind of a takeover on Earth, *Aztec* will be bringing them just the things they need to consolidate and build a solid foothold there. I'd like your approval to call it back for now, pending developments."

"Are we still in normal communication with *Aztec*?" Urzin checked.

"Yes. A routine update came in from Commander Reese a couple of hours ago. There's no reason I can see to suspect anything amiss there."

Urzin thought for a moment. It suggested that whatever might be happening with the other ships, at least they could trust Reese. "Isn't recall a bit drastic?" he said. "Why not let them continue until they reach the vicinity of Earth, but with orders to stand off until further instructions before initiating any contact?"

Vorse pursed his lips. "Just that if there is a hostile situation there, they'd be a long way from home and isolated from any help before they found out."

"But then look at it the other way around," Urzin suggested. "If there is something going on out there, they could represent the only help capable of making a difference right now. Why think of them as just a passive resource to be acquired? Why not a potential active asset?"

"They're a supply ship," Vorse replied. "What could they do if weapons like the ones that disappeared from Rhea have found their way there? And I don't have to tell you what would be involved if *Trojan* shows up."

"I'm not sure what they could do, exactly," Urzin said. "But I have infinite trust in human resourcefulness. One thing I do know is that they can't do anything if they're nowhere near. And precisely because they are such a valuable asset, I don't think the danger to them would be all that great. I'd prefer we do it the way I said."

Vorse drew a deep breath, obviously still far from happy, but nodded shortly. "Very well, Xen. I'll beam Reese accordingly."

CHAPTER THIRTY-SIX

Away from the base and the presence of human works, and now removed even from the confines of the cab and its tiny preserved world of familiar things, the land took on a surreal quality, a feeling of being partly the stuff of dreams. As with the newly formed landscape that he had viewed via the probe over New York, it was the absence of trees that struck Keene the most—or indeed any kind of mature growth or shaping of the land that could be recognized as the work of time. The hills were bare humps of sediment left by the receding oceanic floods, beginning to show scatterings of grass and other vegetation over the upper slopes, but with denser growths still hugging the valleys and hollows. He tried to picture the immense walls of advancing water, miles high in some places, that had been capable of bringing this about in weeks or even days. To the east, beyond the marshes and the broken foothills on their far side, the dark lines of the mountains were new and sharp. Overhead, the gray veils of the sky stood twisted in huge, inverted canyons, revealing briefly in places even a hint of watery blues. It was a young, primeval world once again, arising and taking form out of fresh origins. Keene was reminded of the words he had heard quoted by Reynolds, a Special Forces trooper in the group that had escaped from

Mexico, and also a devout Baptist, while they watched the devastation of Earth from orbit: "Go forth and multiply and *re*populate the Earth." Their significance hadn't fully struck Keene, even then.

They climbed slowly from the edge of the marshland toward a saddle marking a low point between the end of the ridge that they had followed from Serengeti and the lower hills continuing southward. The river that they were seeking lay in that direction, to the west, below the saddle on the far side. The grass was coated with coarse hairs that rasped at their trouser legs, dragging at every step and disgorging clouds of flies. Leathery leaves swished at their faces and stuck to their clothing. The heavy, humid air was dulling and draining of strength. A noisy flock of birds returned to circle and caw at them. Odd forms of life hopped away or slithered among the rocks in the creek beds. Once they spotted a couple of deer-like creatures watching them from a knoll, but the animals kept their distance and it was impossible to make out any details. Keene was beginning to realize that the years not only marked a long absence from laboring under Terran gravity but had taken their inevitable toll in other ways as well. Every effort of dragging a leg upward past the other became a small triumph of will in itself. His breath was coming in quick, painful gasps. Charlie had been right. They would never have made it on foot the whole way.

The light was fading by the time the slope eased and they came over the top of the saddle. It was one of those rare moments when the evening sky actually showed some orange toward the west. But better was the sight that rewarded them when they trudged on over the pebble slopes and runoff gullies at the saddle's high point until the view down the other side opened out before them. They found themselves looking down over the gentler, open folds sloping away to the west. And curving toward them through the gathering darkness and haze lower down was a broad sweep of the river. But there could be no question of completing the journey down to it that night. They would have to bivouac up on the saddle until first light.

They found a dry spot in one of the gullies, sheltered by

rocks from the winds, which were strong and gusting from the west. Their first craving was for something hot and fortifying to drink. While Charlie unpacked coffee and mugs and fiddled around assembling the spirit stove—made specially to order for the Earth mission, since nobody at Kronia camped out or had any use for such a thing—Keene scouted around and collected enough twigs, roots, and bush branches to get a fire of sorts going. They concocted a stew of chicken meat, greens, and reconstituted potato with gravy, accompanied by bread wafers and cheese, followed it with boiled jam pudding, and by the time they sat warming their hands with a second mug of coffee, were finally feeling some relief after the day's shock and tension.

"I was thinking of Reynolds on the way up," Keene said. "Remember him?"

"One of Mitch's guys? The one who was on the shuttle up from Montemorelos? Sounded like Bible Belt." Harvey Mitchell had been the major in command of the Special Forces squad that Cavan had brought from Washington to California.

"Yes."

"What made you think of him?"

"Nothing in particular. Your mind wanders over all kinds of things in a place like this. I think it was something he said about the world starting all over again. It just struck me as ironic. All the fighting that used to go on about old-Earth, young-Earth. Maybe there never was any real conflict. They just weren't talking about the same thing. The same as with so many things."

"What happened to Mitch? Did you keep track of him?" Charlie asked.

"He joined the Security Arm. What else was a guy like Harvey supposed to find to do on Kronia? Cavan said he was earmarked for the *Trojan* mission at one point, but then it was rescinded for some reason. I'm not sure where he went afterward."

Charlie sipped his drink and fell silent for a short while. Then he said, "It makes it sound even more as if *Trojan* is another part of the pattern, doesn't it?"

"How do you mean?"

"Well, suppose you were planning a move like that, and it involved taking over the *Trojan*. Would you want a guy like Mitch around when it happened? Sounds to me as if someone had him pulled because he would have been too dangerous."

It made sense, Keene had to agree. Although inclined to be flamboyant at times, Mitch was a capable leader who would have been a natural rallying point for resistance to organize around. If the Pragmatists had seized the *Trojan* too, they would have wanted more pliable individuals there to deal with—such as SA rookies and freshy graduated SOE trainees supposedly going to Jupiter to gain interplanetary experience. And that was exactly the way it had happened. At least, if it were true, it would mean Robin was okay after all. However, if he and Charlie did manage to make some sort of contact with *Aztec*, he decided he would keep such thoughts to himself. He wouldn't have wanted to raise Vicki's hopes like that, and then be proved wrong.

"Then there was Colby Greene," Charlie said. Colby had been a presidential political aide who had ended up with Keene's party and escaped with them via Mexico. "Kind of a weird sense of humor, but he was okay. I never heard more of him after that last reunion six months before we left Titan."

"I met him a couple of times in Foundation. He was working there with Cavan in whatever Cavan gets mixed up in. Neither of them could stay away from politics very long. I think Leo missed the old Washington underworld."

They talked for a little longer about the others who had been with them then, but Keene could feel himself fading as exhaustion finally overcame him. They had the air beds but not the energy to inflate them. Stretching back among the rocks, he pulled the covers close and fell into total oblivion.

The probe had grounded in a hollow among the rocks on the ridge above Joburg, apparently scraping over some boulders before coming to rest canted sideways and nose-down with some dents in the forward section of its underbelly and one of its stub wings crumpled at the tip. The damage didn't look serious, but Jorff didn't feel it would be wise to risk compounding it further by having Rakki's people drag it down to the open ground below for easier recovery. The technical people from Serengeti could come out and look at it, and decide for themselves how they wanted to deal with the situation. In any case, his thoughts right now were in regions far removed from matters to do with recovering damaged probes.

He sat contentedly in the dusk, his back propped against the probe's motor cowling, legs stretched out along the ground, enjoying the flashes of bare thigh and underwear in the shadows as Leisha stepped into her pants and hitched them back up. In the days back on Earth, he'd always lit up a cigarette at moments like this. Since the habit had never taken on in Kronia's permanently enclosed environments, he made do instead with a swig of coffee from the flask they had brought up with them. No complaints, he told himself again. She certainly lived up to the promise of the body and the eyes.

"You want some?" He gestured with the flask.

"I just did." Leisha laughed, buttoning her top.

"I meant coffee." Jorff poured some into the cup and set it on a rock. "Don't start getting smart with me."

"Well, you should have known better. Words are what I do." She came over out of the darkness and squatted down. "Thanks. . . . Mmm. Tastes good."

"You know, it doesn't pay to be conscientious," Jorff said.

"How do you mean?"

"I'm doing too good a job here. See, Rakki's soldiers are catching on fast, which means they'll be shipping out sooner. So we won't be taking any more walks. And I was just deciding, you know, I could get used to this."

Leisha took it as an invitation and wriggled closer, seeking warmth against the evening chill. "It's better to end these things on a high," she said. "Before they turn sour."

"Why do they have to turn sour?"

She shrugged. "They always do. I suppose it's the way people are."

"You sound like a cynic."

"Just more a realist, I'd say." Leisha stared out at the rocks outlined blackly against the last vestige of fading sky. "That's why I ended up on this side that we're on. They deal in what *is,* with people as they are. To me it makes more sense. It's on solid ground. The others are preoccupied with things that should be. But you have to live in reality." She turned her head toward Jorff. "How about you?"

"Me, what?"

"What's your reason?"

"Oh, nothing so philosophic. I leave that stuff to philosophers. Me? Life was getting too boring, everything predictable. I used to have exciting times here on Earth, you know that? You never knew what was going to happen tomorrow or next week. And I like people who know how to take control. You have to let people know who's in charge. And out here, that's what it's going to take." He nodded his head decisively, as if it had all become clear only at that moment. "I guess that's it. Nothing's too predictable. You don't know what's going to happen. It makes me feel I'm coming back to life again."

Jorff stopped speaking just in time to unmask what sounded like a giggle from somewhere in the darkness, stifled suddenly by an urgent whisper. "What the hell was that?" he demanded, banging the flask down and standing up. He advanced in the direction the sounds had come from, and threw a rock. There were scuffling noises, and two small shapes appeared briefly and ran off into the dark. "Kids!" Jorff exclaimed indignantly. "Would you believe it? Do they change anywhere?"

Leisha straightened up beside him. "You see," she said. "Something always goes wrong with these things. Always complications." She pulled her jacket more tightly around her shoulders. "We should be heading back, anyway. It's starting to get cold. And I need to check with Serengeti to see if the maps were okay."

Zeigler and Kelm, accompanied by a retinue of officers and guards, paced slowly along the perimeter of the compound where the vehicles would be grouped at night, inspecting the arrangements. Things at Joburg were progressing well. A probe would be sent out tomorrow to pinpoint the location of the caves. Zeigler's staff had named the location Carlsbad.

The training program at Joburg was probably one of the fastest courses ever put together for handguns and automatic weapons—but it wasn't as if Rakki's recruits would be making their combat debut against crack troops. The more important thing was to begin recruiting at the earliest opportunity the larger force Zeigler was hoping to raise from Carlsbad. The first phase of the operation—installing Rakki in place of his enemy, Jemmo—had been designated "Usurper."

"The occasion needs to be made big and impressive," Zeigler told Kelm. "We want Rakki to be seen as a superhuman chief appointed by the gods, who will lead them to great victories. We should be there too, to show our support and authority."

"We go to Carlsbad too," Kelm checked.

"Jorff will need an additional flyer at Joburg to transport his team when they're ready. We can depart directly from here, rendezvous with them somewhere, and then proceed to Carlsbad as a unit, all arriving together. That would make more of a spectacle."

"What about Naarmegen and those others in the Scout?" Kelm asked.

"Yes, I've been thinking about them too. We wait until Rakki is secure at Carlsbad, and then have some of his new soldiers from there take care of the Scout for us. We could make it a loyalty test before giving them firearms. Then we let Laelye and her friends send a recovery team out from Serengeti afterwards, so they can see for themselves it was the work of hostile natives. That should put any thoughts of trying something similar out of everyone's mind. It ties all the loose ends up neatly."

Kelm hesitated for a second. "Keene is with them too," he reminded Zeigler. "He's a valuable resource. Can we afford to lose him along with the others?"

"We will manage," Zeigler replied. "He was given his chance to cooperate."

In the power control room, Shayle pushed herself back from the console and stretched gratefully in her chair. Gus had come in to take the next shift and was checking over the log on an adjacent screen. The first thing Shayle was looking forward to when she got back to the dorms was a hot shower to wash away the stickiness from Earth's humid air. Then supper, maybe an hour of reading—Charlie Hu had awakened her interest in Terran geology during the voyage, and she had set herself a study program on the subject—and then an early night. But very likely she'd end up talking with Sariena instead.

"Everything routine and normal," Gus commented. He entered the codes to take over the shift and passed Shayle the log to sign off.

"Nothing wild and exciting," she agreed.

"No more instabilities with the plasma field?" Gus held her eye for just a moment, sharing the private joke and keeping his face straight for the benefit of the guard by the door. The guard detail in the power house had been reduced from two to one.

"Just another one of those things we'll never know, I guess," Shayle replied. She stood up and collected her bag of personal items from a shelf on the wall. "Well, have a good night of it, Gus."

"I'll survive. I've got a couple of good movies lined up. Old Terran mystery thrillers. Great."

"Enjoy."

"Thanks. Goodnight."

"'Night."

Shayle paused outside to take in the fresh air. All around, the base lay subdued as a strange composition of shapes, shadows, and silhouettes in the arc lights. She was about to move away, when she realized that the guard had followed her to the door. Not some kind of hassle now, she groaned inwardly. "Yes?" she said curtly. He moved outside and then a step closer, but hesitantly, in a way that was anything but overbearing.

"The man who worked here with you, the one who went with the group who left. Keene?" The guard kept his voice low, barely more than a whisper. He was tall and broadly built, typically Kronian, but young, hardly past his teens, Shayle guessed.

"What about him?" she asked.

"He was the one Zeigler wanted to be the spokesman."

"Nothing came of it."

"But you're his deputy. You'd be a fairly senior person here, right?"

"I'm not sure how you mean. What's this all about?"

The guard licked his lips. The shaft of light from inside caught his face for a moment. His expression was troubled, almost pleading. "Look, I want you to know that all this . . . what's going on, and the other things that happened. I didn't know it would be like this. I don't want to be a part of it. What should I do?"

Shayle was about to tell him to just walk out; maybe some of the others felt the same way and would follow . . . but then she checked herself. "Are you saying you want to come over? Help put an end to it?" she asked him.

The boy swallowed visibly and nodded. "I guess . . . if I can. I just want someone to know which side I'm on."

Shayle's mind raced for a few moments longer. "What's your name?" she asked.

"Mertak."

"Don't do anything for now. You could be more use to us by remaining on the inside. Keep your eyes and ears open to everything. When we need your help, we'll find a way to let you know."

CHAPTER THIRTY-SEVEN

The first hour the next morning was gruesome. Keene was awakened at dawn by the kind of cold that seems to seep through to the bones. After years of living in Kronia's controlled environments, his body had forgotten how to adapt to conditions like this. When he stirred, every muscle felt as if it had stiffened up. From his muttered groans and hesitant movements, Charlie was evidently having the same problem. They breakfasted sparingly and unenthusiastically on coffee, biscuit, and an insipid cereal preparation, and then packed up their kit, saying little.

The wind was sharp when they emerged from the shelter of the gully. In the gray light of morning, the sight of valley and the river below that had been so welcome to their eyes when they came over the saddle the previous evening now looked bleak and inhospitable. All it seemed to offer now, at the end of an arduous trek down, was the prospect of several hours of back-aching labor, followed by more unknown perils.

Their steps crunched over gravel and squelched through the mud, while their breath made frosty plumes in the chill air. Keene's feet ached, his legs ached, and his shoulders and hips were sore where the pack chafed. Predictably, the ground that had looked to be smooth and easygoing from

a distance turned out to be broken and boggy, slowing them
down with impassable mud-filled hollows and forcing them
into detours. They followed the ribs, picking out the lines
of the high ground. The world contracted to become just
the patch of terrain immediately ahead. Keene found himself playing games in his head, picking out some feature
ahead and counting off the steps until they reached it. "Three
hundred twenty less to go." Then he would repeat it again.
And again. And again . . . He asked himself why they were
doing this, trying to block out the almost certain futility of
it by now. All that came back was another question, asking
what was the alternative. But at least the slope was downward now, aiding their progress and sparing the muscles
racked during the ascent yesterday.

As their bodies warmed and stretched, their pace picked
up to a steadier rhythm. And despite the soreness and the
fatigue, Keene was conscious of a deep-rooted elation at the
sense of being home, in contact and communion with the
elements of Earth once again. It was as if this first close-
ness in years with the air and ground of a world being
reborn were infusing part of its life into his being.

About halfway into the morning they halted by a creek
to rest and snack on drinks mixed from a fruit flavoring
and a confectionary cake. "We're going to need more
water," Charlie remarked, upending one of the bottles they
had brought. "Probably better to refill up here than wait
till we're lower down." Keene agreed. Charlie scouted
around to find a spot where the water was clear and
flowing over rocks. A bird with blue and gray plumage
was watching with jerky, comical motions of its head from
a low bush. Keene flipped it a few crumbs. It hopped down
and investigated them, cautiously, keeping an eye on him
all the time. Several others that had been less forward
joined it. Keene wondered if he had just assured them of
a permanent entourage from here on. Charlie rinsed his
face and then clambered back up from the creek bed with
the water bottle.

"How do you figure it with the Pragmatists, Lan?" he
asked as he began fastening his pack. "All this time they've
been pushing the line that Earth distances are too extended

for any sustained effort, and we should be focusing on Kronia. And then they do a sudden turnabout and want to set themselves up right here. What's going on?"

"The usual power thing," Keene answered. "The first story legitimized a ploy for getting a bigger share in running Kronia. When that failed, they switched it to having their own here instead. It was probably the fallback plan all along."

"All the way out here? With just the resources they could bring on a few ships? Could that be enough to give them a realistic start?"

Keene shrugged. "Wasn't America started from less?"

"They wouldn't have lasted through the first winter without the Indians."

"True. . . . Well, what can I tell you? Evidently, it was a gamble they figured they could take."

They stood up, shouldered their loads, and turned again toward the west. "I'm still astounded that they were able to organize as much as they did and get away with it," Charlie said.

"With Terrans, they wouldn't have," Keene replied. "But you know the kind of heads Kronians have for politics. Cavan tried to make them a bit more cautious and questioning, but this wasn't his home turf."

"You think he saw this coming?"

"Oh, I wouldn't say that. But I know he got close to people like Xen Urzin and Jon Foy. He wanted them to set up an intelligence operation the way anyone back on Earth would have done, so they'd at least have known what was going on. But their whole background makes them take people at face value and accept what they say. In whichever sense you want to take it, they just weren't from the same world."

Lower down, the vegetation became denser, until Lan and Charlie were passing over broad coverings of grasses, dotted with patches of thorn bush and scrub. Although there was still nothing approaching trees, Keene was impressed by the speed with which nature could reinvigorate a new, reworked landscape in just a few years. It brought home more clearly and forcefully than words ever had the things Vicki had said about Earth's biological and geological trans-formations happening much faster than conventional theo-ries had once held. At one point they passed close to a group of animals browsing in a dell. They seemed horse-like but too squat and small, and with odd suggestions of bovine qualities, but Keene didn't know enough to say if they were from a preexisting line or something new. Charlie had no idea either.

The flats bordering the river turned out to be an ill-defined fringe of mud banks, watery incursions, and stagnant reaches of reed-studded marsh. After splashing, sticking, and in some places sinking knee-deep or farther into rank-smelling slime, it became clear that further meaningful progress either out toward the true water's edge or parallel to it was imprac-tical. Yet they still hadn't found any materials they judged suitable for the journey ahead. So they decided to use what they could find to lash the two air mattresses together as a temporary platform and use that to explore the shore further from the water side. Before starting, Keene produced a plastic bag from the assortment of utility items he had packed, wrapped their compads in it, and stowed the package deep inside his pack.

"What kind of reeds do you need for these Bolivian, Egyptian boats, anyway?" he asked Charlie as they splashed about, hacking boughs from bushes and collecting lengths of the thicker vines.

"I don't know. I thought you were the engineer here."

"I build MHD inductor channels and spacecraft reactors. There is a difference, Charlie."

And then when they were partway through figuring out how to hitch together what they had, they realized that they had nothing to propel or steer with. Nothing in the vicin-ity offered any means of fashioning a pole long enough to push from the bottom. While Charlie finished frapping and tying, Keene searched around and experimented with various shapes cut from the waterside growths to make a couple of paddles. He settled on a Y fork with a crosspiece lashed across the open end, and then stitched a doubled patch of fabric cut from a parka over it, using a bradawl piercing tool and twine. But when he tried working the paddle in water, it was too flimsy and it bent. There was nothing for it but to find another forked piece the same shape and lash it along the first as a reinforcement. Then they had to do the same thing for the second one.

By now they were into the latter part of the afternoon. They tried floating their creation, first with Keene on his own, then with them both. The weight was too much to prevent the mattresses from bending and shipping water. The raft would suffice for pottering along the shore and its inlets to search for more materials, but neither of them would have trusted it out in the main current of the river, which they could see moving swiftly in places. It was clear that they would not be casting off on the river portion of the journey until the following day.

They drifted out among islands of root clogged mud and overhanging branches draped with creepers and vines, pushing between floating mats of weed. In places the water was covered in green and yellow scum that released a stench of decomposition when they dipped their paddles, and flowed in over the depressed parts of the mattresses, plastering their clothing and the packs. The air became filled with gnats and mosquitoes that invaded eyes, ears, nostrils, every chink of clothing, and which no amount of slapping could deter. Keene felt his spirits sinking and the first real doubts taking shape that they might have made a serious error of judgment and overestimated their abilities. He kept them to himself; but Charlie's silence and the grim set of his features betrayed that similar feelings were assailing him.

The channels grew wider and less choked, the water cleaner as they came out into the river. They followed its edge of ferns and winding mud flats for maybe a mile, staying close in where the water was sheltered. Then a sandbank protruding from a bend forced them out some way into the stream, but they managed to steer their way back in again on the far side. Farther on, they could now see the mouth of a creek entering between high banks on the left, and beyond it a stretch of what could have been marshy shore or maybe a narrow island running parallel to it, fringed by tall reeds along the waterline with stands of higher cane-like growths behind. From what they had seen of the area, it was probably as good as they were going to get. They glanced at each other, both nodded at the same time without speaking, and began paddling inward.

But as they crossed the mouth of the incoming creek, the flow from it carried them out again into choppy waters, and in the battling between paddles and buffeting, Keene felt the makeshift lashings coming apart. *"We're going in, Charlie!"* he yelled. *"Don't let go of that pack!"* At the same time he grabbed for his own, clamping it down on the mattress with an arm as he floundered down into the water.

The two air mattresses remained tied by a few strands of vine. Charlie clung onto the bindings with one hand and went under, reemerging a few seconds later and dragging his pack up with the other. Keene helped him haul it up from the water and onto the other air mattress. Then, holding on to packs and mattresses like a life raft, they kicked with their legs to propel themselves toward the shore. After about a hundred yards Keene felt down with a leg and touched bottom. Coming into the shallows, they stood and walked the remaining distance, dragging the remnants of the raft and the packs after them—but both the paddles were lost. At the edge they collapsed and sat for a long time recovering their breath and letting the weight of water drain from their clothes.

When they got around to assessing their situation, they found that the pry bar and alloy stake they had brought as weapons were lost. Keene's compad with the map stored in it was still working. He would have felt more secure had he thought to make a hand copy in a notebook as well, but it was too late now. As to building a better raft, there wasn't much in the way of a place to work. The thicket of reeds came to the water's edge, and the cane-like growths farther back were even denser—but they looked useful. The best strategy, they concluded, would be to cut what they needed right there, by the water, and use the clear area that they created as a space to assemble their craft. Not the best workshop in the world, with its roots and cut stems and the waterlogged ground; but it would have to do. They first secured the air beds and packs from floating away. Then, wearily but without any choice, they sorted out the tools they had brought for the purpose and set to work.

This time there were spiders and frogs as well as the ubiquitous mosquitoes and flies. The latter became so irksome that Keene wrapped his head in a waterlogged shirt from his pack. It didn't take long for his hands to begin blistering. When he stooped to begin sawing at another shoot of cane, he stumbled on a snake. It was an ugly gray-black, maybe two inches thick, with yellow eyes, and slithered away among the roots and mud at the disturbance. But somehow it was all he needed. He warned Charlie to be wary of them. From the absence of change in Charlie's slow, painful movements, it wasn't even evident that Charlie had heard. Then Keene noticed the blood trickling down over Charlie's boot. He had gashed his calf on one of the thorny plants. It was bulbous and purple-hued, the thorns thick and flattened, sharp along the edges like blades. Keene bound the wound up as best he could, and they carried on.

Neither of them had any real notion of how to fashion a navigable hull from such materials. It didn't seem like an art that came instantly or easily. Very likely, it was something the Bolivians and the Egyptians had evolved and handed down over generations. They settled for the simple approach of tying reeds in bundles and lashing them together into a rudimentary platform.

By the time darkness began closing in, they weren't even halfway done. They were too wet and cold and tired to think of a meal. There was nowhere to use for preparing one in any case. All they wanted to do was get out of this awful place, but that couldn't be until tomorrow. Yet with the discomfort and the thought of whatever other vermin might be creeping and crawling and slithering around them, neither could there be any sleep. They nibbled on cold oddments and crouched, wet and shivering, through the long blackness of the night. It was the most miserable night Keene could remember spending anytime in his life.

They resumed working at the first hint of light. Both air mattresses had been torn by cut stems and thorns during the night, and were useless. They provided material, instead, for filling the frames of a new set of paddles—four of them this time. In addition, stouter pieces of cane lent themselves as punting poles.

The final construction took the form of two layers of reed bundles laid crossways to each other lengthways, constrained and strengthened by a cane framework. It sat alarmingly low in the water, and Keene couldn't be certain it wouldn't soak in more weight and founder. With ample time, the right tools, space to work, and skills handed down over generations, they probably could have done better; but for now, they would have to settle for it. Yet even with those apprehensions, they set off, conscious only of a sense of relief at being finally on their way at last.

Today, there was little of the talk and spiritedness they had shown on the trek down from the saddle. The night's ordeal had left them cold, hungry, weary, and depressed. As they drifted downstream, still keeping close to the river's edge, Keene stared dully at the monotonously repeating shores and the unchanging flatlands and hills beyond, feeling the wet clothes clinging to his body and the pangs of protesting muscles that seemed to greet every move. Without walking to get circulation moving again and loosen joints, he felt sluggish and drained. His mind was sinking into a state of passive resignation to whatever events the future might unfold, bereft of any will or potency to change them. Another day or more of this, and he was beginning to wonder if they would arrive in a condition to accomplish anything.

Assuming they arrived at all.

CHAPTER THIRTY-EIGHT

At a distance from the Sun corresponding roughly to that of Jupiter's orbit, the course of the *Trojan* was merging toward that of *Eskimo*, boosted on its more direct line from Saturn. The two ships first came within sight of each other as just specks of light moving against the starfield. For the next ten hours as they continued to close, the specks grew brighter and larger, eventually taking on discernible shape and form. Finally, they were riding in parallel, *Trojan* immense by comparison, its annular outer structure and main body turning slowly like a one-wheeled axle; *Eskimo*, unassuming but fattened by its battery of boosters, a local-range transporter built for ferrying between Saturn's moons, now far from home. The docking radars locked with the approach beacons, and *Eskimo* berthed at the locks on *Trojan*'s forward Hub a matter of minutes later.

The reception party waiting to greet Valcroix, Grasse, and their staffs had assembled in the Command Module out at the Rim, where there was simulated gravity. Ceremonies like that were supposed to be carried out with style and dignity, after all, which would have been difficult to achieve with the participants floating about like a slow-motion ballet. The *Trojan*'s honor guard in dress blues snapped to attention and presented arms, and the arriving dignitaries were officially

331

welcomed aboard by Captain Walsh, heading a deputation of the ship's and former SA officers—the latter now renamed the Terran Defense Force. They were then escorted through the customary ritual of inspecting the ranks.

Valcroix gave a speech, broadcast throughout the ship, formally ending the Kronian Pragmatist Movement and merging it into the recently proclaimed Terran Planetary Government, and reaffirming its mission to rebuild Earth along lines of "universal merit and achievement," instead of "the selective elevation of a few self-styled elites." He went on to declare the *Trojan* "reclaimed" by the Terran administration: designed and built as a result of knowledge and technologies originated on Earth, and a small token repayment for the unstinted flow of wealth and resources that Earth had poured into the founding and nurturing of Kronia. Valcroix then announced the promotion of Colonel Nyrom to the rank of general and his new title of Commander-in-Chief of the Terran Defense Force. He handed the platform to Nyrom, who delivered a short message of acknowledgment and pledged himself to defending Earth and its citizens. Nyrom then informed the ship's company and its complement of what had been set as *Trojan*'s first operational objective in the service of the new Terran government.

"The research and supply vessel *Aztec* left Saturn shortly before *Eskimo* was rerouted from Iapetus for the historic meeting we've just celebrated. As some of you may know, the *Aztec* is fitted for trials of the first ship-borne synthetic gravity generators, which will revolutionize every aspect of space travel and habitation. *Aztec* is also carrying the materials and startup equipment for establishing a basic mix of core industries and the technologies necessary for running them. That capability is essential to founding a viable pilot base on Earth and expanding it rapidly later.

"Our first task, now that we are able to operate as a coordinated unit, will be to overhaul, apprehend, and board the *Aztec*. Recognize that this is not an act of war but a legal repossession. Our aim will be to achieve occupation peacefully. Briefings and unit assignments to that end will follow. I'm counting on everyone in the Terran Defense Force that I'm now privileged to command, and Captain Walsh and his crew, to make this a clean and professional first operation in the service of Earth. Thank you."

The senior figures then proceeded to the Captain's Lounge for socializing and refreshments, while the *Trojan*'s honor guard detail returned to quarters. The transfer of personnel and materials from *Eskimo* continued for several hours. Then, left with only a skeleton crew, the smaller craft detached and moved away to stand five miles off while *Trojan* fired its main drives to accelerate toward the inner Solar System. *Eskimo*, its added boosters now spent, was tied to its present velocity and would follow in its own time.

It was a day later when a sergeant showed Robin into General Nyrom's stateroom and office in the Command Module, and then left, closing the door. Robin stood formally, conscious of the gap in ranks between them—more so now that Nyrom had been elevated to General and C-in-C of the entire Terran military command. His immediate superior was Major Ulak. But life in a closed community like the *Trojan*'s encouraged more direct and relaxed contact, and their dealings when Nyrom was a colonel had established something of a precedent.

"At ease, Lieutenant." Nyrom waved toward the metal-frame visitor's chair on the opposite side of the desk. Technically, it was "lieutenant-commander," but Nyrom wasn't going to go through mouthing that every time.

"Thank you, sir."

Nyrom waited until Robin had settled, resting his cap on his knee. "Has it occurred to you that the name of this vessel will very likely go down in history? *Trojan* is the first officially commissioned warship of the New Order that will arise on Earth. While the founding colony is still young and yet to acquire strength, its defense will rest primarily in our hands. I hope you realize the importance and the privilege of the task that places on all of us."

"I'll bear it in mind, sir."

Nyrom sat back, elbows resting on the arms of his chair, and interlaced his fingers. "So what's bothering you?"

"Oh, nothing. This isn't a complaint. More in the line of a suggestion . . . and a request."

"Go on."

"It's to do with the announcement yesterday about commandeering the *Aztec.*"

"I think that 'repossess' would be a more politic word to use, Lieutenant."

"I'm sorry, yes. . . ."

"So, what about it?"

"The President stressed that he wants it to be a peaceful occupation of the ship. And I can see why, if things took a difficult turn—say, because the people on it won't cooperate—and it resulted in force having to be used, that would be a bad thing. The record in history that you just mentioned, for example, might not read so well."

"I'm listening." The look on Nyrom's face said that he still had no idea where this was leading.

Even though Robin had tried rehearsing this several times, the words still came awkwardly. "Well, sir, my mother is aboard the *Aztec.*"

"Yes, I know. A bio-scientist sent by the Academy on Dione."

"She wasn't a Pragmatist supporter. And as things stand, the new Terran government is something she'll be opposed to. Right now, that would probably apply to most of the others there on the *Aztec* too. . . ." Robin made an open-handed gesture. "But I was also with her long enough after we came from Earth to know why she's that way. You see, sir, she deals with Kronian scientists. She's only ever heard one side of it. She doesn't really understand what the New Order means. Because no one's ever really explained it. What they say on the news gets distorted."

"You think it would make a difference?" Nyrom asked. He sounded skeptical.

"Yes, I do, sir. . . . At least, I think it would stand a good chance. Because I know how she really is. And maybe it would make a difference to the others there too if they knew."

"So what are you suggesting?"

"Simply a request to be included in the initial party that

is sent aboard the *Aztec*. If you like, I want to contribute to the success of the mission. I believe that if I talk to her she might see things differently, and if that happens we might be able to influence others. If enough of them come around, it could defuse any resistance before it gets started. So it could help things go smoothly, without trouble, the way everyone wants." Nyrom's expression had softened. He seemed receptive to the idea. Robin showed both hands briefly. "It wouldn't be risking anything to try, sir. But if the whole ship came over as a ready asset to Earth, instead of having to be fought against, it could make a big difference. That's what I'd like to help make happen, if I can."

Nyrom stared at him for several seconds while he considered. "Very well, Lieutenant. I'll propose it to the appropriate people," he replied.

CHAPTER THIRTY-NINE

They came to a bar of gravelly gray sand lying between the main course of the river and a back channel scooped into a bend of low bluffs. It was an island, clean and dry, devoid of reed thickets, cane growth, flies, and snakes, rising out of the water like the back of a long, humpbacked whale. They beached, hauled themselves and the raft up clear from the waterline, and for the first time since the evening of the day before last, tasted a hot meal. And then they slept.

The next morning did not exactly bring the exhilaration of feeling born again into new bodies. But it was an improvement. They actually got to walk from one end of the sandbar to the other, to stretch, bend, draw in deep chestfuls of air, and try a few basic calisthenics, which invigorated Keene but caused twinges of pain in Charlie's injured calf. On checking, they found the wound red and inflamed. Keene cleaned and treated it with what he could find in the medical kit, then bound it up again, after which the last scraps of the food they had brought from the runabout provided a passable breakfast. And then they secured the packs, spare paddles, and poles, pushed off and were on their way once again. Their confidence and technique had improved some by this time, and they were getting more proficient at spotting shallows

and rapids ahead that had to be circumvented on foot, dragging or carrying the raft. At other times, where the flow was
clear, they risked venturing farther out into the stream and
letting the current carry them. Their progress was much faster
than the day before, and Keene estimated they should reach
Joburg with some margin to spare before dark.

"You know, I never thought to ask before," Keene said
as they drifted into a bend, using the paddles to hold direction. "What happened to Cynthia? Are you two still together?"
Cynthia had been one of a couple who joined Keene and
Cavan's group in California. She and Charlie had gravitated
to each other after her original partner went off with some
others to find help after a plane crash, and never returned.

"She was with a survey group that got hit by an impact
storm on Tethys," Charlie answered. "No survivors."

"Oh . . . Sorry to hear that." The silence dragged. Keene
felt a need to add something. "You don't seem to have a
lot of luck in that department, Charlie." When they first met
at JPL, Charlie's wife had just walked out.

"Well, we'll just have to see what the future brings." There
was a silence while they steered around a patch of rocks
and eddies. Then Charlie's voice came again from behind.
"How about you? It used to look like you and Vicki were
going to make it permanent. But it sounds as if you spend
most of your time away."

"You know how it's been, Charlie. Never enough time.
Always more to do . . ."

Truth was, Keene didn't know how he felt. On the occasions when he had gone back to Dione seriously thinking
it was time to make a commitment, always the same restlessness had seized him again, and he had found some reason to put it off.

Early in the afternoon they came to a point where the
river flowed over a fault line in a waterfall of maybe a
hundred feet. The map had given them early warning, and
they pulled in to the shore in good time. Getting past,
however, involved a detour of perhaps half a mile down
rock falls and slippery mud slopes. They were still more
or less on schedule, but Charlie was beginning to limp and

trying not to show it. Once or twice on the awkward stretches, he caught his breath sharply in an audible wince. Keene felt growing concern, but said nothing.

"Tell me again what's in this probe when we get to it," Charlie said from behind, as they carried on, back on the river.

If we find it, Charlie, Keene said to himself. He replied, "They're fitted as mobile emergency posts. Cans of fruit, soup, spongy puddings. Fish and stew. Candy."

"And chocolate? I've got a craving for chocolate."

"Plenty of it. And slabs of that mint stuff that mountain climbers and hikers carry. And of course, coffee and juice to drink. And there's probably more. I only had a quick look while they were showing it to me up in the *Varuna.*"

"Why did you have to mention that? What wouldn't I give to be back up in the *Varuna* right now?"

"To the right, to the right . . . Watch those rocks."

"Clean, dry sheets. Hot water. Showers."

"This paddle's about had it. I need to switch it for one of the spares."

"A squeezer of wine from Mimas. Relax and watch a movie. Maybe one of the old L.A. police detective ones . . ."

"I'll still settle for a good Massachusetts fish restaurant. . . . I wonder what kind of fishing you could get going here. Have the stocks had time to build up again yet? I'd have thought so."

"That's something we haven't really checked out. Maybe the plateau wasn't the best place for a base."

"How's that leg, Charlie?"

"It's got kind of a burning ache . . . but the water helps. Not too bad when the weight's off it."

They came to a brake of tall, broad reeds and pulled in to add another layer of bundles on top of the raft, by now waterlogged and sitting practically level with the surface. The upper part of Charlie's calf had swollen and was stiffening the knee, the wound itself red and angry-looking. The thorn seemed to have infected it with some kind of poison. How virulent it was remained to be seen. When Keene had dressed it, Charlie dragged himself around and tried to help with strengthening the raft. But the movement aggravated the pain, and his stiff leg made it too awkward. He ended up sitting and tying the bundles, letting Keene do the cutting. They still hoped to reach Joburg before dark. Whether they would be able to do much more before the morrow, however, was another matter.

The Joburg settlement lay below rocky slopes that in their upper parts steepened into a ridge of broken crags. It was somewhere up there that the probe had gone down. Below the settlement, easier slopes flanked a ravine containing the creek that ran down to join a long, narrow lake oriented roughly north-to-south, lying to the west. Charlie had guessed that this lake formed part of the course of the river they were on, the river entering at its northern end. After coming ashore, therefore, they would have to work around the settlement to get from the lake below to the ridge above, trusting to care and good fortune that they wouldn't be discovered in the process.

They drifted into the lake without further mishap a little more than an hour before dusk. And it was here that the first difficulty confronted them. For the lake was approximately two miles long, with many inlets and indentations along its eastern bank, and the scale of the map was too small to locate Joburg accurately. They probed their way along the shore, searching the slopes and skyline above for some recognizable landmark—it had become apparent too late that the peaks Keene remembered seeing when he was at Joburg were not visible from the level of the lake. He was beginning to think they would just have to take a chance on landing somewhere and trust to luck, when strange sounds reached their ears: a staccato of five or six reports, muffled and distorted by echos. There was a pause. Then they came again. They seemed to be coming from the far side of a rise sloping down to some bluffs near the water's edge not far ahead. Then another series sounded. Charlie and Keene stared at each other in bewilderment. Neither of them needed to be told what they were hearing. It was gunfire.

They guided the raft into an inlet below the rise and beached among the rocks, hauling the raft out of the water after them. As soon as they began moving up onto higher ground among the bluffs, it became clear that Charlie wouldn't be going far anytime soon—at least, not under his own power. His knee had stiffened completely, racking him with a burning pain at every attempted step. And he was feverish.

"You go on, Lan," he gasped, lowering himself back into a space between the boulders. "There isn't any choice. We can't both stay here, and I can't go on."

Keene couldn't argue. On top of that, the light was running out and they needed to know what the shooting was all about. He unpacked one of the foam-filled quilts to help make Charlie as comfortable as he could, and leaving both packs with him, set off following the rise inland, keeping to the side that was sheltered from the direction the sounds were coming from.

When he had gained some height, he risked moving up to the crest to survey the far side and found himself overlooking a small valley with a creek at the bottom, narrowing to a ravine farther on. It had to be the creek that ran past Joburg and down to the lake. Following the creek farther would take him right past the edge of the settlement area, which would be inviting discovery. He had no choice but to make a detour leftward to get past it.

By the time he rejoined the creek above the settlement, dark was closing in and the gunfire had ceased. He crossed over toward the more open slopes beneath the ridge, which was where it had seemed to be coming from. His only guess was that some kind of fighting had broken out as a result of the events that had taken place at Serengeti. But as he moved up the bank to see, he heard voices and laughing, making him duck hastily back down. Peering from a gap between the rocks, he saw a group of Rakki's Tribesmen moving down in the direction of the huts, some of them swaggering jauntily. All of them were carrying guns. Among them, he recognized Rakki's lieutenant, Enka, with the missing teeth. Then he caught snatches of a voice that sounded familiar.

". . . because I'm the boss, that's why. You just stick to your job. And anyway, even if . . ."

Two of the figures were taller, wearing what looked in the fading light to be Kronian combat garb. The speaker was Jorff.

Keene lay in the darkening shadows, not knowing what to make of it, until a long time after they had gone. For a while he was tempted to work his way closer to the settlement to try and find out something of what was going on, but the recollection that there were dogs there deterred him. As for finding the probe, blundering about up on the ridge in the dark would be more likely to win him a broken leg than anything else, which would be all they needed. There was nothing else for it tonight but to retrace his route back down to where he'd left Charlie. The only thing he was able to offer Charlie when he got back was a refilled water bottle.

As night wore on, Charlie alternated between fits of sweating and shivering, and was not very coherent. Keene gave him the second quilt and made himself as comfortable as he could wedged among rocks with the packs and spare clothing. Thunder boomed distantly to the east. Just to make everything complete, it started to rain. Keene pulled the tatters of his parka close around him and tried to plan for tomorrow.

What were Jorff and Zeigler's guards doing at Joburg? The mood of the party he had seen on their way back down to the huts hadn't spoken of any hostilities. So they had to be training Rakki's warriors in the use of firearms—there had been shooting, and they were carrying guns. Training them for what? The only thing that came to mind was to supplement Zeigler's force at Serengeti. The thought, as Keene pictured it, of Kronians being humiliated by what at present could only be described as little more than savages was distasteful enough; but the further implication was more appalling still. When Valcroix and his supporters arrived, the first small army of oppression would already be waiting to enforce their will. It might be only tiny beginnings, but the pattern of the regime that would grow from it, and the way it would be perpetuated, was already being set. And so the old empires of conquest and exploitation would arise and battle each other again. Unless Kronia could intervene in time to prevent it. But Kronia was ill-prepared for such a task. Since Athena, its energies had been totally absorbed in fighting for its own survival.

More to the immediate point, what was he to do tomorrow? Cold, hungry, wet, and exhausted, he was unable to formulate any clear plan of action. They needed to find the probe, but what to do about Charlie? . . . But surely Rakki's warriors were too few to be worth all the effort. . . . So what was Jorff doing here? . . . Keene fell into a fitful doze with the fragments of thoughts still floating disconnected in his mind.

Another morning came, cold, gray, and damp. Charlie looked bad: pale, clammy, and sunken-eyed, coming out of his stupor only to ramble disjointedly. There could be no question of leaving him as he was for any length of time. And that decided Keene's dilemma for him. He stood up resignedly and turned to commence his route of the previous evening, following the rise up from the lakeshore. This time, however, instead of detouring around, he crossed the creek lower down and headed directly toward the settlement.

But as he came within sight of the huts, the whine of flyer engines reached his ears, coming from behind and to his left, getting louder. It sounded like a craft approaching from the north. He turned to scan the sky and picked it out, following the line of the lake and descending. Then it turned toward the settlement on an approach that would bring it right over him, causing him to take cover hurriedly among some rocks. It was a medium personnel bus—seating up to twenty. Keene watched it pass over the huts to land on the open ground above. Then he emerged and carried on in the same direction as before, but curious now, moving more cautiously, in no haste to reveal his presence. Everyone's attention was on what was happening on the far side of the settlement, and he was able to get quite close.

A new building had appeared, not a makeshift affair like the huts and shelters, but square and solid, and standing apart from them. And on the open ground above, there was another flyer as well, he could now see, smaller than the one that had just landed. That must have been the one that had brought Jorff and his party. Jorff and Rakki were there, with two of Zeigler's troopers from Serengeti, along with Enka, Sims, and a group of what must have been at least a dozen, maybe more, of Rakki's Tribesmen lined up waiting, all carrying arms. As Keene watched, Enka shouted a command, and the Tribesmen began filing into the bus.

CHAPTER FORTY

Yobu remembered more than the younger people did of the world that had existed before times of Terror, when fire and stones rained upon the land, floods roared through the mountains, and the Long Night followed. He remembered the cattle he had tended on the vast estate of a government official who spent most of his time away in the city or out of the country, and life in the shanty village where the domestics and hired hands dwelt.

He had never been to the distant city, but the things he'd heard and seen on the TVs hadn't struck him as appealing. Yes, there was probably more money to be made there, but that had been an obsession of younger men who wanted the chance to change their lives, or to just buy some women, clothes, liquor, and excitement from time to time. But who at Yobu's age would have wanted to change their life, if they were reasonably content and were provided the basics to get by, and then have to start spending the little time they had left having to learn new things all over again?

The coming of the Sky People had reminded him of other things too, that had faded after the more recent and violent happenings. Their machines brought back pictures of the trucks on the road that went to places he had never heard

of; the work going on at their base to the north was like
the construction scenes he'd been to on occasions. But then
the killing that he'd witnessed, and the appearance of an
armed faction assuming power over the rest brought alive
again the feelings of anger and helplessness he'd harbored
toward the strangers who had built their palaces on the land
that had been his people's since the gods of the old legends
created it and gave it to them, and enclosed them behind
wire fences watched by armed soldiers. For a while after
the Terror, he had thought that perhaps the gods were angry
too at what men were making of their gift of the world,
and had swept it all away. But nothing had changed. It was
beginning again, already, and even Sky People who went
to other worlds were unable to stop it. It troubled him.

He stood on the steps of the porch in front of Rakki's
hut, watching the warriors board the large plane that had
just landed—it didn't really resemble the planes he remembered, but he had no other term for it—and the smaller one
that had brought Jorff, Leisha, and the two soldiers earlier.
All were going: Rakki, Enka, Sims, and the fifteen most
proficient with the guns, which meant just about all who
were not youths. So Rakki would get his revenge over Jemmo
at last and become ruler of the caves. And his side of the
bargain would be to allow his people to be trained and
recruited for war. War against whom? It could only be against
the other Sky People at the base, or more who were to
follow. Rakki's warriors would be used as expendables in
fighting the quarrels of others—just as it had always been
before.

And what had Yobu done to stop it? Nothing. He had
encouraged it. He had exhorted the warriors as he had been
expected to, and told them they would find glory and show
their valor in building a bigger, stronger tribe that would
one day become a great nation. Anything else would have
incurred Rakki's anger, and Yobu feared that the most, for
he had seen what it brought upon others. But inside, he
felt shame and contempt for himself. It wasn't those like
Rakki who were responsible for injustices and the suffering that these things brought. Like any others, they were
simply organisms following their nature. It was those like

Yobu, who either helped them through fear, or else did nothing. And were they not following their own inner nature too?

The doors of the two aircraft closed, and the engines started, sending up swirls of dust. The onlookers, meaning just about the entire female and juvenile population that was left, crowded to the side of the settlement to watch. The sounds intensified, and the smaller craft lifted off first to make a slow circuit west above the lake. The larger craft rose to join it as came back over, and the two departed toward the southeast, climbing slowly. The onlookers watched in awe until the two dots were lost against the overcast, and then dispersed to return to their various chores. Yobu turned back to some clay he was mixing. Leisha had shown him some basics of writing, and he was looking for a more permanent way of preserving the markings she had made for him on pieces of paper. Calina, who had been watching the warriors' departure from behind him, was by his table, looking down at them.

"Clay turns hard like rock when it dries," he explained. "I thought we could make the marks in it and keep them from being lost."

"I can help you with this, Yobu," she said distantly.

"You? . . . You know the shapes and how to join them?"

"I did once, a little . . . when I was very young. I had forgotten. Like you, I am remembering things."

Yobu looked at her. "When you were a child . . ." A new possibility that he hadn't thought of opened up in his mind. "We could teach the children too." But even as he spoke the words, the flame died from his eyes.

"It would not be permitted," Calina said, voicing it for him. "Rakki would not let others with an ability he doesn't possess make him look inferior. And he would not have the patience to sit for many hours and learn. His way is for things that are swift and sure."

She was right, of course. Yobu nodded and sighed. Calina looked away suddenly. A commotion was coming from somewhere outside. They moved to the rail at the edge of the porch and looked out. Something was happening below, somewhere by the creek. They moved out from the hut to where they could see. A tall figure, walking unsteadily, was coming up the slope from the direction of the lake. It was one of the Sky People; but Yobu had never before seen one of them looking like this. He was dirty and disheveled, with eyes white and staring from a blackened face, his clothing reduced to tatters and covered in mud. Several of the women who were near began following behind and to the side of the stranger, moving warily, keeping their distance. Three of the youths ran toward him with spears, conscious of their self-imposed status as the settlement's new guardians. They menaced and shouted warnings, but the figure kept coming until he was a few yards from Yobu and Calina.

He uttered some words but Yobu didn't understand. The stranger pointed to himself and gestured back the way he had come, then showed two fingers. "Two . . . Another." He made the same gestures again along with more that involved showing both hands and making waving motions in the air.

"There is another," Calina said. "I think he's saying the other can't move. He must be hurt or sick."

Yobu's first thought was that another aircraft had come down short, but he quickly realized that couldn't be so: the other Sky People would have known and not just left in the way they had. The figure was acting as if it knew Yobu. Yobu looked more closely. After some effort, he realized it was the one who had faced Rakki at the first meeting with the Sky People, and who Rakki had thought was the "head god." From what Yobu had seen, he was not one of those who had given Rakki the guns. So had he come here as a friend or an enemy?

"He was here before," Calina said. "It is the one they call Keene." The Sky Man nodded at the sound of his name.

"Yes, I recognize him." But still Yobu wavered, unsure what to do.

"Put down your spears and help," Calina said to the boys. "Can't you see he can barely stand?" Then she called to Engressi, a female of Uban, who had gone with the warriors. "Get four of the others. Bring vines and skins, thick branches to use as poles, and one of the nets used for fishing. Tell Geel to heat more water and prepare food."

While Engressi ran to and fro, carrying out her directions, Calina nodded to Keene and pointed back the way he had indicated. He turned and began leading the way, Calina and Yobu beside him, the boys following, and a small crowd building up behind.

Keene led them down along the creek, across the head of the ravine, and from there over the rise to descend to the inlet from the lake. Keene's companion was among the rocks a short distance above the water, propped among packs and oddments that they had carried, and covered by padded blankets. Keene conveyed that he was called Charlie. He was feverish with sickness and reacted dully to the arrival of the newcomers, as if hardly aware of their presence. There was no sign of an aircraft or other kind of vehicle by which they might have gotten to that place. Since it was near the water, Yobu could only conclude that they had floated there somehow.

Calina and Engressi used stone blades to cut the rags from Charlie's leg and examined his wound. It looked as if it had been pierced by a thorn of the fangleaf bush, which also grew in the swamplands that Rakki had come from, and which his warriors used to tip their arrows. A preparation of certain leaves would draw the poison and ease the swelling, Calina said. But he was at the time of decision already, and whether or not the measure would succeed, only time would tell. They bound the wound while others constructed a litter from the net that they had brought, tied between two poles that could be carried on shoulders. Then, with followers collecting the packs and other things that were there, the party returned to the settlement.

They took Charlie to Geel's hut, where the women were already heating water for cooking. Calina began crushing leaves, while others cleaned and bathed the wound. But Keene, after taking a few morsels of food and rinsing the worst of the grime from his face, refused to rest and be still. Through signs and gestures, he asked where Rakki and the warriors who had left with him were going and why. Yobu didn't feel it was his place to disclose anything, and pretended not to understand. Keene became more agitated, demanding again to know where Rakki had gone. Yobu grew more obstinate. Calina kept herself to organizing what the women were doing and stayed out of it.

And then Keene noticed two small children, a boy and a girl, playing near the doorway of the hut while their mothers were busy inside. They were using a sharp, bright object to dig stones out of the ground. Keene called to them, and they looked up. He held out an open hand, indicating that he wanted to see what it was. They were unsure and looked to Yobu for guidance. "Let the Sky Man see it," he told them. The boy, who was holding it, gave it to Keene. It was a piece of twisted metal, apparently torn from something. Keene examined it, turning it over in his hands. Evidently, it was something important. He looked up, asking again by signs where it had come from. Yobu didn't know. Keene gestured toward the outside, pointing up at the ridge above Joburg.

Suddenly, Yobu realized what Keene was trying to say. The small plane that Enka had shot an arrow at had crashed up there. Jorff had said it was damaged and would be collected soon, and Rakki had strictly forbidden any interfering with it in the meantime. The children must have taken a piece that had been broken off.

"Is it from the Metal Bird that died up there?" Yobu asked them. "Is that where you found it?"

"Yes," the boy answered. "Where the Sky Warrior and his woman go when they . . ." He looked flustered. The girl with him erupted into a fit of giggling, "Rub bodies."

Yobu looked back at Keene and nodded. "Yes. Is so."

Keene gestured at himself with both hands, then indicated the ridge again. He wanted to go up there. It was urgent.

Anything to keep Keene's mind off Rakki and the warriors, before the argument got any worse, Yobu thought to himself. He called the three boys over, who were still nearby with their spears, keeping a protective eye on things. "Take the Sky Man up there, and show him where the wounded bird lies that Enka brought down with his bow," he instructed.

CHAPTER FORTY-ONE

In the instrumentation bay aboard the orbiting *Varuna* where the survey probes were fitted out and checked, Kerry Heeland floated below a probe in one of the service cradles, disconnecting an underbelly camera that was malfunctioning and would have to come out. He felt frustration and despondency. As a Kronian, he had been outraged by Gallian's murder. And then the whole thing had taken on an additional personal dimension with the shooting and incarceration of Owen Erskine, who had been a close friend of Heeland's as well as a work colleague. He couldn't understand why everyone down there didn't just go for Zeigler's thugs en masse the way Owen had tried to do. Surely there were enough of them. So there was risk, and a few would very likely get hurt. But few worthwhile things in life had been achieved without some kind of risk. Just about everybody else that he had talked to in the *Varuna* felt the same. But there was little they could do up here, isolated in the ship, with all communications to ground routed via Zeigler's headquarters, and the supplies they depended on transferred down to the surface. So they carried on with their jobs as directed. And they waited.

A duty operator from the Probe Director Section drifted in through the far doorway, singled out Heeland, and propelled himself across. "We've got a transmission from the surface coming in on emergency band," he said, keeping his voice low. "It's Landen Keene. He's asking for you personally."

Puzzled, Heeland left what he was doing and followed the operator back into PDS. They stopped at the console of screens monitoring the probes and airmobiles currently deployed. The line flashing red on one of the displays identified the signal as coming from the disabled probe at Joburg. Keene's face, haggard, windblown, and unshaven, was staring from the screen indicated by the alarm signal. "Okay, I'll handle this," Heeland said tersely. The operator nodded and moved away to another station.

"Lan," Heeland muttered. "What in Hell . . . ?"

"Explanations later." Keene's voice was croaky and weak. "You're at Joburg?"

"Yes. Look, I wanted your help on something, but things have gotten even more complicated now. First, can you get access to the *Varuna*'s long-range communications somehow? I need to get a message to the *Aztec* if it isn't too late already. They could be next."

Similar thoughts had crossed Heeland's mind. "That could be a tough one," he replied. "Control is locked into OpCom down on the surface."

"I know. But the channels go out on the ship's lasers. There has to be some way of tapping in up there."

"You're talking to the wrong person for this, Lan."

"I guessed that too. But you're the only one I knew how to contact via this probe's E-band."

"I'll have to check with the comm techs and see," Heeland said after a pause. "What was the other thing?"

"Did you know that Zeigler has been arming the natives here at Joburg and training them?"

Heeland's face hardened. "No, I didn't. But we don't get to learn about much of anything up here."

"Jorff just left here with two flyers carrying Rakki with his pals and all the soldiers. I want to find out where they went and what they're doing."

Heeland shook his head. This was confusing. "Wait a minute. . . . You're there at Joburg, and you know they were training Rakki's guys, but you don't know where they went," he checked. So you weren't with them?"

"Of course not."

"So how did you get there?"

"I said, explanations later. I'm here with Charlie Hu. We started out in one of the site runabouts, but it got wrecked. Charlie's sick but being taken care of. But is there some way of finding out where Jorff and the others went? Can you track nav beacons on the flyers via the sat grid from up there?"

"Normally, yes. But like I said, control is being concentrated at surface OpCom. We're locked out of it." Heeland thought over the possibilities. "Do you think they're being brought in to beef up Zeigler's strength at Serengeti?" he suggested. "His numbers are pretty thin."

"If it were just the troops that left with Jorff, then maybe," Keene replied. "But why Rakki and his general staff too? I've got a hunch something bigger could be going on somewhere else."

"Like what?

"Have you forgotten Pieter Naarmegen and those people in the Scout out there?"

Heeland punched the console in suppressed fury. "But why?" It wasn't that he wouldn't have put it past Zeigler. He just didn't see a reason.

"I don't know, Kerry. But everything has gotten crazy. Who knows what might be going on? Can we get through to someone at Serengeti to find out if they show up there or not? You can patch me through. Let me worry about if I'm traced." Even if Keene had a working compad with him, it wouldn't have the range to connect directly.

"We'd still be identified too," Heeland said. "The incoming message ID would be from here."

"There's got to be a way," Keene insisted.

Heeland thought frantically. If this was his chance to help do something positive, he wasn't about to let it slip away. "The runabout that you abandoned. Were the comms still working in it?"

"I don't know. It did have local functions. I copied some files out of it just before we left. What did you have in mind?"

Heeland answered slowly, still checking through the sequence in his mind. "If I can relay you to the runabout, I might be able to set it to auto-repeat from there. That way the incoming signal at Serengeti would just identify the runabout. I assume it's out in the wilds someplace. If they locate it, you don't care?"

"I already said, let me worry about things like that, Kerry."

"It might work. Can you remember the runabout's number or its net ID code?"

"The vehicle number was SU27. I don't know about the ID. We never used it."

"Let me try that."

Keene thought for a moment longer. "Those high-altitude airmobile platforms that you showed me—that transport and launch probes. Are they still controlled from up there, in the *Varuna*?" he asked.

"Yes. They're primarily for directing planet-wide recon-naissance. Why?"

"Do you have one of them in this area right now?"

"There's one about fifty miles southeast of the base." There was usually a probe on-station in the general vicinity of Serengeti, monitoring weather and geological developments. "It's recently deployed, still with three probes on board."

"Can you move it closer this way?" Keene asked. "As a precaution. Having some high-level eyes up there might be useful."

"Will do." Heeland composed a command to move the center of the airmobile's flight pattern to a new location and sent it off. Then he called up the register of ground vehicles at Serengeti. Site Runabout SU27 was listed as out of service. It responded when he interrogated its ID code.

Sariena was in the labs, reading a report on the plots of meteorites and debris orbiting Earth, when the call from Keene came through on her compad. At least, that was her official task. More surreptitiously, she had become some-thing of a clearing house for information fed back from many eyes and ears around the base. A spirit of resistance was establishing itself that would be ready to erupt when the opportunity presented itself.

She had learned from past experience never to be too surprised at anything that developed once Keene was involved. "You made it? You're at Joburg?" she said without preliminaries.

"Just—last night."

"Why so long?"

"Predictably, we had problems."

"Yes, you look like it. Be careful, Lan. If you don't already know, Jorff is there. He's equipping Rakki's Tribesmen with firearms and training them."

Surprise showed on Keene's face. "How did you know?"

"Shayle has an inside source," Sariena said simply.

Although obviously curious to know more, Keene merely nodded. The details could wait until later. "They left here this morning—Jorff, two of Zeigler's troops, Leisha, Rakki, and the whole squad," he said. "One thought is that they might be coming to Serengeti."

Sariena thought for a moment, then shook her head. "I don't think so, Lan. Kelm also left here earlier with a party of guards. And it seems that Zeigler is getting ready to go somewhere. Something seems to be happening. But whatever it is, it's not here." Keene stared hard from the tiny screen. Behind him, apparently some distance back, Sariena caught a glimpse of a figure holding a spear. "Do you know you have company, Lan?" she asked.

"Yes, don't worry about it. They're my escort. . . . Look, can this source that Shayle has find out more? This is urgent. We need to know now. I think they might be going after Naarmegen and the others in that Scout."

Sariena felt her mouth go dry at the thought. "But why? For what purpose?" she whispered.

"Who knows? To teach everyone else a lesson? To give Rakki's soldiers an easy first-blood lesson and show them that the Sky People aren't invincible? Whatever goes through the minds of people who want things like this."

"I'll go and find Shayle now," Sariena said. "You'll be there?"

"There's not much else in the way of places to go," Keene answered.

✦　　✦　　✦

The rendezvous point chosen for Jorff's two flyers to meet up with the one bringing Kelm and the backup force from Serengeti was a desolate valley on the west side of the central mountain chain known as the Spine, about halfway between Serengeti and Carlsbad, where operation Usurper was to be carried out. The plan was for Rakki's newly trained force to bear the brunt of the action, both as a morale booster for them and to suitably impress the Cave Tribe of how much they stood to gain from coming over as allies once Jemmo was gone. The method to be employed was modeled on former Terran riot and crowd control tactics. Reconnaissance probes were already deployed in the area and would be moved in close to locate Jemmo before the attack went in. When it did, the assault force would be able to go straight for the target, relying on speed and shock to numb any potential resistance into inaction until it was too late. And if something did go wrong that warranted calling in the support, it would be good experience for Kelm's troops too.

Kelm, Jorff, and Leisha stood together on the ground, watching as the three craft that had taken off minutes previously completed their circuit and came down in the same positions they had been in for the three static rehearsals. Sims was the first out of the leading bus, shouting orders and waving Rakki's warriors on as they emerged past him at a run, fanning out to secure the flanks. The smaller personnel flyer that had landed beside it disgorged the snatch squad led by Enka, while the backup team from the second bus slightly farther back advanced to take up covering positions. Considering the insanely short time he'd had to pull anything together, Jorff had done amazingly well, Kelm conceded inwardly. But it wouldn't do to let himself be seen with too soft a public image.

"Too ragged and slow forming up on the left flank," he said. "And the third man along there is going to kill himself or somebody else, holding his weapon like that. Get them back inside, and let's run through it again on the ground."

"Sir," Jorff acknowledged, and began shouting orders.

Kelm turned to Leisha. "How much longer before Zeigler and the others get here?" he asked her.

"Due in just about forty-five minutes," she told him.

Considering the haste, the demonstration they had just seen would no doubt be satisfactory. But Kelm thought they could do even better. "Let's make this a good, snappy one. Then two more drops from circuits," he called to Jorff. "You think we can impress the boss?"

"You bet."

There was some jostling and milling about going on around the doors, Kelm saw. But that wasn't too important. The practice hadn't been to get them back in.

CHAPTER FORTY-TWO

Kronian Interplanetary vessels like the *Osiris* and *Trojan* simulated gravity by the rotation of a wheel-like system of modules carried on spokes that could be trailed at an angle like a partly-open umbrella to produce a normal resultant of centrifugal and linear forces at the Rim. While ingenious, this yielded a large and somewhat ungainly structure whose distortion under thrust set a limit on the acceleration that could be sustained. This meant that they were unable to take full advantage of the performance theoretically attainable from their fusion drives. *Aztec,* by contrast, with its underdeck Yarbat generators, did away with large, deformable geometries, and was trim and compact. When the ship was under thrust, the AG fields were simply generated at a slant to produce the same effect as had previously required enormous works of structural engineering. Hence, though its drives were similar to those used on the earlier craft, *Aztec* could run them to higher power. In addition, even with its greater carrying capacity, *Aztec* was burdened with smaller mass. For both these reasons, it could attain accelerations that were considerably higher. To withstand the resulting forces, the vessel's construction was correspondingly more robust.

If he hadn't known otherwise, he might have thought he

was inside an old Terran ocean liner rather than a space-craft, Jansinick Wernstecki thought to himself as he looked around the aft cargo hold. He had come back to inspect the securing of the "rafts" of massive lithofracture exciters that the ship was carrying. Commander Reese had advised that new orders changing their flight plan were expected from Saturn. With the prospect of course changes and maneuvering, such a check on the heavy cargo was routine. What wasn't routine, of course, was to be anticipating orders to slow down or stand off after all the hurry to get *Aztec* and its payload to Earth as soon as possible.

A call tone sounded from his compad. It was Merlin Friet, Wernstecki's colleague who had come with him from the Tesla Center on Titan. "Jan, how's it going there?" he queried.

"I'm just about done. Nothing amiss. What's up?"

"I'm with Vicki and Luthis in the dining mess. Vicki's been talking about how their planetary theory has been coming together. It's fascinating. I thought you might like to join us."

"Sure. I'm on my way." Wernstecki cut the connection and began making his way forward out of the hold and through the ship.

It was obvious to all by now that something ominous was happening on Earth. Communications were still spasmodic, and then always with the same people. Wernstecki had sent several messages for Keene, but no replies had been forthcoming. The responses to his questions were evasive or nonsensical. The claim of interference from electrical disturbances in Earth's vicinity was wearing thin.

Few now doubted that there had to be some connection with the disappearance at the same time of Valcroix and the Pragmatist leaders at Saturn, and the prevalent guess was that some kind of attempt was being made to seize the Terran base as the beginnings of an independent political system. Many thought that the *Trojan* had to be involved also, although the mechanics of how the different units scattered over such vast distances were to be brought together was unclear.

Wernstecki was unable to relate to the motives or

psychology that would drive men to act in such ways. Born
on Enceladus, a Kronian, he had grown up in tune with
the internal pulse and rhythm of the new cultural organism that was coming into being, expressing its inner
imperative to expand both through space, by encompass-
ing and eventually leaving the Solar System, and through
time by becoming the Future of the human species. Just
as the previous high cultures that had been born, flour-
ished, and then when their span was over, like any other
organism, died—Babylonian, Chinese, Hindu, Egyptian,
Greco-Roman, Arabian, Central American, European, North
American—had been driven to their highest achievements
in thought, art, technical mastery, and social organization
by their religion, so Kronia was an expression of a religion, though not expressed in the same terms as the earlier
ones. Wernstecki was very conscious of the life-force ema-
nating from the collective Kronian soul that was in the
process of awakening, that united him and all others who
shared it.

It wasn't a geographical or territorial thing that had to
do with any place of origin. The pioneers who founded
Kronia had come from every place. What they shared was
a world view that rejected the soulless battlefield of economics that Earth had become, with life itself reduced to
a pointless mechanical process with no other purpose that
the accumulation of money, carrying in them instead the
vision of what could be.

But the forces that had been brought to Kronia when Earth
died, and which were now revealing themselves, had no
place in such an organism. Products of an age that had
already been dead, they would reduce all of life to the level
of animal subsistence and the mechanical caricature that their
sciences had created. Because they comprehended nothing
beyond, the aliens wanted to raise once more to eminence
the accumulation of material wealth as sole object of
existence, and if that were resisted, to impose it by force,
because that was the only way they knew how. And,
indeed, that was the only term to describe the phenomenon,
Wernstecki reflected: *Alien.* A foreign invader in the Kronian
organism, living to a different imperative that was in conflict

with the host. He worried that the host might have recognized the threat and reacted to it too late.

The mess wasn't crowded when Wernstecki arrived. Merlin and Vicki were at a corner table. Tanya, Vicki's cabin mate was with them. He helped himself to a Mimas tea from the self-serve counter by the door and made his way over. A few heads nodded at him perfunctorily. "So what's going on?" he asked, easing himself down onto the bench seat next to Tanya.

"Vicki's latest exchanges with Farzhin at Dione," Merlin replied. "It sounds as if they've got something coming together that could tie it all up. We thought you'd want to hear it."

"Me too. I've only just arrived here," Tanya put in.

Wernstecki sipped his tea. "Well?" He looked around invitingly. "I'm all ears, and panting with suspense." Merlin waved for Vicki to take it. Wernstecki had heard a lot about Vicki as a result of working with Keene on Titan, and gotten to know her himself more during the voyage. She possessed the instincts that made her a natural Kronian too.

"Emil's working with Sariena's people now," Vicki said. "They've been modeling large-scale impacts on internally hot, planet-size bodies. What comes out is consistent with a lot of what we believe happened."

"What are we talking about—the breakup of the Saturnian configuration?" Wernstecki asked.

Vicki shook her head. "Before that. The earlier event. If they're right about Earth being part of a family accompanying a proto-star Saturn, it could have been during the disruption when they encountered whatever the original solar group was."

"They think this is the event that ended the dinosaurs," Tanya said.

"So that didn't happen with the breakup?" Wernstecki checked.

"Not if this latest theory is right."

It was generally accepted that Earth's gravity had undergone a significant increase at some point—things the scale of dinosaurs couldn't have functioned under modern conditions. Many attempts had been made to fit this with the time of Earth's separation from Saturn; the hemisphere phase-locked to face the primary would have experienced a gravity reduction, reverting to full value when Earth became detached. The two problems that this approach had run into, however, were first, no amount of tweaking with the model gave a gravity increase sufficient to account for the effects that had been inferred; and second, it was known that humans had lived at the time of the Saturnian breakup, which was difficult to reconcile with the presence of dinosaurs.

Vicki explained. "It seems there might have been two distinct events. To begin with, Earth was a close-orbiting satellite with reduced gravity on its Saturn-facing side. This produced gigantic life-forms. They lived on a crustal bulge, also a result of the distorted gravity, that stood out from the ocean covering the rest of the planet. A super-continent."

"Pangea," Wernstecki supplied.

"Now, a planet like Earth isn't brittle all through," Vicki said. "It's a crust covering a fluid and sticky interior. An impact by something large isn't going to shatter it into pieces. It'll penetrate and be absorbed to produce a deformed composite body. Imagine Pangea on the far side, fractured by expansion of the opposite surface as the impact shock propagates through."

"How big an object are we talking about?" Wernstecki asked.

"We put it at around twenty percent the volume of the previously existing Earth, and high density—about halfway between that of the crust and the core."

"So you'd get a what? A kind of pear-shaped object?"

"Which over time collapses back to spherical. The increase in radius is small compared to the gain in mass, so surface gravity goes up appreciably. With the figures they used, new animals repopulating the changed environment would have to reduce their body dimensions by around forty percent to retain the same power-weight ratio."

"Is that enough?" Wernstecki looked around questioningly.

"About what you'd need to produce the titanotheres," Vicki answered, referring to the giant mammals of the Pleistocene. Wernstecki nodded. He seemed impressed that it was that large.

"But it gets neater, Jan," Merlin Friet said. "A really economic theory. One cause ties together a whole bunch of things that didn't seem related before."

"Well, so far we've wiped out the dinosaurs and broken up Pangea," Wernstecki agreed. "What else is there?"

"Just about all of plate tectonics," Vicki said. "We know that the movements measured before Athena were just the final, cooling-down phases of processes that once happened a lot faster, and the old time scales of millions of years based on them were wrong. But that also means that shifting whole continents around the globe in a reduced time took something more than the tugs from a passing body that caused the sideways rifting Earth is seeing now." She gestured toward Wernstecki. "You said it yourself a moment ago, Jan. Pear-shaped. The whole hemisphere that the pieces of Pangea are adrift on is elevated way above the surface mean. They slide down the gravitational gradient on layers of molten magma produced by dissipating all the heat." Vicki tossed out a hand casually, as if the rest shouldn't need adding. "And as the shape recovers back toward spherical, surface area shrinks with respect to volume, and crumples. That could give you mountain-chain building and ocean trenches."

"Like I said, neat," Merlin repeated. "One theory does it all."

Wernstecki was intrigued. It fitted with the criticisms he'd heard Vicki express on previous occasions about the reliability of the dating systems once thought to be unquestionable. "Do you have a time for this yet?" he asked her.

"Not really. The whole question of chronology is under revision right now."

"But you're saying it was a different event from the Saturn separation? This is something that happened earlier?"

"Right. The Saturn breakup, we put at about 10,000 B.P. Experienced by people. Described in myths. What caused that is still a good question. We think probably a gravitational interaction with something. It was a less violent event."

"Could it have been a Venus encounter—one of them, or two of them; whichever turns out to be correct?"

"Some people argue that," Vicki said. "Personally, I don't think so. Neither does Emil. He sticks by the Vedas, which put that around five thousand years later. Earth was solidly a planet of the Sun by then."

"There's still lots to do, then," Wernstecki observed, sitting back and raising his cup.

"If we're allowed to get on with it," Vicki sighed.

A short silence signaled the change of mood. "What do you think's going on at Earth, Jan?" Tanya asked finally.

Wernstecki shook his head. "I can only guess. And my guesses are as good as anybody else's."

On the Bridge Deck of the *Aztec*, the Communications Officer reported to Commander Reese that the object detected astern, which had been gaining on them for several hours, had announced itself as the *Trojan*. By the authority of the newly constituted Terran Planetary Government, it declared its intention to put a party aboard the *Aztec* and requested acknowledgment accordingly. It reminded *Aztec*'s commander that it was equipped as a vessel of war with long-range offensive capability, and suggested strongly that a cooperative response would be in the best interests of all.

CHAPTER FORTY-THREE

It was just a kit of survival rations, but Keene couldn't remember food ever tasting so good. He hadn't been able to resist opening some of the packs from the probe's store and nibbling while he used the emergency-band unit to talk to Heeland and Sariena. At the same time, while shielding the compartment with his body, he had surreptitiously removed the automatic and concealed it in his clothing. After finishing the calls, he set aside the medical provisions and a selection of clothing and food items to take back down for Charlie. Now he could do nothing but wait for Sariena to call back, and so sat with his back against the probe's engine, savoring the almost forgotten luxury of cheese, crackers, a mint cake bar, and self-heating coffee. His three young escorts, possibly having acquired a partiality for Kronian food from earlier visits, hadn't been able to resist the temptation either when he offered them samples. At first they had approached warily as if suspecting a trick, but now they were squatting around him, munching chocolate squares and fruit drops approvingly. Keene wondered how much they might know of where the departed expedition was heading.

"Jorff? . . . Sky Soldier who commands." He made signs and gestures that attempted to convey the concept. The youths looked back at him with expressions of what looked like genuine concern to be of help, but total incomprehension. One of them said something and accompanied it with motions that left Keene equally at a loss.

Weariness was creeping over him. Something hot and wet burned his knee. He jerked his head up with a start, realizing he had been fading and let the mug tip in his hand. He tried again, making movements in the air to represent flying vehicles, then indicated the open ground below, where the flyers had landed. One of the youths nodded finally that he understood and pointed to the north. "Sky Base. Serengeti." No, Keene groaned under his breath. He already knew where they had come from. How to get across that he wanted to know where they had gone *to*?

The boy sitting in the center put his hands in the position of holding an imaginary rife and then pointed to his chest. "Me with gun. Shoot," he informed Keene proudly. One of the other two said something that sounded derogatory. The third laughed. Keene accepted that he wasn't going to get anywhere.

His thoughts wandered to the runabout upended back where they had left it, waiting for a call. For some reason he pictured birds perching on it. Why was he thinking about birds? He felt the curve of the probe's side pressing into his back. Probe . . . Up in the *Varuna* . . . Erskine should have known better than to try pulling that stunt. . . . How could a few command that much power? That was the problem. The Kronians had never faced opposition. They never had understood power. . . . Cavan understood. . . . Cavan and Harvey Mitchell with his Special Forces unit, and the plane they had flow in to California . . . Vandenberg when the tide went out, leaving miles of uncovered mud . . . Walls of ocean breaking over the mountains above Pasadena . . .

Beep . . . Beep . . . Beep . . . Beep . . .

The tone from the emergency-unit handset propped on a rock beside him jolted him back to wakefulness. He groped for it blearily and clicked it on. It was Sariena.

"Lan, are you all right?"

"Oh . . . uh? Yeah. . . . Sure. What have you got?"

"You can stop worrying about Pieter and the people in

the Scout. What's going on is more involved. The source couldn't give the whole story, but it seems to have to do with a bigger tribe who live in some caves."

"Caves? That sounds like the place that Rakki and his original group came from."

"That's what I thought too. But now listen to this, Lan." Sariena's face was grave. "As far as the source could make out, the plan is to install Rakki there as chief. Zeigler left to rendezvous with them somewhere. So they'll all be arriving together, making it a big event. He must be using his image to force an alliance of the two tribes. Can you see what this might mean?"

Keene was fully awake now, his eyes wide. He saw exactly what it might mean. "He's building a private army. The larger group they've just found farther east on the coast will be next—and whatever others turn up later. He'll be able to challenge the leadership when they arrive. And that's how the new world will be built."

"Unless Kronia prevents it. Would that be possible?"

"They're too far away to do anything in time. And if Valcroix's people have taken over the *Aztec* and deliver it to Zeigler with the capability it's carrying . . ." Keene's voice trailed away as the plan finally became clear in all its horrifying completeness.

"Lan. What is it?"

He stared hard for several seconds. "The *Trojan* is part of it too. It *didn't* get lost on its way to Jupiter. It's coming here. With its firepower as protection, they'll be able to get a self-sufficient operation going before Kronia can organize anything. After that, they could be practically invulnerable. The only chance is to stop Zeigler now. With no friendly base waiting for them, where do they go?"

"But if they've still got *Trojan* . . ."

"They do what? Destroy Serengeti? How does that benefit anyone?"

"Blackmail, maybe. By threatening the *Varuna*. They might be crazy enough."

Keene sighed. She was right. But what else was there? "We just have to risk it."

"But how? What can we do?"

Keene rummaged through the possibilities in his mind, but nothing immediate leaped out. The only answer he could give was, "I don't know. But whatever the chances are, they exist there, where Zeigler is, not here or at Serengeti, where he isn't."

"But we don't even know where he is," Sariena said. "And even if we did, what could either of us do? We're under armed confinement here. All you have there is a dead probe."

Three faces were watching Keene curiously, aware from his manner and tone that something important was afoot but having no idea what. He thought of Rakki and his warriors meeting with Zeigler somewhere out there in the wild lands to the east. . . .

Somewhere in the area over which Heeland's airmobile was circling.

"There might be a way," Keene said. "Stay tuned."

Since Keene's call, Heeland had been making discreet inquiries about the accessibility of the ship's outgoing communications beam. The situation didn't look promising. Control was exercised from the surface, and the local monitoring stations in the Communications Room were manned by Zeigler's own technicians, covered by guards posted there and in the adjoining Control Center. "Tapping in somewhere" in the way Keene had vaguely suggested sounded all very well in principle, but the reality would require expertise and opportunity of a kind that he hadn't come close to identifying yet. He had remained in the Probe Director Section and was considering what to do next, when Keene came through again.

"Kerry, how far away is that flying mobile?"

"From you? About twenty miles east now."

"I'm playing a hunch. Can we get a scan of the area south and eastward from the base toward the Spine? Sweep for transmissions? A couple of flyers left from here earlier, and more from Serengeti. I think they're heading that way. We need to find them. It's important."

"That's still a big area. You don't have anything more specific?"

"Sorry, that's the best I can do. We'll have to trust to luck."

"I'll move the mobile over."

"Can you launch the probes and use those? Cover more area. I want you to land the mobile here at Joburg. Is there any reason why a person can't get a ride in it?"

"It's not equipped to carry people."

"How about in the probe racks? I'm not looking for first class."

"I guess . . . if we kept the altitude low. It could get pretty cold up there all the same."

"I've got the emergency blanket from the probe that's here. What's the mobile's radiation shielding like?"

"It's adequate. We still have to work around things like mobiles."

"And communications?" Keene asked.

"That could be a problem. Like I said, it isn't intended for passengers. It doesn't carry any." Heeland frowned. On the screen, Keene was racking his brains too to come up with something. "Unless!" Heeland said suddenly.

"What?"

"I only launch two of the probes and keep one in the mobile. Then you can use its local unit and the mobile's on-board relay."

"That'll work. Do it. I'm on the ridge up above Joburg."

"Hit the red button on the panel that says *Locator Beacon.* We'll just follow it on down."

Aztec didn't have a Hub. While *Trojan* stood off at a distance of five miles, the ferry bringing its boarding party docked at the transfer locks situated slightly forward of midships. Minutes after the connection was made, armed parties were spreading out through the *Aztec* to secure it. Commander Reese with his officers received Major Ulak on the Bridge Deck and was formally notified that the vessel was now property of the Terran Planetary Government, and that his command was subordinated to the Defense Force. Ulak then made a surprising request: that the lieutenant-commander seconding the boarding party be permitted to speak privately with Ms. Vicki Delucey, one of the scientists from Kronia, who was traveling with the *Aztec.* She was notified accordingly, and by the time the officer was conducted to her cabin, she was already waiting there. Her expression didn't change as the two guards who had escorted him ushered him through and closed the door.

"Hello, Robin," she said.

Mertak came down from the upper level of OpCom and crossed through the guard quarters to the main door. Moving at a normal pace without show of undue haste, he left the fenced security compound and made his way to the power distribution house. Shayle was alone in the control room. Because of the number that were away with Jorff's and Zeigler's parties, no guard was posted here for the time being. All the same, he kept his voice low.

"They're all together at a rendezvous location on the ground. It's a valley southeast from here, just this side of the Spine. I've got the coordinates. . . ."

Keene had just relayed the numbers to Heeland, when one of his three escorts jumped up suddenly, peering up at the sky. The other two scrambled to their feet also. Keene stood up, following their gaze. His ears caught the muted whine of ducted fans, coming from the east. "Okay, I can hear it now," he said into the handset from the probe.

The dot descending from the gray overhead resolved itself into a bright orange-and-white disk topped by a pair of black tail fins. The boys gazed up apprehensively as it approached, at the same time keeping attention on Keene with nervous glances. He waved up at the airmobile and nodded back at them, trying to look reassuring. "Okay, I've got you on visual," Heeland's voice said from the handset. "Didn't know you had company. What gives?"

"They're okay. Just bring it down right in front of the probe."

"You're not planning on taking those guys too, I hope."

"No, just me."

The mobile landed amid a scattering of dust. Keene picked up the foil-backed survival blanket that he'd taken from the downed probe and moved forward to check the accommodation. Two of the underside racks were empty as Heeland had promised, the third still holding its probe. Keene unsnapped recessed catches locking its emergency compartment cover, then leaned in to activate the comm panel and take out the handset. "Reading?" he checked.

"Loud and clear," Heeland responded on the new channel. Keene shut off the handset he'd been using from the grounded probe. Now he had a channel that would travel with him. He unfolded the blanket and began packing it around inside one of the empty racks. The boys were watching him uncertainly, the leader reaching for his spear now. Keene pointed at the pile of things he had set aside to take back, before the change of plan.

"Back, Joburg," he said, pointing to the direction down from the ridge. "Charlie. For Charlie. You take, yes?" He eased himself down, sliding a leg into the space he had prepared.

"*No!*" the leader barked, brandishing his spear threateningly. It seemed that allowing Keene to go would be a betrayal of responsibility. The other two picked up their spears and came forward to support him. Keene had hoped this wouldn't happen. He produced the automatic that he had retained and leveled it at them. They stopped, confused and afraid. In the last couple of days they had seen enough to know what such a weapon was capable of.

"Sorry, guys. It's not the way I wanted to end things, but I have to insist. Just stay back there, and no one gets hurt." They didn't understand the words, but they got the message. Keene eased himself into the rack, still keeping the boys covered. "Okay, take her away," he told Heeland. The three youths stared helplessly the mobile lifted. As it cleared the ridge, Keene saw figures outside the huts below, some pointing, others running about. Its arrival had obviously caused a commotion. He hoped Charlie would be able to figure out at least something of what it meant. The mobile continued in a turning climb toward the east.

CHAPTER FORTY-FOUR

Wernstecki stood in the *Aztec*'s cargo hold, absorbed in thought as he stared again at the groups of squat, cylindrical AG exciters, each more than six feet across, mounted in their massive steel supporting frames. For transit they were secured solidly to the ship's main structural members, stacked crossways to the vessel's length for symmetrical mass distribution. Capable of generating shaped force-fields to shear blocks weighing hundreds of tons from bedrock, this battery of them could be made to project a region of intense, narrow-focused gravitational potential, like a beam, back from the tail of the ship and across the surrounding space. And sitting out there just a few miles away was the *Trojan*, its construction flimsy and extended compared to the *Aztec*'s ruggedness and compactness. It would be like a ferris wheel caught by a grappling hook thrown from a tank. Exactly what kind of damage, disablement, or other effect might be inflicted in this way, Wernstecki didn't know; that would be for those who knew something about ship design to say. But here was a hostile vessel dictating terms because the *Aztec* was unarmed. But maybe, if properly used, some of the cargo it was carrying could be improvised into an armament that no military mind aboard the *Trojan* had dreamed of.

But how?

He sighed and shook his head. Getting the parameter settings right would need a lot of computing. Then there was the physical problem of running heavy power connections from the ship's fusion converters. How could anything like that be organized or even talked about with the ship occupied? Two guards from the boarding party were watching him from the open doorway at the end of the hold right now. It was impossible.

Approaching footsteps sounded in the corridor outside. Luthis appeared moments later, ignored the guards, and came over. "We're gathering in the staff mess—scientific heads and crew chiefs. You need to be there."

"What's happening?" Wernstecki asked.

Luthis had an almost bemused look on his face, as if he didn't quite understand it himself. "Did you know that Vicki's son is here—one of the officers with the boarding party?"

"Yes, Tanya told me."

"Apparently, the two of them had a long talk at his request. Now she's come out and told Reese that what we've been hearing about the whole . . . everything that's going on, isn't the whole story. There's another side to it that we should be aware of. Reese thinks we should all hear it."

Wernstecki couldn't believe it. After all the vehement opposition he'd heard Vicki voice to the Pragmatists and what they stood for, she could have turned around so easily? He shook his head, equally mystified. Landen Keene had said on a number of occasions that he refused to discuss politics with scientists because they were totally naive when it came to such matters—even Terran ones. So what was a Kronian scientist like Wernstecki supposed to make of it? But there was nothing to be done except at least listen, he supposed.

"Very well," he said. Luthis turned, and they headed back toward the forward part of the ship.

Knives of cold found their way through, however Keene tried to pull the foil-backed blanket around himself. The roar of the fans close-up pounded into his skull, and no matter which way he twisted in the rack space, a bar or an edge or a protuberance of some kind seemed to be digging into him somewhere. He thought of Charlie lying on a soft palliasse in a warm, dry hut, being pampered and fussed over by hordes of women.

Receding away to the right, he could see part of the river that they had followed, continuing below the lake before turning away to the west. Below, the land was a desolate succession of humps and ridges, new sedimentary deposits just starting to acquire a covering of vegetation like the coasts he had seen from the probe over New York: the unworked raw material of land, yet to accumulate the effects of time, the elements, and life in action. Then came the steep eastern scarp, formed by the broken edge of the tilted crustal block. Ahead, to the southeast, across a flat wilderness of sandy basins and marshes, the skyline of mountains loomed larger and higher.

"Okay, got 'em!" Heeland's voice came suddenly from the handset, which Keene had wedged against the side of his head. Keene moved it to where he could see the tiny screen. It showed an aerial slant view from a distance of four objects on the ground. A zoom-in revealed them to be two small personnel carriers and two larger site buses.

"I see them," Keene acknowledged, yelling above the din from the fans. "Where are they?"

"A hundred and twenty-five miles ahead of you. The probe that's sending this is cruising a mile out. I sent the other one farther north before you gave me the coordinates. It's on its way, but it'll be a while."

Figures were standing in line at one of the buses, moving forward and boarding. They were in regular tunics—Zeigler's force from Serengeti, not Rakki's warriors, who must have been already inside the other craft. "Looks like they're leaving," Keene said. "We must have just caught them."

"Looks like it," Heeland agreed.

Even as they watched, the last of the figures entered, the door in the side of the bus closed, and the craft began lifting off. Heeland put the probe into a wide circuit, tracking them as they rose. The four vessels formed up and settled onto a southeast heading, continuing the way both they and Keene had been going, which put him in the position of trailing them. The airmobile was built for endurance not speed, and would fall behind the faster flyers. But the probe would be able to shadow them. He would just have to follow where they led and catch up later, after they arrived.

The mountains ahead grew blacker and more foreboding, opening up into huge walls and jagged towers, with sheer faces plunging into daunting chasms. This was not dead terrain formed from sediment dropped by retreating floods, but violent, untamed storms of rock torn out of the living Earth. Far away to the left, huge palls of smoke unfolded and stood heaped up into the sky, reflecting red glows off their undersides. Heeland kept the craft as low as possible, following the gorges between shoulders and peaks now showing white at the summits and down the gullies. Even so, the airmobile was forced to climb into freezing air and mist. Keene's feet were already numb. He tried to flex his fingers and arms continually, all the time striving to keep his grip through layers of metal foil and blanket wrapped around his hands. He could feel ice forming in his eyebrows and his beard. Heeland came through again to say he only wished he could be down there as well, and get involved directly himself. It was as if he had his own personal score to settle.

In the Command Module of the *Trojan*, Captain Walsh approached Valcroix and Grasse, who were conferring with General Nyrom and several aides. Valcroix turned from the group and nodded for him to go ahead. "We have a communication from Commander Reese of the *Aztec*," Walsh advised.

"Well?"

Walsh raised his eyebrows in the manner of someone pleasantly surprised. "It seems that Ms. Delucey has made an impression on them. Reese agrees that there might be more common ground between us than he had appreciated. Others there feel the same way. They're not committing to anything at this stage, but they agree that any basis for a better understanding should be explored. They're willing to hear us out."

Everyone looked pleased. "Easier than I expected," someone murmured.

"Very encouraging," Grasse said.

"When the lieutenant proposed it, I wrote it off as too much of a long shot," Nyrom confessed. "But worth a try. It just shows, you never know."

Valcroix treated them to one of his rare smiles—thin, but real nevertheless. "Presumably, Reese has realized that if there's a choice, he will find life more amenable as a partner than as a captive," he said to the company. Then, addressing Walsh, "Splendid news, Captain. We will treat this in a civilized manner, accordingly. Tell Reese that we will receive him and a selected deputation of their senior people here, aboard the *Trojan*. Make appropriate arrangements to host them. Cuisine in the Officers' Dining Room would be suitable—but not VIP standard. Limit the number to ten and get a list of the names they intend sending, which I want to see before it's confirmed. Does anyone have anything to add?" Nobody did. Since they were in the superior bargaining position and setting the terms, protocol required that the representatives from the *Aztec* come to them.

"I'll get onto it right away," Walsh said.

"One more thing," Ludwig Grasse put in. Valcroix turned to him. "Zeigler has been holding out against difficult odds there on Earth. To boost his morale, I think we should let him know that interception of the *Aztec* has been accomplished successfully. I doubt if he'll learn of it from elsewhere for some time."

Trojan had maintained communications silence since its takeover en route for Jupiter. Kronia would have been informed of its appearance as soon as it was identified by *Aztec*, but there was nothing anybody could have done to prevent that. Even if those at Kronia had had their suspicions previously, there was no reason why they would communicate them to Earth, more so in view of the uncertain situation that they would have discerned there too. Now that they knew for sure of *Trojan*'s part in the scheme, they would be under no further delusions as to what had happened on Earth. Hence, they wouldn't be sending news there of the success of the *Trojan*'s mission.

"A good point," Valcroix agreed. "Yes, by all means, let's

keep Zeigler in the picture. I'm sure he could use all the good news he can get. Can you take care of that too, Captain Walsh?"

"Right away," Walsh promised.

CHAPTER FORTY-FIVE

The Oldworlders said that men had once lived in palaces—huge structures that they built as level upon level rising higher than the cliffs above the caves. Jemmo had decided that caves were dark, damp, inhospitably shaped, and unbecoming of his status. He wanted to build himself a palace.

The line of rock outcrops connected by earth ramparts that had once been the defensive barrier enclosing the front of the caves was now forming parts of dwelling huts, inner works, and animal pens. The population had grown. And nobody any longer lived down in the swamps, all the people having migrated up to the caves. The extended settlement around the caves was now bounded by a wall built from rocks cemented by dried mud. On the outside of it was a ditch, and on the inside a protected step for defenders, raised posts to provide elevate positions for watchmen and archers. Access was via two gates, one backing the other, made from thick root-wood and branches brought up from the swamps, and woven with thorns. On the heights above the caves was a lookout tower, also built from mud-cemented rocks.

The Oldworlder Wakabe had become Jemmo's builder. Jemmo wanted him to build the palace. But whatever Jemmo wanted, always, it seemed, all anybody could tell him were the problems. He didn't want to hear about what couldn't be done. Just for once, couldn't someone just agree and do it? The problem with building a palace, he was told, was that of bridging the roof.

He scowled as he stood with Wakabe and a couple of Wakabe's helpers in front of the four-walled enclosure that Wakabe had built to try out his latest attempt at a solution. The space between the walls was spanned by a mat of woven vines with mud worked into it to form a solid shell. When the mud dried, Wakabe had added another layer on top, and when that dried, another, the intention being that it would become strong enough to support additional loads above. But the work was showing cracks that had spread and widened more since yesterday, Jemmo wouldn't have risked walking under it, never mind have trusted his weight on top.

"The mud needs to be bound," Wakabe explained. "It has no strength against extension. We've never used it this way before. In the walls it has always been compressed, not extended. It needs grass mixed in to bind it. Or reeds might be better. I have to try different things."

"You said your Oldworld people built palaces higher than the cliff," Jemmo grumbled. "Yet you can't build me just one roof?"

"They had trees then. Beams of wood as thick as a man's thigh, as long as five times a man's height. And metal ones, even longer and stronger. We have to learn to work without such things."

Jemmo seethed inside. But it would only make him look foolish to try and command what could not be. He wanted the cave settlement strengthened and secured in preparation for a campaign to extend his domain to the east. Long-range scouting parties despatched in that direction had encountered other humans survivors from the Great Terror and the Long Night, and engaged them in several skirmishes. But he was still uncertain as to their numbers. It could turn out that he and his people became objects of similar ambitions coming the other way, and so a strong defense was the first essential.

He pointed toward the middle of the space with the rifle

he was holding. The bullets had all been used long ago, but he still carried it as an emblem of status, along with his red headband and hide cape fastened with a clasp. "You need to support it there. Why can't you make a pillar from stones and mud, built as you do with the walls? It needs support in the center."

"Yes. That might help a lot," Wakabe agreed deferentially. "It will be done."

Jemmo felt satisfied, having been seen to add something constructive. He was about to add more, when a shout sounded from the tower above the cliff. People were drawing into groups, chattering excitedly, looking up at the sky. "There!" Wakabe exclaimed, pointing. Jemmo looked.

Outside the wall, something long and pointed, the shape of a spearhead, gray in color, was descending from the sky. It was like a gliding bird, but smoother and straighter in its lines, and much larger—a metal bird such as the Oldworlders spoke of. Others had told of seeing such things in the sky recently, but never this close to the caves. Jemmo had never observed one personally. It moved slowly along the far side of the wall, following its line, as if searching the ground inside. Then it made a sudden move closer, bringing it immediately above the wall, at the same time swinging around to point toward where Jemmo and the others were standing. Jemmo had the eerie feeling that it was searching him out personally. Cold fingers of the fear that comes from confrontation with the totally unknown clawed in his stomach. But he forced them back down and strode several paces forward to glower up at the object defiantly. "My war club!" he called to Iyala, his henchman, who was never far away. "Summon spearmen and archers." But Iyala was already giving the orders.

As warriors began arriving, consternation broke out anew among the onlookers. Four more shapes were approaching fast, coming in over the swamplands in a tight group. They were even larger than the metal bird. They swooped on over the wall with a roaring noise and descended toward the area of ground immediately in front of Jemmo and the assembling warriors, causing the people around them to fall back, and then break and flee in fear. Two of the birds were larger than the other two. One of the larger and one smaller came down ahead, the others a short distance behind them. Openings appeared in the sides, from which figures poured at a run. Figures wielding guns! Before Jemmo could even take in what was happening, they were spreading out quickly on either side. . . . He watched in a daze as his personal guards ran forward and were shot down without even slowing the pace of the attackers. Then a tightly grouped formation emerged in the center, coming straight at him. Jemmo knew he was defenseless, that there could be no resistance. But his pride refused to let him budge. He tightened his grip on his club and brought it back determinedly.

But then, he realized, it was over. While the flanking parties waved back the remaining guards, who had also seen the futility of opposing, the center group converged upon him, covering him with their guns but staying out of his reach. He wouldn't have survived making one false move in any case, even if they came closer.

And then the ranks opened and a figure came through at a shuffling gait, dragging one leg, wearing a strange head-dress and sleeveless jacket of thick Oldworlder material. He was also carrying a gun, but slung across his shoulder was a vicious edged club of Oldworld metal that Jemmo had seen before. His face was a mask of gloating delight. He had been waiting a long time for this.

"Will you hand over your weapon like a warrior who accepts defeat?" he asked. "Or would you be seen to have it taken from you like a child?"

Rakki had returned for his revenge.

Heeland was bringing the probe in high, using its wide-scan imager to view the general area. He reported that the analyzers had picked up the signature of another probe circling close in below at not much above ground level; it wasn't being controlled from the *Varuna* and must have been sent by the ground-control operation at Serengeti, which Zeigler's people had taken over. He had located the four flyers at the edge of some broken highlands, where the ground below sloped away toward a low-lying region of lakes and swamps. They didn't seem to be moving. The zoom cursor centered on them, and the view expanded.

"Still can't see anything," Keene croaked, fumbling the handset in his frozen hands.

"I'm taking it down lower, coming out more to change the angle," Heeland's voice said from the unit. "It looks like they've landed. . . . They're at the bottom of a line of cliffs, inside some kind of perimeter that doesn't look natural." Keene could just make it out on his tiny screen—an embankment or wall curving out for some distance and then back again to form an enclosed area against the face. "I think there are caves there," Heeland said. "Huts, people . . . It's some kind of settlement with a wall around. . . ."

"Something's going on—between where the flyers are and the wall." Keene squinted to try and resolve the detail. "Are those people there, all bunched together? What are they doing, Kerry?"

Figures—a dozen of them, maybe—were standing close together in a line along the inside of the wall. Another line stood facing them from a short distance away, with others formed up behind and to the sides. Another group was clustered around flyers farther back, while what looked like the rest of the population crowded in a background semicircle.

"I can't make out what they're doing," Heeland said.

Keene stared at the screen on the handset. To him it was too obvious. What experience would a Kronian have of such things? "That's a firing squad," he said. "They're executing them."

"Why? Who are they?"

"I know as much as you, but it can't be good. Get me down there."

"You're still minutes away."

"Then break it up. Buzz them with the probe." That was all Keene could think of. It had worked at Joburg.

But instead of enlarging, the view on the screen shifted and tilted, and then sky appeared across one corner. Heeland had put the probe into a climb. A horizon materialized and then vanished, and the cliff line came into view again, this time from vertically overhead. The walled settlement was dead center. Enlarging rapidly . . .

✧   ✧   ✧

For Heeland, on his high-resolution screen, had seen what Keene hadn't. The figures lined up against the wall were natives, the one in the center wearing a red headdress and cape. The squad holding rifles and facing them were also natives, as were the ranks immediately behind. But the group of uniformed figures farther back, standing around the flyers and looking on, were in Kronian garb. The red shoulder tabs on the tunic of the one in the center marked him as the Acting Planetary Governor.

The picture of Gallian staggering back and falling replayed itself in Heeland's mind. Owen Erskine shot down, dragged away, his dead companions . . . He centered the crosslines of the pilot graticule, gunned the probe's motor up to maximum, his jaw clamped grimly. Surrounding details flowed off the edge of the image as it leaped upward. Heads lightened in hue as faces turned suddenly upward in alarm.

"Kerry? What in hell are you doing?"

Heeland thought he caught a glimpse of Zeigler's features, eyes wide in disbelief, mouth gaping, an instant before the image blacked out. Maybe it was just wishful thinking and imagination. But it didn't alter the satisfaction.

CHAPTER FORTY-SIX

The discipline that they had worked so hard to perfect was lost. Half of Rakki's warriors were fleeing this way and that, heedless of Enka's shouts and exhortations, terrified that they would be next, while others stood petrified where they were. Some who had been nearest were groaning or crawling on the ground, hit by flying debris. The rest of the cave population were shouting and boiling around in confusion. Rakki stood stunned, staring at where the four flying war engines of the gods had been just moments before, symbols of the power that was to be his to command one day. Two of them were unrecognizable, just heaps of twisted wreckage, one starting to flare up in flames; the other two had been hurled aside like baskets in a wind storm, one lying on its side, the other overturned, both smashed and broken. Of the gods that he'd thought had proved the mightiest, nothing was left. A smoldering hole in the ground marked where Zeigler, his Warrior Chiefs Jorff and Kelm, the woman who spoke tongues, and the others who had arrived with Zeigler at the meeting point, had been standing. The god-warriors who had stood with them had been struck down and scattered. Rakki couldn't see one who had been missed. What force, unleashed from where, had done this?

His triumph had been complete. Exactly as Jorff and Kelm had foretold, they had come out of the sky with the speed of streaking fire-stars, stormed from their carriers to find Jemmo where the eyes of the metal bird had seen him, and taken him before either he, his bodyguards, or anyone was able even to summon the will to react. Embodying the ultimate of terror and power, Rakki had stood before the ranks of his invincible warriors and proclaimed to the cowed yet marveling Cave People that he, *Rakki*, had returned to claim the overlordship that was his by valor and force of arms, not by the ways of lies, deception, and treachery that were the resorts of cowards. Then he had turned to look contemptuously at Jemmo, disarmed and disgraced, menaced by weapons that he had been able only to wave like a toy but which Rakki's men had mastered, and ordered his warriors to dispose of him.

In the way that Kelm had instructed, they had led Jemmo, with Iyala, Alin, Dorik, and his other lieutenants, and stood them along the wall while the clan looked on. Given his own way, Rakki would have made it a slower and more entertaining business, but Zeigler had been firm that such was not the way of gods. The children of Yellow Hair were led out and stood alongside them too, for she would be Rakki's now, or given to one of his favorites. The moment of culmination of Rakki's years of scheming, planning, and inner burning had arrived.

It must have been one of the devils that White Head spoke of at times. It had come down on them like a giant arrow shot from beyond the sky, with the shriek of a thousand caw-birds signaling bush cats near their nests. Straight and true into the midst of god-warriors who had thought to defy some even greater power before which they were as helpless as grubs in a burning log, blasting them into nothingness with the flash and fury of a thunderbolt. Those had been Rakki's Great Protectors, who had awed and overwhelmed him, and whom he had pledged his clan to serve? What worth was his power now?

Still he stood, dazed and bewildered, while around him his warriors tried to regain order, the Cave People babbled and ran about in disarray, and the injured staggered and fell. He and his men had been spared; yet it was they who had been about to carry out the deed. It was Zeigler and the errant gods, the ones who had conceived it and urged Rakki to do their bidding, who had been destroyed. It meant something. He was being given a message to unravel, a lesson of immense significance to learn and absorb, to make part of himself for the remainder of the life he had been allowed. *But what was the message?*

He became aware, then, of stillness descending around him. Turning numbly and looking around, he saw that the people were staring upward again, some pointing. Another flying vehicle was approaching. He braced himself, thinking this must be his turn to be delivered retribution. . . . But no. This was no thunderbolt of destruction and death. Whatever it was, it came down steadily in a shallow descent . . . gracefully yet somehow commanding. Its form was white above and orange beneath, the colors of the purest sky and the brightest flames. Rakki had a sudden feeling of a presence approaching that represented a power so absolute and assured that demonstrations of violence would be unbecoming, a power without need to prove itself. He let the hand that was holding his rifle fall to his side and stood passively, accepting and unresisting to whatever fate should be decided.

This was surely an emissary from the true realm of the gods. Sleek like the swiftest of birds, yet of smooth and rounded curves, adorned by twin tails of pure black, it came to rest not two tens of paces away from him, while the people fell back to clear the space. Its power poured out in a deep, pulsing drone that seemed to make the earth itself quiver and seize Rakki by his very bones. Murmurs of fear and wonder arose among the people. A God who overthrew the mightiest of god-warriors and their chieftains like playthings was emerging.

Two doors opened like arms on the underside to deliver him to the ground. He moved slowly and unhurriedly, conceding neither to haste nor urgency, masterful in his dignity. His face, framed in a close-fitting mantle, was dark and terrible, eyes of mountain ice blazing above a close-trimmed beard streaked with white. About his body he wore a robe of purest silver gathered at the shoulders and enclosing his arms like a cloak. He advanced with a steady tread, his mouth set tight in a downturned line.

Rakki tried not to let his trembling show as he awaited the verdict. And then his eyes widened, and he peered more closely. He knew this God! It was the one they called Keene, the one Rakki had thought of as the head god, and then abandoned to serve instead the false god, Zeigler. Keene had stopped and was staring at him. He was waiting for Rakki to interpret the message. Rakki's fate would depend on the answer he gave.

Rakki looked away and saw Jemmo, along with the most loyal of Jemmo's followers, the young ones of Yellow Hair, still lined by the wall, as paralyzed and uncomprehending as everyone else. The God looked at them too. He wanted Rakki to contemplate them.

Keene and the long-haired Goddess had tried to teach Rakki other ways. They had told him that the power he sought to share could be his, but it could not be obtained through killing, hatred, and destruction. The huge machines that had brought them from beyond the sky, and the cities that they would rebuild across the world, the knowledge that revealed the mysteries of life and the meaning of why pain and hardship, pleasure and joy existed—these things were achieved by cooperation and trust, by uniting in an effort to overcome the challenges that the world posed, not dividing and striving to overcome each other. The false gods had proclaimed, as Rakki had believed through all the time he had lived, that power came from instilling terror and compelling the obedience of others. And in his wisdom, the God Keene had allowed Rakki to follow that path if he chose, and now he had shown him where it would lead.

The power that Zeigler would have offered had been pitted against that which true Godhood promised. Rakki was looking at the result. And now, in his moment of revelation, it all seemed so simple and self-evident to him. He had seen the intricate fashioning of the interiors of the craft in which the Gods flew over the land, and of the artifacts that filled them; the immense constructions they were erecting at their city to the north; the windows that brought living images from distant places, the light that appeared on command, and countless other arts for manipulating objects and forces, and directing thought of which he had no comprehension. How could the clumsy swinging of a club, the ending of a life, rage, and bloodshed accomplish any of those things? All they could result in had been shown to him in the calamity he had just witnessed. White Head had told him that the whole world had tried to follow the path that Zeigler and the false gods had thought would bring them greatness. And it too had met with its calamity. Had that too been visited by the Gods who were now asking Rakki which world he would rebuild? And he knew his answer, and he knew what he must do.

While the whole of the Cave Tribe looked on, he walked to the wall where Jemmo and the others were standing and drew up in front of him. He brought up the rifle and saw Jemmo's jaw tighten, his body tense. And then Rakki extended his arm back to hand the weapon to Enka, who had followed him. He beckoned to Yellow Hair, and she came across, hesitant and apprehensive. "Take your children and care well for them. They will help us begin a new world," he told her.

And then, to Jemmo, showing his empty hands, "Can we forget the hatreds that are behind us? Our peoples, working together, can learn to build cities and fly beyond the sky. And we can learn to live wisely, as Gods. True Gods."

Keene put out a general announcement via the *Varuna* that Zeigler and the entourage that had gone with him had been wiped out, and their attempt to raise a native force was over. The supporters left at Serengeti and up in the ships were on their own and leaderless. Adreya Laelye came through shortly afterward to say they had capitulated, and she had taken charge at Serengeti.

A medical unit was despatched to Joburg for Charlie Hu. They reported that he was weak but hanging in. The treatment the women there had applied had been effective, and he was expected to recover. A short while later, a flyer landed at Carlsbad to collect Keene.

He left for Serengeti stiff, aching, numb with cold and exhaustion; but inside, weak with relief, and still not really believing things could have worked out this way. A clamorous reception was awaiting when he arrived, but a bath, clean clothes, a meal were all he could really think of. After that, he was sure he would sleep for a week. . . .

Until Sariena informed him that a signal had come in from the *Trojan,* obviously intended for Zeigler. The ship was now the possession of the Terran Planetary Government, in whose name it had intercepted and taken command of the *Aztec.* Both vessels were proceeding to Earth. Valcroix congratulated Zeigler on his dedication and ability in carrying through a difficult and demanding task.

CHAPTER FORTY-SEVEN

Robin reported to Major Ulak on Bridge Deck of the *Aztec*. "Sir, Commander Reese and Elmer Luthis are requesting your presence in the staff dining mess."

"Luthis?"

"The senior member of the ship's scientific contingent. It's with regard to the names they're required to submit for the party to be received aboard *Trojan*."

"Very well. Captain Quoyn will assume watch duty on the Bridge."

"Sir," Quoyn acknowledged.

Ulak detailed two troopers to accompany himself and Robin. They left by a passage passing between communications and control rooms aft of the Bridge, descended two levels of stairs to the quarterdeck, and from there proceeded aft past the officers' day room to a midships bulkhead lock, where one of the guards securing the ship had been posted. On the far side of the bulkhead, a gallery containing air regeneration plant connected to a lateral corridor that was on the way to the section that the scientific staff used. As the party came through the lock into the gallery, Robin grabbed suddenly at one of the handrails by the door; at the same time, a strange thing happened. Somebody turned off the Yarbat generators underneath that section of flooring. The reaction to the crisp military footfalls of the other three sent them soaring upward and floundering in the suddenly zeroed gravity. A moment later the generators came on again, slamming them to the floor with the impact of a well-executed judo throw. Ulak lay dazed, all the breath knocked out of him. He recovered his senses to become aware of Robin relieving him of his firearm and communications equipment. Two other figures that had appeared from behind the machinery were likewise disarming the troopers.

"What? . . . Delucey? . . . Treachery?" Ulak wheezed.

"I regret the necessity for deception," Robin replied. "But sometimes loyalty goes back a long way." More people were coming quickly and silently from the direction of the far corridor.

"We'll take care of them," Merlin Friet said. And to the other arrivals, "Put these three in the utility locker."

The guard posted on the forward side of the lock heard the activity and came through to investigate just in time to be relieved of his weapon and added to the catch.

"Are they ready in the cargo hold?" Robin asked. The guards there should have been dealt with similarly at the same time, and locked in one of the switchgear compartments.

Friet checked, using a compad. "No hitches," he confirmed. "They're moving into place."

On the Bridge Deck, Quoyn took a call from Robin, sounding urgent. *"Captain, emergency situation in the mid cargo hold!* Major Ulak needs you here with nine men immediately!"* Quoyn rattled off names and set out with his squad. They entered the hold at the double through the forward door to find figures milling in some kind of disturbance at the far end. The figures vanished through the after door, which moments later clanged shut. Only then did it register with Quoyn that neither Ulak, nor Delucey, nor any other TDF uniforms had been among them. He turned back in sudden alarm, his men coming to a confused halt around him. . . .

Just in time to see the steel shutter slide down across the forward doorway, too.

✧   ✧   ✧

The sergeant commanding the guard detail in the aft cargo hold also got a call from Robin. "Lieutenant Delucey acting on behalf of Major Ulak. All men in the aft section proceed to the midships quarterdeck immediately to receive further orders."

"Sir."

The route forward led through an instrumentation bay, where the same Yarbat up-then-down-again treatment was repeated. It proved singularly effective with military personnel running at the double, and netted the whole squad.

The skeleton crew that Quoyn had left behind to watch over the Bridge Deck were the only ones left—though they had no notion of the fact—by the time Luthis came along the passage between the ancillary rooms to the rear, followed by a mixed group of senior staff and scientists. The two guards posted at the entry to the Bridge stepped forward as they approached. "Not past this point," one of them told him.

"But Major Ulak told us to assemble here," Luthis retorted indignantly.

"What is it?" The corporal who was now the most senior of those present came across.

"The party due to go over to the *Trojan* with Commander Reese. We were told to come here."

The corporal was uneasy. He hadn't been briefed on this. "I don't have any instructions on that. My understanding was that the list isn't approved yet. Assembly would be in the lock area, not here."

Vicki emerged from the throng and began heading toward where Reese was standing with some ship's officers. "Commander, isn't there—"

"You can't come into the Bridge area, ma'am," one of the guards repeated, moving across to block her.

Luthis, grumbling, edged into the space the guard had vacated. "I refuse to be run back and forth like a lab rat. Call Major Ulak."

Flustered, the corporal produced a compad. More figures were milling in from the passage. The guards who had been left looked to the corporal for direction, but for a few vital seconds his attention was focused on making the call.

Suddenly, guns appeared in the hands of the arrivals. A couple of the guards managed to raise their weapons but they were outnumbered. Luthis trained a pistol on the stupefied corporal, still with his compad raised, gun in his unbuttoned holster, and held out his other hand. "Be sensible. We've got you cold," Luthis said. "Ulak and the others are all harmless and locked away, every one of them. Tell your men to stand down."

The corporal looked from the muzzle aimed at him from a couple of feet away, then around at their hopeless situation. He nodded. "Do as he says," he told them.

Reese emitted a sigh, finally releasing the tension he had been holding down. This last part had needed to be quick and to go without hitches. The party on the Bridge had been maintaining contact with the *Trojan*. "Disarm them and secure them in the officers' day room," he instructed the First Officer.

"Yes, sir!" The FO moved away, grinning.

Reese turned to Vicki. "He pulled it off. That's quite a son."

Vicki was suddenly overcome with relief, too. "I always thought it. But then, when was there a mother who didn't? I thought I'd lost him long ago. I don't mean when the *Trojan* vanished. Long before that—lost him as a person. I still don't have the whole story. But it must have been even harder on him than it was on me."

Robin appeared from the aft direction and joined them as the last of the *Trojan*'s boarding party were being led away. "The engineers are manhandling cables through from the power conversion section now," he reported. "Wernstecki and a couple of his people are setting up their computations. He says they'll need at least half an hour."

Reese indicated the crew station where a channel was open to the *Trojan*. "It's all yours. Stall them as long as you can," he said.

In the *Trojan*'s Command Module, Valcroix paced impatiently and looked up at the clock display above the mural screens on the Control Deck. One of the screens showed the *Aztec*, appearing stationary as it maintained its matching course. He came back to where Grasse was standing with General Nyrom and Captain Walsh. "What's keeping them?" he muttered. "We asked for a simple list of nominations. Wasn't it Reese who initiated this in the first place? Why is it taking so long?"

"Could you check again, General?" Grasse said.

Nyrom turned back to the crew station where an operator was monitoring the channel to the *Aztec*. "Get me Ulak," he instructed. "I want Major Ulak personally this time. Make that plain."

"I'll try, sir."

But it was Lieutenant Commander Delucey's face again that appeared on the screen.

Nyrom's patience had worn thin. "Why are my orders not being followed?" he demanded curtly. "I asked for Major Ulak. Put him on."

"I'm sorry, but the major is not present on the Bridge Deck at the moment, sir."

"Connect me to his personal code."

"We're not getting a response on that circuit, sir. Shall I send another party to locate him?" Evasions, excuses. What was going on there?

"Lieutenant Commander Delucey, I demand an explanation. Where is your commanding officer? Why have we not been able to speak with him?"

"I'm not familiar with the layout of this ship, sir."

"Put Commander Reese of the *Aztec* on!" Nyrom snapped. What had happened all of a sudden? Up until now Delucey had always been a capable, first-rate officer.

"He's conferring with the scientific delegation in another part of the ship, sir."

"*Connect me to him, then!*" Nyrom exploded.

What seemed an interminable wait ensued. Finally, Reese's face appeared on the screen. "General?"

"Commander Reese, I want an explanation. Where is Major Ulak?"

Reese looked puzzled. "The major? He's been waiting for your approval of the nominations list."

"We haven't received any list yet."

"That's strange. I—"

"What is going on over there? I warn you, Commander, if I don't get a satisfactory answer right now, I'll put a full crew aboard your ship and have you and everyone else there locked up for the remainder of the voyage. . . ."

Across the floor, an operator at one of the watch consoles called out suddenly, "*Surveillance alert!* Permission to report?"

Walsh looked over from the group that Nyrom had just left. "Go ahead."

"Sensors are showing thermal signatures on the *Aztec*'s maneuvering thrusters. Radar indicates attitude altering. She's starting to move, sir."

"Commander Reese, what's happening?" Nyrom demanded. "Your ship is moving out of station. What in hell do you think you're doing? Do I have to remind you that we are an armed vessel?"

"Moving? That's absurd. Let me check."

But it was clearly true. On the large screen, the *Aztec* was starting to swing visibly, its tail coming around to bear in *Trojan*'s direction.

"I don't know what they're up to," Grasse called back from the monitor station.

"Prepare for action. Issue a final warning," Valcroix said to Walsh. "If they ignore it, fire to disable, not destroy."

Walsh addressed the Chief Armaments Officer. "Deploy secondary lasers for low kill on stern section. Bring close-range disablers to launch readiness. Pods to Orange standby."

On the screen *Aztec*'s stern was now full-face toward the Trojan. "*Aztec* firing main drive," the watch operator sang out.

"They must be insane," Walsh murmured, shaking his head. "There's no way they can hope to get out of range of what we're carrying."

"Secondary lasers locked on stern section, twenty percent power," the CAO reported. "Ready to fire. Awaiting orders."

"*Aztec* has cut main drive."

Walsh's face creased in bemusement. "It doesn't make any sense. If they're—"

"What—?"

"Argh!"

"*Jesus Christ!*"

It was as if a gigantic, invisible hammer had struck the ship. The entire floor bucked sideways suddenly, sending everyone who had been standing sprawling across the floor and in heaps on top of each other, and pitching console operators from their seats. Loose items flew in torrents off shelves and worktops and tumbled across the floor. Closet doors burst open; drawers slid out and fell off their runners. The air was filled with the juddering and groans of distorted structures protesting. Some figures managed to untangle themselves and pull themselves back to their feet . . . just in time to be bowled over by the next jolt. When they tried to rise again, their bodies felt unnaturally heavy, causing them to flounder more and lose coordination. A lighting fixture detached from its recess in the ceiling and shattered across the floor.

Trojan had the general form of a stepped axle carrying a wheel at the thicker end. The wheel consisted of six spokes with various functional modules at the ends, interconnected by a communications ring. "Down" within the module decks meant outward, the force defining it being generated by a slow rotation of the whole structure. When the ship was accelerating under thrust, the spokes trailed back, tilting the module decks at the correct angle to create a normal gravity simulation.

It had been Tanya's suggestion to position *Aztec* in a direction tangential to *Trojan*'s wheel and direct Wernstecki's stern-pointing AG beam at the approaching side of it, thus speeding it up. But since gravity, like any force, is a two-way affair, this also had the effect of drawing *Aztec* in the opposite direction, toward *Trojan*. *Aztec*, however, had one factor working for it that *Trojan* didn't: Its main drive was aligned with Wernstecki's beam and when fired would oppose it. Hence, using the analogy Wernstecki had given when he first described his inspiration to the others, *Aztec* had the equivalent of something to dig its heels into when throwing its grapnel and jerking on the line.

One complication remained. The sensitive fusion optics in *Aztec*'s stern wouldn't function while the AG beam, coming from the cargo holds forward of the propulsion section, was active. Hence, the procedure they had been forced to adopt was first to fire the main drive to accelerate *Aztec* away from *Trojan;* then cut the drive and energize the AG beam, which would act as a brake and retard it; then repeat the cycle. The momentum acquired by *Aztec* and then lost again was thus transferred to *Trojan* in a series of massive pulses, each one adding to its rotation like successive pushes to a children's carousel. Which of course increased gravity inside all the modules as well as putting all kinds of extra stresses on the spoke and support structures—with hopefully deleterious effect.

It was having other effects too, Wernstecki could see for himself on the screen without having to consult the analyzer readouts—although it had been expected. He was still at the monitor console in the control compartment by the cargo hold, frantically trying to synchronize the beam dynamics with the firing of the ship's drive, which Reese was directing from the Bridge, coordinating via one of Wernstecki's screens. *Trojan* wasn't just increasing rotational speed about its longitudinal axis; the axis itself was building up a tumbling motion of its own. The gravity pulses from *Aztec* were being applied to one side of the wheel only, producing an imbalance of force that was setting the whole structure into gyration like a wobbly spinning top. Carried to completion, this would result in a second, end-over-end mode of rotation superimposed on the first. What the effects would be on the occupants was anyone's guess. Wernstecki had hardly had time to go deeply into it—even if he'd had the inclination.

The additional degree of freedom in *Trojan*'s motion made it necessary now to reorientate *Aztec* into the correct relative position before each fresh AG pulse. This meant predicting when the target portion of *Trojan* would move into alignment with *Aztec*'s stern and at the same time be on a matching approach vector, which involved a tricky computation.

"Hold on *X* . . . coming in on *Z* now, twelve . . . ten-point-three . . . nine-nine . . ." Tanya recited, watching an adjacent panel.

"Dee-phi to five," Wernstecki directed over the link to Reese. "Reduce alpha more."

"Two-second burn on FS2. Retro on MP4, ten percent power," Reese translated to others on the Bridge. "Fire main at ten."

"Main drive firing, ten percent," a voice acknowledged.

Wernstecki took in several displays. "A half on dee-theta. Steady right there. . . . Steady . . . Wait on my count. Ready on beam."

"Ready on beam," the engineer in charge in the hold confirmed.

"Six . . . five . . . four—it's good—three . . . two . . . one . . . *Cut!*"

"Cut main," Reese ordered on the Bridge.

"Main drive out."

The force that had been impelling everyone rearward in their seats vanished as forward acceleration ceased, but all anyone felt was a brief nudge as the underdeck Yarbat arrays compensated. For a brief moment *Aztec* coasted away from *Trojan* in freefall.

"Go, beam."

"Beam on."

This time the transient was beyond the range of the compensators. Wernstecki and the others held on for support as the invisible leash yanked *Aztec* back to a relative standstill.

"Off, beam."

"Beam off."

"What's your reading?" Wernstecki asked Merlin Friet, who was running other calculations at a crew station in the Communications Room.

"Axial multiplier alone should be at four-plus," he replied. It meant that anyone in the *Trojan*'s ring modules would now be in possession of more than four times their normal body weight from just the speed-up, never mind what else the added tumbling did. Wernstecki told Reese that it should be enough to disrupt all the ship's functions for a considerable time to come.

"Then let's hose the Hub and the drive, and get out of here," Reese said. They had already agreed that for good measure they would aim a pulse each at the region of the *Trojan*'s spoke bases, where most of the weaponry was concentrated, and at the tail-end fusion complex—simply in the hope of inducing further dislocation and chaos for those aboard to attend to.

Its mission accomplished, *Aztec* accelerated away flat-out on the fastest intercept course for Earth.

With no external friction to slow it down, an object set spinning in space will continue indefinitely until something acts to retard it. It took almost twelve hours for Walsh and his crew in the crazily turning and toppling *Trojan* to drag themselves together into a functional team and figure out a firing pattern for the maneuvering thrusters that would bring about recovery. Even then it was only partly effective, for some of the spokes had buckled, distorting the ring symmetry and introducing permanent instabilities that couldn't be corrected. The result was that life in the modules took on the feel of crossing a slowly pitching ocean, and a number of the occupants became acutely seasick. Several parts of the vessel that had suffered containment failure and were leaking into space had to be sealed off. Beyond that, the precision targeting instrumentation for the long-range weapons systems was malfunctioning and would have to be reset and recalibrated—which was neither here nor there as far as *Aztec* was concerned, since *Aztec* was long gone—and the main drive focusing system was out of alignment, which would reduce acceleration to thirty percent of normal until repairs could be effected.

But all was not lost. Valcroix delivered a rallying speech to the entire company, reminding them that the base on Earth was held, and with the *Varuna* and *Surya* in their possession, *Trojan* could be restored to full battle-strength before anything to match it could be organized and reach it from Saturn. *Aztec* would never be allowed to pull the same stunt again. So what would it do? If it continued to Earth, it would become their prize. If it returned to Saturn, the opposition on Earth would be reduced accordingly. True, the resources aboard it would have been a valuable asset to own, but they were not essential. *Trojan* itself carried a full complement of conventional industrial seed equipment that had been intended to establish a pilot capability in the Jovian system. With enough will and devotion to their cause, they could still regain Earth and make themselves impregnable. Oratory and inspiring followers was Valcroix's calling. With morale revived and a new determination sharpened by adversity, *Trojan* set course once again.

And then the news came in from Earth that there was no haven to be reached there after all. Zeigler's bid had ended. He and his followers were no more. It was the first anyone on the *Trojan* had heard of Gallian's murder and the deaths of the others there. Adreya Laelye had assumed control in the name of the government of Kronia. An hour later, a signal came in from President Urzin at Saturn. He exonerated Valcroix from direct responsibility for the crimes, since Zeigler had exceeded his orders, promising him and his followers a fair hearing if they recognized the inevitable and gave up. Meanwhile, Kronia was preparing an armed force.

What was there to do? With its armament and propulsion system impaired, its structure damaged, leaking, and likely to undergo further failures at any time, no friendly base available for making repairs, choices were nonexistent. Before his assembled entourage, a tight-lipped Valcroix sent out a message accepting Urzin's terms and announcing that the *Trojan* would make its way to Earth.

The term of the independent Terran Planetary Government was over.

CHAPTER FORTY-EIGHT

It had been a while since the days when anyone with the inclination could come into the upper level of the OpComs dome to watch the shuttles from orbit come down, and to await incoming arrivals. OpComs was still there, but more restricted these days to air and orbital traffic control, which was what it had been built for in the first place. Buses from the new landing silos and service bays on the far side of what had been the pad area now delivered to the Terminal Building, erected a short distance along from the OpComs dome in front of the dorm blocks. The dorm blocks had acquired some individual rooms as well as billeting and were still used for shorter-term and temporary accommodation. However, most of the original inhabitants had moved to a residential complex outside the central work area of the base, which had separate living units as well as communal dining and recreation and offered more comfort and privacy. On the opposite side of the central area, the workshop and production facilities had grown and diversified.

Keene stood with Vicki, Sariena, Wernstecki, and Charlie Hu, some way ahead of an expectant crowd gathered at the edge of the area in front of the Terminal Building, which with orbital traffic now farther away had become the apron for surface aircraft and local flyers. Adreya Laelye waited a few paces in front of them, facing a podium with a microphone and draped with Kronia's colors. On either side of the group, the honor guard stood in two detachments facing each other. A small procession of vehicles approached from the pads, bringing the first contingent to be shuttled down from the Kronian large-capacity interplanetary cruiser *Gallian,* now ten hours in Earth orbit after completing its maiden voyage from Saturn.

The onlookers included Shayle, who had supervised the shutdown of *Agni* and its return to orbit to recombine with the *Varuna* after the permanent power plant delivered by the *Aztec* was assembled and brought online. Also present were Jansinick Wernstecki and Merlin Friet, currently experimenting with using AG methods to transport cut blocks now that the basic lithoforming quarries were operating; Pieter Naarmegen and Elmer Luthis from the *Aztec,* joint-managing Serengeti's biological research activity; Kerry Heeland, on a break from the *Varuna,* still involved with probe reconnaissance and surveys, along with Owen Erskine, patched up and fit again; and Beth, irrevocably stamped as a psychologist now, and Maria Sanchez, highly regarded as the medic who had dug the bullets out of Owen and stitched him up, and who had probably saved Charlie Hu's leg. Adreya had somehow contrived to look formally professional in a dark business dress and shoulder wrap to perform her last function in the capacity in which she had been acting since Zeigler's demise. This was a special occasion.

The vehicles drew to a halt ahead of them, and the arrivals began emerging. The officers of the two guard detachments called their units to attention, then to present arms. The rank on one side was commanded by Mertak and wore the dove-gray uniforms of the recently instituted Kronian Armed Service. With its record of uncertain loyalties and inadequate internal policing, the former Security Arm had suffered too much loss of confidence and prestige, and had been disbanded. Robin had been entrusted with command—by Adreya Laelye—of the Terran part of the operation, and done a commendable job with the restructuring and reorganizing; but he had departed two weeks previously with the repaired and refitted *Trojan,* resuming its original mission to Jupiter.

A major from the *Trojan*'s SA complement who had refused to join the rebel faction and been incarcerated, had assumed temporary command pending the *Gallian*'s arrival.

The other guard detachment was composed of younger, dark-skinned members, equally crisp in their drill and smartly attired in navy-blue tunics devised for a new corps called the Auxiliary Guard. In command of them was Enka, with Rakki and Jemmo standing by to lend a native presence. The rulers of Kronia had accepted that their trust in the inherent universal goodness of human nature had been misplaced and not a little naive. As all of history had shown, elements would arise in any society which, when no other option is left, would seek to impose themselves by force, and could only be met with force. Kronia had made the mistake of thinking that since nothing existed on Earth to oppose its far-flung mission to return, there was nothing to protect against. Kronia had been very lucky.

Keene spotted Cavan's lean form and Alicia with her blond hair among the first to appear. Cavan picked him and Vicki out at once, and even at that distance Keene could see the smile come into the pink face beneath the thinning hair, and the nod of recognition. An assortment of people in typical Kronian tunics, a few jackets and skirts, and more Armed Service uniforms came next—one of them Mylor Vorse from SOE. And then the arriving group opened up to admit to the front a robust, swarthy, silver-haired figure with vaguely Asian features, wearing a maroon robe-like garment. His eyes were as alive and alert as ever, scanning the crowd and taking in details of the base and the general surroundings even as he led the others forward. Kronians didn't need to sag under sudden, unaccustomed weight anymore—they got acclimatized using Yarbat generators well in advance. Adreya Laelye smiled as she moved forward to meet him at the podium. "Welcome to Earth," she greeted.

"Already, I feel I've come home," Jon Foy, the first official Kronian governor, who would be taking over from her, replied.

There was a reception that evening in the former general mess room and cafeteria, now enhanced into being something of a social center. It was both a welcoming party for Foy and his administration, and a delayed celebration of Earth's consolidation as an extension of Kronia. For some reason, an overt display of victory and jubilation before Saturn's ascendancy was formally ratified would not have felt right. Now it seemed that everyone was making an extra effort to make good the lost time.

Of course, there were impromptu speeches and toasts. Naarmegen proposed one to "Landen Keene, Robin Delucey, and Jansinick Wernstecki, the three people who saved Earth and the *Aztec,* and brought about the Pragmatist downfall." Keene objected that they couldn't have done it without Charlie Hu and Kerry Heeland, and Sariena and Shayle . . . and then added Reese, Yarbat, and others not present, finally throwing out his arms and exclaiming, "Hell, it was all of us!" which earned him cheers. Later in the evening, Adreya steered Vicki aside to learn more about the latest ideas on Earth's origins, and he finally got a chance to talk with Vorse and Foy.

Apparently, the motion of Athena was still uncertain.

"It's not over," Vorse told him. "We've been getting better information now that we can coordinate observations from Saturn and Earth. The period we've just been through could turn out to be the end of a lull. Athena is causing another wave of disruption among the Asteroids. Kronia could be facing more danger yet."

"How bad?" Keene asked.

"Nobody can say."

Foy elaborated. "But it's not beyond the bounds of possibility that the culture we've brought into being out at Saturn could be rendered nonviable—at least, for some time. And even pulling everyone back to Earth wouldn't necessarily eliminate all the risks. Things could get bad again here too. Suppose Venus were sent into a repeating resonant pattern in the way that Emil Farzhin says happened five thousand years ago with Mars."

It didn't come as a total surprise. That had been one of the reasons for sending the *Varuna* back to reconnoiter the situation on Earth, after all, and for the rush in sending the equipment that the *Aztec* had brought. The problems entailed in being forced to begin again on Earth should be straightforward enough to deal with compared to those of surviving in airless, lifeless space environments, and all the other things the Kronians had already learned to regard as normal. But as a first essential they would need safe refuges to retire to during periods of meteorite storms, floods, or other generally bad times. Not flimsy frameworks thrown up to maximize short-term rental returns on investment, like those that had constituted most of the cities now swept away or buried, but massive, non-corroding structures in high places, virtually embedded in and forming extensions of the earth itself.

"We've been giving it top priority," Keene said. "Jan and his people are having a great time. They've got half a mountain out there cut into play blocks. It looks like the Nursery of the Gods."

"We saw it on the way down from orbit," Vorse said. "Very impressive. We'll be going out tomorrow to see it."

"It was just as well that we scheduled a further consignment," Foy said.

"Very fortunate," Keene agreed. He eyed Vorse. "Your idea, Mylor?"

Vorse shook his head. "No, it was Jon. Always the optimist."

"Optimism pays off," Foy told them.

The *Gallian* had brought a further consignment of the latest litho-tech equipment from Titan. After its departure from Saturn, more survivors had been found in parts of Asia and both North and South America. Accordingly, more shelter construction was being planned for bases to be sited at highland locations in Tibet, Bolivia, and the Rockies. A contact party put down by a lander from the *Varuna* had reported that the latter group, incredibly, included individuals that Keene himself had known and had last seen leaving in the last plane out from Vandenberg, heading for the Air Force survival fortress beneath Cheyenne Mountain in Colorado. Pressures of other things had so far prevented him going there personally.

"Sariena and Charlie are working out a symbolic system to write our story in stone for posterity," Keene said. "Not dependent on any specific language. But decodable by anyone with the right knowledge."

Foy smiled. "Why? Don't they think we'll still be here five thousand years from now?"

Keene shrugged. "Just in case. We'd like to leave something more permanent this time."

Then Luthis and Shayle joined them, and for a while the talk ranged from native farming projects around Serengeti to Kronian spiritual philosophy. Keene was glad that, while he wouldn't have wanted Gallian's memory forgotten, nobody stood up to start giving an obituary or calling for a memorial moment of silence. The party was going well, and such things were appropriate to other occasions.

And he knew Gallian would have wanted it that way.

After they had helped close the last of the festivities down, Keene and Vicki walked with Cavan and Alicia back toward the newcomers' room in what had been the dorm blocks, which was on the way to the residential area. With all the day's business, it was Keene's first chance to talk with Cavan about anything other than incidental matters. Keene fell quiet as they approached the point where the walkway leading to the building left the path that he and Vicki would continue along. Alicia was talking about her reactions to the first day of being back on Earth.

"Yes, everything was almost totally destroyed, and it will be a long time recovering. But there's a . . . *feeling* that I can't describe. It hit me when I saw the water and the areas starting to turn green again from the shuttle on the way down."

"I know. I felt it too," Vicki said. "It's like suddenly being in touch with Life again. You said it happened to you after you left the base area with Charlie, didn't you, Lan?"

No response.

Alicia nodded. "Yes, that's it exactly! Being part of a living world. All of a sudden you realize how sterile Kronia was. I mean, of course we couldn't have done without it. It preserved knowledge and technology when everything else was lost. And I'm sure that when we expand out of the Solar System, that's where it will be from. But for all the other things, *human* things, we have to rebuild the center of the new civilization here. Kronia will be an outpost. Don't you think so?"

She directed her last words at Keene and Cavan. They had come to the intersection with the path and halted. But Keene was looking at Cavan, as if not hearing her. Cavan was taking in the night scene of the base with its geometric shapes and lights, as if leaving Keene to come to his own conclusions in his own time—but somehow giving the impression of having an intimation of what they might be.

"That was why you did it, wasn't it, Leo," Keene said finally. Cavan turned on a look of feigned innocence that would have been an offense to Keene's intelligence if they hadn't known each other for years. "Why you wanted me on the Earth mission. It was political. You guessed something like that would happen. You tried recruiting me that time when you and Alicia came to Dione, but I said I wasn't interested in politics. So you set me up with Vorse and Foy. You wanted me to know more about what Kronia meant and where it was heading."

"You'd have stayed on Titan, content to let your work on the AG program justify your existence," Cavan agreed, dropping the pretense.

"That whole line of Vorse's about my being needed to supervise *Agni*'s MHD system was part of it. It wasn't necessary. Shayle could have done it."

Vicki was looking from one to the other, puzzled. "Leo had some ulterior agenda for sending you to Earth? Why?"

"I think I can see it now. . . ." Alicia said. "Leo never discussed it with me."

"Not the kind of thing one talks about when the person concerned isn't there," Cavan remarked.

"See what?" Vicki asked again. She had never pretended to harbor any political instinct.

"Look at what Lan did in those last days back on Earth," Cavan said to her. "If you'd had a good idea that Valcroix's people were going to pull off something like they did, wouldn't that be exactly the kind of person you'd want to have here? I'm sorry if it was using you, Lan, and that it put you in personal danger. But as you can see now, a lot more was at stake." He shrugged in a way that said life had to be that way sometimes. "Anyway, as you yourself said a moment ago, I did give you the opportunity to volunteer."

Keene just shook his head, for the moment too taken aback by the enormity of the whole picture that was opening up to respond.

"Are you saying you knew what the Pragmatists were planning?" Alicia asked Cavan.

He shook his head. "Not specifically. If I had known, and could prove it, I'd have taken the evidence straight to Urzin. But I'd been around those kinds of people long enough to be pretty sure they'd try something. They don't concede power easily. The Kronians can work miracles in some areas, but they've got their weak spots too. We saw some of them when they came to Earth. No security-minded government would ever have let the SA become compromised in the way it was. I tried getting it across to people like Urzin and Foy, but they just didn't have the experience."

Now Keene was more confused than offended. "But that's not the way it was, Leo," he objected. "The reason I said I didn't want to get mixed up in political things back then was because I didn't think Valcroix had a chance. And you *agreed*!"

Cavan gave one of the devious smiles that always marked finally getting to the bottom of something he had been involved in. "I agreed he could never have succeeded at *Kronia*," he confirmed. "But I never said anything about their making a bid for control on Earth. The warning signals were there: the SA being packed with disgruntled Terrans; the way Harvey Mitchell was pulled from the *Trojan* mission after I got him assigned to it. They'd always had their sights set on Earth. The whole business about calling for a say in running the Directorates was to create an appearance of legality having failed. It was the obvious target—undefended and too far away for any timely intervention." Cavan sighed and shrugged apologetically, this time at Vicki. "Of course, I didn't know exactly what would be called for. So I arranged to have someone there who I knew from personal previous experience would keep his head in a crisis, know how to improvise when one thing after another went wrong, and who doesn't know how to give up. And look what he did here. How many more people do you know who could have pulled it off?"

Vicki was staring at him fixedly. "When Mitch was pulled . . ." she said slowly. "Robin was your substitute, wasn't he? You'd already set him up as your insider in the SA. He told us the whole story."

Cavan nodded candidly in a way that said there was no point in hiding anything now. "I know it caused you and Landen a lot of grief," he said. "But we were up against professionals who knew all about infiltration and undercover techniques, and hampered by the naivete of people who were too trusting and knew nothing. I needed someone in the SA to keep tabs on what was going on. We didn't dare let you or Landen know. It was imperative for everyone to act naturally. Especially Robin. They had dossiers going way back on everyone they recruited."

"I didn't even know," Alicia informed them.

"What, exactly, did you expect Robin to do?" Keene asked.

"There was no way to be specific," Cavan answered. "But he's from the same kind of mold as yourself. The main thing was for him to just be there. Whatever developed, he would come up with something."

For a moment Keene felt the beginnings of indignation. But then he remembered that what they were talking about here was something that was bigger than individuals, that he had been ready to put before himself when Jon Foy opened his eyes on that day long ago in the tower room at Foundation to the things that Kronia stood for. And in any case, would he have preferred staying back there, immersed in his own world, while Earth was lost and the whole future course of human events set on a path of repeating its same sorry saga all over again?

No. It wasn't in his nature. His inability to strike a compromise between what was right and what wasn't, and the accompanying compulsion to hurl himself totally into doing what needed to be done, regardless of the odds, had caused him to give up a career to spend half his life fighting the establishments of a degenerate science in the world that was gone, and to bring a dozen people out to the new world beginning. And the same qualities had emerged again, when the new world he had pledged himself to was threatened.

As Cavan had known he would.

Keene and Vicki carried on walking slowly between the glinting forms of the domes and structures after Cavan and Alicia had left them. The base didn't look so much like a construction site these days. With the essentials taken care of, a lot of cleaning up had been going on, and Serengeti center was taking on a little style and color. Sapling trees that had been found in some of the lower regions had been brought in and replanted, and plots of grass and shrubs were being carefully nurtured. In the day, bright streaks and patches of iridescent blue in the thinning cloud were becoming commonplace, and flowers were beginning to appear in greater numbers. Beds of them were being fertilized and planted around and through the residential area.

"So did Vorse try to tempt you today with all that exciting work waiting back on Titan?" Vicki said, glancing at him. It was a veiled way of asking if he was going back to Saturn. Vicki would be staying on, to continue her work with Luthis.

Standing policy was to keep at least one long-range vessel stationed at Earth at all times. *Surya* had departed for Kronia some time ago with a consignment mainly of flora and fauna, but with *Aztec* now in orbit, the *Varuna* was being readied for a return trip, to be refitted to more permanent standards and equipped with Yarbat arrays. A recurring topic between Vicki and Keene had been the question of whether, with Earth's immediate emergency now over, he would return to resume his work with Pang Yarbat's group on Titan. Inwardly, Keene had thought he would, since that had been the pattern of his life since coming to Kronia; but he knew too that Vicki had her own personal reasons and hopes for asking, and he hadn't wanted to deal with the issue until it became necessary. So, he had never voiced a final decision one way or the other.

But as he turned over his feelings in his mind, he

became aware that somehow the equations didn't come out the way they had before. On Earth, before and during the Athena crisis, and all through his years at Kronia, always there had been a sense of an overriding imperative that placed its own demands above personal wants and worldly things. Now, suddenly, he felt . . . free. It was as if some power that had laid first claim on him acknowledged that his dues were paid, and was releasing him from its service.

He was being unusually long in replying. Vicki looked at him. When he answered, it was from a completely different direction.

"Do you still have this Kronian belief that you used to talk about with Sariena, of some intelligence, guiding principle—whatever you want to call it—at work behind what goes on, shaping the way it all unfolds?"

Vicki looked surprised. "Yes—more so than ever, after what we're finding out about living things. What . . . ?" But her beginning of a question trailed away, as if she saw there was no reason to complete it.

"Do you think it sometimes reaches down to individuals and enlists them to its purpose when it needs to, and lets them go when it's done? Or do we just project outward something that's really in ourselves?"

"Does it matter? The outcome's still the same."

"We might be building a civilization to go out among the stars looking for something that's not there," Keene said.

"Maybe it isn't where you go, but what you have to do to get there that finds you the answers," Vicki replied.

"The things I had to do are done," Keene told her. "What Alicia said was right. The future we need to be thinking about now is here, not at Saturn."

In the light from the lamps, he saw her eyes moistening. "You're not going back with the *Varuna*?" she said, her voice catching.

He shook his head and slipped an arm around her waist, drawing her closer as they walked. "And anyway, you and I have got a lot of lost time to make up, haven't we?"

"You really mean it?"

He nodded.

Vicki dropped her head against his shoulder, closed her eyes. Around them, the night breeze between the looming shadows of the base was fresh and cool, bringing a hint of rain with the scents and sounds of the new world.

The new world beginning.

FURTHER READING

As requested by numerous readers, below are sources of further information pertaining to some of the topics alluded to in *The Anguished Dawn*.

Gravity Electromagnetics

The suggestion of gravity deriving from electromagnetism was inspired by the work of Dr. Andre Assis, Institute of Physics, Campinas, Brazil. See:

Assis, A.K.T., 1992, "Deriving gravitation from electromagnetism," *Canadian Journal of Physics*, Vol. 70, pp. 330-340.

Assis, A.K.T., 1995, "Gravitation as a Fourth Order Electromagnetic Effect," *Advanced Electromagnetism—Foundations, Theory, and Applications*, Editors T.W. Barrett & D.M. Grimes, World Scientific, Singapore, 1995, pp. 314-331.

Dr. Assis's home page is at http://www.ifi.unicamp.br/~assis.

Inertial Agent Model of Gravity

Van Flandern, Tom, 1993, *Dark Matter, Missing Planets, and New Comets*, North Atlantic Books, Berkeley, CA.

Mars Encounter

The Mars-encounters interpretation of the Sanskrit *Vedas* was based on the work *Firmament and Chaos* by John

Ackerman. Copies can be downloaded from his web site at http://www.firmament-chaos.com.

Problems with Darwinian Evolution
and Related Issues

Behe, Michael J., 1996, *Darwin's Black Box,* Free Press, NY.

Dembski, William A., 1999, *Intelligent Design*, Intervarsity Press, Downers Grove, IL.

Denton, Michael, 1986, *Evolution: A Theory in Crisis.* Adler & Adler, Bethesda, MD.

Ginenthal, Charles, 1994, "Scientific Dating Methods in Ruins," *The Velikovskian,* Vol.2, No.1 pp. 50–79.

Hoyle, Fred, 1983, *The Intelligent Universe*, Michael Joseph, London.

Johnson, Phillip, 1991, *Darwin on Trial,* Regnery, Washington, D.C.

Johnson, Phillip, 1995, *Reason in the Balance*, InterVarsity Press, Downers Grove, IL.

Milton, Richard, 1997, *Shattering the Myths of Darwinism,* Park Street Press, Rochester, VT.

Spetner, Lee, 1997, *Not By Chance!* Judaica Press, New York, NY.

Wells, Jonathan, 2000, *Icons of Evolution*, Regnery, Washington, D.C.

Woodmorappe, John, 1999, *The Mythology of Modern Dating Methods*, ICR, El Cajon, CA.

Impossible Dinosaurs

Holden, Ted, 1993, "Giants of the Earth," *The Velikovskian,* Vol.1, No.4, p. 7.

Also, various papers at www.aeonjournal.com.

Catastrophism

Ginenthal, Charles, 1995, *Carl Sagan & Immanuel Velikovsky,* New Falcon Press, Tempe, AZ.

Over 400 pages presenting findings from space missions and other sources that are consistent with Velikovsky's claims, while contradicting the experts who vilified him.

Velikovsky and Establishment Science

A comprehensive rejoinder to the publication *Scientists Confront Velikovsky*, which followed the 1974 AAAS conference. What really went on, earning Velikovsky a standing ovation that the media didn't mention. 144 pp.

Available from:
Lewis Greenberg
226 Richmond C
Deerfield Beach FL 33442

Raup, David M., 1991: *Extinction: Bad Genes or Bad Luck?* W.W. Norton, New York, NY.

Velikovsky, Immanuel, 1950, *Worlds in Collision*, Buccaneer Books, Cutchogue, NY.

Velikovsky, Immanuel, 1952, *Ages in Chaos*, Buccaneer Books, Cutchogue, NY.

Velikovsky, Immanuel, 1955, *Earth in Upheaval*, Buccaneer Books, Cutchogue, NY.

The Velikovskian

A journal dedicated to studies of the evidence for global catastrophes in human times, along with such related issues as the ancient historic record, evolution and extinction, the dynamics of the Solar System, methods of chronology and dating. Normally 4 issues per year.

Inquiries to:
Charles Ginenthal
Ivy Press
65-35 108th St.
Forest Hill NY 11375
Tel: 718-897-2403

Aeon

A journal of myth, science, and ancient history, frequently exploring theories of different early Solar System configurations, including the Saturn hypothesis. Information at: www.aeonjournal.com or from Ev Cochrane, e-mail ev@ aeonjournal.com.

Society for Interdisciplinary Studies

Biannual catastrophist journal providing articles and papers on a wide range of related topics, books sources and reviews, and digest of Internet coverage.

Inquiries to:
The Membership Secretary
SIS
10 Witley Green
Darley Heights
Stopsley Beds, LU2 8TR
U.K.
Web: http://www.knowledge.co.uk/xxx/cat/sis
E-mail SIS@knowledge.co.uk